PENGUIN CLASSICS

A LITTLE PRINCESS

Frances Hodgson Burnett was born in Manchester, England, in 1849. In 1865, after her father's death, her mother moved the family to rural Tennessee, where they struggled to earn a living. At seventeen, Burnett sold her first story to a magazine, and by the time she was twenty-two she had earned enough to return to England as a tourist. From 1887 until her death, she maintained homes in both England and America. Her two marriages—to Dr. Swan Burnett, with whom she had two sons, from 1874 to 1898, and to the actor Stephen Townsend from 1900 to 1902—ended in divorce. Burnett wrote a number of popular novels for adults, among them *That Lass o' Lowrie's* (1877), *Through One Administration* (1883), and *The Shuttle* (1907), as well as several plays and a memoir of her childhood, *The One I Knew Best of All* (1893). But she is best remembered for her children's novels: *Little Lord Fauntleroy* (1886), *A Little Princess* (1905), an expanded version of the 1888 novella *Sara Crewe* and the 1902 stage play *The Little Princess*, and *The Secret Garden* (1911). Burnett died in 1924 at her home on Long Island.

U. C. Knoepflmacher is a professor of English and the Paton Foundation Professor of Ancient and Modern Literature at Princeton University. He is the author of *Ventures into Childland: Victorians, Fairy Tales, and Femininity* and *Wuthering Heights: A Study* and coeditor of *Forbidden Journeys: Fairy Tales and Fantasies by Victorian Women Writers*. He edited George MacDonald's *The Complete Fairy Tales* for Penguin Classics.

A LITTLE PRINCESS

FRANCES HODGSON BURNETT

EDITED WITH AN
INTRODUCTION AND NOTES BY
U. C. KNOEPFLMACHER

PENGUIN BOOKS

PENGUIN BOOKS

Published by the Penguin Group

Penguin Group (USA) Inc., 375 Hudson Street, New York, New York 10014, U.S.A.

Penguin Books Ltd, 80 Strand, London WC2R 0RL, England

Penguin Books Australia Ltd, 250 Camberwell Road, Camberwell, Victoria 3124, Australia

Penguin Books Canada Ltd, 10 Alcorn Avenue, Toronto, Ontario, Canada M4V 3B2

Penguin Books India (P) Ltd, 11 Community Centre, Panchsheel Park, New Delhi – 110 017, India

Penguin Group (NZ), cnr Airborne and Rosedale Roads, Albany, Auckland 1310, New Zealand

Penguin Books (South Africa) (Pty) Ltd, 24 Sturdee Avenue,
Rosebank, Johannesburg 2196, South Africa

Penguin Books Ltd, Registered Offices: 80 Strand, London WC2R 0RL, England

A Little Princess first published in the United States of America by
Charles Scribner's Sons 1905
This edition with an introduction and notes by U. C. Knoepflmacher
published in Penguin Books 2002

3 5 7 9 10 8 6 4

LIBRARY OF CONGRESS CATALOGING-IN-PUBLICATION DATA

Burnett, Frances Hodgson, 1849–1924.
A little princess / Frances Hodgson Burnett ; edited with an introduction
and notes by U. C. Knoepflmacher.
p. cm. — (Penguin classics)
Summary: Sara Crewe, a pupil at Miss Minchin's London school, is left
in poverty when her father dies but is later rescued by a mysterious benefactor.
ISBN 0-14-243701-8 (pbk. : alk. paper)
[1. Boarding schools—Fiction.   2. Schools—Fiction.   3. Orphans—
Fiction.   4. London (England)—Fiction.]   I. Knoepflmacher, U. C.   II. Title.
III. Series.

PZ7.B934 Lg 2002
[Fic]—dc21   2001036423

Printed in the United States of America
Set in Stempel Garamond

CONTENTS

INTRODUCTION

When Frances Hodgson Burnett published a short novella called *Sara Crewe: Or, What Happened at Miss Minchin's* in three monthly installments from December 1887 to February 1888 in *St. Nicholas Magazine*, she was still basking in the success of *Little Lord Fauntleroy*, the longer novel she had serialized in the same journal in 1886. A best-seller on both sides of the Atlantic, *Fauntleroy* allowed Burnett, an Englishwoman who had come to the United States in her teens, to capture the vast Anglo-American audience coveted by writers such as Henry James and Edith Wharton. She was ready to capitalize on her recent success. By setting *Sara Crewe* in Victorian London and by casting her heroine as a marginalized outsider, Burnett reworked the formula that had worked so well in *Fauntleroy*; there, an endearing American boy protagonist had triumphantly overcome the vicissitudes of his own painful translocation to England.

The relationship between the two narratives was to persist in other ways. Eager to repeat her lucrative transformation of *Fauntleroy* into a stage play performed in London and New York in 1888 and 1889, Burnett resolved to expand *Sara Crewe* into a three-act drama designed for "Children and Grown-Up Children." Initially called *A Little Unfairy Princess* but later known simply as *The Little Princess*, the 1902 play was so enthusiastically received that Burnett decided to rework it once more into a longer novel. Indeed, when that novel appeared in 1905, it came with a preface called "The Whole of the Story" in which the author contended that the drama's popularity had presumably led her publishers to ask "me if I could not write Sara's story over again and put into it all the things and people who had been left out before." She claimed to have discovered "pages and pages of things which had happened that had never been put even into the play." The result, therefore, was an entirely "new" version that included, at long last, all the events that had "actually" transpired at Miss Minchin's.

Burnett's "The Whole of the Story" (reprinted for the first time in this edition) pretends that, in fashioning Sara's thrice-told tale, the author has merely acted as a fact-finding investigative reporter. The incompleteness of the two earlier narratives is thus playfully blamed on faulty real-life informants. Instead of fully identifying themselves out in the open, these shadowy figures had failed to "come forward" to "tap the writing person on the shoulder and say, 'Hallo, what about me?' " But Burnett's tongue-in-cheek complaint that characters supposedly "as real as Sara" ought to have introduced themselves much earlier is more than a joke. For the protestation also serves as a clever advertising ploy. The "writing person" who has fashioned this nineteen-chapter novel can reassure prospective buyers that she is offering them a new product rather than a mere retread of materials already familiar to either the readers of *Sara Crewe* or the audience of *A Little Unfairy Princess*. And, what is more, by pretending to blame her derelict informants, Burnett can coyly absolve herself from any imputation of carelessness. She humorously disarms all those who might well wonder why it took her almost two decades to grasp the import of her "whole story." A less harried writer, after all, might have perfected a faultless text before handsomely profiting from the marketing of two imperfect antecedents of the same plot.

As a prolific transatlantic author, envied for the enormous sales of her works by Henry James, her fastidious neighbor and competitor, Frances Hodgson Burnett often wrote quite hastily. Even *The Secret Garden* (1911), which for many modern readers holds the place of eminence that *Fauntleroy* occupied in the late nineteenth century, is a less polished production than *A Little Princess*. Also originally intended as a novella, the story of "Mistress Mary" quickly ballooned into a full-scale novel without undergoing the slow gestation process of *A Little Princess*. And, with the unexpected prominence given to Colin Craven in the second half of *The Secret Garden*, Mary Lennox suffered a reduction. The girl whose hardiness draws us into the text just as much as Sara Crewe's uniqueness does at the start of *A Little Princess* becomes diminished when she passively observes the endless calisthenics that transform her whimpering cousin into a bronzed athlete and future "master" of Misselthwaite Manor. By way of contrast, Sara's centrality is never jeopardized: on reworking the stage play into *A Little Princess*, Burnett wisely curtailed the antics of little Donald Carmichael—a figure based, like Little Lord Fauntleroy and even Colin Craven, on fond memories of her favorite son, Lionel.

The transformation that *A Little Princess* underwent gave the last version of Sara's odyssey its richest tints and most intricately woven texture. When, in her 1905 preface, Burnett alerts her prospective audience that she has transcended the limits of the original novella and stage play, she tacitly asks us to read her book as a multilayered text. Her invitation seems to have gone largely unheeded. Without access to "The Whole of the Story," only a few students of the novel have paid attention to the particulars of its evolution. That oversight is regrettable. For the metamorphosis of the 1888 novella into the 1902 stage play and the conversion of that superficial comedy into a hauntingly introspective and symbolic text not only help us appreciate the greater complexity of the final 1905 version but also offer us important insights into Burnett's own development as an artist.

This children's book may seem removed from the polished constructs of aesthetes such as Edith Wharton and Henry James, who respectively published *The House of Mirth* and *The Golden Bowl* in the same year; and the consummate craft of Kipling's "They," another popular 1905 text, certainly excels any of Burnett's later ventures into a ghost-story mode that she tried to emulate. Nonetheless, *A Little Princess* unquestionably remains the most exquisitely controlled of all of Frances Hodgson Burnett's fictions. Its textual fabric is not only enhanced by Burnett's retrospective insight into the "whole" implications of her fable but also benefits from her fuller understanding of its place among the major fictions of loss and gain that her culture had to offer. Allusions to traditional fairy tales and to Victorian novels that had before been rather casually introduced have proliferated and acquired a greater density of meaning. Complemented by further analogues that Burnett has, in the interim, found in the writings of major contemporaries such as Twain and Kipling, these allusions now contribute to a much broader frame of reference. When earlier Brontëan touchstones are expanded and when Wordsworth, Keats, and Ruskin are evoked to place the account of Sara's imagination within a distinct literary tradition, we sense that further layers of meaning have been added to this already multilayered narrative. For the 1905 text carefully situates Sara Crewe—and hence Burnett herself—in the company of those nineteenth-century Romantics who had celebrated the transformative powers of the mind.

In chapter V of *A Little Princess*, Sara Crewe, richly attired in a "rose-colored" dancing frock and adorned with a wreath of "some real buds" on her "black locks," returns to her chamber and stumbles upon Becky, the kitchen scullion who has fallen asleep from hunger and exhaustion. Skillfully, Burnett complicates what at first merely seems a cruel contrast between the privileged girl (whose very name means "princess") and an abused member of London's underclass. The "ugly, stunted, worn-out little scullery drudge" may be as comatose as the fairy-tale princess who slumbered "for a hundred years." But the narrator who has introduced the analogy quickly dismisses its extravagance: Becky, we are curtly reminded, hardly looks "like a Sleeping Beauty at all." It is an imaginative Sara, after all, and not the unsentimental narrator, who has transformed Becky into the "ill-used heroine" of a romance. And, to heighten the irony, Sara hardly anticipates that her own aspirations as a romantic heroine will be fulfilled only after she becomes as ill used as poor Becky.

Still, despite Sara's naive embellishment of a sordid reality she has yet to confront herself, the girl also demonstrates her indisputable credentials as Burnett's heroine. Hovering over Becky "like a rose-colored fairy," observing her "with interested eyes," Sara possesses the power to lighten a Victorian cinder girl's burdens. Deftly shifting from one fairy-tale analogue to another, Burnett encourages us to regard this Anglo-Indian heiress as the potential redeemer of an abused Cinderella. The motherless child who has already nurtured marginalized girls at Miss Minchin's genteel seminary can now add a lower-class orphan to her widening list of beneficiaries. She not only offers to provide this stunted adolescent with a steady supply of extra food but also promises to nurture her starved imagination. Having previously noticed the scullery maid's pathetic eagerness to join the children who raptly listened to her revision of Hans Christian Andersen's "Little Mermaid," Sara is willing to serve the special needs of this new auditor. She therefore offers to enlarge her account of a merman prince and a human princess for Becky's exclusive benefit: "I will try to be here and tell you a bit of it every day until it is finished. It's a lovely long one—and I'm always putting new bits to it."

This important scene is brilliantly managed. The overt ironies are significant, of course: stripped of her rose-colored outfit and her optimistic outlook on life, Princess Sara will soon be herself cruelly debased. As a maltreated Cinderella, she will have to deploy her defiant imagination to protect her own threatened identity even more than Becky's. Awed by her still rosy patroness, Becky is struck by Sara's physical similarity to one of Queen Victoria's daughters, a "growed-up young lady" whom she remembers as also being "pink all over—gownd an' cloak, an' flowers an' all." But Sara already entertains a notion of royalty that requires no such outward trappings. Being a "pretend princess," she has decided, will allow her to "scatter largess to the populace." Her determination to cling to this extravagant ideal is about to be painfully tested. The powers of fantasy she has so far placed in the service of others will soon become her sole mode of defense against the deprivations she will suffer.

By the end of the book, hindsight allows this supremely intelligent child to grasp most of the ironies that marked her reversals in fortune. But, as a character in a novel, Sara can hardly be expected to see an overlap between her final self-knowledge and the self-awareness that her empathetic creator gained in the course of perfecting her story. Indeed, *A Little Princess* must be read as the culmination of a gradual process of authorial self-recognition. For this fable of identity formation owes much of its power to Burnett's increasing awareness of the strong affinities that bind her to her heroine. These affinities are far deeper than those linking Sara and Becky as social outcasts; the two girls will remain decidely unequal despite their temporarily shared attic quarters. And even the social parity that ultimately links Sara to Tom Carrisford, the "Indian gentleman" who acts as a debilitated and desexualized version of Cinderella's prince, is not enough to convert this father substitute into her equal. Early in the novel, Sara has animated the doll Emily to replace the father from whom she is forced to separate. She considers Emily, in an echo of a speech in *Wuthering Heights*, that master text about intersubjectivity written by another Emily, to be "more like me than I am like myself." But it is Burnett, of course, who has animated Sara, who is more herself than Emily or Becky or Uncle Tom Carrisford. She remains Princess Sara's only true double.

Although *A Little Princess* is hardly an autobiographical novel, its powerful insights into the hardships suffered by a child who loses her father as well as her social status are rooted in Burnett's painful memories of the aftermath of her own prosperous father's death. The fantasy life of Frances Hodgson sustained her twice: first when, as an introspective small child in England, she read fictions and invented stories for herself that allowed her to escape her family's deracination; and then once again when, as an immigrant teenager in the United States, she succeeded where her mother, uncles, and older brothers had failed. By selling her romances about British heroines ("ill-used" perhaps, but inevitably rewarded) to sundry women's magazines, the future "Mrs. Burnett" gradually recouped her family's fortunes. Increasingly successful in marketing a variety of literary forms, she came to realize that the inventive powers which had twice come to her rescue—therapeutically as well as financially—were at the very core of her recurrent interest in narratives about recuperation.

Many of Burnett's child protagonists, such as the Anglo-American Cedric Errol—better known as "Little Lord Fauntleroy"—or that other memorable Anglo-Indian child, Mary Lennox, are cast as healers. Cedric cures his wounded and testy grandfather while the "sour" Mary cures herself before helping to heal the hypochondriacal Colin Craven and his self-pitying and self-mutilating father, Archibald. Although Sara Crewe, too, eventually nurtures a wounded father figure by helping Tom Carrisford overcome his self-induced invalidism, she differs in one major respect from these other child physicians. The "odd-looking little girl" we meet in the novel's opening possesses an almost clinical understanding of the mechanisms of make-believe. Her exercise of the powers of transference and projection permit her to withstand separation anxieties so acutely painful that they would surely cripple more ordinary children—or any adult devoid of her extraordinary resilience.

Sara's astute grasp of psychological mechanisms is evident in her initial choice of the doll Emily as a fetish that might allow her to detach herself from her imprudent young father. And she manages to soothe him as much as herself when she assures Captain Crewe that he need not fear being forgotten by her. She calmly informs him that his external displacement by Emily has actually transformed him into a permanently introjected presence "inside my heart." Sara's unusually clear sense of the emotional dynamics she tries to explain to this vulnerable child-man gives her the self-control he sorely lacks. Indeed, as we later learn, the boyish Captain Crewe might well have withstood a bout of "jungle fever" had he not also "been driven mad" by his agitation over the apparent financial losses that disenfranchised his daughter.

The sturdier Sara, however, refuses to become the mad girl in the attic. She fends off hunger, cold, and degradation: "I shall die presently," she ruefully notes at one low point, yet soon rallies by banishing such morbidity. Her pensiveness (which gives her an "old look" at the age of seven, when we first meet her) marks her extraordinary maturity. For she can tenaciously hold on to mental resources that neither Ralph Crewe nor Carrisford, his former Eton chum and cricket partner, has ever learned to tap. Like Burnett, Sara knows how to enlist the energies of a metamorphic imagination. Her attic becomes a place of refuge from the demeaning world below. Ensconced in her eyrie, she can translate that soiling lower reality by relying on her ability to "pretend" and to "suppose." Fantasy becomes an absolute necessity. It allows her, quite simply, to survive.

But Sara's exchange with Becky in chapter V reflects even more poignant analogies between Burnett and the resilient child whose fiction-making ability allows her to stave off a physical and mental collapse. For by 1905 the novelist could count on a hindsight of almost twenty years to reflect on the full personal implications of a story of deracination and recovery she had first sketched in a version in which Sara was cast more as a pathetic victim than as an admirable fantasist. Self-reflexiveness and even a certain amount of gentle self-irony thus undeniably mark Burnett's final characterization of Sara as a fellow fabulist. Indeed, when Burnett has Sara promise Becky a longer version of the merman story that the girl so obviously has derived from Andersen, she is probably poking fun at her own freely acknowledged tendency to borrow from well-known writers of both adult and children's texts.

Moreover, Burnett also evokes the textual antecedents of *A Little Princess* itself when she has Sara promise Becky that her retelling would rely on an expandable series of installments with added "new bits." If Sara is a revisionist who adapts Andersen for the benefit of her own listeners in the novel (and who, in the play, adapts Frances Browne's 1856 *Granny's Wonderful Chair*, a text Burnett had herself previously used for one of her own retold fairy tales, "Prince Fairyfoot"), it is Burnett herself who remains the arch-revisionist by expanding the previous two versions of Sara's story. Indeed, Sara's interlocutor in this scene is herself an addition—"a new bit," as it were—for Becky was not a character in the original novella, having been first introduced, along with Lottie and the rat Melchisedec, in the 1902 stage production. And it was not until after she conceptualized the story a third time that Burnett fully realized the role that such figures would have to play in Sara's imaginative efforts to overcome her emotional isolation. Like the doll Emily and the rat Melchisedec, the characters of Ermengarde, Lottie, Becky, and the street child Anne act as relational outlets in Sara's dramatic struggles to avoid self-fragmentation and death. The little girl in the attic must rely on her transformative powers to bridge the gap between body and mind; in the manner of the Romantics whom she so often resembles, Sara must carefully navigate between inner and outer reality, fantasy and actuality, self and not-self.

To read *A Little Princess* as a Romantic text may, at first glance, seem anachronistic. Whereas the Yorkshire moors of *The Secret Garden* befit a pastoral romance that dramatizes the quasi-providential operations of a beneficent Nature, the grimy Victorian London of *A Little Princess* harks back to the materialist urban worlds anatomized by Dickens and Thackeray rather than to the mythic settings of the Brontës. And, as if to reinforce that link, Burnett significantly expands the novelistic coordinates she had already used in *Sara Crewe*.

Even more distinctly than before, Miss Minchin's establishment now resembles Miss Pinkerton's Academy for Young Ladies, the institution that William Thackeray had used as a setting for the opening chapter of his *Vanity Fair* (1847–48). Both schools are run by a mercenary autocrat who dominates her more benevolent younger sister as much as her young wards; both schools are exposed for commodifying a genteel education that is woefully inadequate in preparing female students for life's actual hardships. Like Sara Crewe, Miss Pinkerton's star pupil, Amelia Sedley, is prized for her father's wealth rather than for any accomplishments. Yet whereas the "old"-looking Sara is superior to her boyish father in adjusting to unforeseen reversals, Amelia falls apart after her own father's loss of his fortunes and remains girlish and ill-equipped for her responsibilities as wife, mother, and widow. Hence, whereas Burnett strongly endorses Sara's powers of fantasy as a form of resistance, Thackeray is highly critical of his childish heroine's persistent deformations of reality. He mocks the wishfulness of a child-woman as much as the adolescent delusions of her male counterpart, William Dobbin, whose escapist daydreams about "Sindbad the Sailor in the Valley of Diamonds" Burnett seems to recall in her own novel when she has Sara and her peers indulge in fantasies about *The Arabian Nights* after hearing about Captain Crewe's investment in diamond mines.

Given Thackeray's relentless mockery of a Romantic subjectivity, why did Burnett choose not only to retain but also to expand these and further Thackerayan coordinates? In moving from her novella to the play and the novel, she tried to strengthen her heroine's unique claims on our sympathies. But Thackeray had gone in an exactly contrary direction when he discouraged an attraction to either of the two female figures who could easily have become the heroine of his "Novel Without a Hero": the overemotional and naive Amelia Sedley and the brainy but heartless Becky Sharp. In the first chapter of *Vanity Fair*, in a scene that Burnett recasts in the fourth chapter of her own novel, Thackeray denies his readers an identification that she will reinstate. He first ridicules a weeping Amelia's excessive response to Laura Martin, a tiny orphan who "wistfully" vows forever to "call [Amelia her] mamma," and then aligns Amelia's sentimental reaction to this child with Miss Jemima Pinkerton's misplaced sympathy for Becky Sharp, whom the good lady absurdly romanticizes as a helpless waif. For Thackeray, all such projections are childish deformations of reality. But not for Burnett, who asks her readers to regard projection as a mark of Princess Sara's emotional superiority.

In *Sara Crewe*, Burnett had already given Amelia Sedley's first name to Miss Amelia Minchin, who defers to her tyrannical older sister just as the meek Miss Jemima had deferred to the elder Miss Pinkerton. But Burnett had yet to create Becky and Lottie, figures she enlisted to widen the scope of Sara's influence. She boldly gave the name Becky to the kitchen scullion with whom Sara identifies herself as strongly as Miss Jemima had identified herself with Becky Sharp. And she converted Thackeray's little Laura Martin into the needy Lottie. Whereas little Laura herself had suggested that Amelia Sedley take the place of her dead mother, it is Sara who proposes to Lottie that "I will be your mamma" in a continuing fantasy in which, she vows, "we will play that you are my little girl. And Emily shall be your sister."

That short, unobtrusive sentence—"And Emily shall be your sister"—is brilliantly placed. Lottie's full name is Charlotte, of course, and in the novel's last chapter Sara will discover that still another beneficiary of her powers of projection has been given the name Anne. Burnett, whose last name can be read an anagram for "Brunty" or "Bruntey," the Irish family name that Patrick Brontë had Anglicized, knows her literary history. She is aware that Charlotte Brontë had dedicated the second edition of *Jane Eyre* to William Makepeace Thackeray because the early installments of *Vanity Fair* still had encouraged the notion that his orphaned Becky Sharp might become his novel's heroine and hence play as prominent a role as that which Brontë herself assigned to the defiant orphan she used to tame the Byronic Mr. Rochester. Burnett, who even drew on Elizabeth Gaskell's *Life of Charlotte Brontë* in her naming of Melchisedec, Sara's rat, wants to reclaim an affiliation that was lost when Thackeray turned Becky Sharp into a scheming anti-heroine. Sara's self-projections on Emily, Lottie, and Anne thus help revalidate the Brontëan fables of lonely and isolated hero-ines in need of elective affinities. But they also help to redeem Thackeray's own interest in marginalized heroines and to rekindle his residual sympathy for all those thwarted fantasists who vainly try to project their inner yearnings on the contours of an outside world.

Translated into Thackerayan terms, then, the character of Sara Crewe can be said to blend the superior attributes of his antithetical heroines while eliminating all their shortcomings. Like Becky Sharp, Sara is smart, endowed with the clarity of an outsider's perspective. Both characters earn the enmity of head-mistresses whose total ignorance of French they help expose. Sara is as sharply aware as Becky Sharp of the hypocritical pretensions of an unctious vulgarian who falsely poses as an educator and whose professed gentility merely masks money-grubbing and a desire for domination. Yet whereas Becky uses her mother's French language to humiliate the elder Miss Pinkerton, Sara actually tries to protect Miss Minchin from a similar embarrassment. She repeatedly tries to inform Miss Minchin that she is already fluent in a language which she and her father have used simply because her mamma "had been French." Becky Sharp invents an aristocratic French lineage in order to elevate herself in the eyes of others. But when Sara identifies herself with Marie Antoinette, she does so privately in order to maintain her self-esteem. Like Thackeray's Amelia, Sara resolutely maintains her own genteel standards of propriety even after she has become declassed. And, as a prepubescent child, Sara need not harbor Amelia's romantic illusions about princely male lovers. The suitor best fitted to become her prince—for there are actually two candidates for that role—is even more ineligible as a mate than the kindly William Dobbin who, in *Vanity Fair*, returned from India to refurbish Amelia's own impoverished quarters and lend new meaning to a fallen heiress's life.

Sara's ostensible benefactor is the "Indian gentleman" who moves into the house next door. By restoring Sara's wealth and status, Tom Carrisford may seem to play prince to her Cinderella; and, by allowing her to cure his self-loathing and emotional paralysis, he also plays Beast to her Beauty. But it is really the more active Ram Dass, an exotic figure resembling the disguised sultans and caliphs of Eastern fables, who is single-handedly responsible for making Sara's dreams become consonant with a waking reality. It is this fellow outsider who studies Sara, understands her plight, and ultimately, like the prince in "Sleeping Beauty," alters the evil spell cast on the female space that he has penetrated. In *Sara Crewe*, this rescuer had simply been called "the Lascar" and had been given a much smaller role. But now, endowed with a Sikh name used in several of Kipling's Indian fictions, Ram Dass has become as extraordinary as Sara herself. If she can transcend her victimization as a slave laborer for Miss Minchin, so can this dignified colonial subject, a servant and attic dweller like herself, be as bountiful as any maharaja. The girl who acted as fairy godmother to Becky, Lottie, and Ermengarde gratefully defers to this benevolent genie. Called "The Magician" by Sara before she can identify him as the fellow exile she had already met on the rooftop, he is—besides Burnett—her one true double, more like herself than any of the novel's other characters.

Indeed, Ram Dass's loving redecoration of Sara's room suggests that, even more than Uncle Tom Carrisford, he acts as a father substitute. At the beginning of the novel, Captain Crewe tried to compensate Sara for his absence by eagerly stocking her "pretty bedroom and sitting-room" with an overabundance of material goods. (Burnett's own father, it is worth remembering, had profited, as an interior decorator, from his skills in furnishing the opulent rooms of Manchester magnates.) Ram Dass restores Sara's connection to India by helping her recover the paternal legacy her father had squandered; but his noiseless gliding in and out of windows also makes this "lithe white figure" seem a visitor from a more spectral realm of dead fathers. Through his agency, fantasy and reality, severed as long as Sara tried to make her way through a Thackerayan Vanity Fair, can finally be bridged. A drab actuality has, at long last, become infused with romance. The lamp Ram Dass has placed on Sara's table is covered with a "rosy shade" that no longer casts a cruel light.

As Sara's steadfast observer, Ram Dass comes closest to the omniscience of Burnett's narrator. When Carrisford's secretary finds it surprising that an Indian servant should know such "a great deal about" Sara, Ram Dass hints at the true scope of his knowledge: "All her life each day I know," he asserts. "Her going out I know, and her coming in; her sadness and her poor joys; her coldness and her hunger. I know when she sits alone until midnight, learning from her books; I know when her secret friends steal to her and she is happier—as children can be, even in the midst of poverty." More than a voyeur, Ram Dass is an alter ego, a child's secret friend. And, as his quasi-biblical diction is meant to suggest, he is also a watchful spirit, an alert guardian angel: "If she were ill I should know," he concludes, "and I would come and serve her if it might be done." Although non-Christian, Ram Dass believes in the workings of a providential design; he is confident that Carrisford will someday be reunited with the lost child: "His God may lead her to him yet." Unlike the clueless Mr. Carmichael, Carrisford's lawyer, who is unable to effect that reunion, the Sikh servant who nurtures both his master and Sara will be responsible for bringing them together.

It seems significant that Burnett should signal the momentousness of Ram Dass's entry into the novel by lyrically transforming Sara's physical surroundings. Ram Dass himself will eventually reshape Sara's shabby bedroom as a chamber befitting one whose superiority he instantly recognized on their first meeting. (He addresses her as if she were "the little daughter of a rajah" and later remarks that, though maltreated as a "pariah," Sara has "the bearing of a child who is of the blood of kings.") Yet Burnett acts even more boldly when she radically alters the appearance of an entire cityscape. Having so far maintained a sympathetic distance from Sara's subjectivity, the narrator now resorts to her own metamorphic imagination by unabashedly dissolving a "sooty" netherworld and converting it into a glowing celestial wonderland.

At the opening of chapter XI, called "Ram Dass," Burnett allows Sara to preside over that conversion. Bathed in the colors of the sunset, the grimy city has become transfigured, suddenly at one with the many-hued vault that spans over it much like the rainbow that betokened a new covenant after the Flood. But Burnett does not rely on a Judeo-Christian typology for this transfiguration. Instead, the phenomenon that suddenly makes Sara feel specially chosen, "as if she had all the sky and the world to herself," remains, for all its extraordinariness, wholly natural:

> And there Sara would stand, sometimes turning her face upward to the blue which seemed so friendly and near,—just like a lovely vaulted ceiling,—sometimes watching the west and all the wonderful things that happened there: the clouds melting or drifting or waiting softly to be changed pink or crimson or snow-white or purple or pale dove-gray. Sometimes they made islands or great mountains enclosing lakes of deep turquoise-blue, or liquid amber, or chrysoprase-green; sometimes dark headlands jutted into strange, lost seas; sometimes slender strips of wonderful lands joined other wonderful lands together. There were places where it seemed that one could run or climb or stand and wait to see what next was coming—until, perhaps, as it all melted, one could float away. At least it seemed so to Sara, and nothing had ever been quite so beautiful to her as the things she saw as she stood on the table—her body half out of the skylight—the sparrows twittering with sunset softness on the slates. The sparrows always seemed to her to twitter with a sort of subdued softness just when these marvels were going on.

Burnett here enlists tropes that go back to Romantic poetry and to the prose works of John Ruskin and George MacDonald in order to prepare her readers for the advent of Sara's savior, the deferential Sikh whose emerging top half matches her own skyward-lifted head and torso. When Sara sees the turbaned Easterner, his "dark face" strikes her "as sorrowful and homesick." He seems to answer all her yearnings for a companiable spirit. Asked whether he can "get across," he simply replies, "In a moment." The apparition of this healing man of sorrows may be as providential as Mary Lennox's discovery of the key to the secret garden. But the robin who leads Mary to a key that proves golden and the sad stranger who so readily identifies himself with Sara's martyrdom are cast as non-Christian this-worldly agents. Like the novelist herself, Ram Dass acts as a bridge builder who can help readers in their own crossing from subject to object. It is hardly coincidental that one of the texts on which Burnett draws in this major narrative addition to her earlier versions of Sara's story should be Wordsworth's famous sonnet "Composed upon Westminster Bridge." There, the speaker's realization that the sleeping city is at one with an immanent nature allows him to dissolve the traditional antinomies between matter and spirit.

A Little Princess validates the powers of fantasy by endorsing Sara's belief in a "magic" that carries out something akin to a providential dispensation. The novel suggests that more than sheer accident has prompted Carrisford to occupy the building adjacent to that which houses Miss Minchin's Seminary for Young Ladies. When Sara wishes that a fellow attic dweller might move into the empty garret next to hers, she merely hopes for another "little girl" to materialize there, so that "we could talk to each other through the windows and climb over to see each other, if we were not afraid of falling." When Ram Dass, rather than another Becky, fulfills her wish on that unusual day when "floods of molten gold" cover the sky "as if a glorious tide was sweeping over the world," Sara can become the recipient of a greater plenitude than even she has been able to foresee. Yet bountiful though he may be as a dispenser of spiritual and material gold, this exotic magician is himself a servant, not a supernatural apparition, such as George MacDonald's majestic North Wind or C. S. Lewis's royal Aslan. In At the Back of the North Wind, North Wind removes the boy Diamond from the sordid streets of Victorian London; in The

Magician's Nephew, Aslan is the magnet that draws the children Polly and Digory out of the Edwardian attic into which they have crawled. But Sara's redemption cannot be effected by her transportation into the alternative reality of some allegorical fantasyland. The cloudy, Narnia-like wonderlands the narrator evokes as a purer alternative to the Vanity Fair that has enslaved Sara are brought down to touch the child. Firmly anchored in the realities of Sara's body and mind, Burnett's text is centrifugal, not centripetal. It is not Sara's soul that must be saved to restore her to sanity, but rather her abused and undernourished body.

A Little Princess is a multilayered text that owes much of its success to its author's progressive understanding of the implications of Sara's "whole" story. Subsequent adaptations of the book have profitably extended Burnett's transformation of the earlier novella and play: Film and television productions such as the excellent 1986 version with Amelia Shankley as Sara and Tariq Alibai as Ram Dass have updated the narrative by introducing further layers of meaning. Hindsight may make us more resistant than Burnett's 1905 audience was to the notion that an heiress-turned-philanthropist might single-handedly soften the crass social injustices the book documents. In a century that has witnessed mass starvation and has familiarized us with the inner thoughts of another imaginative attic dweller, Anne Frank, Sara's experiences have acquired resonances that Burnett could hardly have foreseen. All adaptations of the story, however, have rightly retained the novelist's original focus on her protagonist's unique psychology. For Burnett understood that Sara's refusal to succumb to the indifference and denigration of her adult tormentors would attract child readers as much as grown-ups. This psychological romance will continue to draw a dual audience fascinated by an inviolable child mind's resistance to deformation and compromise.

The present edition stresses the evolution of *A Little Princess* and, in its explanatory notes, documents some of the rich intertextual relations with adult and children's classics that Burnett introduced in her final text. It restores the 1905 preface and offers selections from the two earlier versions of the story for purposes of comparison and contrast. The very different opening that Burnett had used in the 1888 *Sara Crewe*, reproduced in Appendix A, allows us to appreciate her later changes in emphasis; similarly, her earlier version of the scene in which Sara wakes up to find that her room has been "magically" transformed by Ram Dass, also reprinted in Appendix A, makes us realize the superior craftsmanship of her revisions. The excerpts from the dramatic version printed in Appendix B help us recognize further turns in Burnett's increasingly complicated plotting and characterization. Lastly, the inclusion of the entire text of Burnett's 1879 story "Behind the White Brick" in Appendix C is intended to call attention to a major antecedent for all three versions of Sara Crewe's story. As my headnote to this last appendix suggests, the clash between Jem and Aunt Hetty—which so closely resembles that between Sara and Miss Minchin—is resolved through the application of fairy-tale conventions that Burnett would further naturalize in her later retellings of the conflicts between a child fantasist and an oppressive adult reality.

U. C. KNOEPFLMACHER

SUGGESTIONS FOR FURTHER READING

EDITIONS

Giovanni and the Other: Children Who Have Made Stories. New York: Scribner's, 1892.

In the Closed Room. New York: Grosset & Dunlap, 1904.

Little Lord Fauntleroy. New York: Scribner's, 1886.

The Little Princess: A Play for Children and Grown-Up Children in Three Acts. 1902. Reprint, New York: Samuel French, 1911.

The Lost Prince. 1915. Reprint, Harmondsworth, U.K.: Puffin, 1986.

The One I Knew the Best of All. 1893. Reprint, London: Warne, 1974.

Racketty-Packetty House. 1907. Reprint, Avenel, N.J.: Derrydale, 1992.

Sara Crewe: or, What Happened at Miss Minchin's. New York: Scribner's, 1888.

The Secret Garden. London: Heinemann, 1911.

"The Story of Prince Fairyfoot," in *Little Saint Elizabeth and Other Stories.* New York: Scribner's, 1894.

FILM VERSIONS

A Little Princess (dir. Marshall Neilan, with Mary Pickford as Sara). Artcraft, 1917.

The Little Princess (dir. Walter Lang, with Shirley Temple as Sara). Twentieth Century Fox, 1939.

A Little Princess (dir. Carol Wiseman, with Amelia Shankley as Sara). London Weekend Television, 1986.

A Little Princess (dir. Alfonso Cuarón, with Liesel Mathews as Sara). Warner Brothers, 1995.

BIOGRAPHIES

Burnett, Vivian. *The Romantick Lady*. New York: Scribner's, 1927.

Thwaite, Ann. *Waiting for the Party: The Life of Frances Hodgson Burnett, 1849–1924*. New York: Scribner's, 1974.

CRITICAL STUDIES

Auerbach, Nina, and U. C. Knoepflmacher. "Subversions." In *Forbidden Journeys: Fairy Tales and Fantasies by Victorian Women Writers*, 129–38. Chicago: University of Chicago Press, 1992.

Bixler, Phyllis. "Tradition and the Individual Talent of Frances Hodgson Burnett: A Generic Analysis of *Little Lord Fauntleroy*, *A Little Princess*, and *The Secret Garden*." *Children's Literature* 7 (1978): 191–207.

———. *Frances Hodgson Burnett*. Boston: Twayne, 1984.

Brown, Marian E. "Three Versions of *A Little Princess*: How the Story Developed." *Children's Literature in Education* 19 (1988): 199–210.

Cadogan, Mary, and Patricia Craig. *You're a Brick, Angela! A New Look at Girls' Fiction from 1839 to 1975*. London: Gollancz, 1976.

Connell, Eileen. "Playing House: Frances Hodgson Burnett's Victorian Fairy Tale." In *Keeping the Victorian House: A Collection of Essays*, edited by Vanessa D. Dickerson, 149–71. New York: Garland, 1995.

Dusinberre, Juliet. "Making Space for a Child." In *Alice to the Lighthouse: Children's Books and Radical Experiments in Art*, 187–219. New York: St. Martin's, 1987.

Gannon, Susan R. " 'The Best Magazine for Children of All Ages': Cross-Editing *St. Nicholas Magazine* (1873–1905)." *Children's Literature* 25 (1997): 153–80.

Gruner, Elizabeth Rose. "Cinderella, Marie Antoinette, and Sara: Roles and Role Models in *A Little Princess*." *The Lion and the Unicorn* 22 (1998): 163–87.

Keyser, Elizabeth Lennox. " 'The Whole of the Story': Frances Hodgson Burnett's 'A Little Princess.' " In *Triumphs of the*

Spirit in Children's Literature, edited by Francelia Butler and Richard Rotert, 230–43. Hamden, Conn.: Library Professional Publications, 1986.

Knoepflmacher, U. C. "Little Girls Without Their Curls: Female Aggression in Victorian Children's Literature." *Children's Literature* 11 (1983): 14–31.

Laski, Marghanita. *Mrs. Ewing, Mrs. Molesworth, and Mrs. Hodgson Burnett*. London: Barker, 1950.

L'Engle, Madeleine. Preface to *A Little Princess*, vii–xii. New York: Bantam, 1987.

McGillis, Roderick. *A Little Princess: Gender and Empire*. New York: Twayne, 1996.

Reimer, Mavis. "Making Princesses, Re-Making *A Little Princess*." In *Voices of the Other: Children's Literature and the Postcolonial Context*, edited by Roderick McGillis, New York: Garland, 1999. 111–34.

Schwartz, Lynne Sharon. Afterword to *A Little Princess*, 223–26. New York: Signet, 1988.

OTHER WORKS CITED

Brontë, Emily. *Wuthering Heights*. 1847. Reprint, edited by William N. Sale and Richard J. Dunn, New York: Norton, 1990.

Browne, Frances. *Granny's Wonderful Chair*. 1856. Reprint, Harmondsworth, U.K.: Puffin, 1985.

Lewis, C. S. *The Magician's Nephew*. 1955. Reprint, New York: Collier, 1970.

MacDonald, George. *At the Back of the North Wind*. 1871. Reprint, Harmondsworth, U.K.: Puffin, 1984.

Thackeray, William Makepeace. *Vanity Fair*. 1847–48. Reprint, edited by John Sutherland, New York: Oxford, 1983.

A NOTE ON THE TEXT

The first edition of *A Little Princess*, subtitled *Being the Whole Story of Sara Crewe Now Told for the First Time*, lavishly illustrated by Ethel Franklin Betts, was published in New York by Charles Scribner's Sons in 1905. It is the text I have adopted, with the exception of a misprint corrected by Frances Hodgson Burnett herself in the copy I own: in the opening sentence of chapter IV, "Lottie," the printer had apparently misread Burnett's "the next two years" as "the next ten years," a mistake perpetuated in every subsequent reprint of the novel. Burnett, who inscribed this volume "with love and thousands of good wishes" to "dear little Betty Houghton," carefully crossed out the "ten" and inserted a "two"; for reasons that remain unclear, however, it seems that she never instructed her publishers to make the same change.

The two selections from "Sara Crewe" in Appendix A are taken from the three-part serialization of the story in *St. Nicholas Magazine* 15 (December 1887 to February 1888), 97–105, 168–74, 252–60. The first excerpt corresponds to pages 97–99 and the second one to pages 172–74 and 252. Burnett actually used the identical text (and the same illustrations by Reginald B. Birch) for the 1888 edition of the novella in book form, published by Charles Scribner's Sons.

The selections from *The Little Princess: A Play for Children and Grown-Up Children in Three Acts* in Appendix B are taken from the 1911 version printed in New York and London by Samuel French, the theatrical publisher; the lavish stage instructions intended for school productions of the play do not seem to have been written by Burnett herself.

Lastly, "Behind the White Brick," the early short story

reprinted in Appendix C, follows the original version published in *St. Nicholas Magazine* 6 (January 1879), 169–75. Burnett again retained the original text when she reprinted the tale in *Little Saint Elizabeth and Other Stories* (New York: Scribner's, 1890), 125–46.

A LITTLE PRINCESS

THE WHOLE OF THE STORY

I DO NOT KNOW whether many people realize how much more than is ever written there really is in a story—how many parts of it are never told—how much more really happened than there is in the book one holds in one's hand and pores over. Stories are something like letters. When a letter is written, how often one remembers things omitted and says, "Ah, why did I not tell them that?" In writing a book one relates all that one remembers at the time, and if one told all that really happened perhaps the book would never end. Between the lines of every story there is another story, and that is one that is never heard and can only be guessed at by the people who are good at guessing. The person who writes the story may never know all of it, but sometimes he does and wishes he had the chance to begin again.

When I wrote the story of "Sara Crewe" I guessed that a great deal more had happened at Miss Minchin's than I had had time to find out just then. I knew, of course, that there must have been chapters full of things going on all the time; and when I began to make a play out of the book and called it "A Little Princess," I discovered three acts full of things. What interested me most was that I found that there had been girls at the school whose names I had not even known before. There was a little girl whose name was Lottie, who was an amusing little person; there was a hungry scullery-maid who was Sara's adoring friend; Ermengarde was much more entertaining than she had seemed at first; things happened in the garret which had never been hinted at in the book; and a certain gentleman whose name was Melchisedec was an intimate friend of Sara's who should never have been left out of the story if he had only walked into it in time. He and Becky and Lottie lived at Miss Minchin's, and I cannot understand why they did not mention themselves to me at first. They were as real as Sara, and it was careless of them not to come out of the story shadowland and say, "Here I am—tell about me." But they did not—which was their fault and not mine. People who live in the story one is writing ought to come forward at the beginning and tap the writing person on the shoulder and say, "Hallo, what about me?" If they don't, no one can be blamed but themselves and their slouching, idle ways.

After the play of "A Little Princess" was produced in New York, and so many children went to see it and liked Becky and Lottie and Melchisedec, my publishers asked me if I could not write Sara's story over again and put into it all the things and people who had been left out before, and so I have done it; and when I began I found there were actually pages and pages of things which had happened that had never been put even into the play, so in this new "Little Princess" I have put all I have been able to discover.

FRANCES HODGSON BURNETT

CHAPTER I

Sara

ONCE ON A DARK WINTER'S DAY, when the yellow fog hung so thick and heavy in the streets of London that the lamps were lighted and the shop windows blazed with gas as they do at night, an odd-looking little girl sat in a cab with her father and was driven rather slowly through the big thoroughfares.[1]

She sat with her feet tucked under her, and leaned against her father, who held her in his arm, as she stared out of the window at the passing people with a queer old-fashioned thoughtfulness in her big eyes.

She was such a little girl that one did not expect to see such a look on her small face. It would have been an old look for a child of twelve, and Sara Crewe was only seven.[2] The fact was, however, that she was always dreaming and thinking odd things and could not herself remember any time when she had not been thinking things about grown-up people and the world they belonged to. She felt as if she had lived a long, long time.

At this moment she was remembering the voyage she had just made from Bombay with her father, Captain Crewe. She was thinking of the big ship, of the Lascars[3] passing silently to and fro on it, of the children playing about on the hot deck, and of some young officers' wives who used to try to make her talk to them and laugh at the things she said.

Principally, she was thinking of what a queer thing it was that at one time one was in India in the blazing sun, and then in the middle of the ocean, and then driving in a strange vehicle through strange streets where the day was as dark as the night. She found this so puzzling that she moved closer to her father.

"Papa," she said in low, mysterious little voice which was almost a whisper, "papa."

"What is it, darling?" Captain Crewe answered, holding

her closer and looking down into her face. "What is Sara thinking of?"

"Is this the place?" Sara whispered, cuddling still closer to
him. "Is it, papa?"

"Yes, little Sara, it is. We have reached it at last." And though
she was only seven years old, she knew that he felt sad when he
said it.

It seemed to her many years since he had begun to prepare
her mind for "the place," as she always called it. Her mother
had died when she was born, so she had never known or missed
her. Her young, handsome, rich, petting father seemed to be the
only relation she had in the world. They had always played together and been fond of each other. She only knew he was rich
because she had heard people say so when they thought she was
not listening, and she had also heard them say that when she
grew up she would be rich, too. She did not know all that being
rich meant. She had always lived in a beautiful bungalow, and
had been used to seeing many servants who made salaams to
her and called her "Missee Sahib," and gave her her own way in
everything. She had had toys and pets and an ayah[4] who worshipped her, and she had gradually learned that people who
were rich had these things. That, however, was all she knew
about it.

During her short life only one thing had troubled her, and
that thing was "the place" she was to be taken to some day. The
climate of India was very bad for children, and as soon as possible they were sent away from it—generally to England and to
school. She had seen other children go away, and had heard
their fathers and mothers talk about the letters they received
from them. She had known that she would be obliged to go
also, and though sometimes her father's stories of the voyage
and the new country had attracted her, she had been troubled
by the thought that he could not stay with her.

"Couldn't you go to that place with me, papa?" she had
asked when she was five years old. "Couldn't you go to school,
too? I would help you with your lessons."

"But you will not have to stay for a very long time, little
Sara," he had always said. "You will go to a nice house where
there will be a lot of little girls, and you will play together, and

I will send you plenty of books, and you will grow so fast that it will seem scarcely a year before you are big enough and clever enough to come back and take care of papa."

She had liked to think of that. To keep the house for her father; to ride with him, and sit at the head of his table when he had dinner-parties; to talk to him and read his books—that would be what she would like most in the world, and if one must go away to "the place" in England to attain it, she must make up her mind to go. She did not care very much for other little girls, but if she had plenty of books she could console herself. She liked books more than anything else, and was, in fact, always inventing stories of beautiful things and telling them to herself. Sometimes she had told them to her father, and he had liked them as much as she did.

"Well, papa," she said softly, "if we are here I suppose we must be resigned."

He laughed at her old-fashioned speech and kissed her. He was really not at all resigned himself, though he knew he must keep that a secret. His quaint little Sara had been a great companion to him, and he felt he should be a lonely fellow when, on his return to India, he went into his bungalow knowing he need not expect to see the small figure in its white frock come forward to meet him. So he held her very closely in his arm as the cab rolled into the big, dull square in which stood the house which was their destination.

It was a big, dull, brick house, exactly like all the others in its row, but that on the front door there shone a brass plate on which was engraved in black letters:

MISS MINCHIN,[5]
SELECT SEMINARY FOR YOUNG LADIES.

"Here we are, Sara," said Captain Crewe, making his voice sound as cheerful as possible. Then he lifted her out of the cab and they mounted the steps and rang the bell. Sara often thought afterward that the house was somehow exactly like Miss Minchin. It was respectable and well furnished, but everything in it was ugly; and the very arm-chairs seemed to have hard bones in them. In the hall everything was hard and polished—even the red cheeks of the moon face on the tall clock in the corner had a severe varnished look. The drawing-room into which they were ushered was covered by a carpet with a square pattern upon it, the chairs were square, and a heavy marble timepiece stood upon the heavy marble mantel.

As she sat down in one of the stiff mahogany chairs, Sara cast one of her quick looks about her.

"I don't like it, papa," she said. "But then I dare say soldiers—even brave ones—don't really *like* going into battle."

Captain Crewe laughed outright at this. He was young and full of fun, and he never tired of hearing Sara's queer speeches.

"Oh, little Sara," he said. "What shall I do when I have no one to say solemn things to me? No one else is quite as solemn as you are."

"But why do solemn things make you laugh so?" inquired Sara.

"Because you are such fun when you say them," he answered, laughing still more. And then suddenly he swept her into his arms and kissed her very hard, stopping laughing all at once and looking almost as if tears had come into his eyes.

It was just then that Miss Minchin entered the room. She was very like her house, Sara felt: tall and dull, and respectable and ugly. She had large, cold, fishy eyes, and a large, cold, fishy smile. It spread itself into a very large smile when she saw Sara and Captain Crewe. She had heard a great many desirable things of the young soldier from the lady who had recommended her school to him. Among other things, she had heard that he was a rich father who was willing to spend a great deal of money on his little daughter.

"It will be a great privilege to have charge of such a beautiful and promising child, Captain Crewe," she said, taking Sara's hand and stroking it. "Lady Meredith has told me of her unusual cleverness.[6] A clever child is a great treasure in an establishment like mine."

Sara stood quietly, with her eyes fixed upon Miss Minchin's face. She was thinking something odd, as usual.

"Why does she say I am a beautiful child," she was thinking. "I am not beautiful at all. Colonel Grange's little girl, Isobel, is beautiful. She has dimples and rose-colored cheeks, and long hair the color of gold. I have short black hair and green eyes; besides which, I am a thin child and not fair in the least. I am one of the ugliest children I ever saw. She is beginning by telling a story."

She was mistaken, however, in thinking she was an ugly child. She was not in the least like Isobel Grange, who had been the beauty of the regiment, but she had an odd charm of her own. She was a slim, supple creature, rather tall for her age, and had an intense, attractive little face. Her hair was heavy and quite black and only curled at the tips; her eyes were greenish gray, it is true, but they were big, wonderful eyes with long, black lashes, and though she herself did not like the color of them, many other people did. Still she was very firm in her belief that she was an ugly little girl, and she was not at all elated by Miss Minchin's flattery.

"I should be telling a story if I said she was beautiful," she thought; "and I should know I was telling a story. I believe I am as ugly as she is—in my way. What did she say that for?"

After she had known Miss Minchin longer she learned why she had said it. She discovered that she said the same thing to each papa and mamma who brought a child to her school.

Sara stood near her father and listened while he and Miss Minchin talked. She had been brought to the seminary because Lady Meredith's two little girls had been educated there, and Captain Crewe had a great respect for Lady Meredith's experience. Sara was to be what was known as "a parlor-boarder," and she was to enjoy even greater privileges than parlor-boarders usually did. She was to have a pretty bedroom and sitting-room of her own; she was to have a pony and a carriage, and a maid to take the place of the ayah who had been her nurse in India.

"I am not in the least anxious about her education," Captain Crewe said, with his gay laugh, as he held Sara's hand and patted it. "The difficulty will be to keep her from learning too fast and too much. She is always sitting with her little nose burrowing into books. She doesn't read them, Miss Minchin; she gobbles them up as if she were a little wolf instead of a little girl. She is always starving for new books to gobble, and she wants grown-up books—great, big, fat ones—French and German as well as English—history and biography and poets, and all sorts of things. Drag her away from her books when she reads too much. Make her ride her pony in the Row or go out and buy a new doll. She ought to play more with dolls."

"Papa," said Sara. "You see, if I went out and bought a new doll every few days I should have more than I could be fond of. Dolls ought to be intimate friends. Emily is going to be my intimate friend."[7]

Captain Crewe looked at Miss Minchin and Miss Minchin looked at Captain Crewe.

"Who is Emily?" she inquired.

"Tell her, Sara," Captain Crewe said, smiling.

Sara's green-gray eyes looked very solemn and quite soft as she answered.

"She is a doll I haven't got yet," she said. "She is a doll papa is going to buy for me. We are going out together to find her. I have called her Emily. She is going to be my friend when papa is gone. I want her to talk to about him."

Miss Minchin's large, fishy smile became very flattering indeed.

"What an original child!" she said. "What a darling little creature!"

"Yes," said Captain Crewe, drawing Sara close. "She is a darling little creature. Take great care of her for me, Miss Minchin."

Sara stayed with her father at his hotel for several days; in fact, she remained with him until he sailed away again to India. They went out and visited many big shops together, and bought a great many things. They bought, indeed, a great many more things than Sara needed; but Captain Crewe was a rash, innocent young man and wanted his little girl to have everything she admired and everything he admired himself, so between them they collected a wardrobe much too grand for a child of seven. There were velvet dresses trimmed with costly furs, and lace dresses, and embroidered ones, and hats with great, soft ostrich feathers, and ermine coats and muffs, and boxes of tiny gloves and handkerchiefs and silk stockings in such abundant supplies that the polite young women behind the counters whispered to each other that the odd little girl with the big, solemn eyes must be at least some foreign princess—perhaps the little daughter of an Indian rajah.

And at last they found Emily, but they went to a number of toy-shops and looked at a great many dolls before they finally discovered her.

"I want her to look as if she wasn't a doll really," Sara said.[8] "I want her to look as if she *listens* when I talk to her. The trouble with dolls, papa"—and she put her head on one side and reflected as she said it—"the trouble with dolls is that they never seem to *hear*." So they looked at big ones and little ones—at dolls with black eyes and dolls with blue—at dolls with brown curls and dolls with golden braids, dolls dressed and dolls undressed.

"You see," Sara said when they were examining one who had no clothes. "If, when I find her, she has no frocks, we can take her to a dressmaker and have her things made to fit. They will fit better if they are tried on."

After a number of disappointments they decided to walk and look in at the shop windows and let the cab follow them. They had passed two or three places without even going in, when, as they were approaching a shop which was really not a very large one, Sara suddenly started and clutched her father's arm.

"Oh, papa!" she cried. "There is Emily!"

A flush had risen to her face and there was an expression in her green-gray eyes as if she had just recognized some one she was intimate with and fond of.

"She is actually waiting for us!" she said. "Let us go in to her."

"Dear me!" said Captain Crewe; "I feel as if we ought to have some one to introduce us."

"You must introduce me and I will introduce you," said Sara. "But I knew her the minute I saw her—so perhaps she knew me, too."

Perhaps she had known her. She had certainly a very intelligent expression in her eyes when Sara took her in her arms. She was a large doll, but not too large to carry about easily; she had naturally curling golden-brown hair, which hung like a mantle about her, and her eyes were a deep, clear, gray blue, with soft, thick eyelashes which were real eyelashes and not mere painted lines.

"Of course," said Sara, looking into her face as she held her on her knee—"of course, papa, this is Emily."

So Emily was bought and actually taken to a children's outfitter's shop, and measured for a wardrobe as grand as Sara's own. She had lace frocks, too, and velvet and muslin ones, and hats and coats and beautiful lace-trimmed underclothes, and gloves and handkerchiefs and furs.

"I should like her always to look as if she was a child with a good mother," said Sara. "I'm her mother, though I am going to make a companion of her."

Captain Crewe would really have enjoyed the shopping tremendously, but that a sad thought kept tugging at his heart. This all meant that he was going to be separated from his beloved, quaint little comrade.

He got out of his bed in the middle of that night and went and stood looking down at Sara, who lay asleep with Emily in her arms. Her black hair was spread out on the pillow and Emily's golden-brown hair mingled with it, both of them had lace-ruffled night-gowns, and both had long eyelashes which lay and curled up on their cheeks. Emily looked so like a real child that Captain Crewe felt glad she was there. He drew a big sigh and pulled his mustache with a boyish expression.

"Heigh-ho, little Sara!" he said to himself. "I don't believe you know how much your daddy will miss you."

The next day he took her to Miss Minchin's and left her there. He was to sail away the next morning. He explained to Miss Minchin that his solicitors, Messrs. Barrow & Skipworth, had charge of his affairs in England and would give her any advice she wanted, and that they would pay the bills she sent in for Sara's expenses. He would write to Sara twice a week, and she was to be given every pleasure she asked for.

"She is a sensible little thing, and she never wants anything it isn't safe to give her," he said.

Then he went with Sara into her little sitting-room and they bade each other good-by. Sara sat on his knee and held the lapels of his coat in her small hands, and looked long and hard at his face.

"Are you learning me by heart, little Sara," he said, stroking her hair.

"No," she answered. "I know you by heart. You are inside my heart." And they put their arms round each other and kissed as if they would never let each other go.

When the cab drove away from the door, Sara was sitting on the floor of her sitting-room, with her hands under her chin and her eyes following it until it had turned the corner of the square. Emily was sitting by her, and she looked after it, too. When Miss Minchin sent her sister, Miss Amelia, to see what the child was doing, she found she could not open the door.[9]

"I have locked it," said a queer, polite little voice from inside. "I want to be quite by myself, if you please."

Miss Amelia was fat and dumpy, and stood very much in awe of her sister. She was really the better-natured person of the two, but she never disobeyed Miss Minchin. She went down-stairs again, looking almost alarmed.

"I never saw such a funny, old-fashioned child, sister," she said. "She has locked herself in, and she is not making the least particle of noise."

"It is much better than if she kicked and screamed, as some of them do," Miss Minchin answered. "I expected that a child as much spoiled as she is would set the whole house in an uproar. If ever a child was given her own way in everything, she is."

"I've been opening her trunks and putting her things away," said Miss Amelia. "I never saw anything like them—sable and ermine on her coats, and real Valenciennes lace on her underclothing.[10] You have seen some of her clothes. What *do* you think of them?"

"I think they are perfectly ridiculous," replied Miss Minchin, sharply; "but they will look very well at the head of the line when we take the school-children to church on Sunday. She has been provided for as if she were a little princess."

And up-stairs in the locked room Sara and Emily sat on the floor and stared at the corner round which the cab had disappeared, while Captain Crewe looked backward, waving and kissing his hand as if he could not bear to stop.

CHAPTER II

A French Lesson

WHEN SARA entered the school-room the next morning everybody looked at her with wide, interested eyes. By that time every pupil—from Lavinia Herbert, who was nearly thirteen and felt quite grown up, to Lottie Legh, who was only just four and the baby of the school—had heard a great deal about her.[1] They knew very certainly that she was Miss Minchin's show pupil and was considered a credit to the establishment. One or two of them had even caught a glimpse of her French maid, Mariette, who had arrived the evening before.[2] Lavinia had managed to pass Sara's room when the door was open, and had seen Mariette opening a box which had arrived late from some shop.

"It was full of petticoats with lace frills on them—frills and frills," she whispered to her friend Jessie as she bent over her geography. "I saw her shaking them out. I heard Miss Minchin say to Miss Amelia that her clothes were so grand that they were ridiculous for a child. My mamma says that children should be dressed simply. She has got one of those petticoats on now. I saw it when she sat down."

"She has silk stockings on!" whispered Jessie, bending over her geography also. "And what little feet! I never saw such little feet."[3]

"Oh," sniffed Lavinia, spitefully, "that is the way her slippers are made. My mamma says that even big feet can be made to look small if you have a clever shoemaker. I don't think she is pretty at all. Her eyes are such a queer color."

"She isn't pretty as other pretty people are," said Jessie, stealing a glance across the room; "but she makes you want to look at her again. She has tremendously long eyelashes, but her eyes are almost green."

Sara was sitting quietly in her seat, waiting to be told what to do. She had been placed near Miss Minchin's desk. She was not abashed at all by the many pairs of eyes watching her. She was interested and looked back quietly at the children who looked at her. She wondered what they were thinking of, and if they liked Miss Minchin, and if they cared for their lessons, and if any of them had a papa at all like her own. She had had a long talk with Emily about her papa that morning.

"He is on the sea now, Emily," she had said. "We must be very great friends to each other and tell each other things. Emily, look at me. You have the nicest eyes I ever saw,—but I wish you could speak."

She was a child full of imaginings and whimsical thoughts, and one of her fancies was that there would be a great deal of comfort in even pretending that Emily was alive and really heard and understood.[4] After Mariette had dressed her in her dark-blue school-room frock and tied her hair with a dark-blue ribbon, she went to Emily, who sat in a chair of her own, and gave her a book.

"You can read that while I am down-stairs," she said; and, seeing Mariette looking at her curiously, she spoke to her with a serious little face.

"What I believe about dolls," she said, "is that they can do things they will not let us know about. Perhaps, really, Emily can read and talk and walk, but she will only do it when people are out of the room. That is her secret. You see, if people knew that dolls could do things, they would make them work. So, perhaps, they have promised each other to keep it a secret. If you stay in the room, Emily will just sit there and stare; but if you go out, she will begin to read, perhaps, or go and look out of the window. Then if she heard either of us coming, she would just run back and jump into her chair and pretend she had been there all the time."

"*Comme elle est drôle!*"[5] Mariette said to herself, and when she went down-stairs she told the head housemaid about it. But she had already begun to like this odd little girl who had such an intelligent small face and such perfect manners. She had taken care of children before who were not so polite. Sara was a very fine little person, and had a gentle, appreciative way of saying, "If you please, Mariette," "Thank you, Mariette," which was very charming. Mariette told the head housemaid that she thanked her as if she was thanking a lady.

"*Elle a l'air d'une princesse, cette petite,*" she said.[6] Indeed, she was very much pleased with her new little mistress and liked her place greatly.

After Sara had sat in her seat in the school-room for a few minutes, being looked at by the pupils, Miss Minchin rapped in a dignified manner upon her desk.

"Young ladies," she said, "I wish to introduce you to your new companion." All the little girls rose in their places, and Sara rose also. "I shall expect you all to be very agreeable to Miss Crewe; she has just come to us from a great distance—in fact, from India. As soon as lessons are over you must make each other's acquaintance."

The pupils bowed ceremoniously, and Sara made a little courtesy, and then they sat down and looked at each other again.

"Sara," said Miss Minchin in her school-room manner, "come here to me."

She had taken a book from the desk and was turning over its leaves. Sara went to her politely.

"As your papa has engaged a French maid for you," she began, "I conclude that he wishes you to make a special study of the French language."

Sara felt a little awkward.

"I think he engaged her," she said, "because he—he thought I would like her, Miss Minchin."

"I am afraid," said Miss Minchin, with a slightly sour smile, "that you have been a very spoiled little girl and always imagine that things are done because you like them. My impression is that your papa wished you to learn French."

If Sara had been older or less punctilious about being quite polite to people, she could have explained herself in a very few words. But, as it was, she felt a flush rising on her cheeks. Miss Minchin was a very severe and imposing person, and she seemed so absolutely sure that Sara knew nothing whatever of French that she felt as if it would be almost rude to correct her. The truth was that Sara could not remember the time when she had not seemed to know French. Her father had often spoken it to her when she had been a baby. Her mother had been a Frenchwoman, and Captain Crewe had loved her language, so it happened that Sara had always heard and been familiar with it.[7]

"I—I have never really learned French, but—but—" she began, trying shyly to make herself clear.

One of Miss Minchin's chief secret annoyances was that she did not speak French herself, and was desirous of concealing the irritating fact.[8] She, therefore, had no intention of discussing the matter and laying herself open to innocent questioning by a new little pupil.

"That is enough," she said with polite tartness. "If you have not learned, you must begin at once. The French master, Monsieur Dufarge, will be here in a few minutes. Take this book and look at it until he arrives."

Sara's cheeks felt warm. She went back to her seat and opened the book. She looked at the first page with a grave face. She knew it would be rude to smile, and she was very determined not to be rude. But it was very odd to find herself expected to study a page which told her that "*le père*" meant "the father," and "*la mère*" meant "the mother."

Miss Minchin glanced toward her scrutinizingly.

"You look rather cross, Sara," she said. "I am sorry you do not like the idea of learning French."

"I am very fond of it," answered Sara, thinking she would try again; "but—"

"You must not say 'but' when you are told to do things," said Miss Minchin. "Look at your book again."

And Sara did so, and did not smile, even when she found that "*le fils*" meant "the son," and "*le frère*" meant "the brother."

"When Monsieur Dufarge comes," she thought, "I can make him understand."

Monsieur Dufarge arrived very shortly afterward. He was a very nice, intelligent, middle-aged Frenchman, and he looked interested when his eyes fell upon Sara trying politely to seem absorbed in her little book of phrases.

"Is this a new pupil for me, madame?" he said to Miss Minchin. "I hope that is my good fortune."

"Her papa—Captain Crewe—is very anxious that she should begin the language. But I am afraid she has a childish prejudice against it. She does not seem to wish to learn," said Miss Minchin.

"I am sorry of that, mademoiselle," he said kindly to Sara. "Perhaps, when we begin to study together, I may show you that it is a charming tongue."

Little Sara rose in her seat. She was beginning to feel rather desperate, as if she were almost in disgrace. She looked up into Monsieur Dufarge's face with her big, green-gray eyes, and they were quite innocently appealing. She knew that he would understand as soon as she spoke. She began to explain quite simply in pretty and fluent French. Madame had not understood. She had not learned French exactly,—not out of books,—but her papa and other people had always spoken it to her, and she had read it and written it as she had read and written English. Her papa loved it, and she loved it because he did. Her dear mamma, who had died when she was born, had been French. She would be glad to learn anything monsieur would teach her, but what she had tried to explain to madame was that she already knew the words in this book—and she held out the little book of phrases.

When she began to speak Miss Minchin started quite violently and sat staring at her over her eye-glasses, almost indignantly, until she had finished. Monsieur Dufarge began to smile, and his smile was one of great pleasure. To hear this pretty childish voice speaking his own language so simply and charmingly made him feel almost as if he were in his native land—which in dark, foggy days in London sometimes seemed worlds away. When she had finished, he took the phrase-book from her, with a look almost affectionate. But he spoke to Miss Minchin.

"Ah, madame," he said, "there is not much I can teach her. She has not *learned* French; she *is* French. Her accent is exquisite."

"You ought to have told me," exclaimed Miss Minchin, much mortified, turning on Sara.

"I—I tried," said Sara. "I—I suppose I did not begin right."

Miss Minchin knew she had tried, and that it had not been

her fault that she was not allowed to explain. And when she saw that the pupils had been listening and that Lavinia and Jessie were giggling behind their French grammars, she felt infuriated.

"Silence, young ladies!" she said severely, rapping upon the desk. "Silence at once!"

And she began from that minute to feel rather a grudge against her show pupil.

CHAPTER III

Ermengarde

ON THAT FIRST MORNING, when Sara sat at Miss Minchin's side, aware that the whole school-room was devoting itself to observing her, she had noticed very soon one little girl, about her own age, who looked at her very hard with a pair of light, rather dull, blue eyes. She was a fat child who did not look as if she were in the least clever, but she had a good-naturedly pouting mouth. Her flaxen hair was braided in a tight pigtail, tied with a ribbon, and she had pulled this pigtail round her neck, and was biting the end of the ribbon, resting her elbows on the desk, as she stared wonderingly at the new pupil. When Monsieur Dufarge began to speak to Sara, she looked a little frightened; and when Sara stepped forward and, looking at him with the innocent, appealing eyes, answered him, without any warning, in French, the fat little girl gave a startled jump, and grew quite red in her awed amazement. Having wept hopeless tears for weeks in her efforts to remember that "*la mère*" meant "the mother," and "*le père*," "the father,"—when one spoke sensible English,—it was almost too much for her to suddenly find herself listening to a child her own age who seemed not only quite familiar with these words, but apparently knew any number of others, and could mix them up with verbs as if they were mere trifles.

She stared so hard and bit the ribbon on her pigtail so fast that she attracted the attention of Miss Minchin, who, feeling extremely cross at the moment, immediately pounced upon her.

"Miss St. John!" she exclaimed severely. "What do you mean by such conduct? Remove your elbows! Take your ribbon out of your mouth! Sit up at once!"

Upon which Miss St. John gave another jump, and when Lavinia and Jessie tittered she became redder than ever—so red, indeed, that she almost looked as if tears were coming into her poor, dull, childish eyes; and Sara saw her and was so sorry for her that she began to rather like her and want to be her friend. It was a way of hers always to want to spring into any fray in which some one was made uncomfortable or unhappy.

"If Sara had been a boy and lived a few centuries ago," her father used to say, "she would have gone about the country with her sword drawn, rescuing and defending every one in distress. She always wants to fight when she sees people in trouble."[1]

So she took rather a fancy to fat, slow, little Miss St. John, and kept glancing toward her through the morning. She saw that lessons were no easy matter to her, and that there was no danger of her ever being spoiled by being treated as a show pupil. Her French lesson was a pathetic thing. Her pronunciation made even Monsieur Dufarge smile in spite of himself, and Lavinia and Jessie and the more fortunate girls either giggled or looked at her in wondering disdain. But Sara did not laugh. She tried to look as if she did not hear when Miss St. John called "*le bon pain*," "*lee bong pang.*" She had a fine, hot little temper of her own, and it made her feel rather savage when she heard the titters and saw the poor, stupid, distressed child's face.

"It isn't funny, really," she said between her teeth, as she bent over her book. "They ought not to laugh."

When lessons were over and the pupils gathered together in groups to talk, Sara looked for Miss St. John, and finding her bundled rather disconsolately in a window-seat, she walked over to her and spoke.[2] She only said the kind of thing little girls always say to each other by way of beginning an acquaintance, but there was something nice and friendly about Sara, and people always felt it.

"What is your name?" she said.

To explain Miss St. John's amazement one must recall that a new pupil is, for a short time, a somewhat uncertain thing; and of this new pupil the entire school had talked the night before until it fell asleep quite exhausted by excitement and contradictory stories. A new pupil with a carriage and a pony and a maid, and a voyage from India to discuss, was not an ordinary acquaintance.

"My name's Ermengarde St. John,"[3] she answered.

"Mine is Sara Crewe," said Sara. "Yours is very pretty. It sounds like a story-book."

"Do you like it?" fluttered Ermengarde. "I—I like yours."

Miss St. John's chief trouble in life was that she had a clever father. Sometimes this seemed to her a dreadful calamity. If you have a father who knows everything, who speaks seven or eight languages, and has thousands of volumes which he has apparently learned by heart, he frequently expects you to be familiar with the contents of your lesson-books at least; and it is not improbable that he will feel you ought to be able to remember a few incidents of history and to write a French exercise. Ermengarde was a severe trial to Mr. St. John.[4] He could not understand how a child of his could be a notably and unmistakably dull creature who never shone in anything.

"Good heavens!" he had said more than once, as he stared at her, "there are times when I think she is as stupid as her Aunt Eliza!"

If her Aunt Eliza had been slow to learn and quick to forget a thing entirely when she had learned it, Ermengarde was strikingly like her. She was the monumental dunce of the school, and it could not be denied.

"She must be *made* to learn," her father said to Miss Minchin.

Consequently Ermengarde spent the greater part of her life in disgrace or in tears. She learned things and forgot them; or, if she remembered them, she did not understand them. So it was natural that, having made Sara's acquaintance, she should sit and stare at her with profound admiration.

"You can speak French, can't you?" she said respectfully.

Sara got on to the window-seat, which was a big, deep one, and, tucking up her feet, sat with her hands clasped round her knees.

"I can speak it because I have heard it all my life," she answered. "You could speak it if you had always heard it."

"Oh, no, I couldn't," said Ermengarde. "I *never* could speak it!"

"Why?" inquired Sara, curiously.

Ermengarde shook her head so that the pigtail wabbled.

"You heard me just now," she said. "I'm always like that. I can't *say* the words. They're so queer."

She paused a moment, and then added with a touch of awe in her voice:

"You are *clever*, aren't you?"

Sara looked out of the window into the dingy square, where the sparrows were hopping and twittering on the wet, iron railings and the sooty branches of the trees. She reflected a few moments. She had heard it said very often that she was "clever," and she wondered if she was,—and *if* she was, how it had happened.

"I don't know," she said. "I can't tell." Then, seeing a mournful look on the round, chubby face, she gave a little laugh and changed the subject.

"Would you like to see Emily?" she inquired.

"Who is Emily?" Ermengarde asked, just as Miss Minchin had done.

"Come up to my room and see," said Sara, holding out her hand.

They jumped down from the window-seat together, and went up-stairs.

"Is it true," Ermengarde whispered, as they went through the hall—"is it true that you have a play-room all to yourself?"

"Yes," Sara answered. "Papa asked Miss Minchin to let me have one, because—well, it was because when I play I make up stories and tell them to myself, and I don't like people to hear me. It spoils it if I think people listen."

They had reached the passage leading to Sara's room by this time, and Ermengarde stopped short, staring, and quite losing her breath.

"You *make up* stories!" she gasped. "Can you do that—as well as speak French? *Can* you?"

Sara looked at her in simple surprise.

"Why, any one can make up things," she said. "Have you never tried?"

She put her hand warningly on Ermengarde's.

"Let us go very quietly to the door," she whispered, "and then I will open it quite suddenly; perhaps we may catch her."

She was half laughing, but there was a touch of mysterious

hope in her eyes which fascinated Ermengarde, though she had not the remotest idea what it meant, or whom it was she wanted to "catch," or why she wanted to catch her. Whatsoever she meant, Ermengarde was sure it was something delightfully exciting. So, quite thrilled with expectation, she followed her on tiptoe along the passage. They made not the least noise until they reached the door. Then Sara suddenly turned the handle, and threw it wide open. Its opening revealed the room quite neat and quiet, a fire gently burning in the grate, and a wonderful doll sitting in a chair by it, apparently reading a book.

"Oh, she got back to her seat before we could see her!" Sara exclaimed. "Of course they always do. They are as quick as lightning."

Ermengarde looked from her to the doll and back again.

"Can she—walk?" she asked breathlessly.

"Yes," answered Sara. "At least I believe she can. At least I *pretend* I believe she can. And that makes it seem as if it were true. Have you never pretended things?"

"No," said Ermengarde. "Never. I—tell me about it."

She was so bewitched by this odd, new companion that she actually stared at Sara instead of at Emily—notwithstanding that Emily was the most attractive doll person she had ever seen.

"Let us sit down," said Sara, "and I will tell you. It's so easy that when you begin you can't stop. You just go on and on doing it always. And it's beautiful. Emily, you must listen. This is Ermengarde St. John, Emily. Ermengarde, this is Emily. Would you like to hold her?"

"Oh, may I?" said Ermengarde. "May I, really? She *is* beautiful!" And Emily was put into her arms.

Never in her dull, short life had Miss St. John dreamed of such an hour as the one she spent with the queer new pupil before they heard the lunch-bell ring and were obliged to go down-stairs.

Sara sat upon the hearth-rug and told her strange things. She sat rather huddled up, and her green eyes shone and her cheeks flushed. She told stories of the voyage, and stories of India; but what fascinated Ermengarde the most was her fancy about the dolls who walked and talked, and who could do anything they chose when the human beings were out of the room, but who must keep their powers a secret and so flew back to their places "like lightning" when people returned to the room.

"*We* couldn't do it," said Sara, seriously. "You see, it's a kind of magic."

Once, when she was relating the story of the search for Emily, Ermengarde saw her face suddenly change. A cloud seemed to pass over it and put out the light in her shining eyes. She drew her breath in so sharply that it made a funny, sad little sound, and then she shut her lips and held them tightly closed, as if she was determined either to do or *not* to do something. Ermengarde had an idea that if she had been like any other little girl, she might have suddenly burst out sobbing and crying. But she did not.

"Have you a—a pain?" Ermengarde ventured.

"Yes," Sara answered, after a moment's silence. "But it is not in my body." Then she added something in a low voice which she tried to keep quite steady, and it was this: "Do you love your father more than anything else in all the whole world?"

Ermengarde's mouth fell open a little. She knew that it would be far from behaving like a respectable child at a select seminary to say that it had never occurred to you that you *could* love your father, that you would do anything desperate to avoid being left alone in his society for ten minutes. She was, indeed, greatly embarrassed.

"I—I scarcely ever see him," she stammered. "He is always in the library—reading things."

"I love mine more than all the world ten times over," Sara said. "That is what my pain is. He has gone away."

She put her head quietly down on her little, huddled-up knees, and sat very still for a few minutes.

"She's going to cry out loud," thought Ermengarde, fearfully.

But she did not. Her short, black locks tumbled about her ears, and she sat still. Then she spoke without lifting her head.

"I promised him I would bear it," she said. "And I will. You have to bear things. Think what soldiers bear! Papa is a soldier.

If there was a war he would have to bear marching and thirstiness and, perhaps, deep wounds. And he would never say a word—not one word."

Ermengarde could only gaze at her, but she felt that she was beginning to adore her. She was so wonderful and different from any one else.

Presently, she lifted her face and shook back her black locks, with a queer little smile.

"If I go on talking and talking," she said, "and telling you things about pretending, I shall bear it better. You don't forget, but you bear it better."

Ermengarde did not know why a lump came into her throat and her eyes felt as if tears were in them.

"Lavinia and Jessie are 'best friends,'" she said rather huskily. "I wish we could be 'best friends.' Would you have me for yours? You're clever, and I'm the stupidest child in the school, but I—oh, I do so like you!"

"I'm glad of that," said Sara. "It makes you thankful when you are liked. Yes. We will be friends. And I'll tell you what"— a sudden gleam lighting her face—"I can help you with your French lessons."

CHAPTER IV

Lottie

IF SARA HAD BEEN a different kind of child, the life she led at Miss Minchin's Select Seminary for the next two years would not have been at all good for her.[1] She was treated more as if she were a distinguished guest at the establishment than as if she were a mere little girl. If she had been a self-opinionated, domineering child, she might have become disagreeable enough to be unbearable through being so much indulged and flattered. If she had been an indolent child, she would have learned nothing. Privately Miss Minchin disliked her, but she was far too worldly a woman to do or say anything which might make such a desirable pupil wish to leave her school. She knew quite well that if Sara wrote to her papa to tell him she was uncomfortable or unhappy, Captain Crewe would remove her at once. Miss Minchin's opinion was that if a child were continually praised and never forbidden to do what she liked, she would be sure to be fond of the place where she was so treated. Accordingly, Sara was praised for her quickness at her lessons, for her good manners, for her amiability to her fellow-pupils, for her generosity if she gave sixpence to a beggar out of her full little purse; the simplest thing she did was treated as if it were a virtue, and if she had not had a disposition and a clever little brain, she might have been a very self-satisfied young person. But the clever little brain told her a great many sensible and true things about herself and her circumstances, and now and then she talked these things over to Ermengarde as time went on.

"Things happen to people by accident," she used to say. "A lot of nice accidents have happened to me. It just *happened* that I always liked lessons and books, and could remember things when I learned them. It just happened that I was born with a father who was beautiful and nice and clever, and could give me

27

everything I liked. Perhaps I have not really a good temper at all, but if you have everything you want and every one is kind to you, how can you help but be good-tempered? I don't know"—looking quite serious—"how I shall ever find out whether I am really a nice child or a horrid one. Perhaps I'm a *hideous* child, and no one will ever know, just because I never have any trials."

"Lavinia has no trials," said Ermengarde, stolidly, "and she is horrid enough."

Sara rubbed the end of her little nose reflectively, as she thought the matter over.

"Well," she said at last, "perhaps—perhaps that is because Lavinia is *growing.*"

This was the result of a charitable recollection of having heard Miss Amelia say that Lavinia was growing so fast that she believed it affected her health and temper.

Lavinia, in fact, was spiteful. She was inordinately jealous of Sara. Until the new pupil's arrival, she had felt herself the leader in the school. She had led because she was capable of making herself extremely disagreeable if the others did not follow her. She domineered over the little children, and assumed grand airs with those big enough to be her companions. She was rather pretty, and had been the best-dressed pupil in the procession when the Select Seminary walked out two by two, until Sara's velvet coats and sable muffs appeared, combined with drooping ostrich feathers, and were led by Miss Minchin at the head of the line. This, at the beginning, had been bitter enough; but as time went on it became apparent that Sara was a leader, too, and not because she could make herself disagreeable, but because she never did.

"There's one thing about Sara Crewe," Jessie had enraged her "best friend" by saying honestly,—"she's never 'grand' about herself the least bit, and you know she might be, Lavvie. I believe I couldn't help being—just a little—if I had so many fine things and was made such a fuss over. It's disgusting, the way Miss Minchin shows her off when parents come."

" 'Dear Sara must come into the drawing-room and talk to Mrs. Musgrave about India,' " mimicked Lavinia, in her most highly flavored imitation of Miss Minchin. " 'Dear Sara must speak French to Lady Pitkin. Her accent is so perfect.' She didn't learn her French at the Seminary, at any rate. And there's nothing so clever in her knowing it. She says herself she didn't learn it at all. She just picked it up, because she always heard her papa speak it. And, as to her papa, there is nothing so grand in being an Indian officer."

"Well," said Jessie, slowly, "he's killed tigers. He killed the one in the skin Sara has in her room. That's why she likes it so. She lies on it and strokes its head, and talks to it as if it was a cat."

"She's always doing something silly," snapped Lavinia. "My mamma says that way of hers of pretending things is silly. She says she will grow up eccentric."

It was quite true that Sara was never "grand." She was a friendly little soul, and shared her privileges and belongings with a free hand. The little ones, who were accustomed to being disdained and ordered out of the way by mature ladies aged ten and twelve, were never made to cry by this most envied of them all. She was a motherly young person, and when people fell down and scraped their knees, she ran and helped them up and patted them, or found in her pocket a bonbon or some other article of a soothing nature. She never pushed them out of her way or alluded to their years as a humiliation and a blot upon their small characters.

"If you are four you are four," she said severely to Lavinia on an occasion of her having—it must be confessed—slapped Lottie and called her "a brat"; "but you will be five next year, and six the year after that. And," opening large, convicting eyes, "it only takes sixteen years to make you twenty."

"Dear me!" said Lavinia; "how we can calculate!" In fact, it was not to be denied that sixteen and four made twenty,—and twenty was an age the most daring were scarcely bold enough to dream of.

So the younger children adored Sara. More than once she had been known to have a tea-party, made up of these despised ones, in her own room. And Emily had been played with, and Emily's own tea-service used—the one with cups which held quite a lot of much-sweetened weak tea and had blue flowers on them. No one had seen such a very real doll's tea-set before.

From that afternoon Sara was regarded as a goddess and a queen by the entire alphabet class.

Lottie Legh worshipped her to such an extent that if Sara had not been a motherly person, she would have found her tiresome. Lottie had been sent to school by a rather flighty young papa who could not imagine what else to do with her. Her young mother had died, and as the child had been treated like a favorite doll or a very spoiled pet monkey or lap-dog ever since the first hour of her life, she was a very appalling little creature. When she wanted anything or did not want anything she wept and howled; and, as she always wanted the things she could not have, and did not want the things that were best for her, her shrill little voice was usually to be heard uplifted in wails in one part of the house or another.

Her strongest weapon was that in some mysterious way she had found out that a very small girl who had lost her mother was a person who ought to be pitied and made much of. She had probably heard some grown-up people talking her over in the early days, after her mother's death. So it became her habit to make great use of this knowledge.

The first time Sara took her in charge was one morning when, on passing a sitting-room, she heard both Miss Minchin and Miss Amelia trying to suppress the angry wails of some child who, evidently, refused to be silenced. She refused so strenuously indeed that Miss Minchin was obliged to almost shout—in a stately and severe manner—to make herself heard.

"What *is* she crying for?" she almost yelled.

"Oh—oh—oh!" Sara heard; "I haven't got any mam—ma-a!"

"Oh, Lottie!" screamed Miss Amelia. "Do stop, darling! Don't cry! Please don't!"

"Oh! oh! oh!" Lottie howled tempestuously. "Haven't—got—any—mam—ma-a!"

"She ought to be whipped," Miss Minchin proclaimed. "You *shall* be whipped, you naughty child!"

Lottie wailed more loudly than ever. Miss Amelia began to cry. Miss Minchin's voice rose until it almost thundered, then suddenly she sprang up from her chair in impotent indignation and flounced out of the room, leaving Miss Amelia to arrange the matter.

Sara had paused in the hall, wondering if she ought to go into the room, because she had recently begun a friendly acquaintance with Lottie and might be able to quiet her. When Miss Minchin came out and saw her, she looked rather annoyed. She realized that her voice, as heard from inside the room, could not have sounded either dignified or amiable.

"Oh, Sara!" she exclaimed, endeavoring to produce a suitable smile.

"I stopped," explained Sara, "because I knew it was Lottie,—and I thought, perhaps—just perhaps, I could make her be quiet. May I try, Miss Minchin?"

"If you can. You are a clever child," answered Miss Minchin, drawing in her mouth sharply. Then, seeing that Sara looked slightly chilled by her asperity, she changed her manner. "But you are clever in everything," she said in her approving way. "I dare say you can manage her. Go in." And she left her.

When Sara entered the room, Lottie was lying upon the floor, screaming and kicking her small fat legs violently, and Miss Amelia was bending over her in consternation and despair, looking quite red and damp with heat. Lottie had always found, when in her own nursery at home, that kicking and screaming would always be quieted by any means she insisted on. Poor plump Miss Amelia was trying first one method, and then another.

"Poor darling!" she said one moment; "I know you haven't any mamma, poor—" Then in quite another tone: "If you don't stop, Lottie, I will shake you. Poor little angel! There—there! You wicked, bad, detestable child, I will smack you! I will!"

Sara went to them quietly. She did not know at all what she was going to do, but she had a vague inward conviction that it would be better not to say such different kinds of things quite so helplessly and excitedly.

"Miss Amelia," she said in a low voice, "Miss Minchin says I may try to make her stop—may I?"

Miss Amelia turned and looked at her hopelessly. "Oh, *do* you think you can?" she gasped.

"I don't know whether I *can*," answered Sara, still in her half-whisper; "but I will try."

Miss Amelia stumbled up from her knees with a heavy sigh, and Lottie's fat little legs kicked as hard as ever.

"If you will steal out of the room," said Sara, "I will stay with her."

"Oh, Sara!" almost whimpered Miss Amelia. "We never had such a dreadful child before. I don't believe we *can* keep her."

But she crept out of the room, and was very much relieved to find an excuse for doing it.

Sara stood by the howling, furious child for a few moments, and looked down at her without saying anything.[2] Then she sat down flat on the floor beside her and waited. Except for Lottie's angry screams, the room was quite quiet. This was a new state of affairs for little Miss Legh, who was accustomed, when she screamed, to hear other people protest and implore and command and coax by turns. To lie and kick and shriek, and find the only person near you not seeming to mind in the least, attracted her attention. She opened her tight-shut streaming eyes to see who this person was. And it was only another little girl. But it was the one who owned Emily and all the nice things. And she was looking at her steadily and as if she was merely thinking. Having paused for a few seconds to find this out, Lottie thought she must begin again, but the quiet of the room and of Sara's odd, interested face made her first howl rather half-hearted.

"I—haven't—any—ma—ma—ma-a!" she announced; but her voice was not so strong.

Sara looked at her still more steadily, but with a sort of understanding in her eyes.

"Neither have I," she said.

This was so unexpected that it was astounding. Lottie actually dropped her legs, gave a wriggle, and lay and stared. A new idea will stop a crying child when nothing else will. Also it was true that while Lottie disliked Miss Minchin, who was cross, and Miss Amelia, who was foolishly indulgent, she rather liked Sara, little as she knew her. She did not want to give up her grievance, but her thoughts were distracted from it, so she wriggled again, and, after a sulky sob, said:

"Where is she?"

Sara paused a moment. Because she had been told that her mamma was in heaven, she had thought a great deal about the matter, and her thoughts had not been quite like those of other people.

"She went to heaven," she said. "But I am sure she comes out sometimes to see me—though I don't see her. So does yours. Perhaps they can both see us now. Perhaps they are both in this room."

Lottie sat bolt upright, and looked about her. She was a pretty, little, curly-headed creature, and her round eyes were like wet forget-me-nots. If her mamma had seen her during the last half-hour, she might not have thought her the kind of child who ought to be related to an angel.

Sara went on talking. Perhaps some people might think that what she said was rather like a fairy story, but it was all so real to her own imagination that Lottie began to listen in spite of herself. She had been told that her mamma had wings and a crown, and she had been shown pictures of ladies in beautiful white night-gowns, who were said to be angels. But Sara seemed to be telling a real story about a lovely country where real people were.

"There are fields and fields of flowers," she said, forgetting herself, as usual, when she began, and talking rather as if she were in a dream—"fields and fields of lilies—and when the soft wind blows over them it wafts the scent of them into the air—and everybody always breathes it, because the soft wind is always blowing. And little children run about in the lily-fields and gather armsful of them, and laugh and make little wreaths. And the streets are shining. And no one is ever tired, however far they walk. They can float anywhere they like. And there are walls made of pearl and gold all round the city, but they are low enough for the people to go and lean on them, and look down on to the earth and smile, and send beautiful messages."[3]

Whatsoever story she had begun to tell, Lottie would, no doubt, have stopped crying, and been fascinated into listening; but there was no denying that this story was prettier than most others. She dragged herself close to Sara, and drank in every

word until the end came—far too soon. When it did come, she
was so sorry that she put up her lip ominously.

"I want to go there," she cried. "I—haven't any mamma in
this school."

Sara saw the danger-signal, and came out of her dream. She
took hold of the chubby hand and pulled her close to her side
with a coaxing little laugh.

"I will be your mamma," she said.[4] "We will play that you
are my little girl. And Emily shall be your sister."[5]

Lottie's dimples all began to show themselves.

"Shall she?" she said.

"Yes," answered Sara, jumping to her feet. "Let us go and
tell her. And then I will wash your face and brush your hair."

To which Lottie agreed quite cheerfully, and trotted out of
the room and up-stairs with her, without seeming even to remember that the whole of the last hour's tragedy had been
caused by the fact that she had refused to be washed and
brushed for lunch and Miss Minchin had been called in to use
her majestic authority.

And from that time Sara was an adopted mother.

CHAPTER V

Becky

OF COURSE THE GREATEST POWER Sara possessed and the one which gained her even more followers than her luxuries and the fact that she was "the show pupil," the power that Lavinia and certain other girls were most envious of, and at the same time most fascinated by in spite of themselves, was her power of telling stories and of making everything she talked about seem like a story, whether it was one or not.[1]

Any one who has been at school with a teller of stories knows what the wonder means—how he or she is followed about and besought in a whisper to relate romances; how groups gather round and hang on the outskirts of the favored party in the hope of being allowed to join it and listen. Sara not only could tell stories, but she adored telling them. When she sat or stood in the midst of a circle and began to invent wonderful things, her green eyes grew big and shining, her cheeks flushed, and, without knowing that she was doing it, she began to act and made what she told lovely or alarming by the raising or dropping of her voice, the bend and sway of her slim body, and the dramatic movement of her hands. She forgot that she was talking to listening children; she saw and lived with the fairy folk, or the kings and queens and beautiful ladies, whose adventures she was narrating. Sometimes when she had finished her story, she was quite out of breath with excitement, and would lay her hand on her thin, little, quick-rising chest, and half laugh as if at herself.

"When I am telling it," she would say, "it doesn't seem as if it was only made up. It seems more real than you are—more real than the school-room. I feel as if I were all the people in the story—one after the other. It *is* queer."

She had been at Miss Minchin's school about two years when, one foggy winter's afternoon, as she was getting out of her carriage, comfortably wrapped up in her warmest velvets and furs and looking very much grander than she knew, she caught sight, as she crossed the pavement, of a dingy little figure standing on the area steps, and stretching its neck so that its wide-open eyes might peer at her through the railings. Something in the eagerness and timidity of the smudgy face made her look at it, and when she looked she smiled because it was her way to smile at people.[2]

But the owner of the smudgy face and the wide-open eyes evidently was afraid that she ought not to have been caught looking at pupils of importance. She dodged out of sight like a Jack-in-the-box and scurried back into the kitchen, disappearing so suddenly that if she had not been such a poor, little forlorn thing, Sara would have laughed in spite of herself. That very evening, as Sara was sitting in the midst of a group of listeners in a corner of the school-room telling one of her stories, the very same figure timidly entered the room, carrying a coalbox much too heavy for her, and knelt down upon the hearthrug to replenish the fire and sweep up the ashes.[3]

She was cleaner than she had been when she peeped through the area railings, but she looked just as frightened. She was evidently afraid to look at the children or seem to be listening. She put on pieces of coal cautiously with her fingers so that she might make no disturbing noise, and she swept about the fireirons very softly. But Sara saw in two minutes that she was deeply interested in what was going on, and that she was doing her work slowly in the hope of catching a word here and there. And realizing this, she raised her voice and spoke more clearly.

"The Mermaids swam softly about in the crystal-green water, and dragged after them a fishing-net woven of deep-sea pearls," she said. "The Princess sat on the white rock and watched them."

It was a wonderful story about a princess who was loved by a Prince Merman, and went to live with him in shining caves under the sea.[4]

The small drudge before the grate swept the hearth once and then swept it again. Having done it twice, she did it three times; and, as she was doing it the third time, the sound of the story so lured her to listen that she fell under the spell and actually forgot that she had no right to listen at all, and also forgot every-thing else. She sat down upon her heels as she knelt on the hearth-rug, and the brush hung idly in her fingers. The voice of the story-teller went on and drew her with it into winding grot-tos under the sea, glowing with soft, clear blue light, and paved with pure golden sands. Strange sea flowers and grasses waved about her, and far away faint singing and music echoed.

The hearth-brush fell from the work-roughened hand, and Lavinia Herbert looked round.

"That girl has been listening," she said.

The culprit snatched up her brush, and scrambled to her feet. She caught at the coal-box and simply scuttled out of the room like a frightened rabbit.

Sara felt rather hot-tempered.

"I knew she was listening," she said. "Why shouldn't she?"

Lavinia tossed her head with great elegance.

"Well," she remarked, "I do not know whether your mamma would like you to tell stories to servant girls, but I know *my* mamma wouldn't like *me* to do it."

"My mamma!" said Sara, looking odd. "I don't believe she would mind in the least. She knows that stories belong to everybody."

"I thought," retorted Lavinia, in severe recollection, "that your mamma was dead. How can she know things?"

"Do you think she *doesn't* know things?" said Sara, in her stern little voice. Sometimes she had a rather stern little voice.

"Sara's mamma knows everything," piped in Lottie. "So does my mamma—'cept Sara is my mamma at Miss Minchin's—my other one knows everything. The streets are shining, and there are fields and fields of lilies, and everybody gathers them. Sara tells me when she puts me to bed."

"You wicked thing," said Lavinia, turning on Sara; "making fairy stories about heaven."

"There are much more splendid stories in Revelation," re-turned Sara. "Just look and see! How do you know mine are fairy stories?[5] But I can tell you"—with a fine bit of unheavenly temper—"you will never find out whether they are or not if you're not kinder to people than you are now. Come along, Lottie." And she marched out of the room, rather hoping that

she might see the little servant again somewhere, but she found
no trace of her when she got into the hall.

"Who is that little girl who makes the fires?" she asked Mariette that night.

Mariette broke forth into a flow of description.

Ah, indeed, Mademoiselle Sara might well ask. She was a
forlorn little thing who had just taken the place of scullery-
maid—though, as to being scullery-maid, she was everything
else besides. She blacked boots and grates, and carried heavy
coal-scuttles up and down stairs, and scrubbed floors and
cleaned windows, and was ordered about by everybody. She
was fourteen years old, but was so stunted in growth that
she looked about twelve. In truth, Mariette was sorry for her.
She was so timid that if one chanced to speak to her it appeared
as if her poor, frightened eyes would jump out of her head.

"What is her name?" asked Sara, who had sat by the table,
with her chin on her hands, as she listened absorbedly to the
recital.

Her name was Becky. Mariette heard every one below-stairs
calling, "Becky, do this," and "Becky, do that," every five minutes in the day.

Sara sat and looked into the fire, reflecting on Becky for
some time after Mariette left her. She made up a story of which
Becky was the ill-used heroine.[6] She thought she looked as if
she had never had quite enough to eat. Her very eyes were hungry. She hoped she should see her again, but though she caught
sight of her carrying things up or down stairs on several occasions, she always seemed in such a hurry and so afraid of being
seen that it was impossible to speak to her.

But a few weeks later, on another foggy afternoon, when she
entered her sitting-room she found herself confronting a rather
pathetic picture. In her own special and pet easy-chair before
the bright fire, Becky—with a coal smudge on her nose and
several on her apron, with her poor little cap hanging half off
her head, and an empty coal-box on the floor near her—sat fast
asleep, tired out beyond even the endurance of her hard-
working young body. She had been sent up to put the bedrooms in order for the evening. There were a great many of
them, and she had been running about all day. Sara's rooms she

had saved until the last. They were not like the other rooms, which were plain and bare. Ordinary pupils were expected to be satisfied with mere necessaries. Sara's comfortable sitting-room seemed a bower of luxury to the scullery-maid, though it was, in fact, merely a nice, bright little room. But there were pictures and books in it, and curious things from India; there was a sofa and the low, soft chair; Emily sat in a chair of her own, with the air of a presiding goddess, and there was always a glowing fire and a polished grate. Becky saved it until the end of her afternoon's work, because it rested her to go into it, and she always hoped to snatch a few minutes to sit down in the soft chair and look about her, and think about the wonderful good fortune of the child who owned such surroundings and who went out on the cold days in beautiful hats and coats one tried to catch a glimpse of through the area railing.

On this afternoon, when she had sat down, the sensation of relief to her short, aching legs had been so wonderful and de-lightful that it had seemed to soothe her whole body, and the glow of warmth and comfort from the fire had crept over her like a spell, until, as she looked at the red coals, a tired, slow smile stole over her smudged face, her head nodded forward without her being aware of it, her eyes drooped, and she fell fast asleep. She had really been only about ten minutes in the room when Sara entered, but she was in as deep a sleep as if she had been, like the Sleeping Beauty, slumbering for a hundred years.[7] But she did not look—poor Becky!—like a Sleeping Beauty at all. She looked only like an ugly, stunted, worn-out little scullery drudge.

Sara seemed as much unlike her as if she were a creature from another world.

On this particular afternoon she had been taking her dancing-lesson, and the afternoon on which the dancing-master appeared was rather a grand occasion at the seminary, though it occurred every week. The pupils were attired in their prettiest frocks, and as Sara danced particularly well, she was very much brought forward, and Mariette was requested to make her as diaphanous and fine as possible.

To-day a frock the color of a rose had been put on her, and Mariette had bought some real buds and made her a wreath to wear on her black locks. She had been learning a new, delightful dance in which she had been skimming and flying about the room, like a large rose-colored butterfly, and the enjoyment and exercise had brought a brilliant, happy glow into her face.

When she entered the room, she floated in with a few of the butterfly steps,—and there sat Becky, nodding her cap sideways off her head.

"Oh!" cried Sara, softly, when she saw her. "That poor thing!"

It did not occur to her to feel cross at finding her pet chair occupied by the small, dingy figure. To tell the truth, she was quite glad to find it there. When the ill-used heroine of her story wakened, she could talk to her. She crept toward her quietly, and stood looking at her. Becky gave a little snore.

"I wish she'd waken herself," Sara said. "I don't like to waken her. But Miss Minchin would be cross if she found out. I'll just wait a few minutes."

She took a seat on the edge of the table, and sat swinging her slim, rose-colored legs, and wondering what it would be best to do. Miss Amelia might come in at any moment, and if she did, Becky would be sure to be scolded.

"But she is so tired," she thought. "She *is* so tired!"

A piece of flaming coal ended her perplexity for her that very moment. It broke off from a large lump and fell on to the fender. Becky started, and opened her eyes with a frightened gasp. She did not know she had fallen asleep. She had only sat down for one moment and felt the beautiful glow—and here she found herself staring in wild alarm at the wonderful pupil, who sat perched quite near her, like a rose-colored fairy, with interested eyes.

She sprang up and clutched at her cap. She felt it dangling over her ear, and tried wildly to put it straight. Oh, she had got herself into trouble now with a vengeance! To have impudently fallen asleep on such a young lady's chair! She would be turned out of doors without wages.

She made a sound like a big breathless sob.

"Oh, miss! Oh, miss!" she stuttered. "I arst yer pardon, miss![8] Oh, I do, miss!"

Sara jumped down, and came quite close to her.

"Don't be frightened," she said, quite as if she had been speaking to a little girl like herself. "It doesn't matter the least bit."

"I didn't go to do it, miss," protested Becky. "It was the warm fire—an' me bein' so tired. It—it *wasn't* imperence!"[9]

Sara broke into a friendly little laugh, and put her hand on her shoulder.

"You were tired," she said; "you could not help it. You are not really awake yet."

How poor Becky stared at her! In fact, she had never heard such a nice, friendly sound in any one's voice before. She was used to being ordered about and scolded, and having her ears boxed. And this one—in her rose-colored dancing afternoon splendor—was looking at her as if she were not a culprit at all—as if she had a right to be tired—even to fall asleep! The touch of the soft, slim little paw on her shoulder was the most amazing thing she had ever known.

"Ain't—ain't yer angry, miss?" she gasped. "Ain't yer goin' to tell the missus?"

"No," cried out Sara. "Of course I'm not."

The woful fright in the coal-smutted face made her suddenly so sorry that she could scarcely bear it. One of her queer thoughts rushed into her mind. She put her hand against Becky's cheek.

"Why," she said, "we are just the same—I am only a little girl like you. It's just an accident that I am not you, and you are not me!"

Becky did not understand in the least. Her mind could not grasp such amazing thoughts, and "an accident" meant to her a calamity in which some one was run over or fell off a ladder and was carried to "the 'orspital."

"A' accident, miss," she fluttered respectfully. "Is it?"

"Yes," Sara answered, and she looked at her dreamily for a moment. But the next she spoke in a different tone. She realized that Becky did not know what she meant.

"Have you done your work?" she asked. "Dare you stay here a few minutes?"

Becky lost her breath again.

"Here, miss? Me?"

Sara ran to the door, opened it, and looked out and listened.

"No one is anywhere about," she explained. "If your bedrooms are finished, perhaps you might stay a tiny while. I thought—perhaps—you might like a piece of cake."

The next ten minutes seemed to Becky like a sort of delirium. Sara opened a cupboard, and gave her a thick slice of cake. She seemed to rejoice when it was devoured in hungry bites. She talked and asked questions, and laughed until Becky's fears actually began to calm themselves, and she once or twice gathered boldness enough to ask a question or so herself, daring as she felt it to be.

"Is that—" she ventured, looking longingly at the rose-colored frock. And she asked it almost in a whisper. "Is that there your best?"

"It is one of my dancing-frocks," answered Sara. "I like it, don't you?"

For a few seconds Becky was almost speechless with admiration. Then she said in an awed voice:

"Onct I see a princess. I was standin' in the street with the crowd outside Covin' Garden, watchin' the swells go inter the operer. An' there was one every one stared at most. They ses to each other, 'That's the princess.' She was a growed-up young lady, but she was pink all over—gownd an' cloak, an' flowers an' all. I called her to mind the minnit I see you, sittin' there on the table, miss. You looked like her."

"I've often thought," said Sara, in her reflecting voice, "that I should like to be a princess; I wonder what it feels like. I believe I will begin pretending I am one."

Becky stared at her admiringly, and, as before, did not understand her in the least. She watched her with a sort of adoration. Very soon Sara left her reflections and turned to her with a new question.

"Becky," she said, "weren't you listening to that story?"

"Yes, miss," confessed Becky, a little alarmed again. "I knowed I hadn't orter, but it was that beautiful I—I couldn't help it."[10]

"I liked you to listen to it," said Sara. "If you tell stories, you like nothing so much as to tell them to people who want to listen. I don't know why it is. Would you like to hear the rest?"

Becky lost her breath again.

"Me hear it?" she cried. "Like as if I was a pupil, miss! All about the Prince—and the little white Mer-babies swimming about laughing—with stars in their hair?"

Sara nodded.

"You haven't time to hear it now, I'm afraid," she said; "but if you will tell me just what time you come to do my rooms, I will try to be here and tell you a bit of it every day until it is finished. It's a lovely long one—and I'm always putting new bits to it."

"Then," breathed Becky, devoutly, "I wouldn't mind *how* heavy the coal-boxes was—or *what* the cook done to me, if—if I might have that to think of."

"You may," said Sara. "I'll tell it *all* to you."

When Becky went down-stairs, she was not the same Becky who had staggered up, loaded down by the weight of the coal-scuttle. She had an extra piece of cake in her pocket, and she had been fed and warmed, but not only by cake and fire. Something else had warmed and fed her, and the something else was Sara.

When she was gone Sara sat on her favorite perch on the end of her table. Her feet were on a chair, her elbows on her knees, and her chin in her hands.

"If I *was* a princess—a *real* princess," she murmured, "I could scatter largess to the populace. But even if I am only a pretend princess, I can invent little things to do for people. Things like this. She was just as happy as if it was largess. I'll pretend that to do things people like is scattering largess. I've scattered largess."

CHAPTER VI

The Diamond-Mines

Not very long after this a very exciting thing happened. Not only Sara, but the entire school, found it exciting, and made it the chief subject of conversation for weeks after it occurred. In one of his letters Captain Crewe told a most interesting story. A friend who had been at school with him when he was a boy had unexpectedly come to see him in India. He was the owner of a large tract of land upon which diamonds had been found, and he was engaged in developing the mines. If all went as was confidently expected, he would become possessed of such wealth as it made one dizzy to think of; and because he was fond of the friend of his school-days, he had given him an opportunity to share in this enormous fortune by becoming a partner in his scheme. This, at least, was what Sara gathered from his letters. It is true that any other business scheme, however magnificent, would have had but small attraction for her or for the school-room; but "diamond-mines" sounded so like the "Arabian Nights" that no one could be indifferent.[1] Sara thought them enchanting, and painted pictures, for Ermengarde and Lottie, of labyrinthine passages in the bowels of the earth, where sparkling stones studded the walls and roofs and ceilings, and strange, dark men dug them out with heavy picks.[2] Ermengarde delighted in the story, and Lottie insisted on its being retold to her every evening. Lavinia was very spiteful about it, and told Jessie that she didn't believe such things as diamond-mines existed.

"My mamma has a diamond ring which cost forty pounds," she said. "And it is not a big one, either. If there were mines full of diamonds, people would be so rich it would be ridiculous."

"Perhaps Sara will be so rich that she will be ridiculous," giggled Jessie.

"She's ridiculous without being rich," Lavinia sniffed.

"I believe you hate her," said Jessie.

"No, I don't," snapped Lavinia. "But I don't believe in mines full of diamonds."

"Well, people have to get them from somewhere," said Jessie. "Lavinia,"—with a new giggle,—"what do you think Gertrude says?"

"I don't know, I'm sure; and I don't care if it's something more about that everlasting Sara."

"Well, it is. One of her 'pretends' is that she is a princess. She plays it all the time—even in school. She says it makes her learn her lessons better. She wants Ermengarde to be one, too, but Ermengarde says she is too fat."

"She *is* too fat," said Lavinia. "And Sara is too thin."

Naturally, Jessie giggled again.

"She says it has nothing to do with what you look like, or what you have. It has only to do with what you *think* of, and what you *do*."

"I suppose she thinks she could be a princess if she was a beggar," said Lavinia. "Let us begin to call her Your Royal Highness."

Lessons for the day were over, and they were sitting before the school-room fire, enjoying the time they liked best. It was the time when Miss Minchin and Miss Amelia were taking their tea in the sitting-room sacred to themselves. At this hour a great deal of talking was done, and a great many secrets changed hands, particularly if the younger pupils behaved themselves well, and did not squabble or run about noisily, which it must be confessed they usually did. When they made an uproar the older girls usually interfered with scoldings and shakes. They were expected to keep order, and there was danger that if they did not, Miss Minchin or Miss Amelia would appear and put an end to festivities. Even as Lavinia spoke the door opened and Sara entered with Lottie, whose habit was to trot everywhere after her like a little dog.

"There she is, with that horrid child!" exclaimed Lavinia, in a whisper. "If she's so fond of her, why doesn't she keep her in her own room? She will begin howling about something minutes."

It happened that Lottie had been seized with a sudde

to play in the school-room, and had begged her adopted parent
to come with her. She joined a group of little ones who were
playing in a corner. Sara curled herself up in the window-seat,
opened a book, and began to read.[3] It was a book about the
French Revolution, and she was soon lost in a harrowing picture of the prisoners in the Bastille—men who had spent so
many years in dungeons that when they were dragged out by
those who rescued them, their long, gray hair and beards almost hid their faces, and they had forgotten that an outside
world existed at all, and were like beings in a dream.

She was so far away from the school-room that it was not
agreeable to be dragged back suddenly by a howl from Lottie.
Never did she find anything so difficult as to keep herself from
losing her temper when she was suddenly disturbed while absorbed in a book. People who are fond of books know the feeling of irritation which sweeps over them at such a moment. The
temptation to be unreasonable and snappish is one not easy to
manage.

"It makes me feel as if some one had hit me," Sara had told
Ermengarde once in confidence.[4] "And as if I want to hit back.
I have to remember things quickly to keep from saying some-
thing ill-tempered."

She had to remember things quickly when she laid her book
on the window-seat and jumped down from her comfortable
corner.

Lottie had been sliding across the school-room floor, and,
having first irritated Lavinia and Jessie by making a noise, had
ended by falling down and hurting her fat knee. She was
screaming and dancing up and down in the midst of a group of
friends and enemies, who were alternately coaxing and scolding her.

"Stop this minute, you cry-baby! Stop this minute!" Lavinia
commanded.[5]

"I'm not a cry-baby—I'm not!" wailed Lottie. "Sara,
Sa—ra!"

"If she doesn't stop, Miss Minchin will hear her," cried
Jessie. "Lottie darling, I'll give you a penny!"

"I don't want your penny," sobbed Lottie; and she looked

down at the fat knee, and, seeing a drop of blood on it, burst forth again.

Sara flew across the room and, kneeling down, put her arms round her.

"Now, Lottie," she said. "Now, Lottie, you *promised* Sara."

"She said I was a cry-baby," wept Lottie.

Sara patted her, but spoke in the steady voice Lottie knew.

"But if you cry, you will be one, Lottie pet. You *promised.*"

Lottie remembered that she had promised, but she preferred to lift up her voice.

"I haven't any mamma," she proclaimed. "I haven't—a bit—of mamma."

"Yes, you have," said Sara, cheerfully. "Have you forgotten? Don't you know that Sara is your mamma? Don't you want Sara for your mamma?"

Lottie cuddled up to her with a consoled sniff.

"Come and sit in the window-seat with me," Sara went on, "and I'll whisper a story to you."

"Will you?" whimpered Lottie. "Will you—tell me—about the diamond-mines?"

"The diamond-mines?" broke out Lavinia. "Nasty, little spoiled thing, I should like to *slap* her!"

Sara got up quickly on her feet. It must be remembered that she had been very deeply absorbed in the book about the Bastille, and she had had to recall several things rapidly when she realized that she must go and take care of her adopted child. She was not an angel, and she was not fond of Lavinia.

"Well," she said, with some fire, "I should like to slap *you,*—but I don't want to slap you!" restraining herself. "At least I both want to slap you—and I should *like* to slap you,—but I *won't* slap you. We are not little gutter children. We are both old enough to know better."

Here was Lavinia's opportunity.

"Ah, yes, your royal highness," she said. "We are princesses, I believe. At least one of us is. The school ought to be very fashionable now Miss Minchin has a princess for a pupil."

Sara started toward her. She looked as if she were going to box her ears. Perhaps she was. Her trick of pretending things was the joy of her life. She never spoke of it to girls she was not fond of. Her new "pretend" about being a princess was very near to her heart, and she was shy and sensitive about it. She had meant it to be rather a secret, and here was Lavinia deriding it before nearly all the school. She felt the blood rush up into her face and tingle in her ears. She only just saved herself. If you were a princess, you did not fly into rages. Her hand dropped, and she stood quite still a moment. When she spoke it was in a quiet, steady voice; she held her head up, and everybody listened to her.

"It's true," she said. "Sometimes I do pretend I am a princess. I pretend I am a princess, so that I can try and behave like one."

Lavinia could not think of exactly the right thing to say. Several times she had found that she could not think of a satisfactory reply when she was dealing with Sara. The reason of this was that, somehow, the rest always seemed to be vaguely in sympathy with her opponent. She saw now that they were pricking up their ears interestedly. The truth was, they liked princesses, and they all hoped they might hear something more definite about this one, and drew nearer Sara accordingly.

Lavinia could only invent one remark, and it fell rather flat.

"Dear me!" she said; "I hope, when you ascend the throne, you won't forget us."

"I won't," said Sara, and she did not utter another word, but stood quite still, and stared at her steadily as she saw her take Jessie's arm and turn away.

After this, the girls who were jealous of her used to speak of her as "Princess Sara" whenever they wished to be particularly disdainful, and those who were fond of her gave her the name among themselves as a term of affection. No one called her "princess" instead of "Sara," but her adorers were much pleased with the picturesqueness and grandeur of the title, and Miss Minchin, hearing of it, mentioned it more than once to visiting parents, feeling that it rather suggested a sort of royal boarding-school.

To Becky it seemed the most appropriate thing in the world. The acquaintance begun on the foggy afternoon when she had jumped up terrified from her sleep in the comfortable chair, had ripened and grown, though it must be confessed that Miss Minchin and Miss Amelia knew very little about it. They were aware that Sara was "kind" to the scullery-maid, but they knew nothing of certain delightful moments snatched perilously when, the up-stairs rooms being set in order with lightning rapidity, Sara's sitting-room was reached, and the heavy coal-box set down with a sigh of joy. At such times stories were told by instalments, things of a satisfying nature were either produced and eaten or hastily tucked into pockets to be disposed of at night, when Becky went up-stairs to her attic to bed.

"But I has to eat 'em careful, miss," she said once; " 'cos if I leaves crumbs the rats come out to get 'em."

"Rats!" exclaimed Sara, in horror. "Are there *rats* there?"

"Lots of 'em, miss," Becky answered in quite a matter-of-fact manner. "There mostly is rats an' mice in attics. You gets used to the noise they makes scuttling about. I've got so I don't mind 'em s' long as they don't run over my piller."

"Ugh!" said Sara.

"You gets used to anythin' after a bit," said Becky. "You have to, miss, if you're born a scullery-maid. I'd rather have rats than cockroaches."

"So would I," said Sara; "I suppose you might make friends with a rat in time, but I don't believe I should like to make friends with a cockroach."

Sometimes Becky did not dare to spend more than a few minutes in the bright, warm room, and when this was the case perhaps only a few words could be exchanged, and a small purchase slipped into the old-fashioned pocket Becky carried under her dress skirt, tied round her waist with a band of tape. The search for and discovery of satisfying things to eat which could be packed into small compass, added a new interest to Sara's existence. When she drove or walked out, she used to look into shop windows eagerly. The first time it occurred to her to bring home two or three little meat-pies, she felt that she had hit upon a discovery. When she exhibited them, Becky's eyes quite sparkled.

"Oh, miss!" she murmured. "Them will be nice an' fillin'. It's fillin'ness that's best. Sponge-cake's a 'evingly thing, but it melts away like—if you understand, miss. These'll just *stay* in yer stummick."

"Well," hesitated Sara, "I don't think it would be good if they stayed always, but I do believe they will be satisfying."

They were satisfying,—and so were beef sandwiches, bought at a cook-shop,—and so were rolls and Bologna sausage. In time, Becky began to lose her hungry, tired feeling, and the coal-box did not seem so unbearably heavy.

However heavy it was, and whatsoever the temper of the cook, and the hardness of the work heaped upon her shoulders, she had always the chance of the afternoon to look forward to—the chance that Miss Sara would be able to be in her sitting-room. In fact, the mere seeing of Miss Sara would have been enough without meat-pies. If there was time only for a few words, they were always friendly, merry words that put heart into one; and if there was time for more, then there was an instalment of a story to be told, or some other thing one remembered afterward and sometimes lay awake in one's bed in the attic to think over. Sara—who was only doing what she unconsciously liked better than anything else, Nature having made her for a giver—had not the least idea what she meant to poor Becky, and how wonderful a benefactor she seemed. If Nature has made you for a giver, your hands are born open, and so is your heart; and though there may be times when your hands are empty, your heart is always full, and you can give things out of that—warm things, kind things, sweet things,—help and comfort and laughter,—and sometimes gay, kind laughter is the best help of all.

Becky had scarcely known what laughter was through all her poor, little hard-driven life. Sara made her laugh, and laughed with her; and, though neither of them quite knew it, the laughter was as "fillin' " as the meat-pies.

A few weeks before Sara's eleventh birthday a letter came to her from her father, which did not seem to be written in such boyish high spirits as usual. He was not very well, and was evidently overweighted by the business connected with the diamond-mines.

"You see, little Sara," he wrote, "your daddy is not a business man at all, and figures and documents bother him. He does not really understand them, and all this seems so enormous. Perhaps, if I was not feverish I should not be awake, tossing about, one half of the night and spend the other half in troublesome dreams. If my little missus were here, I dare say she would give me some solemn, good advice. You would, wouldn't you, little missus?"

One of his many jokes had been to call her his "little missus" because she had such an old-fashioned air.

He had made wonderful preparations for her birthday. Among other things, a new doll had been ordered in Paris, and her wardrobe was to be, indeed, a marvel of splendid perfection. When she had replied to the letter asking her if the doll would be an acceptable present, Sara had been very quaint.

"I am getting very old," she wrote; "you see, I shall never live to have another doll given me. This will be my last doll. There is something solemn about it. If I could write poetry, I am sure a poem about 'A Last Doll' would be very nice. But I cannot write poetry. I have tried, and it made me laugh. It did not sound like Watts or Coleridge or Shakespeare at all.[6] No one could ever take Emily's place, but I should respect the Last Doll very much; and I am sure the school would love it. They all like dolls, though some of the big ones—the almost fifteen ones—pretend they are too grown up."

Captain Crewe had a splitting headache when he read this letter in his bungalow in India. The table before him was heaped with papers and letters which were alarming him and filling him with anxious dread, but he laughed as he had not laughed for weeks.

"Oh," he said, "she's better fun every year she lives. God grant this business may right itself and leave me free to run home and see her. What wouldn't I give to have her little arms round my neck this minute! What *wouldn't* I give!"

The birthday was to be celebrated by great festivities. The school-room was to be decorated, and there was to be a party. The boxes containing the presents were to be opened with great ceremony, and there was to a be a glittering feast spread in Miss Minchin's sacred room. When the day arrived the whole house was in a whirl of excitement. How the morning passed nobody quite knew, because there seemed such preparations to be made. The school-room was being decked with garlands of holly; the desks had been moved away, and red covers had been put on the forms which were arrayed round the room against the wall.[7]

When Sara went into her sitting-room in the morning, she found on the table a small, dumpy package, tied up in a piece of brown paper. She knew it was a present, and she thought she could guess whom it came from. She opened it quite tenderly. It was a square pincushion, made of not quite clean red flannel, and black pins had been stuck carefully into it to form the words, "Menny hapy returns."

"Oh!" cried Sara, with a warm feeling in her heart. "What pains she has taken! I like it so, it—it makes me feel sorrowful."

But the next moment she was mystified. On the under side of the pincushion was secured a card, bearing in neat letters the name "Miss Amelia Minchin."

Sara turned it over and over.

"Miss Amelia!" she said to herself. "How *can* it be!"

And just at that very moment she heard the door being cautiously pushed open and saw Becky peeping round it.

There was an affectionate, happy grin on her face, and she shuffled forward and stood nervously pulling at her fingers.

"Do yer like it, Miss Sara?" she said. "Do yer?"

"Like it?" cried Sara. "You darling Becky, you made it all yourself."

Becky gave a hysteric but joyful sniff, and her eyes looked quite moist with delight.

"It ain't nothin' but flannin, an' the flannin ain't new; but I wanted to give yer somethin' an' I made it of nights. I knew yer could *pretend* it was satin with diamond pins in. *I* tried to when I was makin' it. The card, miss," rather doubtfully; " 't warn't wrong of me to pick it up out o' the dust-bin, was it? Miss 'Meliar had throwed it away. I hadn't no card o' my own, an' I knowed it wouldn't be a proper presink if I didn't pin a card on—so I pinned Miss 'Meliar's."

Sara flew at her and hugged her. She could not have told herself or any one else why there was a lump in her throat.

"Oh, Becky!" she cried out, with a queer little laugh. "I love you, Becky,—I do, I do!"

"Oh, miss!" breathed Becky. "Thank yer, miss, kindly. It ain't good enough for that. The—the flannin wasn't new."

CHAPTER VII

The Diamond-Mines Again

WHEN SARA ENTERED the holly-hung school-room in the afternoon, she did so as the head of a sort of procession. Miss Minchin, in her grandest silk dress, led her by the hand. A man-servant followed, carrying the box containing the Last Doll, a housemaid carried a second box, and Becky brought up the rear, carrying a third and wearing a clean apron and a new cap. Sara would have much preferred to enter in the usual way, but Miss Minchin had sent for her, and, after an interview in her private sitting-room, had expressed her wishes.

"This is not an ordinary occasion," she said. "I do not desire that it should be treated as one."

So Sara was led grandly in and felt shy when, on her entry, the big girls stared at her and touched each other's elbows, and the little ones began to squirm joyously in their seats.

"Silence, young ladies!" said Miss Minchin, at the murmur which arose. "James, place the box on the table and remove the lid. Emma, put yours upon a chair.[1] Becky!" suddenly and severely.

Becky had quite forgotten herself in her excitement, and was grinning at Lottie, who was wriggling with rapturous expectation. She almost dropped her box, the disapproving voice so startled her, and her frightened, bobbing courtesy of apology was so funny that Lavinia and Jessie tittered.

"It is not your place to look at the young ladies," said Miss Minchin. "You forget yourself. Put your box down."

Becky obeyed with alarmed haste and hastily backed toward the door.

"You may leave us," Miss Minchin announced to the servants with a wave of her hand.

Becky stepped aside respectfully to allow the superior servants to pass out first. She could not help casting a longing glance at the box on the table. Something made of blue satin was peeping from between the folds of tissue-paper.

"If you please, Miss Minchin," said Sara, suddenly, "mayn't Becky stay?"

It was a bold thing to do. Miss Minchin was betrayed into something like a slight jump. Then she put her eye-glass up, and gazed at her show pupil disturbedly.

"Becky!" she exclaimed. "My dearest Sara!"

Sara advanced a step toward her.

"I want her because I know she will like to see the presents," she explained. "She is a little girl, too, you know."

Miss Minchin was scandalized. She glanced from one figure to the other.

"My dear Sara," she said, "Becky is the scullery-maid. Scullery-maids—er—are not little girls."

It really had not occurred to her to think of them in that light. Scullery-maids were machines who carried coal-scuttles and made fires.[2]

"But Becky is," said Sara. "And I know she would enjoy herself. Please let her stay—because it is my birthday."

Miss Minchin replied with much dignity:

"As you ask it as a birthday favor—she may stay. Rebecca, thank Miss Sara for her great kindess."

Becky had been backing into the corner, twisting the hem of her apron in delighted suspense. She came forward, bobbing courtesies, but between Sara's eyes and her own there passed a gleam of friendly understanding, while her words tumbled over each other.

"Oh, if you please, miss! I'm that grateful, miss! I did want to see the doll, miss, that I did. Thank you, miss. And thank you, ma'am,"—turning and making an alarmed bob to Miss Minchin,—"for letting me take the liberty."

Miss Minchin waved her hand again—this time it was in the direction of the corner near the door.

"Go and stand there," she commanded. "Not too near the young ladies."

Becky went to her place, grinning. She did not care where she was sent, so that she might have the luck of being inside the room, instead of being down-stairs in the scullery, while these delights were going on. She did not even mind when Miss Minchin cleared her throat ominously and spoke again.

"Now, young ladies, I have a few words to say to you," she announced.

"She's going to make a speech," whispered one of the girls. "I wish it was over."

Sara felt rather uncomfortable. As this was her party, it was probable that the speech was about her. It is not agreeable to stand in a school-room and have a speech made about you.

"You are aware, young ladies," the speech began,—for it was a speech,—"that dear Sara is eleven years old today."

"*Dear* Sara!" murmured Lavinia.

"Several of you here have also been eleven years old, but Sara's birthdays are rather different from other little girls' birthdays. When she is older she will be heiress to a large fortune, which it will be her duty to spend in a meritorious manner."

"The diamond-mines," giggled Jessie, in a whisper.

Sara did not hear her; but as she stood with her green-gray eyes fixed steadily on Miss Minchin, she felt herself growing rather hot. When Miss Minchin talked about money, she felt somehow that she always hated her—and, of course, it was disrespectful to hate grown-up people.

"When her dear papa, Captain Crewe, brought her from India and gave her into my care," the speech proceeded, "he said to me, in a jesting way, 'I am afraid she will be very rich, Miss Minchin.' My reply was, 'Her education at my seminary, Captain Crewe, shall be such as will adorn the largest fortune.' Sara has become my most accomplished pupil. Her French and her dancing are a credit to the seminary. Her manners—which have caused you to call her Princess Sara—are perfect. Her amiability she exhibits by giving you this afternoon's party. I hope you appreciate her generosity. I wish you to express your appreciation of it by saying aloud all together, 'Thank you, Sara!' "

The entire school-room rose to its feet as it had done the morning Sara remembered so well.

"Thank you, Sara!" it said, and it must be confessed that Lottie jumped up and down. Sara looked rather shy for a moment. She made a courtesy—and it was a very nice one.

"Thank you," she said, "for coming to my party."

"Very pretty, indeed, Sara," approved Miss Minchin. "That is what a real princess does when the populace applauds her. Lavinia,"—scathingly,—"the sound you just made was extremely like a snort. If you are jealous of your fellow-pupil, I beg you will express your feelings in some more ladylike manner. Now I will leave you to enjoy yourselves."

The instant she had swept out of the room the spell her presence always had upon them was broken. The door had scarcely closed before every seat was empty. The little girls jumped or tumbled out of theirs; the older ones wasted no time in deserting theirs. There was a rush toward the boxes. Sara had bent over one of them with a delighted face.

"These are books, I know," she said.

The little children broke into a rueful murmur, and Ermengarde looked aghast.

"Does your papa send you books for a birthday present?" she exclaimed. "Why, he's as bad as mine. Don't open them, Sara."

"I like them," Sara laughed, but she turned to the biggest box. When she took out the Last Doll it was so magnificent that the children uttered delighted groans of joy, and actually drew back to gaze at it in breathless rapture.

"She is almost as big as Lottie," some one gasped.

Lottie clapped her hands and danced about, giggling.

"She's dressed for the theatre," said Lavinia. "Her cloak is lined with ermine."

"Oh!" cried Ermengarde, darting forward, "she has an opera-glass in her hand—a blue-and-gold one."

"Here is her trunk," said Sara. "Let us open it and look at her things."

She sat down upon the floor and turned the key. The children crowded clamoring around her, as she lifted tray after tray and revealed their contents. Never had the school-room been in such an uproar. There were lace collars and silk stockings and handkerchiefs; there was a jewel-case containing a necklace and a tiara which looked quite as if they were made of real diamonds; there was a long sealskin and muff; there were ball dresses and walking dresses and visiting dresses; there were hats and tea-gowns and fans. Even Lavinia and Jessie forgot that they were too elderly to care for dolls, and uttered exclamations of delight and caught up things to look at them.

"Suppose," Sara said, as she stood by the table, putting a large, black-velvet hat on the impassively smiling owner of all these splendors—"suppose she understands human talk and feels proud of being admired."

"You are always supposing things," said Lavinia, and her air was very superior.

"I know I am," answered Sara, undisturbedly. "I like it. There is nothing so nice as supposing. It's almost like being a fairy. If you suppose anything hard enough it seems as if it were real."

"It's all very well to suppose things if you have everything," said Lavinia. "Could you suppose and pretend if you were a beggar and lived in a garret?"

Sara stopped arranging the Last Doll's ostrich plumes, and looked thoughtful.

"I *believe* I could," she said. "If one was a beggar, one would have to suppose and pretend all the time. But it mightn't be easy."

She often thought afterward how strange it was that just as she had finished saying this—just at that very moment—Miss Amelia came into the room.

"Sara," she said, "your papa's solicitor, Mr. Barrow, has called to see Miss Minchin, and, as she must talk to him alone and the refreshments are laid in her parlor, you had all better come and have your feast now, so that my sister can have her interview here in the school-room."

Refreshments were not likely to be disdained at any hour, and many pairs of eyes gleamed. Miss Amelia arranged the procession into decorum, and then, with Sara at her side heading it, she led it away, leaving the Last Doll sitting upon a chair with the glories of her wardrobe scattered about her; dresses and coats hung upon chair backs, piles of lace-frilled petticoats lying upon their seats.

Becky, who was not expected to partake of refreshments, had the indiscretion to linger a moment to look at these beauties—it really was an indiscretion.

"Go back to your work, Becky," Miss Amelia had said; but she had stopped to reverently pick up first a muff and then a coat, and while she stood looking at them adoringly, she heard Miss Minchin upon the threshold, and, being smitten with terror at the thought of being accused of taking liberties, she rashly darted under the table, which hid her by its table-cloth.

Miss Minchin came into the room, accompanied by a sharp-featured, dry little gentleman, who looked rather disturbed. Miss Minchin herself also looked rather disturbed, it must be admitted, and she gazed at the dry little gentleman with an irritated and puzzled expression.

She sat down with stiff dignity, and waved him to a chair.

"Pray, be seated, Mr. Barrow," she said.

Mr. Barrow did not sit down at once. His attention seemed attracted by the Last Doll and the things which surrounded her. He settled his eye-glasses and looked at them in nervous disapproval. The Last Doll herself did not seem to mind this in the least. She merely sat upright and returned his gaze indifferently.

"A hundred pounds," Mr. Barrow remarked succinctly. "All expensive material, and made at a Parisian modiste's. He spent money lavishly enough, that young man."

Miss Minchin felt offended. This seemed to be a disparagement of her best patron and was a liberty.

Even solicitors had no right to take liberties.

"I beg your pardon, Mr. Barrow," she said stiffly. "I do not understand."

"Birthday presents," said Mr. Barrow in the same critical manner, "to a child eleven years old! Mad extravagance, I call it."

Miss Minchin drew herself up still more rigidly.

"Captain Crewe is a man of fortune," she said. "The diamond-mines alone—"

Mr. Barrow wheeled round upon her.

"Diamond-mines!" he broke out. "There are none! Never were!"

Miss Minchin actually got up from her chair.

"What!" she cried. "What do you mean?"

"At any rate," answered Mr. Barrow, quite snappishly, "it would have been much better if there never had been any."

"Any diamond-mines?" ejaculated Miss Minchin, catching at the back of a chair and feeling as if a splendid dream was fading away from her.

"Diamond-mines spell ruin oftener than they spell wealth," said Mr. Barrow. "When a man is in the hands of a very dear friend and is not a business man himself, he had better steer clear of the dear friend's diamond-mines, or gold-mines, or any other kind of mines dear friends want his money to put into. The late Captain Crewe—"

Here Miss Minchin stopped him with a gasp.

"The *late* Captain Crewe!" she cried out; "the *late!* You don't come to tell me that Captain Crewe is—"

"He's dead, ma'am," Mr. Barrow answered with jerky brusqueness. "Died of jungle fever and business troubles combined. The jungle fever might not have killed him if he had not been driven mad by the business troubles, and the business troubles might not have put an end to him if the jungle fever had not assisted. Captain Crewe is dead!"

Miss Minchin dropped into her chair again. The words he had spoken filled her with alarm.

"What *were* his business troubles?" she said. "What *were* they?"

"Diamond-mines," answered Mr. Barrow, "and dear friends—and ruin."

Miss Minchin lost her breath.

"Ruin!" she gasped out.

"Lost every penny. That young man had too much money. The dear friend was mad on the subject of the diamond-mine. He put all his own money into it, and all Captain Crewe's. Then the dear friend ran away—Captain Crewe was already stricken with fever when the news came. The shock was too much for him. He died delirious, raving about his little girl—and didn't leave a penny."

Now Miss Minchin understood, and never had she received such a blow in her life. Her show pupil, her show patron, swept away from the Select Seminary at one blow. She felt as if she had been outraged and robbed, and that Captain Crewe and Sara and Mr. Barrow were equally to blame.

"Do you mean to tell me," she cried out, "that he left *noth-*

ing! That Sara will have no fortune! That the child is a beggar! That she is left on my hands a little pauper instead of an heiress?"[3]

Mr. Barrow was a shrewd business man, and felt it as well to make his own freedom from responsibility quite clear without any delay.

"She is certainly left a beggar," he replied. "And she is certainly left on your hands, ma'am,—as she hasn't a relation in the world that we know of."[4]

Miss Minchin started forward. She looked as if she was going to open the door and rush out of the room to stop the festivities going on joyfully and rather noisily that moment over the refreshments.

"It is monstrous!" she said. "She's in my sitting-room at this moment, dressed in silk gauze and lace petticoats, giving a party at my expense."

"She's giving it at your expense, madam, if she's giving it," said Mr. Barrow, calmly. "Barrow & Skipworth are not responsible for anything. There never was a cleaner sweep made of a man's fortune. Captain Crewe died without paying *our* last bill—and it was a big one."

Miss Minchin turned back from the door in increased indignation. This was worse than any one could have dreamed of its being.

"That is what has happened to me!" she cried. "I was always so sure of his payments that I went to all sorts of ridiculous expenses for the child. I paid the bills for that ridiculous doll and her ridiculous fantastic wardrobe. The child was to have anything she wanted. She has a carriage and a pony and a maid, and I've paid for all of them since the last cheque came."

Mr. Barrow evidently did not intend to remain to listen to the story of Miss Minchin's grievances after he had made the position of his firm clear and related the mere dry facts. He did not feel any particular sympathy for irate keepers of boarding-schools.

"You had better not pay for anything more, ma'am," he remarked, "unless you want to make presents to the young lady. No one will remember you. She hasn't a brass farthing to call her own."

"But what am I to do?" demanded Miss Minchin, as if she felt it entirely his duty to make the matter right. "What am I to do?"

"There isn't anything to do," said Mr. Barrow, folding up his eye-glasses and slipping them into his pocket. "Captain Crewe is dead. The child is left a pauper. Nobody is responsible for her but you."

"I am not responsible for her, and I refuse to be made responsible!"

Miss Minchin became quite white with rage.

Mr. Barrow turned to go.

"I have nothing to do with that, madam," he said uninterestedly. "Barrow & Skipworth are not responsible. Very sorry the thing has happened, of course."

"If you think she is to be foisted off on me, you are greatly mistaken," Miss Minchin gasped. "I have been robbed and cheated; I will turn her into the street!"

If she had not been so furious, she would have been too discreet to say quite so much. She saw herself burdened with an extravagantly brought-up child whom she had always resented, and she lost all self-control.

Mr. Barrow undisturbedly moved toward the door.

"I wouldn't do that, madam," he commented; "it wouldn't look well. Unpleasant story to get about in connection with the establishment. Pupil bundled out penniless and without friends."

He was a clever business man, and he knew what he was saying. He also knew that Miss Minchin was a business woman, and would be shrewd enough to see the truth. She could not afford to do a thing which would make people speak of her as cruel and hard-hearted.

"Better keep her and make use of her," he added. "She's a clever child, I believe. You can get a good deal out of her as she grows older."

"I will get a good deal out of her before she grows older!" exclaimed Miss Minchin.

"I am sure you will, ma'am," said Mr. Barrow, with a little sinister smile. "I am sure you will. Good morning!"

He bowed himself out and closed the door, and it must be

confessed that Miss Minchin stood for a few moments and glared at it. What he had said was quite true. She knew it. She had absolutely no redress. Her show pupil had melted into nothingness, leaving only a friendless, beggared little girl. Such money as she herself had advanced was lost and could not be regained.

And as she stood there breathless under her sense of injury, there fell upon her ears a burst of gay voices from her own sacred room, which had actually been given up to the feast. She could at least stop this.

But as she started toward the door it was opened by Miss Amelia, who, when she caught sight of the changed, angry face, fell back a step in alarm.

"What *is* the matter, sister?" she ejaculated.

Miss Minchin's voice was almost fierce when she answered:

"Where is Sara Crewe?"

Miss Amelia was bewildered.

"Sara!" she stammered. "Why, she's with the children in your room, of course."

"Has she a black frock in her sumptuous wardrobe?"—in bitter irony.

"A black frock?" Miss Amelia stammered again. "A *black* one?"

"She has frocks of every other color. Has she a black one?"

Miss Amelia began to turn pale.

"No—ye-es!" she said. "But it is too short for her. She has only the old black velvet, and she has outgrown it."

"Go and tell her to take off that preposterous pink silk gauze, and put the black one on, whether it is too short or not. She has done with finery!"

Then Miss Amelia began to wring her fat hands and cry.

"Oh, sister!" she sniffed. "Oh, sister! What *can* have happened?"

Miss Minchin wasted no words.

"Captain Crewe is dead," she said. "He has died without a penny. That spoiled, pampered, fanciful child is left a pauper on my hands."

Miss Amelia sat down quite heavily in the nearest chair.

"Hundreds of pounds have I spent on nonsense for her. And I shall never see a penny of it. Put a stop to this ridiculous party of hers. Go and make her change her frock at once."

"I?" panted Miss Amelia. "M-must I go and tell her now?"

"This moment!" was the fierce answer. "Don't sit staring like a goose. Go!"

Poor Miss Amelia was accustomed to being called a goose. She knew, in fact, that she was rather a goose, and that it was left to geese to do a great many disagreeable things. It was a somewhat embarrassing thing to go into the midst of a room full of delighted children, and tell the giver of the feast that she had suddenly been transformed into a little beggar, and must go up-stairs and put on an old black frock which was too small for her. But the thing must be done. This was evidently not the time when questions might be asked.

She rubbed her eyes with her handkerchief until they looked quite red. After which she got up and went out of the room, without venturing to say another word. When her older sister looked and spoke as she had done just now, the wisest course to pursue was to obey orders without any comment. Miss Minchin walked across the room. She spoke to herself aloud without knowing that she was doing it. During the last year the story of the diamond-mines had suggested all sorts of possibilities to her. Even proprietors of seminaries might make fortunes in stocks, with the aid of owners of mines. And now, instead of looking forward to gains, she was left to look back upon losses.

"The Princess Sara, indeed!" she said. "The child has been pampered as if she were a *queen*."

She was sweeping angrily past the corner table as she said it, and the next moment she started at the sound of a loud, sobbing sniff which issued from under the cover.

"What is that!" she exclaimed angrily. The loud, sobbing sniff was heard again, and she stooped and raised the hanging folds of the table-cover.

"How *dare* you!" she cried out. "How *dare* you! Come out immediately!"

It was poor Becky who crawled out, and her cap was

knocked on one side, and her face was red with repressed crying.

"If you please, 'm—it's me, mum," she explained. "I know I hadn't ought to. But I was lookin' at the doll, mum—an' I was frightened when you come in—an' slipped under the table."

"You have been there all the time, listening," said Miss Minchin.

"No, mum," Becky protested, bobbing courtesies. "Not listenin'—I thought I could slip out without your noticin', but I couldn't an' I had to stay. But I didn't listen, mum—I wouldn't for nothin'. But I couldn't help hearin'."

Suddenly it seemed almost as if she lost all fear of the awful lady before her. She burst into fresh tears.

"Oh, please, 'm," she said; "I dare say you'll give me warnin', mum,—but I'm so sorry for poor Miss Sara—I'm so sorry!"

"Leave the room!" ordered Miss Minchin.

Becky courtesied again, the tears openly streaming down her cheeks.

"Yes, 'm; I will, 'm," she said, trembling; "but oh, I just wanted to arst you: Miss Sara—she's been such a rich young lady, an' she's been waited on, 'and and foot; an' what will she do now, mum, without no maid? If—if, oh please, would you let me wait on her after I've done my pots an' kettles? I'd do 'em that quick—if you'd let me wait on her now she's poor. Oh,"—breaking out afresh,—"poor little Miss Sara, mum—that was called a princess."

Somehow, she made Miss Minchin feel more angry than ever. That the very scullery-maid should range herself on the side of this child—whom she realized more fully than ever that she had never liked—was too much. She actually stamped her foot.

"No—certainly not," she said. "She will wait on herself, and on other people, too. Leave the room this instant, or you'll leave your place."

Becky threw her apron over her head and fled. She ran out of the room and down the steps into the scullery, and there she sat down among her pots and kettles, and wept as if her heart would break.

"It's exactly like the ones in the stories," she wailed. "Them pore princess ones that was drove into the world."[5]

Miss Minchin had never looked quite so still and hard as she did when Sara came to her, a few hours later, in response to a message she had sent her.

Even by that time it seemed to Sara as if the birthday party had either been a dream or a thing which had happened years ago, and had happened in the life of quite another little girl.

Every sign of the festivities had been swept away; the holly had been removed from the school-room walls, and the forms and desks put back into their places. Miss Minchin's sitting-room looked as it always did—all traces of the feast were gone, and Miss Minchin had resumed her usual dress. The pupils had been ordered to lay aside their party frocks; and this having been done, they had returned to the school-room and huddled together in groups, whispering and talking excitedly.

"Tell Sara to come to my room," Miss Minchin had said to her sister. "And explain to her clearly that I will have no crying or unpleasant scenes."

"Sister," replied Miss Amelia, "she is the strangest child I ever saw. She has actually made no fuss at all. You remember she made none when Captain Crewe went back to India. When I told her what had happened, she just stood quite still and looked at me without making a sound. Her eyes seemed to get bigger and bigger, and she went quite pale. When I had finished, she still stood staring for a few seconds, and then her chin began to shake, and she turned round and ran out of the room and up-stairs. Several of the other children began to cry, but she did not seem to hear them or to be alive to anything but just what I was saying. It made me feel quite queer not to be answered; and when you tell anything sudden and strange, you expect people will say *something*—whatever it is."

Nobody but Sara herself ever knew what had happened in her room after she had run up-stairs and locked her door. In fact, she herself scarcely remembered anything but that she walked up and down, saying over and over again to herself in a voice which did not seem her own:

"My papa is dead! My papa is dead!"

Once she stopped before Emily, who sat watching her from her chair, and cried out wildly:

"Emily! Do you hear? Do you hear—papa is dead? He is dead in India—thousands of miles away."

When she came into Miss Minchin's sitting-room in answer to her summons, her face was white and her eyes had dark rings around them. Her mouth was set as if she did not wish it to reveal what she had suffered and was suffering. She did not look in the least like the rose-colored butterfly child who had flown about from one of her treasures to the other in the decorated school-room. She looked instead a strange, desolate, almost grotesque little figure.

She had put on, without Mariette's help, the cast-aside black-velvet frock. It was too short and tight, and her slender legs looked long and thin, showing themselves from beneath the brief skirt. As she had not found a piece of black ribbon, her short, thick, black hair tumbled loosely about her face and contrasted strongly with its pallor. She held Emily tightly in one arm, and Emily was swathed in a piece of black material.

"Put down your doll," said Miss Minchin. "What do you mean by bringing her here?"

"No," Sara answered. "I will not put her down. She is all I have. My papa gave her to me."

She had always made Miss Minchin feel secretly uncomfortable, and she did so now. She did not speak with rudeness so much as with a cold steadiness with which Miss Minchin felt it difficult to cope—perhaps because she knew she was doing a heartless and inhuman thing.

"You will have no time for dolls in future," she said. "You will have to work and improve yourself and make yourself useful."

Sara kept her big, strange eyes fixed on her, and said not a word.

"Everything will be very different now," Miss Minchin went on. "I suppose Miss Amelia has explained matters to you."

"Yes," answered Sara. "My papa is dead. He left me no money. I am quite poor."

"You are a beggar," said Miss Minchin, her temper rising at the recollection of what all this meant. "It appears that you have no relations and no home, and no one to take care of you."

For a moment the thin, pale little face twitched, but Sara again said nothing.

"What are you staring at?" demanded Miss Minchin, sharply. "Are you so stupid that you cannot understand? I tell you that you are quite alone in the world, and have no one to do anything for you, unless I choose to keep you here out of charity."

"I understand," answered Sara, in a low tone; and there was a sound as if she had gulped down something which rose in her throat. "I understand."

"That doll," cried Miss Minchin, pointing to the splendid birthday gift seated near—"that ridiculous doll, with all her nonsensical, extravagant things—*I* actually paid the bill for her!"

Sara turned her head toward the chair.

"The Last Doll," she said. "The Last Doll." And her little mournful voice had an odd sound.

"The Last Doll, indeed!" said Miss Minchin. "And she is mine, not yours. Everything you own is mine."

"Please take it away from me, then," said Sara. "I do not want it."[6]

If she had cried and sobbed and seemed frightened, Miss Minchin might almost have had more patience with her. She was a woman who liked to domineer and feel her power, and as she looked at Sara's pale little steadfast face and heard her proud little voice, she quite felt as if her might was being set at naught.

"Don't put on grand airs," she said. "The time for that sort of thing is past. You are not a princess any longer. Your carriage and your pony will be sent away—your maid will be dismissed. You will wear your oldest and plainest clothes—your extravagant ones are no longer suited to your station. You are like Becky—you must work for your living."

To her surprise, a faint gleam of light came into the child's eyes—a shade of relief.

"Can I work?" she said. "If I can work it will not matter so much. What can I do?"

"You can do anything you are told," was the answer. "You

are a sharp child, and pick up things readily.[7] If you make yourself useful I may let you stay here. You speak French well, and
you can help with the younger children."

"May I?" exclaimed Sara. "Oh, please let me! I know I can
teach them. I like them, and they like me."

"Don't talk nonsense about people liking you," said Miss
Minchin. "You will have to do more than teach the little ones.
You will run errands and help in the kitchen as well as in the
school-room. If you don't please me, you will be sent away.
Remember that. Now go."

Sara stood still just a moment, looking at her. In her young
soul, she was thinking deep and strange things. Then she turned
to leave the room.

"Stop!" said Miss Minchin. "Don't you intend to thank me?"

Sara paused, and all the deep, strange thoughts surged up in
her breast.

"What for?" she said.

"For my kindness to you," replied Miss Minchin. "For my
kindness in giving you a home."

Sara made two or three steps toward her. Her thin little chest
heaved up and down, and she spoke in a strange, unchildishly
fierce way.

"You are not kind," she said. "You are *not* kind, and it is *not*
a home." And she had turned and run out of the room before
Miss Minchin could stop her or do anything but stare after her
with stony anger.

She went up the stairs slowly, but panting for breath, and she
held Emily tightly against her side.

"I wish she could talk," she said to herself. "If she could
speak—if she could speak!"

She meant to go to her room and lie down on the tiger-skin,
with her cheek upon the great cat's head, and look into the fire
and think and think and think. But just before she reached the
landing Miss Amelia came out of the door and closed it behind
her, and stood before it, looking nervous and awkward. The
truth was that she felt secretly ashamed of the thing she had
been ordered to do.

"You—you are not to go in there," she said.

"Not go in?" exclaimed Sara, and she fell back a pace.

"That is not your room now," Miss Amelia answered, reddening a little.

Somehow, all at once, Sara understood. She realized that this was the beginning of the change Miss Minchin had spoken of.

"Where is my room?" she asked, hoping very much that her voice did not shake.

"You are to sleep in the attic next to Becky."

Sara knew where it was. Becky had told her about it. She turned, and mounted up two flights of stairs. The last one was narrow, and covered with shabby strips of old carpet. She felt as if she were walking away and leaving far behind her the world in which that other child, who no longer seemed herself, had lived. This child, in her short, tight old frock, climbing the stairs to the attic, was quite a different creature.

When she reached the attic door and opened it, her heart gave a dreary little thump. Then she shut the door and stood against it and looked about her.

Yes, this was another world. The room had a slanting roof and was whitewashed. The whitewash was dingy and had fallen off in places. There was a rusty grate, an old iron bedstead, and a hard bed covered with a faded coverlet. Some pieces of furniture too much worn to be used down-stairs had been sent up. Under the skylight in the roof, which showed nothing but an oblong piece of dull gray sky, there stood an old battered red footstool. Sara went to it and sat down. She seldom cried. She did not cry now. She laid Emily across her knees and put her face down upon her and her arms around her, and sat there, her little black head resting on the black draperies, not saying one word, not making one sound.

And as she sat in this silence there came a low tap at the door—such a low, humble one that she did not at first hear it, and, indeed, was not roused until the door was timidly pushed open and a poor tear-smeared face appeared peeping round it. It was Becky's face, and Becky had been crying furtively for hours and rubbing her eyes with her kitchen apron until she looked strange indeed.

"Oh, miss," she said under her breath. "Might I—would you allow me—jest to come in?"

Sara lifted her head and looked at her. She tried to begin a smile, and somehow she could not. Suddenly—and it was all through the loving mournfulness of Becky's streaming eyes—her face looked more like a child's not so much too old for her years. She held out her hand and gave a little sob.

"Oh, Becky," she said. "I told you we were just the same—only two little girls—just two little girls.[8] You see how true it is. There's no difference now. I'm not a princess any more."

Becky ran to her and caught her hand, and hugged it to her breast, kneeling beside her and sobbing with love and pain.

"Yes, miss, you are," she cried, and her words were all broken. "Whats'ever 'appens to you—whats'ever—you'd be a princess all the same—an' nothin' couldn't make you nothin' different."

CHAPTER VIII

In the Attic

THE FIRST NIGHT she spent in her attic was a thing Sara never forgot. During its passing, she lived through a wild, un-childlike woe of which she never spoke to any one about her.[1] There was no one who would have understood. It was, indeed, well for her that as she lay awake in the darkness her mind was forcibly distracted, now and then, by the strangeness of her surroundings. It was, perhaps, well for her that she was reminded by her small body of material things. If this had not been so, the anguish of her young mind might have been too great for a child to bear. But, really, while the night was passing she scarcely knew that she had a body at all or remembered any other thing than one.

"My papa is dead!" she kept whispering to herself. "My papa is dead!"

It was not until long afterward that she realized that her bed had been so hard that she turned over and over in it to find a place to rest, that the darkness seemed more intense than any she had ever known, and that the wind howled over the roof among the chimneys like something which wailed aloud. Then there was something worse. This was certain scufflings and scratchings and squeakings in the walls and behind the skirting boards. She knew what they meant, because Becky had described them. They meant rats and mice who were either fighting with each other or playing together. Once or twice she even heard sharp-toed feet scurrying across the floor, and she remembered in those after days, when she recalled things, that when first she heard them she started up in bed and sat trembling, and when she lay down again covered her head with the bedclothes.

The change in her life did not come about gradually, but was made all at once.

"She must begin as she is to go on," Miss Minchin said to Miss Amelia. "She must be taught at once what she is to expect."

Mariette had left the house the next morning. The glimpse Sara caught of her sitting-room, as she passed its open door, showed her that everything had been changed. Her ornaments and luxuries had been removed, and a bed had been placed in a corner to transform it into a new pupil's bedroom.

When she went down to breakfast she saw that her seat at Miss Minchin's side was occupied by Lavinia, and Miss Minchin spoke to her coldly.

"You will begin your new duties, Sara," she said, "by taking your seat with the younger children at a smaller table. You must keep them quiet, and see that they behave well and do not waste their food. You ought to have been down earlier. Lottie has already upset her tea."

That was the beginning, and from day to day the duties given to her were added to. She taught the younger children French and heard their other lessons, and these were the least of her labors. It was found that she could be made use of in numberless directions. She could be sent on errands at any time and in all weathers. She could be told to do things other people neglected. The cook and the housemaids took their tone from Miss Minchin, and rather enjoyed ordering about the "young one" who had been made so much fuss over for so long. They were not servants of the best class, and had neither good manners nor good tempers, and it was frequently convenient to have at hand some one on whom blame could be laid.

During the first month or two, Sara thought that her willingness to do things as well as she could, and her silence under reproof, might soften those who drove her so hard. In her proud little heart she wanted them to see that she was trying to earn her living and not accepting charity. But the time came when she saw that no one was softened at all; and the more willing she was to do as she was told, the more domineering and exacting careless housemaids became, and the more ready a scolding cook was to blame her.

If she had been older, Miss Minchin would have given her the bigger girls to teach and saved money by dismissing an instructress; but while she remained and looked like a child, she could be made more useful as a sort of little superior errand girl and maid of all work. An ordinary errand boy would not have been so clever and reliable. Sara could be trusted with difficult commissions and complicated messages. She could even go and pay bills, and she combined with this the ability to dust a room well and to set things in order.

Her own lessons became things of the past. She was taught nothing, and only after long and busy days spent in running here and there at everybody's orders was she grudgingly allowed to go into the deserted school-room, with a pile of old books, and study alone at night.

"If I do not remind myself of the things I have learned, perhaps I may forget them," she said to herself. "I am almost a scullery-maid, and if I am a scullery-maid who knows nothing, I shall be like poor Becky. I wonder if I could *quite* forget and begin to drop my *h*'s and not remember that Henry the Eighth had six wives."[2]

One of the most curious things in her new existence was her changed position among the pupils. Instead of being a sort of small royal personage among them, she no longer seemed to be one of their number at all. She was kept so constantly at work that she scarcely ever had an opportunity of speaking to any of them, and she could not avoid seeing that Miss Minchin preferred that she should live a life apart from that of the occupants of the school-room.

"I will not have her forming intimacies and talking to the other children," that lady said. "Girls like a grievance, and if she begins to tell romantic stories about herself, she will become an ill-used heroine, and parents will be given a wrong impression.[3] It is better that she should live a separate life—one suited to her circumstances. I am giving her a home, and that is more than she has any right to expect from me."

Sara did not expect much, and was far too proud to try to continue to be intimate with girls who evidently felt rather awkward and uncertain about her. The fact was that Miss Minchin's pupils were a set of dull, matter-of-fact young people. They were accustomed to being rich and comfortable, and as Sara's frocks grew shorter and shabbier and queerer-looking, and it became an established fact that she wore shoes with holes in them and was sent out to buy groceries and carry them through the streets in a basket on her arm when the cook wanted them in a hurry, they felt rather as if, when they spoke to her, they were addressing an under servant.

"To think that she was the girl with the diamond-mines," Lavinia commented. "She does look an object. And she's queerer than ever. I never liked her much, but I can't bear that way she has now of looking at people without speaking—just as if she was finding them out."

"I am," said Sara, promptly, when she heard of this. "That's what I look at some people for. I like to know about them. I think them over afterward."

The truth was that she had saved herself annoyance several times by keeping her eye on Lavinia, who was quite ready to make mischief, and would have been rather pleased to have made it for the ex-show pupil.

Sara never made any mischief herself, or interfered with any one. She worked like a drudge; she tramped through the wet streets, carrying parcels and baskets; she labored with the childish inattention of the little ones' French lessons; as she became shabbier and more forlorn-looking, she was told that she had better take her meals down-stairs; she was treated as if she was nobody's concern, and her heart grew proud and sore, but she never told any one what she felt.

"Soldiers don't complain," she would say between her small, shut teeth. "I am not going to do it; I will pretend this is part of a war."[4]

But there were hours when her child heart might almost have broken with loneliness but for three people.

The first, it must be owned, was Becky—just Becky. Throughout all that first night spent in the garret, she had felt a vague comfort in knowing that on the other side of the wall in which the rats scuffled and squeaked there was another young human creature. And during the nights that followed the sense of comfort grew. They had little chance to speak to each other during the day. Each had her own tasks to perform, and any attempt at conversation would have been regarded as a tendency to loiter and lose time.

"Don't mind me, miss," Becky whispered during the first morning, "if I don't say nothin' polite. Some un 'd be down on us if I did. I *means* 'please' an' 'thank you' an' 'beg pardon,' but I dassn't to take time to say it."

But before daybreak she used to slip into Sara's attic and button her dress and give her such help as she required before she went down-stairs to light the kitchen fire. And when night came Sara always heard the humble knock at her door which meant that her handmaid was ready to help her again if she was needed. During the first weeks of her grief Sara felt as if she were too stupefied to talk, so it happened that some time passed before they saw each other much or exchanged visits. Becky's heart told her that it was best that people in trouble should be left alone.

The second of the trio of comforters was Ermengarde, but odd things happened before Ermengarde found her place.

When Sara's mind seemed to awaken again to the life about her, she realized that she had forgotten that an Ermengarde lived in the world. The two had always been friends, but Sara had felt as if she were years the older. It could not be contested that Ermengarde was as dull as she was affectionate. She clung to Sara in a simple, helpless way; she brought her lessons to her that she might be helped; she listened to her every word and besieged her with requests for stories. But she had nothing interesting to say herself, and she loathed books of every description. She was, in fact, not a person one would remember when one was caught in the storm of a great trouble, and Sara forgot her.

It had been all the easier to forget her because she had been suddenly called home for a few weeks. When she came back she did not see Sara for a day or two, and when she met her for the first time she encountered her coming down a corridor with her arms full of garments which were to be taken down-stairs to be mended. Sara herself had already been taught to mend them. She looked pale and unlike herself, and she was attired in the queer, outgrown frock whose shortness showed so much thin black leg.

Ermengarde was too slow a girl to be equal to such a situation. She could not think of anything to say. She knew what

had happened, but, somehow, she had never imagined Sara
could look like this—so odd and poor and almost like a servant.
It made her quite miserable, and she could do nothing but
break into a short hysterical laugh and exclaim—aimlessly and
as if without any meaning:

"Oh, Sara! is that you?"

"Yes," answered Sara, and suddenly a strange thought passed
through her mind and made her face flush.

She held the pile of garments in her arms, and her chin rested
upon the top of it to keep it steady. Something in the look of
her straight-gazing eyes made Ermengarde lose her wits still
more. She felt as if Sara had changed into a new kind of girl, and
she had never known her before. Perhaps it was because she
had suddenly grown poor and had to mend things and work
like Becky.

"Oh," she stammered. "How—how are you?"

"I don't know," Sara replied. "How are you?"

"I'm—I'm quite well," said Ermengarde, overwhelmed with
shyness. Then spasmodically she thought of something to say
which seemed more intimate. "Are you—are you very unhappy?" she said in a rush.

Then Sara was guilty of an injustice. Just at that moment her
torn heart swelled within her, and she felt that if any one was as
stupid as that, one had better get away from her.

"What do you think?" she said. "Do you think I am very
happy?" and she marched past her without another word.

In course of time she realized that if her wretchedness had
not made her forget things, she would have known that poor,
dull Ermengarde was not to be blamed for her unready, awkward ways. She was always awkward, and the more she felt, the
more stupid she was given to being.

But the sudden thought which had flashed upon her had
made her over-sensitive.

"She is like the others," she had thought. "She does not really want to talk to me. She knows no one does."

So for several weeks a barrier stood between them. When
they met by chance Sara looked the other way, and Ermengarde
felt too stiff and embarrassed to speak. Sometimes they nodded

to each other in passing, but there were times when they did not even exchange a greeting.

"If she would rather not talk to me," Sara thought, "I will keep out of her way. Miss Minchin makes that easy enough."

Miss Minchin made it so easy that at last they scarcely saw each other at all. At that time it was noticed that Ermengarde was more stupid than ever, and that she looked listless and unhappy. She used to sit in the window-seat, huddled in a heap, and stare out of the window without speaking. Once Jessie, who was passing, stopped to look at her curiously.

"What are you crying for, Ermengarde?" she asked.

"I'm not crying," answered Ermengarde, in a muffled, unsteady voice.

"You are," said Jessie. "A great big tear just rolled down the bridge of your nose and dropped off at the end of it. And there goes another."

"Well," said Ermengarde, "I'm miserable—and no one need interfere." And she turned her plump back and took out her handkerchief and boldly hid her face in it.

That night, when Sara went to her attic, she was later than usual. She had been kept at work until after the hour at which the pupils went to bed, and after that she had gone to her lessons in the lonely school-room. When she reached the top of the stairs, she was surprised to see a glimmer of light coming from under the attic door.

"Nobody goes there but myself," she thought quickly; "but some one has lighted a candle."

Some one had, indeed, lighted a candle, and it was not burning in the kitchen candlestick she was expected to use, but in one of those belonging to the pupils' bedrooms. The some one was sitting upon the battered footstool, and was dressed in her night-gown and wrapped up in a red shawl. It was Ermengarde.

"Ermengarde!" cried Sara. She was so startled that she was almost frightened. "You will get into trouble."

Ermengarde stumbled up from her footstool. She shuffled across the attic in her bedroom slippers, which were too large for her. Her eyes and nose were pink with crying.

"I know I shall—if I'm found out," she said. "But I don't

care—I don't care a bit. Oh, Sara, please tell me. What *is* the matter? Why don't you like me any more?"

Something in her voice made the familiar lump rise in Sara's throat. It was so affectionate and simple—so like the old Ermengarde who had asked her to be "best friends." It sounded as if she had not meant what she had seemed to mean during these past weeks.

"I do like you," Sara answered. "I thought—you see, everything is different now. I thought you—were different."

Ermengarde opened her wet eyes wide.

"Why, it was you who were different!" she cried. "You didn't want to talk to me. I didn't know what to do. It was you who were different after I came back."

Sara thought a moment. She saw she had made a mistake.

"I *am* different," she explained, "though not in the way you think. Miss Minchin does not want me to talk to the girls. Most of them don't want to talk to me. I thought—perhaps—you didn't. So I tried to keep out of your way."

"Oh, Sara," Ermengarde almost wailed in her reproachful dismay. And then after one more look they rushed into each other's arms. It must be confessed that Sara's small black head lay for some minutes on the shoulder covered by the red shawl. When Ermengarde had seemed to desert her, she had felt horribly lonely.

Afterward they sat down upon the floor together, Sara clasping her knees with her arms, and Ermengarde rolled up in her shawl. Ermengarde looked at the odd, big-eyed little face adoringly.

"I couldn't bear it any more," she said. "I dare say you could live without me, Sara; but I couldn't live without you. I was nearly *dead*. So to-night, when I was crying under the bed-clothes, I thought all at once of creeping up here and just begging you to let us be friends again."

"You are nicer than I am," said Sara. "I was too proud to try and make friends. You see, now that trials have come, they have shown that I am *not* a nice child. I was afraid they would. Perhaps"—wrinkling her forehead wisely—"that is what they were sent for."

"I don't see any good in them," said Ermengarde, stoutly.

"Neither do I—to speak the truth," admitted Sara, frankly. "But I suppose there *might* be good in things, even if we don't see it. There *might*"—doubtfully—"be good in Miss Minchin."

Ermengarde looked round the attic with a rather fearsome curiosity.

"Sara," she said, "do you think you can bear living here?"

Sara looked round also.

"If I pretend it's quite different, I can," she answered; "or if I pretend it is a place in a story."

She spoke slowly. Her imagination was beginning to work for her. It had not worked for her at all since her troubles had come upon her. She had felt as if it had been stunned.

"Other people have lived in worse places. Think of the Count of Monte Cristo in the dungeons of the Château d'If. And think of the people in the Bastille!"[5]

"The Bastille," half whispered Ermengarde, watching her and beginning to be fascinated. She remembered stories of the French Revolution which Sara had been able to fix in her mind by her dramatic relation of them. No one but Sara could have done it.

A well-known glow came into Sara's eyes.

"Yes," she said, hugging her knees. "That will be a good place to pretend about. I am a prisoner in the Bastille. I have been here for years and years—and years; and everybody has forgotten about me. Miss Minchin is the jailer—and Becky"—a sudden light adding itself to the glow in her eyes—"Becky is the prisoner in the next cell."

She turned to Ermengarde, looking quite like the old Sara.

"I shall pretend that," she said; "and it will be a great comfort."

Ermengarde was at once enraptured and awed.

"And will you tell me all about it?" she said. "May I creep up here at night, whenever it is safe, and hear the things you have made up in the day? It will seem as if we were more 'best friends' than ever."

"Yes," answered Sara, nodding. "Adversity tries people, and mine has tried you and proved how nice you are."

CHAPTER IX

Melchisedec

THE THIRD PERSON in the trio was Lottie. She was a small thing and did not know what adversity meant, and was much bewildered by the alteration she saw in her young adopted mother. She had heard it rumored that strange things had happened to Sara, but she could not understand why she looked different—why she wore an old black frock and came into the school-room only to teach instead of to sit in her place of honor and learn lessons herself. There had been much whispering among the little ones when it had been discovered that Sara no longer lived in the rooms in which Emily had so long sat in state. Lottie's chief difficulty was that Sara said so little when one asked her questions. At seven mysteries must be made very clear if one is to understand them.

"Are you very poor now, Sara?" she had asked confidentially the first morning her friend took charge of the small French class. "Are you as poor as a beggar?" She thrust a fat hand into the slim one and opened round, tearful eyes. "I don't want you to be as poor as a beggar."

She looked as if she was going to cry, and Sara hurriedly consoled her.

"Beggars have nowhere to live," she said courageously. "I have a place to live in."

"Where do you live?" persisted Lottie. "The new girl sleeps in your room, and it isn't pretty any more."

"I live in another room," said Sara.

"Is it a nice one?" inquired Lottie. "I want to go and see it."

"You must not talk," said Sara. "Miss Minchin is looking at us. She will be angry with me for letting you whisper."

She had found out already that she was to be held accountable for everything which was objected to. If the children were not attentive, if they talked, if they were restless, it was she who would be reproved.

But Lottie was a determined little person. If Sara would not tell her where she lived, she would find out in some other way. She talked to her small companions and hung about the elder girls and listened when they were gossiping; and acting upon certain information they had unconsciously let drop, she started late one afternoon on a voyage of discovery, climbing stairs she had never known the existence of, until she reached the attic floor. There she found two doors near each other, and opening one, she saw her beloved Sara standing upon an old table and looking out of a window.

"Sara!" she cried, aghast. "Mamma Sara!" She was aghast because the attic was so bare and ugly and seemed so far away from all the world. Her short legs had seemed to have been mounting hundreds of stairs.

Sara turned round at the sound of her voice. It was her turn to be aghast. What would happen now? If Lottie began to cry and any one chanced to hear, they were both lost. She jumped down from her table and ran to the child.

"Don't cry and make a noise," she implored. "I shall be scolded if you do, and I have been scolded all day. It's—it's not such a bad room, Lottie."

"Isn't it?" gasped Lottie, and as she looked round it she bit her lip. She was a spoiled child yet, but she was fond enough of her adopted parent to make an effort to control herself for her sake. Then, somehow, it was quite possible that any place in which Sara lived might turn out to be nice. "Why isn't it, Sara?" she almost whispered.

Sara hugged her close and tried to laugh. There was a sort of comfort in the warmth of the plump, childish body. She had had a hard day and had been staring out of the windows with hot eyes.

"You can see all sorts of things you can't see down-stairs," she said.

"What sort of things?" demanded Lottie, with that curiosity Sara could always awaken even in bigger girls.

"Chimneys—quite close to us—with smoke curling up in

wreaths and clouds and going up into the sky,—and sparrows hopping about and talking to each other just as if they were people,—and other attic windows where heads may pop out any minute and you can wonder who they belong to. And it all feels as high up—as if it was another world."

"Oh, let me see it!" cried Lottie. "Lift me up!"

Sara lifted her up, and they stood on the old table together and leaned on the edge of the flat window in the roof, and looked out.

Any one who has not done this does not know what a different world they saw. The slates spread out on either side of them and slanted down into the rain gutter-pipes. The sparrows, being at home there, twittered and hopped about quite without fear. Two of them perched on the chimney-top nearest and quarrelled with each other fiercely until one pecked the other and drove him away. The garret window next to theirs was shut because the house next door was empty.

"I wish some one lived there," Sara said. "It is so close that if there was a little girl in the attic, we could talk to each other through the windows and climb over to see each other, if we were not afraid of falling."

The sky seemed so much nearer than when one saw it from the street, that Lottie was enchanted. From the attic window, among the chimney-pots, the things which were happening in the world below seemed almost unreal. One scarcely believed in the existence of Miss Minchin and Miss Amelia and the school-room, and the roll of wheels in the square seemed a sound belonging to another existence.

"Oh, Sara!" cried Lottie, cuddling in her guarding arm. "I like this attic—I like it! It is nicer than down-stairs!"

"Look at that sparrow," whispered Sara. "I wish I had some crumbs to throw to him."

"I have some!" came in a little shriek from Lottie. "I have part of a bun in my pocket; I bought it with my penny yesterday, and I saved a bit."

When they threw out a few crumbs the sparrow jumped and flew away to an adjacent chimney-top. He was evidently not accustomed to intimates in attics, and unexpected crumbs startled him. But when Lottie remained quite still and Sara chirped very softly—almost as if she were a sparrow herself—he saw that the thing which had alarmed him represented hospitality, after all.[1] He put his head on one side, and from his perch on the chimney looked down at the crumbs with twinkling eyes. Lottie could scarcely keep still.

"Will he come? Will he come?" she whispered.

"His eyes look as if he would," Sara whispered back. "He is thinking and thinking whether he dare. Yes, he will! Yes, he is coming!"

He flew down and hopped toward the crumbs, but stopped a few inches away from them, putting his head on one side again, as if reflecting on the chances that Sara and Lottie might turn out to be big cats and jump on him. At last his heart told him they were really nicer than they looked, and he hopped nearer and nearer, darted at the biggest crumb with a lightning peck, seized it, and carried it away to the other side of his chimney.

"Now he *knows*," said Sara. "And he will come back for the others."

He did come back, and even brought a friend, and the friend went away and brought a relative, and among them they made a hearty meal over which they twittered and chattered and exclaimed, stopping every now and then to put their heads on one side and examine Lottie and Sara. Lottie was so delighted that she quite forgot her first shocked impression of the attic. In fact, when she was lifted down from the table and returned to earthly things as it were, Sara was able to point out to her many beauties in the room which she herself would not have suspected the existence of.

"It is so little and so high above everything," she said, "that it is almost like a nest in a tree.[2] The slanting ceiling is so funny. See, you can scarcely stand up at this end of the room; and when the morning begins to come I can lie in bed and look right up into the sky through that flat window in the roof. It is like a square patch of light. If the sun is going to shine, little pink clouds float about, and I feel as if I could touch them. And if it rains, the drops patter and patter as if they were saying something nice. Then if there are stars, you can lie and try to count how many go into the patch. It takes such a lot. And just look at that tiny, rusty grate in the corner. If it was polished and there was a fire in it, just think how nice it would be. You see, it's really a beautiful little room."

She was walking round the small place, holding Lottie's hand and making gestures which described all the beauties she was making herself see. She quite made Lottie see them, too. Lottie could always believe in the things Sara made pictures of.

"You see," she said, "there could be a thick, soft blue Indian rug on the floor; and in that corner there could be a soft little sofa, with cushions to curl up on; and just over it could be a shelf full of books so that one could reach them easily; and there could be a fur rug before the fire, and hangings on the wall to cover up the whitewash, and pictures. They would have to be little ones, but they could be beautiful; and there could be a lamp with a deep rose-colored shade; and a table in the middle, with things to have tea with; and a little fat copper kettle singing on the hob; and the bed could be quite different. It could be made soft and covered with a lovely silk coverlet. It could be beautiful. And perhaps we could coax the sparrows until we made such friends with them that they would come and peck at the window and ask to be let in."

"Oh, Sara!" cried Lottie; "I should like to live here!"

When Sara had persuaded her to go down-stairs again, and, after setting her in her way, had come back to her attic, she stood in the middle of it and looked about her. The enchantment of her imaginings for Lottie had died away. The bed was hard and covered with its dingy quilt. The whitewashed wall showed its broken patches, the floor was cold and bare, the grate was broken and rusty, and the battered footstool, tilted sideways on its injured leg, the only seat in the room. She sat down on it for a few minutes and let her head drop in her hands. The mere fact that Lottie had come and gone away again made things seem a little worse—just as perhaps prisoners feel a little more desolate after visitors come and go, leaving them behind.

"It's a lonely place," she said. "Sometimes it's the loneliest place in the world."

She was sitting in this way when her attention was attracted by a slight sound near her. She lifted her head to see where it came from, and if she had been a nervous child she would have left her seat on the battered footstool in a great hurry. A large rat was sitting up on his hind quarters and sniffing the air in an interested manner. Some of Lottie's crumbs had dropped upon the floor and their scent had drawn him out of his hole.

He looked so queer and so like a gray-whiskered dwarf or gnome that Sara was rather fascinated.[3] He looked at her with his bright eyes, as if he were asking a question. He was evidently so doubtful that one of the child's queer thoughts came into her mind.

"I dare say it is rather hard to be a rat," she mused. "Nobody likes you. People jump and run away and scream out, 'Oh, a horrid rat!' I shouldn't like people to scream and jump and say, 'Oh, a horrid Sara!' the moment they saw me. And set traps for me, and pretend they were dinner. It's so different to be a sparrow. But nobody asked this rat if he wanted to be a rat when he was made. Nobody said, 'Wouldn't you rather be a sparrow?' "

She had sat so quietly that the rat had begun to take courage. He was very much afraid of her, but perhaps he had a heart like the sparrow and it told him that she was not a thing which pounced. He was very hungry. He had a wife and a large family in the wall, and they had had frightfully bad luck for several days. He had left the children crying bitterly, and felt he would risk a good deal for a few crumbs, so he cautiously dropped upon his feet.

"Come on," said Sara; "I'm not a trap. You can have them, poor thing! Prisoners in the Bastille used to make friends with rats. Suppose I make friends with you."

How it is that animals understand things I do not know, but it is certain that they do understand.[4] Perhaps there is a language which is not made of words and everything in the world understands it. Perhaps there is a soul hidden in everything and it can always speak, without even making a sound, to another soul. But whatsoever was the reason, the rat knew from that moment that he was safe—even though he was a rat. He knew that this young human being sitting on the red footstool would not jump up and terrify him with wild, sharp noises or throw heavy objects at him which, if they did not fall and crush him, would send him limping in his scurry back to his hole. He was really a very nice rat, and did not mean the least harm. When he had stood on his hind legs and sniffed the air, with his bright eyes fixed on Sara, he had hoped that she would understand this, and would not begin by hating him as an enemy. When the mysterious thing which speaks without saying any words told him that she would not, he went softly toward the crumbs and began to eat them. As he did it he glanced every now and then at Sara, just as the sparrows had done, and his expression was so very apologetic that it touched her heart.

She sat and watched him without making any movement. One crumb was very much larger than the others—in fact, it could scarcely be called a crumb. It was evident that he wanted that piece very much, but it lay quite near the footstool and he was still rather timid.

"I believe he wants it to carry to his family in the wall," Sara thought. "If I do not stir at all, perhaps he will come and get it."

She scarcely allowed herself to breathe, she was so deeply interested. The rat shuffled a little nearer and ate a few more crumbs, then he stopped and sniffed delicately, giving a side glance at the occupant of the footstool; then he darted at the piece of bun with something very like the sudden boldness of the sparrow, and the instant he had possession of it fled back to the wall, slipped down a crack in the skirting board, and was gone.

"I knew he wanted it for his children," said Sara. "I do believe I could make friends with him."

A week or so afterward, on one of the rare nights when Ermengarde found it safe to steal up to the attic, when she tapped on the door with the tips of her fingers Sara did not come to her for two or three minutes. There was, indeed, such a silence in the room at first that Ermengarde wondered if she could have fallen asleep. Then, to her surprise, she heard her utter a little, low laugh and speak coaxingly to some one.

"There!" Ermengarde heard her say. "Take it and go home, Melchisedec![5] Go home to your wife!"

Almost immediately Sara opened the door, and when she did so she found Ermengarde standing with alarmed eyes upon the threshold.

"Who—who *are* you talking to, Sara?" she gasped out.

Sara drew her in cautiously, but she looked as if something pleased and amused her.

"You must promise not to be frightened—not to scream the least bit, or I can't tell you," she answered.

Ermengarde felt almost inclined to scream on the spot, but managed to control herself. She looked all round the attic and saw no one. And yet Sara had certainly been speaking *to* some one. She thought of ghosts.

"Is it—something that will frighten me?" she asked timorously.

"Some people are afraid of them," said Sara. "I was at first,—but I am not now."

"Was it—a ghost?" quaked Ermengarde.

"No," said Sara, laughing. "It was my rat."[6]

Ermengarde made one bound, and landed in the middle of the little dingy bed. She tucked her feet under her night-gown and the red shawl. She did not scream, but she gasped with fright.

"Oh! oh!" she cried under her breath. "A rat! A rat!"

"I was afraid you would be frightened," said Sara. "But you needn't be. I am making him tame. He actually knows me and comes out when I call him. Are you too frightened to want to see him?"

The truth was that, as the days had gone on and, with the aid of scraps brought up from the kitchen, her curious friendship had developed, she had gradually forgotten that the timid creature she was becoming familiar with was a mere rat.

At first Ermengarde was too much alarmed to do anything but huddle in a heap upon the bed and tuck up her feet, but the sight of Sara's composed little countenance and the story of Melchisedec's first appearance began at last to rouse her curiosity, and she leaned forward over the edge of the bed and watched Sara go and kneel down by the hole in the skirting board.

"He—he won't run out quickly and jump on the bed, will he?" she said.

"No," answered Sara. "He's as polite as we are. He is just like a person. Now watch!"

She began to make a low, whistling sound—so low and coaxing that it could only have been heard in entire stillness. She did
it several times, looking entirely absorbed in it. Ermengarde
thought she looked as if she were working a spell. And at last,
evidently in response to it, a gray-whiskered, bright-eyed head
peeped out of the hole. Sara had some crumbs in her hand. She
dropped them, and Melchisedec came quietly forth and ate
them. A piece of larger size than the rest he took and carried in
the most businesslike manner back to his home.

"You see," said Sara, "that is for his wife and children. He is
very nice. He only eats the little bits. After he goes back I can
always hear his family squeaking for joy. There are three kinds
of squeaks. One kind is the children's, and one is Mrs.
Melchisedec's, and one is Melchisedec's own."

Ermengarde began to laugh.

"Oh, Sara!" she said. "You *are* queer,—but you are nice."

"I know I am queer," admitted Sara, cheerfully; "and I *try* to
be nice." She rubbed her forehead with her little brown paw,
and a puzzled, tender look came into her face. "Papa always
laughed at me," she said; "but I liked it. He thought I was
queer, but he liked me to make up things. I—I can't help making up things. If I didn't, I don't believe I could live." She
paused and glanced round the attic. "I'm sure I couldn't live
here," she added in a low voice.

Ermengarde was interested, as she always was. "When you
talk about things," she said, "they seem as if they grew real.
You talk about Melchisedec as if he was a person."

"He *is* a person," said Sara. "He gets hungry and frightened,
just as we do; and he is married and has children. How do we
know he doesn't think things, just as we do? His eyes look as if
he was a person. That was why I gave him a name."

She sat down on the floor in her favorite attitude, holding
her knees.

"Besides," she said, "he is a Bastille rat sent to be my friend.
I can always get a bit of bread the cook has thrown away, and it
is quite enough to support him."

"Is it the Bastille yet?" asked Ermengarde, eagerly. "Do you
always pretend it is the Bastille?"

"Nearly always," answered Sara. "Sometimes I try to pretend it is another kind of place; but the Bastille is generally easiest—particularly when it is cold."

Just at that moment Ermengarde almost jumped off the bed, she was so startled by a sound she heard. It was like two distinct knocks on the wall.

"What is that?" she exclaimed.

Sara got up from the floor and answered quite dramatically: "It is the prisoner in the next cell."

"Becky!" cried Ermengarde, enraptured.

"Yes," said Sara. "Listen; the two knocks meant, 'Prisoner, are you there?' "

She knocked three times on the wall herself, as if in answer.

"That means, 'Yes, I am here, and all is well.' "

Four knocks came from Becky's side of the wall.

"That means," explained Sara, " 'Then, fellow-sufferer, we will sleep in peace. Good-night.' "

Ermengarde quite beamed with delight.

"Oh, Sara!" she whispered joyfully. "It is like a story!"

"It *is* a story," said Sara. "*Everything*'s a story. You are a story—I am a story. Miss Minchin is a story."[7]

And she sat down again and talked until Ermengarde forgot that she was a sort of escaped prisoner herself, and had to be reminded by Sara that she could not remain in the Bastille all night, but must steal noiselessly down-stairs again and creep back into her deserted bed.

CHAPTER X

The Indian Gentleman

BUT IT WAS A PERILOUS THING for Ermengarde and Lottie to make pilgrimages to the attic. They could never be quite sure when Sara would be there, and they could scarcely ever be certain that Miss Amelia would not make a tour of inspection through the bedrooms after the pupils were supposed to be asleep. So their visits were rare ones, and Sara lived a strange and lonely life. It was a lonelier life when she was down-stairs than when she was in her attic. She had no one to talk to; and when she was sent out on errands and walked through the streets, a forlorn little figure carrying a basket or a parcel, trying to hold her hat on when the wind was blowing, and feeling the water soak through her shoes when it was raining, she felt as if the crowds hurrying past her made her loneliness greater. When she had been the Princess Sara, driving through the streets in her brougham, or walking, attended by Mariette, the sight of her bright, eager little face and picturesque coats and hats had often caused people to look after her. A happy, beautifully cared for little girl naturally attracts attention. Shabby, poorly dressed children are not rare enough and pretty enough to make people turn around to look at them and smile. No one looked at Sara in these days, and no one seemed to see her as she hurried along the crowded pavements. She had begun to grow very fast, and, as she was dressed only in such clothes as the plainer remnants of her wardrobe would supply, she knew she looked very queer, indeed. All her valuable garments had been disposed of, and such as had been left for her use she was expected to wear so long as she could put them on at all. Sometimes, when she passed a shop window with a mirror in it, she almost laughed outright on catching a glimpse of herself, and sometimes her face went red and she bit her lip and turned away.

In the evening, when she passed houses whose windows were lighted up, she used to look into the warm rooms and amuse herself by imagining things about the people she saw sitting before the fires or about the tables. It always interested her to catch glimpses of rooms before the shutters were closed. There were several families in the square in which Miss Minchin lived, with which she had become quite familiar in a way of her own. The one she liked best she called the Large Family. She called it the Large Family not because the members of it were big,—for, indeed, most of them were little,—but because there were so many of them. There were eight children in the Large Family, and a stout, rosy mother, and a stout, rosy father, and a stout, rosy grandmother, and any number of servants. The eight children were always either being taken out to walk or to ride in perambulators by comfortable nurses, or they were going to drive with their mamma, or they were flying to the door in the evening to meet their papa and kiss him and dance around him and drag off his overcoat and look in the pockets for packages, or they were crowding about the nursery windows and looking out and pushing each other and laughing—in fact, they were always doing something enjoyable and suited to the tastes of a large family. Sara was quite fond of them, and had given them names out of books—quite romantic names. She called them the Montmorencys when she did not call them the Large Family.[1] The fat, fair baby with the lace cap was Ethelberta Beauchamp Montmorency; the next baby was Violet Cholmondeley Montmorency; the little boy who could just stagger and who had such round legs was Sydney Cecil Vivian Montmorency; and then came Lilian Evangeline Maud Marion, Rosalind Gladys, Guy Clarence, Veronica Eustacia, and Claude Harold Hector.

One evening a very funny thing happened—though, perhaps, in one sense it was not a funny thing at all.[2]

Several of the Montmorencys were evidently going to a children's party, and just as Sara was about to pass the door they were crossing the pavement to get into the carriage which was waiting for them. Veronica Eustacia and Rosalind Gladys, in white-lace frocks and lovely sashes, had just got in, and Guy Clarence, aged five, was following them. He was such a pretty fellow and had such rosy cheeks and blue eyes, and such a darling little round head covered with curls, that Sara forgot her basket and shabby cloak altogether—in fact, forgot everything but that she wanted to look at him for a moment. So she paused and looked.

It was Christmas time, and the Large Family had been hearing many stories about children who were poor and had no mammas and papas to fill their stockings and take them to the pantomime—children who were, in fact, cold and thinly clad and hungry. In the stories, kind people—sometimes little boys and girls with tender hearts—invariably saw the poor children and gave them money or rich gifts, or took them home to beautiful dinners. Guy Clarence had been affected to tears that very afternoon by the reading of such a story, and he had burned with a desire to find such a poor child and give her a certain sixpence he possessed, and thus provide for her for life. An entire sixpence, he was sure, would mean affluence for evermore. As he crossed the strip of red carpet laid across the pavement from the door to the carriage, he had this very sixpence in the pocket of his very short man-o'-war trousers. And just as Rosalind Gladys got into the vehicle and jumped on to the seat in order to feel the cushions spring under her, he saw Sara standing on the wet pavement in her shabby frock and hat, with her old basket on her arm, looking at him hungrily.

He thought that her eyes looked hungry because she had perhaps had nothing to eat for a long time. He did not know that they looked so because she was hungry for the warm, merry life his home held and his rosy face spoke of, and that she had a hungry wish to snatch him in her arms and kiss him. He only knew that she had big eyes and a thin face and thin legs and a common basket and poor clothes. So he put his hand in his pocket and found his sixpence and walked up to her benignly.

"Here, poor little girl," he said. "Here is a sixpence. I will give it to you."

Sara started, and all at once realized that she looked exactly like poor children she had seen, in her better days, waiting on the pavement to watch her as she got out of her brougham. And she had given them pennies many a time. Her face went red and then it went pale, and for a second she felt as if she could not take the dear little sixpence.

"Oh, no!" she said. "Oh, no, thank you; I mustn't take it, indeed!"

Her voice was so unlike an ordinary street child's voice and her manner was so like the manner of a well-bred little person that Veronica Eustacia (whose real name was Janet) and Rosalind Gladys (who was really called Nora) leaned forward to listen.

But Guy Clarence was not to be thwarted in his benevolence. He thrust the sixpence into her hand.

"Yes, you must take it, poor little girl!" he insisted stoutly. "You can buy things to eat with it. It is a whole sixpence!"

There was something so honest and kind in his face, and he looked so likely to be heartbrokenly disappointed if she did not take it, that Sara knew she must not refuse him. To be as proud as that would be a cruel thing. So she actually put her pride in her pocket, though it must be admitted her cheeks burned.

"Thank you," she said. "You are a kind, kind little darling thing." And as he scrambled joyfully into the carriage she went away, trying to smile, though she caught her breath quickly and her eyes were shining through a mist. She had known that she looked odd and shabby, but until now she had not known that she might be taken for a beggar.

As the Large Family's carriage drove away, the children inside it were talking with interested excitement.

"Oh, Donald" (this was Guy Clarence's name), Janet exclaimed alarmedly, "why did you offer that little girl your sixpence? I'm sure she is not a beggar!"

"She didn't speak like a beggar!" cried Nora; "and her face didn't really look like a beggar's face!"

"Besides, she didn't beg," said Janet. "I was so afraid she might be angry with you. You know, it makes people angry to be taken for beggars when they are not beggars."

"She wasn't angry," said Donald, a trifle dismayed, but still firm. "She laughed a little, and she said I was a kind, kind little darling thing. And I was!"—stoutly. "It was my whole sixpence."

Janet and Nora exchanged glances.

"A beggar girl would never have said that," decided Janet. "She would have said, 'Thank yer kindly, little gentleman—thank yer, sir'; and perhaps she would have bobbed a courtesy."

Sara knew nothing about the fact, but from that time the Large Family was as profoundly interested in her as she was in it. Faces used to appear at the nursery windows when she passed, and many discussions concerning her were held round the fire.

"She is a kind of servant at the seminary," Janet said. "I don't believe she belongs to anybody. I believe she is an orphan. But she is not a beggar, however shabby she looks."

And afterward she was called by all of them, "The-little-girl-who-is-not-a-beggar," which was, of course, rather a long name, and sounded very funny sometimes when the youngest ones said it in a hurry.

Sara managed to bore a hole in the sixpence and hung it on an old bit of narrow ribbon round her neck. Her affection for the Large Family increased—as, indeed, her affection for everything she could love increased. She grew fonder and fonder of Becky, and she used to look forward to the two mornings a week when she went into the school-room to give the little ones their French lesson. Her small pupils loved her, and strove with each other for the privilege of standing close to her and insinuating their small hands into hers. It fed her hungry heart to feel them nestling up to her. She made such friends with the sparrows that when she stood upon the table, put her head and shoulders out of the attic window, and chirped, she heard almost immediately a flutter of wings and answering twitters, and a little flock of dingy town birds appeared and alighted on the slates to talk to her and make much of the crumbs she scattered. With Melchisedec she had become so intimate that he actually brought Mrs. Melchisedec with him sometimes, and now and then one or two of his children. She used to talk to him, and, somehow, he looked quite as if he understood.

There had grown in her mind rather a strange feeling about Emily, who always sat and looked on at everything. It arose in one of her moments of great desolateness. She would have liked to believe or pretend to believe that Emily understood and sympathized with her. She did not like to own to herself that her only companion could feel and hear nothing. She used to put her in a chair sometimes and sit opposite to her on the old red footstool, and stare and pretend about her until her own eyes would grow large with something which was almost like fear—particularly at night when everything was so still, when the only sound in the attic was the occasional sudden scurry and squeak of Melchisedec's family in the wall. One of her "pretends" was that Emily was a kind of good witch who could protect her. Sometimes, after she had stared at her until she was wrought up to the highest pitch of fancifulness, she would ask her questions and find herself *almost* feeling as if she would presently answer. But she never did.

"As to answering, though," said Sara, trying to console herself, "I don't answer very often. I never answer when I can help it. When people are insulting you, there is nothing so good for them as not to say a word—just to look at them and *think*. Miss Minchin turns pale with rage when I do it, Miss Amelia looks frightened, and so do the girls. When you will not fly into a passion people know you are stronger than they are, because you are strong enough to hold in your rage, and they are not, and they say stupid things they wish they hadn't said afterward. There's nothing so strong as rage, except what makes you hold it in—that's stronger. It's a good thing not to answer your enemies. I scarcely ever do. Perhaps Emily is more like me than I am like myself.[3] Perhaps she would rather not answer her friends, even. She keeps it all in her heart."

But though she tried to satisfy herself with these arguments, she did not find it easy. When, after a long, hard day, in which she had been sent here and there, sometimes on long errands through wind and cold and rain, she came in wet and hungry, and was sent out again because nobody chose to remember that she was only a child, and that her slim legs might be tired and her small body might be chilled; when she had been given only harsh words and cold, slighting looks for thanks; when the cook had been vulgar and insolent; when Miss Minchin had been in her worst mood, and when she had seen the girls sneering among themselves at her shabbiness—then she was not always able to comfort her sore, proud, desolate heart with fancies when Emily merely sat upright in her old chair and stared.

One of these nights, when she came up to the attic cold and hungry, with a tempest raging in her young breast, Emily's stare seemed so vacant, her sawdust legs and arms so inexpressive, that Sara lost all control over herself. There was nobody but Emily—no one in the world. And there she sat.

"I shall die presently," she said at first.

Emily simply stared.

"I can't bear this," said the poor child, trembling. "I know I shall die. I'm cold; I'm wet; I'm starving to death. I've walked a thousand miles to-day, and they have done nothing but scold me from morning until night. And because I could not find that last thing the cook sent me for, they would not give me any supper. Some men laughed at me because my old shoes made me slip down in the mud. I'm covered with mud now. And they laughed. Do you hear?"

She looked at the staring glass eyes and complacent face, and suddenly a sort of heartbroken rage seized her. She lifted her little savage hand and knocked Emily off the chair, bursting into a passion of sobbing,—Sara who never cried.

"You are nothing but a *doll!*" she cried; "nothing but a doll—doll—doll! You care for nothing. You are stuffed with sawdust. You never had a heart. Nothing could ever make you feel. You are a *doll!*"

Emily lay on the floor, with her legs ignominiously doubled up over her head, and a new flat place on the end of her nose; but she was calm, even dignified. Sara hid her face in her arms. The rats in the wall began to fight and bite each other and squeak and scramble. Melchisedec was chastising some of his family.

Sara's sobs gradually quieted themselves. It was so unlike her to break down that she was surprised at herself. After a while she raised her face and looked at Emily, who seemed to be gazing at her round the side of one angle, and, somehow, by this time actually with a kind of glassy-eyed sympathy. Sara bent and picked her up. Remorse overtook her. She even smiled at herself a very little smile.

"You can't help being a doll," she said with a resigned sigh, "any more than Lavinia and Jessie can help not having any sense. We are not all made alike. Perhaps you do your sawdust best." And she kissed her and shook her clothes straight, and put her back upon her chair.

She had wished very much that some one would take the empty house next door. She wished it because of the attic window which was so near hers. It seemed as if it would be so nice to see it propped open some day and a head and shoulders rising out of the square aperture.

"If it looked a nice head," she thought, "I might begin by saying, 'Good morning,' and all sorts of things might happen.[4] But, of course, it's not really likely that any one but under servants would sleep there."

One morning, on turning the corner of the square after a visit to the grocer's, the butcher's, and the baker's, she saw, to her great delight, that during her rather prolonged absence, a van full of furniture had stopped before the next house, the front doors were thrown open, and men in shirt sleeves were going in and out carrying heavy packages and pieces of furniture.

"It's taken!" she said. "It really *is* taken! Oh, I do hope a nice head will look out of the attic window!"

She would almost have liked to join the group of loiterers who had stopped on the pavement to watch the things carried in. She had an idea that if she could see some of the furniture she could guess something about the people it belonged to.

"Miss Minchin's tables and chairs are just like her," she thought; "I remember thinking that the first minute I saw her, even though I was so little. I told papa afterward, and he laughed and said it was true. I am sure the Large Family have fat, comfortable arm-chairs and sofas, and I can see that their red-flowery wall-paper is exactly like them. It's warm and cheerful and kind-looking and happy."

She was sent out for parsley to the greengrocer's later in the day, and when she came up the area steps her heart gave quite a quick beat of recognition. Several pieces of furniture had been set out of the van upon the pavement. There was a beautiful table of elaborately wrought teak-wood, and some chairs, and a screen covered with rich Oriental embroidery. The sight of them gave her a weird, homesick feeling. She had seen things so like them in India. One of the things Miss Minchin had taken from her was a carved teak-wood desk her father had sent her.

"They are beautiful things," she said; "they look as if they ought to belong to a nice person. All the things look rather grand. I suppose it is a rich family."

The vans of furniture came and were unloaded and gave place to others all the day. Several times it so happened that Sara had an opportunity of seeing things carried in. It became plain that she had been right in guessing that the new-comers were people of large means. All the furniture was rich and beautiful, and a great deal of it was Oriental. Wonderful rugs and draperies and ornaments were taken from the vans, many pictures, and books enough for a library. Among other things there was a superb god Buddha in a splendid shrine.

"Some one in the family *must* have been in India," Sara thought. "They have got used to Indian things and like them. I *am* glad. I shall feel as if they were friends, even if a head never looks out of the attic window."

When she was taking in the evening's milk for the cook (there was really no odd job she was not called upon to do), she saw something occur which made the situation more interesting than ever. The handsome, rosy man who was the father of the Large Family walked across the square in the most matter-of-fact manner, and ran up the steps of the next-door house. He ran up them as if he felt quite at home and expected to run up and down them many a time in the future. He stayed inside quite a long time, and several times came out and gave directions to the workmen, as if he had a right to do so. It was quite certain that he was in some intimate way connected with the newcomers and was acting for them.

"If the new people have children," Sara speculated, "the Large Family children will be sure to come and play with them, and they *might* come up into the attic just for fun."

At night, after her work was done, Becky came in to see her fellow-prisoner and bring her news.

"It's a' Nindian gentleman that's comin' to live next door, miss," she said. "I don't know whether he's a black gentleman or not, but he's a Nindian one. He's very rich, an' he's ill, an' the gentleman of the Large Family is his lawyer. He's had a lot of trouble, an' it's made him ill an' low in his mind. He worships idols, miss. He's an 'eathen an' bows down to wood an' stone. I seen a' idol bein' carried in for him to worship. Somebody had oughter send him a trac'.[5] You can get a trac' for a penny."

Sara laughed a little.

"I don't believe he worships that idol," she said; "some people like to keep them to look at because they are interesting. My papa had a beautiful one, and he did not worship it."

But Becky was rather inclined to prefer to believe that the new neighbor was "an 'eathen." It sounded so much more romantic than that he should merely be the ordinary kind of gentleman who went to church with a prayer-book. She sat and talked long that night of what he would be like, of what his wife would be like if he had one, and of what his children would be like if they had children. Sara saw that privately she could not help hoping very much that they would all be black, and would wear turbans, and, above all, that—like their parent—they would all be " 'eathens."

"I never lived next door to no 'eathens, miss," she said; "I should like to see what sort o' ways they'd have."

It was several weeks before her curiosity was satisfied, and then it was revealed that the new occupant had neither wife nor children. He was a solitary man with no family at all, and it was evident that he was shattered in health and unhappy in mind.

A carriage drove up one day and stopped before the house. When the footman dismounted from the box and opened the door the gentleman who was the father of the Large Family got out first. After him there descended a nurse in uniform, then came down the steps two men-servants. They came to assist their master, who, when he was helped out of the carriage, proved to be a man with a haggard, distressed face, and a skeleton body wrapped in furs. He was carried up the steps, and the head of the Large Family went with him, looking very anxious. Shortly afterward a doctor's carriage arrived, and the doctor went in—plainly to take care of him.

"There is such a yellow gentleman next door, Sara," Lottie whispered at the French class afterward. "Do you think he is a Chinee? The geography says the Chinee men are yellow."

"No, he is not Chinese," Sara whispered back; "he is very ill. Go on with your exercise, Lottie. '*Non, monsieur. Je n'ai pas le canif de mon oncle.*' "[6]

That was the beginning of the story of the Indian gentleman.

CHAPTER XI

Ram Dass

THERE WERE FINE SUNSETS even in the square, sometimes. One could only see parts of them, however, between the chimneys and over the roofs. From the kitchen windows one could not see them at all, and could only guess that they were going on because the bricks looked warm and the air rosy or yellow for a while, or perhaps one saw a blazing glow strike a particular pane of glass somewhere. There was, however, one place from which one could see all the splendor of them: the piles of red or gold clouds in the west; or the purple ones edged with dazzling brightness; or the little fleecy, floating ones, tinged with rose-color and looking like flights of pink doves scurrying across the blue in a great hurry if there was a wind. The place where one could see all this, and seem at the same time to breathe a purer air, was, of course, the attic window. When the square suddenly seemed to begin to glow in an enchanted way and look wonderful in spite of its sooty trees and railings, Sara knew something was going on in the sky; and when it was at all possible to leave the kitchen without being missed or called back, she invariably stole away and crept up the flights of stairs, and, climbing on the old table, got her head and body as far out of the window as possible. When she had accomplished this, she always drew a long breath and looked all round her. It used to seem as if she had all the sky and the world to herself. No one else ever looked out of the other attics. Generally the skylights were closed; but even if they were propped open to admit air, no one seemed to come near them. And there Sara would stand, sometimes turning her face upward to the blue which seemed so friendly and near,—just like a lovely vaulted ceiling,—sometimes watching the west and all the wonderful things that happened there: the clouds melting or drifting or waiting softly to be changed pink or crimson or snow-white or purple or pale dove-gray. Sometimes they made islands or great mountains enclosing lakes of deep turquoise-blue, or liquid amber, or chrysoprase-green; sometimes dark headlands jutted into strange, lost seas; sometimes slender strips of wonderful lands joined other wonderful lands together.[1] There were places where it seemed that one could run or climb or stand and wait to see what next was coming—until, perhaps, as it all melted, one could float away. At least it seemed so to Sara, and nothing had ever been quite so beautiful to her as the things she saw as she stood on the table—her body half out of the skylight—the sparrows twittering with sunset softness on the slates. The sparrows always seemed to her to twitter with a sort of subdued softness just when these marvels were going on.

There was such a sunset as this a few days after the Indian gentleman was brought to his new home; and, as it fortunately happened that the afternoon's work was done in the kitchen and nobody had ordered her to go anywhere or perform any task, Sara found it easier than usual to slip away and go upstairs.

She mounted her table and stood looking out. It was a wonderful moment. There were floods of molten gold covering the west, as if a glorious tide was sweeping over the world.[2] A deep, rich yellow light filled the air; the birds flying across the tops of the houses showed quite black against it.

"It's a Splendid one," said Sara, softly, to herself. "It makes me feel almost afraid—as if something strange was just going to happen. The Splendid ones always make me feel like that."

She suddenly turned her head because she heard a sound a few yards away from her. It was an odd sound like a queer little squeaky chattering. It came from the window of the next attic. Some one had come to look at the sunset as she had. There was a head and part of a body emerging from the skylight, but it was not the head or body of a little girl or a housemaid; it was the picturesque white-swathed form and dark-faced, gleaming-eyed, white-turbaned head of a native Indian man-servant,—"a Lascar," Sara said to herself quickly,—and the sound she had heard came from a small monkey he held in his arms as if he were fond of it, and which was snuggling and chattering against his breast.[3]

As Sara looked toward him he looked toward her. The first thing she thought was that his dark face looked sorrowful and homesick. She felt absolutely sure he had come up to look at the sun, because he had seen it so seldom in England that he longed for a sight of it. She looked at him interestedly for a second, and then smiled across the slates. She had learned to know how comforting a smile, even from a stranger, may be.

Hers was evidently a pleasure to him. His whole expression altered, and he showed such gleaming white teeth as he smiled back that it was as if a light had been illuminated in his dusky face. The friendly look in Sara's eyes was always very effective when people felt tired or dull.

It was perhaps in making his salute to her that he loosened his hold on the monkey. He was an impish monkey and always ready for adventure, and it is probable that the sight of a little girl excited him. He suddenly broke loose, jumped on to the slates, ran across them chattering, and actually leaped on to Sara's shoulder, and from there down into her attic room. It made her laugh and delighted her; but she knew he must be restored to his master,—if the Lascar was his master,—and she wondered how this was to be done. Would he let her catch him, or would he be naughty and refuse to be caught, and perhaps get away and run off over the roofs and be lost? That would not do at all. Perhaps he belonged to the Indian gentleman, and the poor man was fond of him.

She turned to the Lascar, feeling glad that she remembered still some of the Hindustani she had learned when she lived with her father. She could make the man understand. She spoke to him in the language he knew.

"Will he let me catch him?" she asked.

She thought she had never seen more surprise and delight than the dark face expressed when she spoke in the familiar tongue. The truth was that the poor fellow felt as if his gods had intervened, and the kind little voice came from heaven itself. At once Sara saw that he had been accustomed to European children. He poured forth a flood of respectful thanks. He was the servant of Missee Sahib. The monkey was a good monkey and would not bite; but, unfortunately, he was difficult to catch. He would flee from one spot to another, like the lightning. He was disobedient, though not evil. Ram Dass knew him as if he were his child, and Ram Dass he would sometimes obey, but not always.[4] If Missee Sahib would permit Ram Dass, he himself could cross the roof to her room, enter the windows, and regain the unworthy little animal. But he was evidently afraid Sara might think he was taking a great liberty and perhaps would not let him come.

But Sara gave him leave at once.

"Can you get across?" she inquired.

"In a moment," he answered her.

"Then come," she said; "he is flying from side to side of the room as if he was frightened."

Ram Dass slipped through his attic window and crossed to hers as steadily and lightly as if he had walked on roofs all his life. He slipped through the skylight and dropped upon his feet without a sound. Then he turned to Sara and salaamed again. The monkey saw him and uttered a little scream. Ram Dass hastily took the precaution of shutting the skylight, and then went in chase of him. It was not a very long chase. The monkey prolonged it a few minutes evidently for the mere fun of it, but presently he sprang chattering on to Ram Dass's shoulder and sat there chattering and clinging to his neck with a weird little skinny arm.

Ram Dass thanked Sara profoundly. She had seen that his quick native eyes had taken in at a glance all the bare shabbiness of the room, but he spoke to her as if he were speaking to the little daughter of a rajah, and pretended that he observed nothing. He did not presume to remain more than a few moments after he had caught the monkey, and those moments were given to further deep and grateful obeisance to her in return for her indulgence. This little evil one, he said, stroking the monkey, was, in truth, not so evil as he seemed, and his master, who was ill, was sometimes amused by him. He would have been made sad if his favorite had run away and been lost. Then he salaamed once more and got through the skylight and across the slates again with as much agility as the monkey himself had displayed.

When he had gone Sara stood in the middle of her attic and

thought of many things his face and his manner had brought back to her. The sight of his native costume and the profound reverence of his manner stirred all her past memories. It seemed a strange thing to remember that she—the drudge whom the cook had said insulting things to an hour ago—had only a few years ago been surrounded by people who all treated her as Ram Dass had treated her; who salaamed when she went by, whose foreheads almost touched the ground when she spoke to them, who were her servants and her slaves. It was like a sort of dream. It was all over, and it could never come back. It certainly seemed that there was no way in which any change could take place. She knew what Miss Minchin intended that her future should be. So long as she was too young to be used as a regular teacher, she would be used as an errand girl and servant and yet expected to remember what she had learned and in some mysterious way to learn more. The greater number of her evenings she was supposed to spend at study, and at various indefinite intervals she was examined and knew she would have been severely admonished if she had not advanced as was expected of her. The truth, indeed, was that Miss Minchin knew that she was too anxious to learn to require teachers. Give her books, and she would devour them and end by knowing them by heart. She might be trusted to be equal to teaching a good deal in the course of a few years. This was what would happen: when she was older she would be expected to drudge in the school-room as she drudged now in various parts of the house; they would be obliged to give her more respectable clothes, but they would be sure to be plain and ugly and to make her look somehow like a servant. That was all there seemed to be to look forward to, and Sara stood quite still for several minutes and thought it over.

Then a thought came back to her which made the color rise in her cheek and a spark light itself in her eyes. She straightened her thin little body and lifted her head.

"Whatever comes," she said, "cannot alter one thing. If I am a princess in rags and tatters, I can be a princess inside. It would be easy to be a princess if I were dressed in cloth of gold, but it is a great deal more of a triumph to be one all the time when no one knows it. There was Marie Antoinette when she was in prison and her throne was gone and she had only a black gown on, and her hair was white, and they insulted her and called her Widow Capet. She was a great deal more like a queen then than when she was so gay and everything was so grand. I like her best then. Those howling mobs of people did not frighten her. She was stronger than they were, even when they cut her head off."

This was not a new thought, but quite an old one, by this time. It had consoled her through many a bitter day, and she had gone about the house with an expression in her face which Miss Minchin could not understand and which was a source of great annoyance to her, as it seemed as if the child were mentally living a life which held her above the rest of the world. It was as if she scarcely heard the rude and acid things said to her; or, if she heard them, did not care for them at all. Sometimes, when she was in the midst of some harsh, domineering speech, Miss Minchin would find the still, unchildish eyes fixed upon her with something like a proud smile in them. At such times she did not know that Sara was saying to herself:

"You don't know that you are saying these things to a princess, and that if I chose I could wave my hand and order you to execution. I only spare you because I *am* a princess, and you are a poor, stupid, unkind, vulgar old thing, and don't know any better."

This used to interest and amuse her more than anything else; and queer and fanciful as it was, she found comfort in it and it was a good thing for her. While the thought held possession of her, she could not be made rude and malicious by the rudeness and malice of those about her.

"A princess must be polite," she said to herself.

And so when the servants, taking their tone from their mistress, were insolent and ordered her about, she would hold her head erect and reply to them with a quaint civility which often made them stare at her.

"She's got more airs and graces than if she come from Buckingham Palace, that young one," said the cook, chuckling a little sometimes; "I lose my temper with her often enough, but I

will say she never forgets her manners. 'If you please, cook;'
'Will you be so kind, cook?' 'I beg your pardon, cook;' 'May I
trouble you, cook?' She drops 'em about the kitchen as if they
was nothing."

The morning after the interview with Ram Dass and his
monkey, Sara was in the school-room with her small pupils.
Having finished giving them their lessons, she was putting the
French exercise-books together and thinking, as she did it, of
the various things royal personages in disguise were called
upon to do: Alfred the Great, for instance, burning the cakes
and getting his ears boxed by the wife of the neatherd.[5] How
frightened she must have been when she found out what she
had done. If Miss Minchin should find out that she—Sara,
whose toes were almost sticking out of her boots—was a
princess—a real one! The look in her eyes was exactly the look
which Miss Minchin most disliked. She would not have it; she
was quite near her and was so enraged that she actually flew at
her and boxed her ears—exactly as the neatherd's wife had
boxed King Alfred's. It made Sara start. She wakened from her
dream at the shock, and, catching her breath, stood still a second. Then, not knowing she was going to do it, she broke into
a little laugh.

"What are you laughing at, you bold, impudent child?" Miss
Minchin exclaimed.

It took Sara a few seconds to control herself sufficiently to
remember that she was a princess. Her cheeks were red and
smarting from the blows she had received.

"I was thinking," she answered.

"Beg my pardon immediately," said Miss Minchin.

Sara hesitated a second before she replied.

"I will beg your pardon for laughing, if it was rude," she said
then; "but I won't beg your pardon for thinking."

"What were you thinking?" demanded Miss Minchin. "How
dare you think? What were you thinking?"

Jessie tittered, and she and Lavinia nudged each other in uni-
son. All the girls looked up from their books to listen. Really, it
always interested them a little when Miss Minchin attacked
Sara. Sara always said something queer, and never seemed the

least bit frightened. She was not in the least frightened now, though her boxed ears were scarlet and her eyes were as bright as stars.

"I was thinking," she answered grandly and politely, "that you did not know what you were doing."

"That I did not know what I was doing?" Miss Minchin fairly gasped.

"Yes," said Sara, "and I was thinking what would happen if I were a princess and you boxed my ears—what I should do to you. And I was thinking that if I were one, you would never dare to do it, whatever I said or did. And I was thinking how surprised and frightened you would be if you suddenly found out—"

She had the imagined future so clearly before her eyes that she spoke in a manner which had an effect even upon Miss Minchin. It almost seemed for the moment to her narrow, unimaginative mind that there must be some real power hidden behind this candid daring.

"What?" she exclaimed. "Found out what?"

"That I really was a princess," said Sara, "and could do anything—anything I liked."

Every pair of eyes in the room widened to its full limit. Lavinia leaned forward on her seat to look.

"Go to your room," cried Miss Minchin, breathlessly, "this instant! Leave the school-room! Attend to your lessons, young ladies!"

Sara made a little bow.

"Excuse me for laughing if it was impolite," she said, and walked out of the room, leaving Miss Minchin struggling with her rage, and the girls whispering over their books.

"Did you see her? Did you see how queer she looked?" Jessie broke out. "I shouldn't be at all surprised if she did turn out to be something. Suppose she should!"

CHAPTER XII

The Other Side of the Wall

WHEN ONE LIVES in a row of houses, it is interesting to think of the things which are being done and said on the other side of the wall of the very rooms one is living in. Sara was fond of amusing herself by trying to imagine the things hidden by the wall which divided the Select Seminary from the Indian gentleman's house. She knew that the school-room was next to the Indian gentleman's study, and she hoped that the wall was thick so that the noise made sometimes after lesson hours would not disturb him.

"I am growing quite fond of him," she said to Ermengarde; "I should not like him to be disturbed. I have adopted him for a friend. You can do that with people you never speak to at all. You can just watch them, and think about them and be sorry for them, until they seem almost like relations. I'm quite anxious sometimes when I see the doctor call twice a day."

"I have very few relations," said Ermengarde, reflectively, "and I'm very glad of it. I don't like those I have. My two aunts are always saying, 'Dear me, Ermengarde! You are very fat. You shouldn't eat sweets,' and my uncle is always asking me things like, 'When did Edward the Third ascend the throne?' and, 'Who died of a surfeit of lampreys?' "[1]

Sara laughed.

"People you never speak to can't ask you questions like that," she said; "and I'm sure the Indian gentleman wouldn't even if he was quite intimate with you. I am fond of him."

She had become fond of the Large Family because they looked happy; but she had become fond of the Indian gentleman because he looked unhappy. He had evidently not fully recovered from some very severe illness. In the kitchen—where, of course, the servants, through some mysterious means, knew everything—there was much discussion of his case. He was not an Indian gentleman really, but an Englishman who had lived in India. He had met with great misfortunes which had for a time so imperilled his whole fortune that he had thought himself ruined and disgraced forever. The shock had been so great that he had almost died of brain-fever; and ever since he had been shattered in health, though his fortunes had changed and all his possessions had been restored to him.[2] His trouble and peril had been connected with mines.

"And mines with diamonds in 'em!" said the cook. "No savin's of mine never goes into no mines—particular diamond ones"—with a side glance at Sara. "We all know somethin' of *them.*"

"He felt as my papa felt," Sara thought. "He was ill as my papa was; but he did not die."

So her heart was more drawn to him than before. When she was sent out at night she used sometimes to feel quite glad, because there was always a chance that the curtains of the house next door might not yet be closed and she could look into the warm room and see her adopted friend. When no one was about she used sometimes to stop, and, holding to the iron railings, wish him good night as if he could hear her.

"Perhaps you can *feel* if you can't hear," was her fancy. "Perhaps kind thoughts reach people somehow, even through windows and doors and walls. Perhaps you feel a little warm and comforted, and don't know why, when I am standing here in the cold and hoping you will get well and happy again. I am so sorry for you," she would whisper in an intense little voice. "I wish you had a 'Little Missus' who could pet you as I used to pet papa when he had a headache. I should like to be your 'Little Missus' myself, poor dear! Good night—good night. God bless you!"

She would go away, feeling quite comforted and a little warmer herself. Her sympathy was so strong that it seemed as if it *must* reach him somehow as he sat alone in his arm-chair by the fire, nearly always in a great dressing-gown, and nearly always with his forehead resting in his hand as he gazed hopelessly into the fire. He looked to Sara like a man who had a trouble on his mind still, not merely like one whose troubles lay all in the past.

"He always seems as if he were thinking of something that hurts him *now*," she said to herself; "but he has got his money back and he will get over his brain-fever in time, so he ought not to look like that. I wonder if there is something else."

If there was something else,—something even servants did not hear of,—she could not help believing that the father of the Large Family knew it—the gentleman she called Mr. Montmorency. Mr. Montmorency went to see him often, and Mrs. Montmorency and all the little Montmorencys went, too, though less often. He seemed particularly fond of the two elder little girls—the Janet and Nora who had been so alarmed when their small brother Donald had given Sara his sixpence. He had, in fact, a very tender place in his heart for all children, and particularly for little girls. Janet and Nora were as fond of him as he was of them, and looked forward with the greatest pleasure to the afternoons when they were allowed to cross the square and make their well-behaved little visits to him. They were extremely decorous little visits because he was an invalid.

"He is a poor thing," said Janet, "and he says we cheer him up. We try to cheer him up very quietly."

Janet was the head of the family, and kept the rest of it in order. It was she who decided when it was discreet to ask the Indian gentleman to tell stories about India, and it was she who saw when he was tired and it was the time to steal quietly away and tell Ram Dass to go to him. They were very fond of Ram Dass. He could have told any number of stories if he had been able to speak anything but Hindustani.[3] The Indian gentleman's real name was Mr. Carrisford, and Janet told Mr. Carrisford about the encounter with the little-girl-who-was-not-a-beggar. He was very much interested, and all the more so when he heard from Ram Dass of the adventure of the monkey on the roof. Ram Dass made for him a very clear picture of the attic and its desolateness—of the bare floor and broken plaster, the rusty, empty grate, and the hard, narrow bed.

"Carmichael," he said to the father of the Large Family, after he had heard this description; "I wonder how many of the attics in this square are like that one, and how many wretched little servant girls sleep on such beds, while I toss on my down pillows, loaded and harassed by wealth that is, most of it—not mine."

"My dear fellow," Mr. Carmichael answered cheerily, "the sooner you cease tormenting yourself the better it will be for you. If you possessed all the wealth of all the Indies, you could not set right all the discomforts in the world, and if you began to refurnish all the attics in this square, there would still remain all the attics in all the other squares and streets to put in order. And there you are!"

Mr. Carrisford sat and bit his nails as he looked into the glowing bed of coals in the grate.

"Do you suppose," he said slowly, after a pause—"do you think it is possible that the other child—the child I never cease thinking of, I believe—could be—could *possibly* be reduced to any such condition as the poor little soul next door?"

Mr. Carmichael looked at him uneasily. He knew that the worst thing the man could do for himself, for his reason and his health, was to begin to think in this particular way of this particular subject.

"If the child at Madame Pascal's school in Paris was the one you are in search of," he answered soothingly, "she would seem to be in the hands of people who can afford to take care of her. They adopted her because she had been the favorite companion of their little daughter who died. They had no other children, and Madame Pascal said that they were extremely well-to-do Russians."

"And the wretched woman actually did not know where they had taken her!" exclaimed Mr. Carrisford.

Mr. Carmichael shrugged his shoulders.

"She was a shrewd, worldly Frenchwoman, and was evidently only too glad to get the child so comfortably off her hands when the father's death left her totally unprovided for.[4] Women of her type do not trouble themselves about the futures of children who might prove burdens. The adopted parents apparently disappeared and left no trace."

"But you say '*if*' the child was the one I am in search of. You say 'if.' We are not sure. There was a difference in the name."

"Madame Pascal pronounced it as if it were Carew instead of Crewe,—but that might be merely a matter of pronunciation.

The circumstances were curiously similar. An English officer in India had placed his motherless little girl at the school. He had died suddenly after losing his fortune." Mr. Carmichael paused a moment, as if a new thought had occurred to him. "Are you *sure* the child was left at a school in Paris? Are you sure it was Paris?"

"My dear fellow," broke forth Carrisford, with restless bitterness, "I am *sure* of nothing. I never saw either the child or her mother. Ralph Crewe and I loved each other as boys, but we had not met since our school-days, until we met in India. I was absorbed in the magnificent promise of the mines. He became absorbed, too. The whole thing was so huge and glittering that we half lost our heads. When we met we scarcely spoke of anything else. I only knew that the child had been sent to school somewhere. I do not even remember, now, *how* I knew it."

He was beginning to be excited. He always became excited when his still weakened brain was stirred by memories of the catastrophes of the past.

Mr. Carmichael watched him anxiously. It was necessary to ask some questions, but they must be put quietly and with caution.

"But you had reason to think the school *was* in Paris?"

"Yes," was the answer, "because her mother was a Frenchwoman, and I had heard that she wished her child to be educated in Paris. It seemed only likely that she would be there."

"Yes," Mr. Carmichael said, "it seems more than probable."

The Indian gentleman leaned forward and struck the table with a long, wasted hand.

"Carmichael," he said, "I *must* find her. If she is alive, she is somewhere. If she is friendless and penniless, it is through my fault. How is a man to get back his nerve with a thing like that on his mind? This sudden change of luck at the mines has made realities of all our most fantastic dreams, and poor Crewe's child may be begging in the street!"

"No, no," said Carmichael. "Try to be calm. Console yourself with the fact that when she is found you have a fortune to hand over to her."

"Why was I not man enough to stand my ground when

things looked black?" Carrisford groaned in petulant misery. "I believe I should have stood my ground if I had not been responsible for other people's money as well as my own. Poor Crewe had put into the scheme every penny that he owned. He trusted me—he *loved* me. And he died thinking I had ruined him—I—Tom Carrisford, who played cricket at Eton with him. What a villain he must have thought me!"

"Don't reproach yourself so bitterly."

"I don't reproach myself because the speculation threatened to fail—I reproach myself for losing my courage. I ran away like a swindler and a thief, because I could not face my best friend and tell him I had ruined him and his child."

The good-hearted father of the Large Family put his hand on his shoulder comfortingly.

"You ran away because your brain had given way under the strain of mental torture," he said. "You were half delirious already. If you had not been you would have stayed and fought it out. You were in a hospital, strapped down in bed, raving with brain-fever, two days after you left the place. Remember that."

Carrisford dropped his forehead in his hands.

"Good God! Yes," he said. "I was driven mad with dread and horror. I had not slept for weeks. The night I staggered out of my house all the air seemed full of hideous things mocking and mouthing at me."

"That is explanation enough in itself," said Mr. Carmichael. "How could a man on the verge of brain-fever judge sanely!"

Carrisford shook his drooping head.

"And when I returned to consciousness poor Crewe was dead—and buried. And I seemed to remember nothing.[5] I did not remember the child for months and months. Even when I began to recall her existence everything seemed in a sort of haze."

He stopped a moment and rubbed his forehead. "It sometimes seems so now when I try to remember. Surely I must sometime have heard Crewe speak of the school she was sent to. Don't you think so?"

"He might not have spoken of it definitely. You never seem even to have heard her real name."

"He used to call her by an odd pet name he had invented. He

called her his 'Little Missus.' But the wretched mines drove everything else out of our heads. We talked of nothing else. If he spoke of the school, I forgot—I forgot. And now I shall never remember."

"Come, come," said Carmichael. "We shall find her yet. We will continue to search for Madame Pascal's good-natured Russians. She seemed to have a vague idea that they lived in Moscow. We will take that as a clue. I will go to Moscow."

"If I were able to travel, I would go with you," said Carrisford; "but I can only sit here wrapped in furs and stare at the fire. And when I look into it I seem to see Crewe's gay young face gazing back at me. He looks as if he were asking me a question. Sometimes I dream of him at night, and he always stands before me and asks the same question in words. Can you guess what he says, Carmichael?"

Mr. Carmichael answered him in a rather low voice.

"Not exactly," he said.

"He always says, 'Tom, old man—Tom—where is the Little Missus?' " He caught at Carmichael's hand and clung to it. "I must be able to answer him—I must!" he said. "Help me to find her. Help me."

On the other side of the wall Sara was sitting in her garret talking to Melchisedec, who had come out for his evening meal.

"It has been hard to be a princess to-day, Melchisedec," she said. "It has been harder than usual. It gets harder as the weather grows colder and the streets get more sloppy. When Lavinia laughed at my muddy skirt as I passed her in the hall, I thought of something to say all in a flash—and I only just stopped myself in time. You can't sneer back at people like that—if you are a princess. But you have to bite your tongue to hold yourself in. I bit mine. It was a cold afternoon, Melchisedec. And it's a cold night."

Quite suddenly she put her black head down in her arms, as she often did when she was alone.

"Oh, papa," she whispered, "what a long time it seems since I was your 'Little Missus'!"

This was what happened that day on both sides of the wall.

CHAPTER XIII

One of the Populace

THE WINTER WAS A WRETCHED ONE. There were days on which Sara tramped through snow when she went on her errands; there were worse days when the snow melted and combined itself with mud to form slush; there were others when the fog was so thick that the lamps in the street were lighted all day and London looked as it had looked the afternoon, several years ago, when the cab had driven through the thoroughfares with Sara tucked up on its seat, leaning against her father's shoulder. On such days the windows of the house of the Large Family always looked delightfully cosey and alluring, and the study in which the Indian gentleman sat glowed with warmth and rich color. But the attic was dismal beyond words. There were no longer sunsets or sunrises to look at, and scarcely ever any stars, it seemed to Sara. The clouds hung low over the skylight and were either gray or mud-color, or dropping heavy rain. At four o'clock in the afternoon, even when there was no special fog, the daylight was at an end. If it was necessary to go to her attic for anything, Sara was obliged to light a candle. The women in the kitchen were depressed, and that made them more ill-tempered than ever. Becky was driven like a little slave.

" 'T warn't for you, miss," she said hoarsely to Sara one night when she had crept into the attic—" 't warn't for you, an' the Bastille, an' bein' the prisoner in the next cell, I should die. That there does seem real now, doesn't it? The missus is more like the head jailer every day she lives. I can jest see them big keys you say she carries. The cook she's like one of the underjailers. Tell me some more, please, miss—tell me about the subt'ranean passage we've dug under the walls."

"I'll tell you something warmer," shivered Sara. "Get your coverlet and wrap it round you, and I'll get mine, and we will huddle close together on the bed, and I'll tell you about the tropical forest where the Indian gentleman's monkey used to live. When I see him sitting on the table near the window and looking out into the street with that mournful expression, I always feel sure he is thinking about the tropical forest where he used to swing by his tail from cocoanut-trees. I wonder who caught him, and if he left a family behind who had depended on him for cocoanuts."

"That is warmer, miss," said Becky, gratefully; "but, someways, even the Bastille is sort of heatin' when you gets to tellin' about it."

"That is because it makes you think of something else," said Sara, wrapping the coverlet round her until only her small dark face was to be seen looking out of it. "I've noticed this. What you have to do with your mind, when your body is miserable, is to make it think of something else."

"Can you do it, miss?" faltered Becky, regarding her with admiring eyes.

Sara knitted her brows a moment.

"Sometimes I can and sometimes I can't," she said stoutly. "But when I *can* I'm all right. And what I believe is that we always could—if we practised enough. I've been practising a good deal lately, and it's beginning to be easier than it used to be. When things are horrible—just horrible—I think as hard as ever I can of being a princess. I say to myself, 'I am a princess, and I am a fairy one, and because I am a fairy nothing can hurt me or make me uncomfortable.' You don't know how it makes you forget,"—with a laugh.

She had many opportunities of making her mind think of something else, and many opportunities of proving to herself whether or not she was a princess. But one of the strongest tests she was ever put to came on a certain dreadful day which, she often thought afterward, would never quite fade out of her memory even in the years to come.

For several days it had rained continuously; the streets were chilly and sloppy and full of dreary, cold mist; there was mud everywhere,—sticky London mud,—and over everything the pall of drizzle and fog. Of course there were several long and tiresome errands to be done,—there always were on days like this,—and Sara was sent out again and again, until her shabby clothes were damp through. The absurd old feathers on her for-lorn hat were more draggled and absurd than ever, and her downtrodden shoes were so wet that they could not hold any more water. Added to this, she had been deprived of her dinner, because Miss Minchin had chosen to punish her. She was so cold and hungry and tired that her face began to have a pinched look, and now and then some kind-hearted person passing her in the street glanced at her with sudden sympathy. But she did not know that. She hurried on, trying to make her mind think of something else. It was really very necessary. Her way of do-ing it was to "pretend" and "suppose" with all the strength that was left in her. But really this time it was harder than she had ever found it, and once or twice she thought it almost made her more cold and hungry instead of less so. But she persevered ob-stinately, and as the muddy water squelched through her bro-ken shoes and the wind seemed trying to drag her thin jacket from her, she talked to herself as she walked, though she did not speak aloud or even move her lips.

"Suppose I had dry clothes on," she thought. "Suppose I had good shoes and a long, thick coat and merino stockings and a whole umbrella. And suppose—suppose—just when I was near a baker's where they sold hot buns, I should find sixpence—which belonged to nobody. *Suppose*, if I did, I should go into the shop and buy six of the hottest buns and eat them all with-out stopping."

Some very odd things happen in this world sometimes.

It certainly was an odd thing that happened to Sara. She had to cross the street just when she was saying this to herself. The mud was dreadful—she almost had to wade. She picked her way as carefully as she could, but she could not save herself much; only, in picking her way, she had to look down at her feet and the mud, and in looking down—just as she reached the pavement—she saw something shining in the gutter. It was ac-tually a piece of silver—a tiny piece trodden upon by many feet, but still with spirit enough left to shine a little. Not quite a sixpence, but the next thing to it—a fourpenny piece.

In one second it was in her cold little red-and-blue hand.

"Oh," she gasped, "it is true! It is true!"

And then, if you will believe me, she looked straight at the shop directly facing her.[1] And it was a baker's shop, and a cheerful, stout, motherly woman with rosy cheeks was putting into the window a tray of delicious newly baked hot buns, fresh from the oven—large, plump, shiny buns, with currants in them.

It almost made Sara feel faint for a few seconds—the shock, and the sight of the buns, and the delightful odors of warm bread floating up through the baker's cellar window.

She knew she need not hesitate to use the little piece of money. It had evidently been lying in the mud for some time, and its owner was completely lost in the stream of passing people who crowded and jostled each other all day long.

"But I'll go and ask the baker woman if she has lost anything," she said to herself, rather faintly. So she crossed the pavement and put her wet foot on the step. As she did so she saw something that made her stop.

It was a little figure more forlorn even than herself—a little figure which was not much more than a bundle of rags, from which small, bare, red muddy feet peeped out, only because the rags with which their owner was trying to cover them were not long enough. Above the rags appeared a shock head of tangled hair, and a dirty face with big, hollow, hungry eyes.

Sara knew they were hungry eyes the moment she saw them, and she felt a sudden sympathy.

"This," she said to herself, with a little sigh, "is one of the populace—and she is hungrier than I am."

The child—this "one of the populace"—stared up at Sara, and shuffled herself aside a little, so as to give her room to pass. She was used to being made to give room to everybody. She knew that if a policeman chanced to see her he would tell her to "move on."[2]

Sara clutched her little fourpenny piece and hesitated a few seconds. Then she spoke to her.

"Are you hungry?" she asked.

The child shuffled herself and her rags a little more.

"Ain't I jist?" she said in a hoarse voice. "Jist ain't I?"

"Haven't you had any dinner?" said Sara.

"No dinner,"—more hoarsely still and with more shuffling. "Nor yet no bre'fast—nor yet no supper. No nothin'."

"Since when?" asked Sara.

"Dunno. Never got nothin' to-day—nowhere. I've axed an' axed."

Just to look at her made Sara more hungry and faint. But those queer little thoughts were at work in her brain, and she was talking to herself, though she was sick at heart.

"If I'm a princess," she was saying—"if I'm a princess—when they were poor and driven from their thrones—they always shared—with the populace—if they met one poorer and hungrier than themselves. They always shared. Buns are a penny each. If it had been sixpence I could have eaten six. It won't be enough for either of us. But it will be better than nothing."

"Wait a minute," she said to the beggar child.

She went into the shop. It was warm and smelled deliciously. The woman was just going to put some more hot buns into the window.

"If you please," said Sara, "have you lost fourpence—a silver fourpence?" And she held the forlorn little piece of money out to her.

The woman looked at it and then at her—at her intense little face and draggled, once fine clothes.

"Bless us! no," she answered. "Did you find it?"

"Yes," said Sara. "In the gutter."

"Keep it, then," said the woman. "It may have been there for a week, and goodness knows who lost it. *You* could never find out."

"I know that," said Sara, "but I thought I would ask you."

"Not many would," said the woman, looking puzzled and interested and good-natured all at once.

"Do you want to buy something?" she added, as she saw Sara glance at the buns.

"Four buns, if you please," said Sara. "Those at a penny each."

The woman went to the window and put some in a paper bag.

Sara noticed that she put in six.

"I said four, if you please," she explained. "I have only fourpence."

"I'll throw in two for makeweight," said the woman, with her good-natured look. "I dare say you can eat them sometime. Aren't you hungry?"

A mist rose before Sara's eyes.

"Yes," she answered. "I am very hungry, and I am much obliged to you for your kindness; and"—she was going to add—"there is a child outside who is hungrier than I am." But just at that moment two or three customers came in at once, and each one seemed in a hurry, so she could only thank the woman again and go out.

The beggar girl was still huddled up in the corner of the step. She looked frightful in her wet and dirty rags. She was staring straight before her with a stupid look of suffering, and Sara saw her suddenly draw the back of her roughened black hand across her eyes to rub away the tears which seemed to have surprised her by forcing their way from under her lids. She was muttering to herself.

Sara opened the paper bag and took out one of the hot buns, which had already warmed her own cold hands a little.

"See," she said, putting the bun in the ragged lap, "this is nice and hot. Eat it, and you will not feel so hungry."

The child started and stared up at her, as if such sudden, amazing good luck almost frightened her; then she snatched up the bun and began to cram it into her mouth with great wolfish bites.

"Oh, my! Oh, my!" Sara heard her say hoarsely, in wild delight. "*Oh, my!*"

Sara took out three more buns and put them down.

The sound in the hoarse, ravenous voice was awful.

"She is hungrier than I am," she said to herself. "She's starving." But her hand trembled when she put down the fourth bun. "I'm not starving," she said—and she put down the fifth.

The little ravening London savage was still snatching and devouring when she turned away. She was too ravenous to give any thanks, even if she had ever been taught politeness—which she had not. She was only a poor little wild animal.

"Good-by," said Sara.

When she reached the other side of the street she looked back. The child had a bun in each hand and had stopped in the middle of a bite to watch her. Sara gave her a little nod, and the child, after another stare,—a curious lingering stare,—jerked her shaggy head in response, and until Sara was out of sight she did not take another bite or even finish the one she had begun.

At that moment the baker-woman looked out of her shop window.

"Well, I never!" she exclaimed. "If that young un hasn't given her buns to a beggar child! It wasn't because she didn't want them, either. Well, well, she looked hungry enough. I'd give something to know what she did it for."

She stood behind her window for a few moments and pondered. Then her curiosity got the better of her. She went to the door and spoke to the beggar child.

"Who gave you those buns?" she asked her.

The child nodded her head toward Sara's vanishing figure.

"What did she say?" inquired the woman.

"Axed me if I was 'ungry," replied the hoarse voice.

"What did you say?"

"Said I was jist."

"And then she came in and got the buns, and gave them to you, did she?"

The child nodded.

"How many?"

"Five."

The woman thought it over.

"Left just one for herself," she said in a low voice. "And she could have eaten the whole six—I saw it in her eyes."

She looked after the little draggled far-away figure and felt more disturbed in her usually comfortable mind than she had felt for many a day.

"I wish she hadn't gone so quick," she said. "I'm blest if she shouldn't have had a dozen." Then she turned to the child.

"Are you hungry yet?" she said.

"I'm allus hungry," was the answer, "but 't ain't as bad as it was."

"Come in here," said the woman, and she held open the shop door.

The child got up and shuffled in. To be invited into a warm

place full of bread seemed an incredible thing. She did not know what was going to happen. She did not care, even.

"Get yourself warm," said the woman, pointing to a fire in the tiny back room. "And look here; when you are hard up for a bit of bread, you can come in here and ask for it. I'm blest if I won't give it to you for that young one's sake."

Sara found some comfort in her remaining bun. At all events, it was very hot, and it was better than nothing. As she walked along she broke off small pieces and ate them slowly to make them last longer.

"Suppose it was a magic bun," she said, "and a bite was as much as a whole dinner. I should be overeating myself if I went on like this."

It was dark when she reached the square where the Select Seminary was situated. The lights in the houses were all lighted. The blinds were not yet drawn in the windows of the room where she nearly always caught glimpses of members of the Large Family. Frequently at this hour she could see the gentleman she called Mr. Montmorency sitting in a big chair, with a small swarm round him, talking, laughing, perching on the arms of his seat or on his knees or leaning against them. This evening the swarm was about him, but he was not seated. On the contrary, there was a good deal of excitement going on. It was evident that a journey was to be taken, and it was Mr. Montmorency who was to take it. A brougham stood before the door, and a big portmanteau had been strapped upon it.[3] The children were dancing about, chattering and hanging on to their father. The pretty rosy mother was standing near him, talking as if she was asking final questions. Sara paused a moment to see the little ones lifted up and kissed and the bigger ones bent over and kissed also.

"I wonder if he will stay away long," she thought. "The portmanteau is rather big. Oh, dear, how they will miss him! I shall miss him myself—even though he doesn't know I am alive."

When the door opened she moved away,—remembering the sixpence,—but she saw the traveller come out and stand against the background of the warmly lighted hall, the older children still hovering about him.

"Will Moscow be covered with snow?" said the little girl Janet. "Will there be ice everywhere?"

"Shall you drive in a drosky?" cried another.[4] "Shall you see the Czar?"

"I will write and tell you all about it," he answered, laughing. "And I will send you pictures of muzhiks and things.[5] Run into the house. It is a hideous damp night. I would rather stay with you than go to Moscow. Good night! Good night, duckies! God bless you!" And he ran down the steps and jumped into the brougham.

"If you find the little girl, give her our love," shouted Guy Clarence, jumping up and down on the door-mat.

Then they went in and shut the door.

"Did you see," said Janet to Nora, as they went back to the room—"the little-girl-who-is-not-a-beggar was passing? She looked all cold and wet, and I saw her turn her head over her shoulder and look at us. Mamma says her clothes always look as if they had been given her by some one who was quite rich—some one who only let her have them because they were too shabby to wear. The people at the school always send her out on errands on the horridest days and nights there are."

Sara crossed the square to Miss Minchin's area steps, feeling faint and shaky.

"I wonder who the little girl is," she thought—"the little girl he is going to look for."

And she went down the area steps, lugging her basket and finding it very heavy indeed, as the father of the Large Family drove quickly on his way to the station to take the train which was to carry him to Moscow, where he was to make his best efforts to search for the lost little daughter of Captain Crewe.

CHAPTER XIV

What Melchisedec Heard and Saw

ON THIS VERY AFTERNOON, while Sara was out, a strange thing happened in the attic. Only Melchisedec saw and heard it; and he was so much alarmed and mystified that he scuttled back to his hole and hid there, and really quaked and trembled as he peeped out furtively and with great caution to watch what was going on.

The attic had been very still all the day after Sara had left it in the early morning. The stillness had only been broken by the pattering of the rain upon the slates and the skylight. Melchisedec had, in fact, found it rather dull; and when the rain ceased to patter and perfect silence reigned, he decided to come out and reconnoitre, though experience taught him that Sara would not return for some time. He had been rambling and sniffing about, and had just found a totally unexpected and un-explained crumb left from his last meal, when his attention was attracted by a sound on the roof. He stopped to listen with a palpitating heart. The sound suggested that something was moving on the roof. It was approaching the skylight; it reached the skylight. The skylight was being mysteriously opened. A dark face peered into the attic; then another face appeared be-hind it, and both looked in with signs of caution and interest. Two men were outside on the roof, and were making silent preparations to enter through the skylight itself. One was Ram Dass, and the other was a young man who was the Indian gen-tleman's secretary; but of course Melchisedec did not know this. He only knew that the men were invading the silence and privacy of the attic; and as the one with the dark face let himself down through the aperture with such lightness and dexterity that he did not make the slightest sound, Melchisedec turned tail and fled precipitately back to his hole. He was frightened to death. He had ceased to be timid with Sara, and knew she would never throw anything but crumbs, and would never make any sound other than the soft, low, coaxing whistling; but strange men were dangerous things to remain near. He lay close and flat near the entrance of his home, just managing to peep through the crack with a bright, alarmed eye. How much he understood of the talk he heard I am not in the least able to say; but, even if he had understood it all, he would probably have remained greatly mystified.

The secretary, who was light and young, slipped through the skylight as noiselessly as Ram Dass had done; and he caught a last glimpse of Melchisedec's vanishing tail.

"Was that a rat?" he asked Ram Dass in a whisper.

"Yes; a rat, Sahib," answered Ram Dass, also whispering. "There are many in the walls."

"Ugh!" exclaimed the young man; "it is a wonder the child is not terrified of them."

Ram Dass made a gesture with his hands. He also smiled respectfully. He was in this place as the intimate exponent of Sara, though she had only spoken to him once.

"The child is the little friend of all things, Sahib," he answered.[1] "She is not as other children. I see her when she does not see me. I slip across the slates and look at her many nights to see that she is safe. I watch her from my window when she does not know I am near. She stands on the table there and looks out at the sky as if it spoke to her. The sparrows come at her call. The rat she has fed and tamed in her loneliness. The poor slave of the house comes to her for comfort. There is a little child who comes to her in secret; there is one older who worships her and would listen to her forever if she might. This I have seen when I have crept across the roof. By the mistress of the house—who is an evil woman—she is treated like a pariah; but she has the bearing of a child who is of the blood of kings!"

"You seem to know a great deal about her," the secretary said.

"All her life each day I know," answered Ram Dass. "Her going out I know, and her coming in; her sadness and her poor joys; her coldness and her hunger. I know when she sits alone until midnight, learning from her books; I know when her secret friends steal to her and she is happier—as children can be, even in the midst of poverty—because they come and she may laugh and talk with them in whispers. If she were ill I should know, and I would come and serve her if it might be done."

"You are sure no one comes near this place but herself, and that she will not return and surprise us. She would be frightened if she found us here, and the Sahib Carrisford's plan would be spoiled."

Ram Dass crossed noiselessly to the door and stood close to it.

"None mount here but herself, Sahib," he said. "She has gone out with her basket and may be gone for hours. If I stand here I can hear any step before it reaches the last flight of the stairs."

The secretary took a pencil and a tablet from his breast pocket.

"Keep your ears open," he said; and he began to walk slowly and softly round the miserable little room, making rapid notes on his tablet as he looked at things.

First he went to the narrow bed. He pressed his hand upon the mattress and uttered an exclamation.

"As hard as a stone," he said. "That will have to be altered some day when she is out. A special journey can be made to bring it across. It cannot be done to-night." He lifted the covering and examined the one thin pillow.

"Coverlet dingy and worn, blanket thin, sheets patched and ragged," he said. "What a bed for a child to sleep in—and in a house which calls itself respectable! There has not been a fire in that grate for many a day," glancing at the rusty fireplace.

"Never since I have seen it," said Ram Dass. "The mistress of the house is not one who remembers that another than herself may be cold."

The secretary was writing quickly on his tablet. He looked up from it as he tore off a leaf and slipped it into his breast pocket.

"It is a strange way of doing the thing," he said. "Who planned it?"

Ram Dass made a modestly apologetic obeisance.

"It is true that the first thought was mine, Sahib," he said; "though it was naught but a fancy. I am fond of this child; we are both lonely. It is her way to relate her visions to her secret friends. Being sad one night, I lay close to the open skylight and listened. The vision she related told what this miserable room might be if it had comforts in it. She seemed to see it as she talked, and she grew cheered and warmed as she spoke. Then she came to this fancy; and the next day, the Sahib being ill and wretched, I told him of the thing to amuse him.[2] It seemed then but a dream, but it pleased the Sahib. To hear of the child's doings gave him entertainment. He became interested in her and asked questions. At last he began to please himself with the thought of making her visions real things."

"You think that it can be done while she sleeps? Suppose she awakened," suggested the secretary; and it was evident that whatsoever the plan referred to was, it had caught and pleased his fancy as well as the Sahib Carrisford's.

"I can move as if my feet were of velvet," Ram Dass replied; "and children sleep soundly—even the unhappy ones. I could have entered this room in the night many times, and without causing her to turn upon her pillow. If the other bearer passes to me the things through the window, I can do all and she will not stir. When she awakens she will think a magician has been here."

He smiled as if his heart warmed under his white robe, and the secretary smiled back at him.

"It will be like a story from the 'Arabian Nights,' " he said. "Only an Oriental could have planned it. It does not belong to London fogs."

They did not remain very long, to the great relief of Melchisedec, who, as he probably did not comprehend their conversation, felt their movements and whispers ominous. The young secretary seemed interested in everything. He wrote down things about the floor, the fireplace, the broken footstool, the old table, the walls—which last he touched with his hand again and again, seeming much pleased when he found that a number of old nails had been driven in various places.

"You can hang things on them," he said.

Ram Dass smiled mysteriously.

"Yesterday, when she was out," he said, "I entered, bringing with me small, sharp nails which can be pressed into the wall without blows from a hammer. I placed many in the plaster where I may need them. They are ready."

The Indian gentleman's secretary stood still and looked round him as he thrust his tablets back into his pocket.

"I think I have made notes enough; we can go now," he said. "The Sahib Carrisford has a warm heart. It is a thousand pities that he has not found the lost child."

"If he should find her his strength would be restored to him," said Ram Dass. "His God may lead her to him yet."[3]

Then they slipped through the skylight as noiselessly as they had entered it. And, after he was quite sure they had gone, Melchisedec was greatly relieved, and in the course of a few minutes felt it safe to emerge from his hole again and scuffle about in the hope that even such alarming human beings as these might have chanced to carry crumbs in their pockets and drop one or two of them.

CHAPTER XV

The Magic

When Sara had passed the house next door she had seen Ram Dass closing the shutters, and caught her glimpse of this room also.

"It is a long time since I saw a nice place from the inside," was the thought which crossed her mind.

There was the usual bright fire glowing in the grate, and the Indian gentleman was sitting before it. His head was resting in his hand, and he looked as lonely and unhappy as ever.

"Poor man!" said Sara; "I wonder what *you* are supposing."

And this was what he was "supposing" at that very moment.

"Suppose," he was thinking, "suppose—even if Carmichael traces the people to Moscow—the little girl they took from Madame Pascal's school in Paris is *not* the one we are in search of. Suppose she proves to be quite a different child. What steps shall I take next?"

When Sara went into the house she met Miss Minchin, who had come down-stairs to scold the cook.

"Where have you wasted your time?" she demanded. "You have been out for hours."

"It was so wet and muddy," Sara answered, "it was hard to walk, because my shoes were so bad and slipped about."

"Make no excuses," said Miss Minchin, "and tell no falsehoods."

Sara went in to the cook. The cook had received a severe lecture and was in a fearful temper as a result. She was only too rejoiced to have some one to vent her rage on, and Sara was a convenience, as usual.

"Why didn't you stay all night?" she snapped.

Sara laid her purchases on the table.

"Here are the things," she said.

The cook looked them over, grumbling. She was in a very savage humor indeed.

"May I have something to eat?" Sara asked rather faintly.

"Tea's over and done with," was the answer. "Did you expect me to keep it hot for you?"

Sara stood silent for a second.

"I had no dinner," she said next, and her voice was quite low. She made it low because she was afraid it would tremble.

"There's some bread in the pantry," said the cook. "That's all you'll get at this time of day."

Sara went and found the bread. It was old and hard and dry. The cook was in too vicious a humor to give her anything to eat with it. It was always safe and easy to vent her spite on Sara. Really, it was hard for the child to climb the three long flights of stairs leading to her attic. She often found them long and steep when she was tired; but to-night it seemed as if she would never reach the top. Several times she was obliged to stop to rest. When she reached the top landing she was glad to see the glimmer of a light coming from under her door. That meant that Ermengarde had managed to creep up to pay her a visit. There was some comfort in that. It was better than to go into the room alone and find it empty and desolate. The mere presence of plump, comfortable Ermengarde, wrapped in her red shawl, would warm it a little.

Yes; there Ermengarde was when she opened the door. She was sitting in the middle of the bed, with her feet tucked safely under her. She had never become intimate with Melchisedec and his family, though they rather fascinated her. When she found herself alone in the attic she always preferred to sit on the bed until Sara arrived. She had, in fact, on this occasion had time to become rather nervous, because Melchisedec had appeared and sniffed about a good deal, and once had made her utter a repressed squeal by sitting up on his hind legs and, while he looked at her, sniffing pointedly in her direction.

"Oh, Sara," she cried out, "I *am* glad you have come. Melchy *would* sniff about so. I tried to coax him to go back, but he wouldn't for such a long time. I like him, you know; but it does frighten me when he sniffs right at me. Do you think he ever *would* jump?"

"No," answered Sara.

Ermengarde crawled forward on the bed to look at her.

"You *do* look tired, Sara," she said; "you are quite pale."

"I *am* tired," said Sara, dropping on to the lop-sided footstool. "Oh, there's Melchisedec, poor thing. He's come to ask for his supper."

Melchisedec had come out of his hole as if he had been listening for her footstep. Sara was quite sure he knew it. He came forward with an affectionate, expectant expression as Sara put her hand in her pocket and turned it inside out, shaking her head.

"I'm very sorry," she said. "I haven't one crumb left. Go home, Melchisedec, and tell your wife there was nothing in my pocket. I'm afraid I forgot because the cook and Miss Minchin were so cross."

Melchisedec seemed to understand. He shuffled resignedly, if not contentedly, back to his home.

"I did not expect to see you to-night, Ermie," Sara said.

Ermengarde hugged herself in the red shawl.

"Miss Amelia has gone out to spend the night with her old aunt," she explained. "No one else ever comes and looks into the bedrooms after we are in bed. I could stay here until morning if I wanted to."

She pointed toward the table under the skylight. Sara had not looked toward it as she came in. A number of books were piled upon it. Ermengarde's gesture was a dejected one.

"Papa has sent me some more books, Sara," she said. "There they are."

Sara looked round and got up at once. She ran to the table, and picking up the top volume, turned over its leaves quickly. For the moment she forgot her discomforts.

"Ah," she cried out, "how beautiful! Carlyle's 'French Revolution.'[1] I have *so* wanted to read that!"

"I haven't," said Ermengarde. "And papa will be so cross if I don't. He'll expect me to know all about it when I go home for the holidays. What *shall* I do?"

Sara stopped turning over the leaves and looked at her with an excited flush on her cheeks.

"Look here," she cried, "if you'll lend me these books, *I'll* read them—and tell you everything that's in them afterward—and I'll tell it so that you will remember it, too."

"Oh, goodness!" exclaimed Ermengarde. "Do you think you can?"

"I know I can," Sara answered. "The little ones always remember what I tell them."

"Sara," said Ermengarde, hope gleaming in her round face, "if you'll do that, and make me remember, I'll—I'll give you anything."

"I don't want you to give me anything," said Sara. "I want your books—I want them!" And her eyes grew big, and her chest heaved.

"Take them, then," said Ermengarde. "I wish I wanted them—but I don't. I'm not clever, and my father is, and he thinks I ought to be."

Sara was opening one book after the other. "What are you going to tell your father?" she asked, a slight doubt dawning in her mind.

"Oh, he needn't know," answered Ermengarde. "He'll think I've read them."

Sara put down her book and shook her head slowly. "That's almost like telling lies," she said. "And lies—well, you see, they are not only wicked—they're *vulgar*. Sometimes"—reflectively—"I've thought perhaps I might do something wicked,—I might suddenly fly into a rage and kill Miss Minchin, you know, when she was ill-treating me,—but I *couldn't* be vulgar.[2] Why can't you tell your father *I* read them?"

"He wants me to read them," said Ermengarde, a little discouraged by this unexpected turn of affairs.

"He wants you to know what is in them," said Sara. "And if I can tell it to you in an easy way and make you remember it, I should think he would like that."

"He'll like it if I learn anything in *any* way," said rueful Ermengarde. "You would if you were my father."

"It's not your fault that—" began Sara. She pulled herself up and stopped rather suddenly. She had been going to say, "It's not your fault that you are stupid."

"That what?" Ermengarde asked.

"That you can't learn things quickly," amended Sara. "If you can't, you can't. If I can—why, I can; that's all."

She always felt very tender of Ermengarde, and tried not to let her feel too strongly the difference between being able to learn anything at once, and not being able to learn anything at all. As she looked at her plump face, one of her wise, old-fashioned thoughts came to her.

"Perhaps," she said, "to be able to learn things quickly isn't everything. To be kind is worth a great deal to other people. If Miss Minchin knew everything on earth and was like what she is now, she'd still be a detestable thing, and everybody would hate her. Lots of clever people have done harm and have been wicked. Look at Robespierre—"[3]

She stopped and examined Ermengarde's countenance, which was beginning to look bewildered. "Don't you remember?" she demanded. "I told you about him not long ago. I believe you've forgotten."

"Well, I don't remember *all* of it," admitted Ermengarde.

"Well, you wait a minute," said Sara, "and I'll take off my wet things and wrap myself in the coverlet and tell you over again."

She took off her hat and coat and hung them on a nail against the wall, and she changed her wet shoes for an old pair of slippers. Then she jumped on the bed, and drawing the coverlet about her shoulders, sat with her arms round her knees.

"Now, listen," she said.

She plunged into the gory records of the French Revolution, and told such stories of it that Ermengarde's eyes grew round with alarm and she held her breath. But though she was rather terrified, there was a delightful thrill in listening, and she was not likely to forget Robespierre again, or to have any doubts about the Princesse de Lamballe.

"You know they put her head on a pike and danced round it," Sara explained. "And she had beautiful floating blonde hair; and when I think of her, I never see her head on her body, but always on a pike, with those furious people dancing and howling."[4]

It was agreed that Mr. St. John was to be told the plan they had made, and for the present the books were to be left in the attic.

"Now let's tell each other things," said Sara. "How are you getting on with your French lessons?"

"Ever so much better since the last time I came up here and you explained the conjugations. Miss Minchin could not understand why I did my exercises so well that first morning."

Sara laughed a little and hugged her knees.

"She doesn't understand why Lottie is doing her sums so well," she said; "but it is because she creeps up here, too, and I help her." She glanced round the room. "The attic would be rather nice—if it wasn't so dreadful," she said, laughing again. "It's a good place to pretend in."

The truth was that Ermengarde did not know anything of the sometimes almost unbearable side of life in the attic, and she had not a sufficiently vivid imagination to depict it for herself. On the rare occasions that she could reach Sara's room she only saw that side of it which was made exciting by things which were "pretended" and stories which were told. Her visits partook of the character of adventures; and though sometimes Sara looked rather pale, and it was not to be denied that she had grown very thin, her proud little spirit would not admit of complaints. She had never confessed that at times she was almost ravenous with hunger, as she was to-night. She was growing rapidly, and her constant walking and running about would have given her a keen appetite even if she had had abundant and regular meals of a much more nourishing nature than the unappetizing, inferior food snatched at such odd times as suited the kitchen convenience. She was growing used to a certain gnawing feeling in her young stomach.

"I suppose soldiers feel like this when they are on a long and weary march," she often said to herself. She liked the sound of the phrase, "long and weary march." It made her feel rather like a soldier. She had also a quaint sense of being a hostess in the attic.

"If I lived in a castle," she argued, "and Ermengarde was the lady of another castle, and came to see me, with knights and squires and vassals riding with her, and pennons flying; when I heard the clarions sounding outside the drawbridge I should go down to receive her, and I should spread feasts in the banquet-hall and call in minstrels to sing and play and relate romances. When she comes into the attic I can't spread feasts, but I can tell stories, and not let her know disagreeable things. I dare say poor chatelaines had to do that in times of famine, when their lands had been pillaged."[5] She was a proud, brave little chatelaine, and dispensed generously the one hospitality she could offer—the dreams she dreamed—the visions she saw—the imaginings which were her joy and comfort.

So, as they sat together, Ermengarde did not know that she was faint as well as ravenous, and that while she talked she now and then wondered if her hunger would let her sleep when she was left alone. She felt as if she had never been quite so hungry before.

"I wish I was as thin as you, Sara," Ermengarde said suddenly. "I believe you are thinner than you used to be. Your eyes look so big, and look at the sharp little bones sticking out of your elbow!"

Sara pulled down her sleeve, which had pushed itself up.

"I always was a thin child," she said bravely, "and I always had big green eyes."

"I love your queer eyes," said Ermengarde, looking into them with affectionate admiration. "They always look as if they saw such a long way. I love them—and I love them to be green—though they look black generally."

"They are cat's eyes," laughed Sara; "but I can't see in the dark with them—because I have tried, and I couldn't—I wish I could."

It was just at this minute that something happened at the skylight which neither of them saw. If either of them had chanced to turn and look, she would have been startled by the sight of a dark face which peered cautiously into the room and disappeared as quickly and almost as silently as it had appeared. Not *quite* as silently, however. Sara, who had keen ears, suddenly turned a little and looked up at the roof.

"That didn't sound like Melchisedec," she said. "It wasn't scratchy enough."

"What?" said Ermengarde, a little startled.

"Didn't you think you heard something?" asked Sara.

"N-no," Ermengarde faltered. "Did you?"

"Perhaps I didn't," said Sara; "but I thought I did. It sounded as if something was on the slates—something that dragged softly."

"What could it be?" said Ermengarde. "Could it be—robbers?"

"No," Sara began cheerfully. "There is nothing to steal—"

She broke off in the middle of her words. They both heard the sound that checked her. It was not on the slates, but on the stairs below, and it was Miss Minchin's angry voice. Sara sprang off the bed, and put out the candle.

"She is scolding Becky," she whispered, as she stood in the darkness. "She is making her cry."

"Will she come in here?" Ermengarde whispered back, panic-stricken.

"No. She will think I am in bed. Don't stir."

It was very seldom that Miss Minchin mounted the last flight of stairs. Sara could only remember that she had done it once before. But now she was angry enough to be coming at least part of the way up, and it sounded as if she was driving Becky before her.

"You impudent, dishonest child!" they heard her say. "Cook tells me she has missed things repeatedly."

" 'T warn't me, mum," said Becky, sobbing. "I was 'ungry enough, but 't warn't me—never!"

"You deserve to be sent to prison," said Miss Minchin's voice. "Picking and stealing! Half a meat-pie, indeed!"

" 'T warn't me," wept Becky. "I could 'ave eat a whole un—but I never laid a finger on it."

Miss Minchin was out of breath between temper and mounting the stairs. The meat-pie had been intended for her special late supper. It became apparent that she boxed Becky's ears.

"Don't tell falsehoods," she said. "Go to your room this instant."

Both Sara and Ermengarde heard the slap, and then heard Becky run in her slip-shod shoes up the stairs and into her attic. They heard her door shut, and knew that she threw herself upon her bed.

"I could 'ave e't two of 'em," they heard her cry into her pil-

low. "An' I never took a bite. 'T was cook give it to her policeman."

Sara stood in the middle of the room in the darkness. She
was clenching her little teeth and opening and shutting fiercely
her outstretched hands. She could scarcely stand still, but she
dared not move until Miss Minchin had gone down the stairs
and all was still.

"The wicked, cruel thing!" she burst forth. "The cook takes
things herself and then says Becky steals them. She *doesn't!* She
doesn't! She's so hungry sometimes that she eats crusts out of
the ash-barrel!"[6] She pressed her hands hard against her face
and burst into passionate little sobs, and Ermengarde, hearing
this unusual thing, was overawed by it. Sara was crying! The
unconquerable Sara! It seemed to denote something new—
some mood she had never known. Suppose—! Suppose—! A
new dread possibility presented itself to her kind, slow, little
mind all at once. She crept off the bed in the dark and found her
way to the table where the candle stood. She struck a match and
lit the candle. When she had lighted it, she bent forward and
looked at Sara, with her new thought growing to definite fear in
her eyes.

"Sara," she said in a timid, almost awe-stricken voice, "are—
are—you never told me—I don't want to be rude, but—are *you*
ever hungry?"

It was too much just at that moment. The barrier broke
down. Sara lifted her face from her hands.

"Yes," she said in a new passionate way. "Yes, I am. I'm so
hungry now that I could almost eat *you.* And it makes it worse
to hear poor Becky. She's hungrier than I am."

Ermengarde gasped.

"Oh! Oh!" she cried wofully; "and I never knew!"

"I didn't want you to know," Sara said. "It would have made
me feel like a street beggar. I know I look like a street beggar."

"No, you don't—you don't!" Ermengarde broke in. "Your
clothes are a little queer,—but you *couldn't* look like a street
beggar. You haven't a street-beggar face."

"A little boy once gave me a sixpence for charity," said Sara,
with a short little laugh in spite of herself. "Here it is." And she
pulled out the thin ribbon from her neck. "He wouldn't have

given me his Christmas sixpence if I hadn't looked as if I needed it."

Somehow the sight of the dear little sixpence was good for both of them. It made them laugh a little, though they both had tears in their eyes.

"Who was he?" asked Ermengarde, looking at it quite as if it had not been a mere ordinary silver sixpence.

"He was a darling little thing going to a party," said Sara. "He was one of the Large Family, the little one with the round legs—the one I call Guy Clarence. I suppose his nursery was crammed with Christmas presents and hampers full of cakes and things, and he could see I had had nothing."

Ermengarde gave a little jump backward. The last sentences had recalled something to her troubled mind and given her a sudden inspiration.

"Oh, Sara!" she cried. "What a silly thing I am not to have thought of it!"

"Of what?"

"Something splendid!" said Ermengarde, in an excited hurry. "This very afternoon my nicest aunt sent me a box. It is full of good things. I never touched it, I had so much pudding at dinner, and I was so bothered about papa's books." Her words began to tumble over each other. "It's got cake in it, and little meat-pies, and jam-tarts and buns, and oranges and red-currant wine, and figs and chocolate. I'll creep back to my room and get it this minute, and we'll eat it now."

Sara almost reeled. When one is faint with hunger the mention of food has sometimes a curious effect. She clutched Ermengarde's arm.

"Do you think—you *could?*" she ejaculated.

"I know I could," answered Ermengarde, and she ran to the door—opened it softly—put her head out into the darkness, and listened. Then she went back to Sara. "The lights are out. Everybody's in bed. I can creep—and creep—and no one will hear."

It was so delightful that they caught each other's hands and a sudden light sprang into Sara's eyes.

"Ermie!" she said. "Let us *pretend!* Let us pretend it's a party! And oh, won't you invite the prisoner in the next cell?"

"Yes! Yes! Let us knock on the wall now. The jailer won't hear."

Sara went to the wall. Through it she could hear poor Becky crying more softly. She knocked four times.

"That means, 'Come to me through the secret passage under the wall,' she explained. 'I have something to communicate.' "

Five quick knocks answered her.

"She is coming," she said.

Almost immediately the door of the attic opened and Becky appeared. Her eyes were red and her cap was sliding off, and when she caught sight of Ermengarde she began to rub her face nervously with her apron.

"Don't mind me a bit, Becky!" cried Ermengarde.

"Miss Ermengarde has asked you to come in," said Sara, "because she is going to bring a box of good things up here to us."

Becky's cap almost fell off entirely, she broke in with such excitement.

"To eat, miss?" she said. "Things that's good to eat?"

"Yes," answered Sara, "and we are going to pretend a party."

"And you shall have as much as you *want* to eat," put in Ermengarde. "I'll go this minute!"

She was in such haste that as she tiptoed out of the attic she dropped her red shawl and did not know it had fallen. No one saw it for a minute or so. Becky was too much overpowered by the good luck which had befallen her.

"Oh, miss! oh, miss!" she gasped; "I know it was you that asked her to let me come. It—it makes me cry to think of it." And she went to Sara's side and stood and looked at her worshippingly.

But in Sara's hungry eyes the old light had begun to glow and transform her world for her. Here in the attic—with the cold night outside—with the afternoon in the sloppy streets barely passed—with the memory of the awful unfed look in the beggar child's eyes not yet faded—this simple, cheerful thing had happened like a thing of magic.

She caught her breath.

"Somehow, something always happens," she cried, "just before things get to the very worst. It is as if the Magic did it. If I could only just remember that always. The worst thing never *quite* comes."

She gave Becky a little cheerful shake.

"No, no! You mustn't cry!" she said. "We must make haste and set the table."

"Set the table, miss?" said Becky, gazing round the room. "What'll we set it with?"

Sara looked round the attic, too.

"There doesn't seem to be much," she answered, half laughing.

That moment she saw something and pounced upon it. It was Ermengarde's red shawl which lay upon the floor.

"Here's the shawl," she cried. "I know she won't mind it. It will make such a nice red table-cloth."

They pulled the old table forward, and threw the shawl over it. Red is a wonderfully kind and comfortable color. It began to make the room look furnished directly.

"How nice a red rug would look on the floor!" exclaimed Sara. "We must pretend there is one!"

Her eye swept the bare boards with a swift glance of admiration. The rug was laid down directly.

"How soft and thick it is!" she said, with the little laugh which Becky knew the meaning of; and she raised and set her foot down again delicately, as if she felt something under it.

"Yes, miss," answered Becky, watching her with serious rapture. She was always quite serious.

"What next, now?" said Sara, and she stood still and put her hands over her eyes. "Something will come if I think and wait a little"—in a soft, expectant voice. "The Magic will tell me."

One of her favorite fancies was that on "the outside," as she called it, thoughts were waiting for people to call them. Becky had seen her stand and wait many a time before, and knew that in a few seconds she would uncover an enlightened, laughing face.

In a moment she did.

"There!" she cried. "It has come! I know now! I must look among the things in the old trunk I had when I was a princess."

She flew to its corner and kneeled down. It had not been put in the attic for her benefit, but because there was no room for it elsewhere. Nothing had been left in it but rubbish. But she knew she should find something. The Magic always arranged that kind of thing in one way or another.

In a corner lay a package so insignificant-looking that it had been overlooked, and when she herself had found it she had kept it as a relic. It contained a dozen small white handkerchiefs. She seized them joyfully and ran to the table. She began to arrange them upon the red table-cover, patting and coaxing them into shape with the narrow lace edge curling outward, her Magic working its spells for her as she did it.

"These are the plates," she said. "They are golden plates. These are the richly embroidered napkins. Nuns worked them in convents in Spain."

"Did they, miss?" breathed Becky, her very soul uplifted by the information.

"You must pretend it," said Sara. "If you pretend it enough, you will see them."

"Yes, miss," said Becky; and as Sara returned to the trunk she devoted herself to the effort of accomplishing an end so much to be desired.

Sara turned suddenly to find her standing by the table, looking very queer indeed. She had shut her eyes, and was twisting her face in strange, convulsive contortions, her hands hanging stiffly clenched at her sides. She looked as if she was trying to lift some enormous weight.

"What is the matter, Becky?" Sara cried. "What are you doing?"

Becky opened her eyes with a start.

"I was a-'pretendin',' miss," she answered a little sheepishly; "I was tryin' to see it like you do. I almost did," with a hopeful grin. "But it takes a lot o' stren'th."

"Perhaps it does if you are not used to it," said Sara, with friendly sympathy; "but you don't know how easy it is when you've done it often. I wouldn't try so hard just at first. It will come to you after a while. I'll just tell you what things are. Look at these."

She held an old summer hat in her hand which she had fished out of the bottom of the trunk. There was a wreath of flowers on it. She pulled the wreath off.

"These are garlands for the feast," she said grandly. "They fill all the air with perfume. There's a mug on the wash-stand, Becky. Oh—and bring the soap-dish for a centrepiece."

Becky handed them to her reverently.

"What are they now, miss?" she inquired. "You'd think they was made of crockery,—but I know they ain't."

"This is a carven flagon," said Sara, arranging tendrils of the wreath about the mug.[7] "And this"—bending tenderly over the soap-dish and heaping it with roses—"is purest alabaster encrusted with gems."

She touched the things gently, a happy smile hovering about her lips which made her look as if she were a creature in a dream.

"My, ain't it lovely!" whispered Becky.

"If we just had something for bonbon-dishes," Sara murmured. "There!"—darting to the trunk again. "I remember I saw something this minute."

It was only a bundle of wool wrapped in red and white tissue-paper, but the tissue-paper was soon twisted into the form of little dishes, and was combined with the remaining flowers to ornament the candlestick which was to light the feast. Only the Magic could have made it more than an old table covered with a red shawl and set with rubbish from a long-unopened trunk. But Sara drew back and gazed at it, seeing wonders; and Becky, after staring in delight, spoke with bated breath.

"This 'ere," she suggested, with a glance round the attic—"is it the Bastille now—or has it turned into somethin' different?"

"Oh, yes, yes!" said Sara; "quite different. It is a banquet-hall!"

"My eye, miss!" ejaculated Becky. "A blanket-'all!" and she turned to view the splendors about her with awed bewilderment.

"A banquet-hall," said Sara. "A vast chamber where feasts are given. It has a vaulted roof, and a minstrels' gallery, and a huge chimney filled with blazing oaken logs, and it is brilliant with waxen tapers twinkling on every side."

"My eye, Miss Sara!" gasped Becky again.

Then the door opened, and Ermengarde came in, rather stag-

gering under the weight of her hamper. She started back with
an exclamation of joy. To enter from the chill darkness outside,
and find one's self confronted by a totally unanticipated fes-
tal board, draped with red, adorned with white napery, and
wreathed with flowers, was to feel that the preparations were
brilliant indeed.

"Oh, Sara!" she cried out. "You are the cleverest girl I
ever saw!"

"Isn't it nice?" said Sara. "They are things out of my old
trunk. I asked my Magic, and it told me to go and look."

"But oh, miss," cried Becky, "wait till she's told you what
they are! They ain't just—oh, miss, please tell her," appealing to
Sara.

So Sara told her, and because her Magic helped her she made
her *almost* see it all: the golden platters—the vaulted spaces—
the blazing logs—the twinkling waxen tapers. As the things
were taken out of the hamper—the frosted cakes—the fruits—
the bonbons and the wine—the feast became a splendid thing.

"It's like a real party!" cried Ermengarde.

"It's like a queen's table," sighed Becky.

Then Ermengarde had a sudden brilliant thought.

"I'll tell you what, Sara," she said. "Pretend you are a princess now and this is a royal feast."

"But it's your feast," said Sara; "you must be the princess,
and we will be your maids of honor."

"Oh, I can't," said Ermengarde. "I'm too fat, and I don't
know how. *You* be her."

"Well, if you want me to," said Sara.

But suddenly she thought of something else and ran to the
rusty grate.

"There is a lot of paper and rubbish stuffed in here!" she exclaimed. "If we light it, there will be a bright blaze for a few
minutes, and we shall feel as if it was a real fire." She struck a
match and lighted it up with a great specious glow which illuminated the room.

"By the time it stops blazing," Sara said, "we shall forget
about its not being real."

She stood in the dancing glow and smiled.

"Doesn't it *look* real?" she said. "Now we will begin the party."

She led the way to the table. She waved her hand graciously to Ermengarde and Becky. She was in the midst of her dream.

"Advance, fair damsels," she said in her happy dream-voice, "and be seated at the banquet-table. My noble father, the king, who is absent on a long journey, has commanded me to feast you." She turned her head slightly toward the corner of the room. "What, ho! there, minstrels! Strike up with your viols and bassoons. Princesses," she explained rapidly to Ermengarde and Becky, "always had minstrels to play at their feasts. Pretend there is a minstrel gallery up there in the corner. Now we will begin."

They had barely had time to take their pieces of cake into their hands—not one of them had time to do more, when—they all three sprang to their feet and turned pale faces toward the door—listening—listening.

Some one was coming up the stairs. There was no mistake about it. Each of them recognized the angry, mounting tread and knew that the end of all things had come.

"It's—the missus!" choked Becky, and dropped her piece of cake upon the floor.

"Yes," said Sara, her eyes growing shocked and large in her small white face. "Miss Minchin has found us out."

Miss Minchin struck the door open with a blow of her hand. She was pale herself, but it was with rage. She looked from the frightened faces to the banquet-table, and from the banquet-table to the last flicker of the burnt paper in the grate.

"I have been suspecting something of this sort," she exclaimed; "but I did not dream of such audacity. Lavinia was telling the truth."

So they knew that it was Lavinia who had somehow guessed their secret and had betrayed them. Miss Minchin strode over to Becky and boxed her ears for a second time.

"You impudent creature!" she said. "You leave the house in the morning!"

Sara stood quite still, her eyes growing larger, her face paler. Ermengarde burst into tears.

"Oh, don't send her away," she sobbed. "My aunt sent me the hamper. We're—only—having a party."

"So I see," said Miss Minchin, witheringly. "With the Princess Sara at the head of the table." She turned fiercely on Sara. "It is your doing, I know," she cried. "Ermengarde would never have thought of such a thing. You decorated the table, I suppose—with this rubbish." She stamped her foot at Becky. "Go to your attic!" she commanded, and Becky stole away, her face hidden in her apron, he shoulders shaking.

Then it was Sara's turn again.

"I will attend to you to-morrow. You shall have neither breakfast, dinner, nor supper!"

"I have not had either dinner or supper to-day, Miss Minchin," said Sara, rather faintly.

"Then all the better. You will have something to remember. Don't stand there. Put those things into the hamper again."

She began to sweep them off the table into the hamper herself, and caught sight of Ermengarde's new books.

"And you"—to Ermengarde—"have brought your beautiful new books into this dirty attic. Take them up and go back to bed. You will stay there all day to-morrow, and I shall write to your papa. What would *he* say if he knew where you are to-night?"

Something she saw in Sara's grave, fixed gaze at this moment made her turn on her fiercely.

"What are you thinking of?" she demanded. "Why do you look at me like that?"

"I was wondering," answered Sara, as she had answered that notable day in the school-room.

"What were you wondering?"

It was very like the scene in the school-room. There was no pertness in Sara's manner. It was only sad and quiet.

"I was wondering," she said in a low voice, "what *my* papa would say if he knew where I am to-night."

Miss Minchin was infuriated just as she had been before, and her anger expressed itself, as before, in an intemperate fashion. She flew at her and shook her.

"You insolent, unmanageable child!" she cried. "How dare you! How dare you!"

She picked up the books, swept the rest of the feast back into the hamper in a jumbled heap, thrust it into Ermengarde's arms, and pushed her before her toward the door.

"I will leave you to wonder," she said. "Go to bed this instant." And she shut the door behind herself and poor stumbling Ermengarde, and left Sara standing quite alone.

The dream was quite at an end. The last spark had died out of the paper in the grate and left only black tinder; the table was left bare, the golden plates and richly embroidered napkins, and the garlands were transformed again into old handkerchiefs, scraps of red and white paper, and discarded artificial flowers all scattered on the floor; the minstrels in the minstrel gallery had stolen away, and the viols and bassoons were still. Emily was sitting with her back against the wall, staring very hard. Sara saw her, and went and picked her up with trembling hands.

"There isn't any banquet left, Emily," she said.[8] "And there isn't any princess. There is nothing left but the prisoners in the Bastille." And she sat down and hid her face.

What would have happened if she had not hidden it just then, and if she had chanced to look up at the skylight at the wrong moment, I do not know—perhaps the end of this chapter might have been quite different—because if she had glanced at the skylight she would certainly have been startled by what she would have seen. She would have seen exactly the same face pressed against the glass and peering in at her as it had peered in earlier in the evening when she had been talking to Ermengarde.

But she did not look up. She sat with her little black head in her arms for some time. She always sat like that when she was trying to bear something in silence. Then she got up and went slowly to the bed.

"I can't pretend anything else—while I am awake," she said.[9] "There wouldn't be any use in trying. If I go to sleep, perhaps a dream will come and pretend for me."

She suddenly felt so tired—perhaps through want of food—that she sat down on the edge of the bed quite weakly.

"Suppose there was a bright fire in the grate, with lots of little dancing flames," she murmured. "Suppose there was a comfortable chair before it—and suppose there was a small table near, with a little hot—hot supper on it. And suppose"—as she drew the thin coverings over her—"suppose this was a beautiful soft bed, with fleecy blankets and large downy pillows. Suppose—suppose—" And her very weariness was good to her, for her eyes closed and she fell fast asleep.

She did not know how long she slept. But she had been tired enough to sleep deeply and profoundly—too deeply and soundly to be disturbed by anything, even by the squeaks and scamperings of Melchisedec's entire family, if all his sons and daughters had chosen to come out of their hole to fight and tumble and play.

When she awakened it was rather suddenly, and she did not know that any particular thing had called her out of her sleep. The truth was, however, that it was a sound which had called her back—a real sound—the click of the skylight as it fell in closing after a lithe white figure which slipped through it and crouched down close by upon the slates of the roof—just near enough to see what happened in the attic, but not near enough to be seen.

At first she did not open her eyes. She felt too sleepy and— curiously enough—too warm and comfortable. She was so warm and comfortable, indeed, that she did not believe she was really awake. She never was as warm and cosey as this except in some lovely vision.

"What a nice dream!" she murmured. "I feel quite warm. I— don't—want—to—wake—up."

Of course it was a dream. She felt as if warm, delightful bed-clothes were heaped upon her. She could actually *feel* blankets, and when she put out her hand it touched something exactly like a satin-covered eider-down quilt. She must not awaken from this delight—she must be quite still and make it last.

But she could not—even though she kept her eyes closed tightly, she could not. Something was forcing her to awaken— something in the room. It was a sense of light, and a sound— the sound of a crackling, roaring little fire.

"Oh, I am awakening," she said mournfully. "I can't help it—I can't."

Her eyes opened in spite of herself. And then she actually

smiled—for what she saw she had never seen in the attic before, and knew she never should see.

"Oh, I *haven't* awakened," she whispered, daring to rise on her elbow and look all about her. "I am dreaming yet." She knew it *must* be a dream, for if she were awake such things could not—could not be.

Do you wonder that she felt sure she had not come back to earth? This is what she saw. In the grate there was a glowing, blazing fire; on the hob was a little brass kettle hissing and boiling;[10] spread upon the floor was a thick, warm crimson rug; before the fire a folding-chair, unfolded, and with cushions on it; by the chair a small folding-table, unfolded, covered with a white cloth, and upon it spread small covered dishes, a cup, a saucer, a tea-pot; on the bed were new warm coverings and a satin-covered down quilt; at the foot a curious wadded silk robe, a pair of quilted slippers, and some books. The room of her dream seemed changed into fairyland—and it was flooded with warm light, for a bright lamp stood on the table covered with a rosy shade.

She sat up, resting on her elbow, and her breathing came short and fast.

"It does not—melt away," she panted. "Oh, I never had such a dream before." She scarcely dared to stir; but at last she pushed the bedclothes aside, and put her feet on the floor with a rapturous smile.

"I am dreaming—I am getting out of bed," she heard her own voice say; and then, as she stood up in the midst of it all, turning slowly from side to side,—"I am dreaming it stays— real! I'm dreaming it *feels* real. It's bewitched—or I'm bewitched. I only *think* I see it all." Her words began to hurry themselves. "If I can only keep on thinking it," she cried, "I don't care! I don't care!"

She stood panting a moment longer, and then cried out again.

"Oh, it isn't true!" she said. "It *can't* be true! But oh, how true it seems!"

The blazing fire drew her to it, and she knelt down and held out her hands close to it—so close that the heat made her start back.

"A fire I only dreamed wouldn't be *hot*," she cried.

She sprang up, touched the table, the dishes, the rug; she went to the bed and touched the blankets. She took up the soft wadded dressing-gown, and suddenly clutched it to her breast and held it to her cheek.

"It's warm. It's soft!" she almost sobbed. "It's real. It must be!"

She threw it over her shoulders, and put her feet into the slippers.

"They are real, too. It's all real!" she cried. "I am *not*—I am *not* dreaming!"

She almost staggered to the books and opened the one which lay upon the top. Something was written on the fly-leaf—just a few words, and they were these:

"To the little girl in the attic. From a friend."

When she saw that—wasn't it a strange thing for her to do?—she put her face down upon the page and burst into tears.

"I don't know who it is," she said; "but somebody cares for me a little. I have a friend."

She took her candle and stole out of her own room and into Becky's, and stood by her bedside.

"Becky, Becky!" she whispered as loudly as she dared. "Wake up!"

When Becky wakened, and she sat upright staring aghast, her face still smudged with traces of tears, beside her stood a little figure in a luxurious wadded robe of crimson silk. The face she saw was a shining, wonderful thing. The Princess Sara—as she remembered her—stood at her very bedside, holding a candle in her hand.

"Come," she said. "Oh, Becky, come!"

Becky was too frightened to speak. She simply got up and followed her, with her mouth and eyes open, and without a word.

And when they crossed the threshold, Sara shut the door gently and drew her into the warm, glowing midst of things which made her brain reel and her hungry senses faint.

"It's true! It's true!" she cried. "I've touched them all. They are as real as we are. The Magic has come and done it, Becky, while we were asleep—the Magic that won't let those worst things *ever* quite happen."

CHAPTER XVI

The Visitor

IMAGINE, if you can, what the rest of the evening was like. How they crouched by the fire which blazed and leaped and made so much of itself in the little grate. How they removed the covers of the dishes, and found rich, hot, savory soup, which was a meal in itself, and sandwiches and toast and muffins enough for both of them. The mug from the washstand was used as Becky's tea-cup, and the tea was so delicious that it was not necessary to pretend that it was anything else but tea. They were warm and full-fed and happy, and it was just like Sara that, having found her strange good fortune real, she should give herself up to the enjoyment of it to the utmost. She had lived such a life of imaginings that she was quite equal to accepting any wonderful thing that happened, and almost to cease, in a short time, to find it bewildering.

"I don't know any one in the world who could have done it," she said; "but there has been some one. And here we are sitting by their fire—and—and—it's *true!* And whoever it is— wherever they are—I have a friend, Becky—some one is my friend."

It cannot be denied that as they sat before the blazing fire, and ate the nourishing, comfortable food, they felt a kind of rapturous awe, and looked into each other's eyes with something like doubt.

"Do you think." Becky faltered once, in a whisper— "do you think it could melt away, miss? Hadn't we better be quick?" And she hastily crammed her sandwich into her mouth. If it was only a dream, kitchen manners would be overlooked.

"No, it won't melt away," said Sara. "I am *eating* this muffin, and I can taste it. You never really eat things in dreams. You only think you are going to eat them. Besides, I keep giving

151

myself pinches; and I touched a hot piece of coal just now, on purpose."

The sleepy comfort which at length almost overpowered them was a heavenly thing. It was the drowsiness of happy, well-fed childhood, and they sat in the fire-glow and luxuriated in it until Sara found herself turning to look at her transformed bed.

There were even blankets enough to share with Becky. The narrow couch in the next attic was more comfortable that night than its occupant had ever dreamed that it could be.

As she went out of the room, Becky turned upon the threshold and looked about her with devouring eyes.

"If it ain't here in the mornin', miss," she said, "it's been here to-night, anyways, an' I sha'n't never forget it." She looked at each particular thing, as if to commit it to memory. "The fire was *there*," pointing with her finger, "an' the table was before it; an' the lamp was there, an' the light looked rosy red; an' there was a satin cover on your bed, an' a warm rug on the floor, an' everythin' looked beautiful; an' "—she paused a second, and laid her hand on her stomach tenderly—"there *was* soup an' sandwiches an' muffins—there *was*." And, with this conviction a reality at least, she went away.

Through the mysterious agency which works in schools and among servants, it was quite well known in the morning that Sara Crewe was in horrible disgrace, that Ermengarde was under punishment, and that Becky would have been packed out of the house before breakfast, but that a scullery-maid could not be dispensed with at once. The servants knew that she was allowed to stay because Miss Minchin could not easily find another creature helpless and humble enough to work like a bounden slave for so few shillings a week. The elder girls in the school-room knew that if Miss Minchin did not send Sara away it was for practical reasons of her own.

"She's growing so fast and learning such a lot, somehow," said Jessie to Lavinia, "that she will be given classes soon, and Miss Minchin knows she will have to work for nothing. It was rather nasty of you, Lavvy, to tell about her having fun in the garret. How did you find it out?"

"I got it out of Lottie. She's such a baby she didn't know she was telling me. There was nothing nasty at all in speaking to Miss Minchin. I felt it my duty"—priggishly. "She was being deceitful. And it's ridiculous that she should look so grand, and be made so much of, in her rags and tatters!"

"What were they doing when Miss Minchin caught them?"

"Pretending some silly thing. Ermengarde had taken up her hamper to share with Sara and Becky. She never invites us to share things. Not that I care, but it's rather vulgar of her to share with servant-girls in attics. I wonder Miss Minchin didn't turn Sara out—even if she does want her for a teacher."

"If she was turned out where would she go?" inquired Jessie, a trifle anxiously.

"How do I know?" snapped Lavinia. "She'll look rather queer when she comes into the school-room this morning, I should think—after what's happened. She had no dinner yesterday, and she's not to have any to-day."

Jessie was not as ill-natured as she was silly. She picked up her book with a little jerk.

"Well, I think it's horrid," she said. "They've no right to starve her to death."

When Sara went into the kitchen that morning the cook looked askance at her, and so did the housemaids; but she passed them hurriedly. She had, in fact, overslept herself a little, and as Becky had done the same, neither had had time to see the other, and each had come down-stairs in haste.

Sara went into the scullery. Becky was violently scrubbing a kettle, and was actually gurgling a little song in her throat. She looked up with a wildly elated face.

"It was there when I wakened, miss—the blanket," she whispered excitedly. "It was as real as it was last night."

"So was mine," said Sara. "It is all there now—all of it. While I was dressing I ate some of the cold things we left."

"Oh, laws! oh, laws!" Becky uttered the exclamation in a sort of rapturous groan, and ducked her head over her kettle just in time, as the cook came in from the kitchen.

Miss Minchin had expected to see in Sara, when she appeared in the school-room, very much what Lavinia had expected to see. Sara had always been an annoying puzzle to her, because severity never made her cry or look frightened. When she was scolded she stood still and listened politely with a grave face; when she was punished she performed her extra tasks or went without her meals, making no complaint or outward sign of rebellion. The very fact that she never made an impudent answer seemed to Miss Minchin a kind of impudence in itself. But after yesterday's deprivation of meals, the violent scene of last night, the prospect of hunger to-day, she must surely have broken down. It would be strange indeed if she did not come down-stairs with pale cheeks and red eyes and an unhappy, humbled face.

Miss Minchin saw her for the first time when she entered the school-room to hear the little French class its lessons and superintend its exercises. And she came in with a springing step, color in her cheeks, and a smile hovering about the corners of her mouth. It was the most astonishing thing Miss Minchin had ever known. It gave her quite a shock. What was the child made of? What could such a thing mean? She called her at once to her desk.

"You do not look as if you realize that you are in disgrace," she said. "Are you absolutely hardened?"

The truth is that when one is still a child—or even if one is grown up—and has been well fed, and has slept long and softly and warm; when one has gone to sleep in the midst of a fairy story, and has wakened to find it real, one cannot be unhappy or even look as if one were; and one could not, if one tried, keep a glow of joy out of one's eyes. Miss Minchin was almost struck dumb by the look of Sara's eyes when she lifted them and made her perfectly respectful answer.

"I beg your pardon, Miss Minchin," she said; "I know that I am in disgrace."

"Be good enough not to forget it and look as if you had come into a fortune. It is an impertinence. And remember you are to have no food to-day."

"Yes, Miss Minchin," Sara answered; but as she turned away her heart leaped with the memory of what yesterday had been. "If the Magic had not saved me just in time," she thought, "how horrible it would have been!"

"She can't be very hungry," whispered Lavinia. "Just look at her. Perhaps she is pretending she has had a good breakfast"—with a spiteful laugh.

"She's different from other people," said Jessie, watching Sara with her class. "Sometimes I'm a bit frightened of her."

"Ridiculous thing!" ejaculated Lavinia.

All through the day the light was in Sara's face, and the color in her cheek. The servants cast puzzled glances at her, and whispered to each other, and Miss Amelia's small blue eyes wore an expression of bewilderment. What such an audacious look of well-being, under august displeasure, could mean she could not understand. It was, however, just like Sara's singular obstinate way. She was probably determined to brave the matter out.

One thing Sara had resolved upon, as she thought things over. The wonders which had happened must be kept a secret, if such a thing were possible. If Miss Minchin should choose to mount to the attic again, of course all would be discovered. But it did not seem likely that she would do so for some time at least, unless she was led by suspicion. Ermengarde and Lottie would be watched with such strictness that they would not dare to steal out of their beds again. Ermengarde could be told the story and trusted to keep it secret. If Lottie made any discoveries, she could be bound to secrecy also. Perhaps the Magic itself would help to hide its own marvels.

"But whatever happens," Sara kept saying to herself all day—"what*ever* happens, somewhere in the world there is a heavenly kind person who is my friend—my friend. If I never know who it is—if I never can even thank him—I shall never feel quite so lonely.[1] Oh, the Magic was *good* to me!"

If it was possible for weather to be worse than it had been the day before, it was worse this day—wetter, muddier, colder. There were more errands to be done, the cook was more irritable, and, knowing that Sara was in disgrace, she was more savage. But what does anything matter when one's Magic has just proved itself one's friend. Sara's supper of the night before had given her strength, she knew that she should sleep well and warmly, and, even though she had naturally begun to be hungry again before evening, she felt that she could bear it until breakfast-time on the following day, when her meals would surely be given to her again. It was quite late when she was at last allowed to go up-stairs. She had been told to go into the school-room and study until ten o'clock, and she had become interested in her work, and remained over her books later.

When she reached the top flight of stairs and stood before the attic door, it must be confessed that her heart beat rather fast.

"Of course it *might* all have been taken away," she whispered, trying to be brave. "It might only have been lent to me for just that one awful night. But it *was* lent to me—I had it. It was real."

She pushed the door open and went in. Once inside, she gasped slightly, shut the door, and stood with her back against it, looking from side to side.

The Magic had been there again. It actually had, and it had done even more than before. The fire was blazing, in lovely leaping flames, more merrily than ever. A number of new things had been brought into the attic which so altered the look of it that if she had not been past doubting, she would have rubbed her eyes. Upon the low table another supper stood— this time with cups and plates for Becky as well as herself; a piece of bright, heavy, strange embroidery covered the battered mantel, and on it some ornaments had been placed. All the bare, ugly things which could be covered with draperies had been concealed and made to look quite pretty. Some odd materials of rich colors had been fastened against the wall with fine, sharp tacks—so sharp that they could be pressed into the wood and plaster without hammering. Some brilliant fans were pinned up, and there were several large cushions, big and substantial enough to use as seats. A wooden box was covered with a rug, and some cushions lay on it, so that it wore quite the air of a sofa.

Sara slowly moved away from the door and simply sat down and looked and looked again.

"It is exactly like something fairy come true," she said. "There isn't the least difference. I feel as if I might wish for anything—diamonds or bags of gold—and they would appear! *That* wouldn't be any stranger than this. Is this my garret? Am I the same cold, ragged, damp Sara? And to think I used to pretend and pretend and wish there were fairies! The one thing I always wanted was to see a fairy story come true. I am *living* in a fairy story. I feel as if I might be a fairy myself, and able to turn things into anything else."

She rose and knocked upon the wall for the prisoner in the next cell, and the prisoner came.

When she entered she almost dropped in a heap upon the floor. For a few seconds she quite lost her breath.

"Oh, laws!" she gasped, "Oh, laws, miss!" just as she had done in the scullery.

"You see," said Sara.

On this night Becky sat on a cushion upon the hearth-rug and had a cup and saucer of her own.

When Sara went to bed she found that she had a new thick mattress and big downy pillows. Her old mattress and pillow had been removed to Becky's bedstead, and, consequently, with these additions Becky had been supplied with unheard-of comfort.

"Where does it all come from?" Becky broke forth once. "Laws! who does it, miss?"

"Don't let us even *ask*," said Sara. "If it were not that I want to say, 'Oh, thank you,' I would rather not know. It makes it more beautiful."

From that time life became more wonderful day by day. The fairy story continued. Almost every day something new was done. Some new comfort or ornament appeared each time Sara opened the door at night, until in a short time the attic was a beautiful little room full of all sorts of odd and luxurious things. The ugly walls were gradually entirely covered with pictures and draperies, ingenious pieces of folding furniture appeared, a book-shelf was hung up and filled with books, new comforts and conveniences appeared one by one, until there seemed nothing left to be desired. When Sara went down-stairs in the morning, the remains of the supper were on the table; and when she returned to the attic in the evening, the magician had removed them and left another nice little meal. Miss Minchin was as harsh and insulting as ever, Miss Amelia as peevish, and the servants were as vulgar and rude. Sara was sent on errands in all weathers, and scolded and driven hither and thither; she was scarcely allowed to speak to Ermengarde and

Lottie; Lavinia sneered at the increasing shabbiness of her clothes; and the other girls stared curiously at her when she appeared in the school-room. But what did it all matter while she was living in this wonderful mysterious story? It was more romantic and delightful than anything she had ever invented to comfort her starved young soul and save herself from despair. Sometimes, when she was scolded, she could scarcely keep from smiling.

"If you only knew!" she was saying to herself. "If you only knew!"

The comfort and happiness she enjoyed were making her stronger, and she had them always to look forward to. If she came home from her errands wet and tired and hungry, she knew she would soon be warm and well fed after she had climbed the stairs. During the hardest day she could occupy herself blissfully by thinking of what she should see when she opened the attic door, and wondering what new delight had been prepared for her. In a very short time she began to look less thin. Color came into her cheeks, and her eyes did not seem so much too big for her face.

"Sara Crewe looks wonderfully well," Miss Minchin remarked disapprovingly to her sister.

"Yes," answered poor, silly Miss Amelia. "She is absolutely fattening. She was beginning to look like a little starved crow."

"Starved!" exclaimed Miss Minchin, angrily. "There was no reason why she should look starved. She always had plenty to eat!"

"Of—of course," agreed Miss Amelia, humbly, alarmed to find that she had, as usual, said the wrong thing.

"There is something very disagreeable in seeing that sort of thing in a child of her age," said Miss Minchin, with haughty vagueness.

"What—sort of thing?" Miss Amelia ventured.

"It might almost be called defiance," answered Miss Minchin, feeling annoyed because she knew the thing she resented was nothing like defiance, and she did not know what other unpleasant term to use. "The spirit and will of any other child would have been entirely humbled and broken by—by the changes she has had to submit to. But, upon my word, she seems as little subdued as if—as if she were a princess."

"Do you remember," put in the unwise Miss Amelia, "what she said to you that day in the school-room about what you would do if you found out that she was—"

"No, I don't," said Miss Minchin. "Don't talk nonsense." But she remembered very clearly indeed.

Very naturally, even Becky was beginning to look plumper and less frightened. She could not help it. She had her share in the secret fairy story, too. She had two mattresses, two pillows, plenty of bed-covering, and every night a hot supper and a seat on the cushions by the fire. The Bastille had melted away, the prisoners no longer existed. Two comforted children sat in the midst of delights. Sometimes Sara read aloud from her books, sometimes she learned her own lessons, sometimes she sat and looked into the fire and tried to imagine who her friend could be, and wished she could say to him some of the things in her heart.

Then it came about that another wonderful thing happened. A man came to the door and left several parcels. All were addressed in large letters, "To the Little Girl in the right-hand attic."

Sara herself was sent to open the door and took them in. She laid the two largest parcels on the hall table, and was looking at the address, when Miss Minchin came down the stairs and saw her.

"Take the things to the young lady to whom they belong," she said severely. "Don't stand there staring at them."

"They belong to me," answered Sara, quietly.

"To you?" exclaimed Miss Minchin. "What do you mean?"

"I don't know where they come from," said Sara, "but they are addressed to me. I sleep in the right-hand attic. Becky has the other one."

Miss Minchin came to her side and looked at the parcels with an excited expression.

"What is in them?" she demanded.

"I don't know," replied Sara.

"Open them," she ordered.

Sara did as she was told. When the packages were unfolded Miss Minchin's countenance wore suddenly a singular expression. What she saw was pretty and comfortable clothing—clothing of different kinds: shoes, stockings, and gloves, and a warm and beautiful coat. There were even a nice hat and an umbrella. They were all good and expensive things, and on the pocket of the coat was pinned a paper, on which were written these words: "To be worn every day.—Will be replaced by others when necessary."

Miss Minchin was quite agitated. This was an incident which suggested strange things to her sordid mind. Could it be that she had made a mistake, after all, and that the neglected child had some powerful though eccentric friend in the background—perhaps some previously unknown relation, who had suddenly traced her whereabouts, and chose to provide for her in this mysterious and fantastic way? Relations were sometimes very odd—particularly rich old bachelor uncles, who did not care for having children near them. A man of that sort might prefer to overlook his young relation's welfare at a distance. Such a person, however, would be sure to be crotchety and hot-tempered enough to be easily offended. It would not be very pleasant if there were such a one, and he should learn all the truth about the thin, shabby clothes, the scant food, and the hard work. She felt very queer indeed, and very uncertain, and she gave a side glance at Sara.

"Well," she said, in a voice such as she had never used since the little girl lost her father, "some one is very kind to you. As the things have been sent, and you are to have new ones when they are worn out, you may as well go and put them on and look respectable. After you are dressed you may come down-stairs and learn your lessons in the school-room. You need not go out on any more errands to-day."

About half an hour afterward, when the school-room door opened and Sara walked in, the entire seminary was struck dumb with amazement.

"My word!" ejaculated Jessie, jogging Lavinia's elbow. "Look at the Princess Sara!"

Everybody was looking, and when Lavinia looked she turned quite red.

It was the Princess Sara indeed. At least, since the days when she had been a princess, Sara had never looked as she did now. She did not seem the Sara they had seen come down the back stairs a few hours ago. She was dressed in the kind of frock Lavinia had been used to envying her the possession of. It was deep and warm in color, and beautifully made. Her slender feet looked as they had done when Jessie had admired them, and the hair, whose heavy locks had made her look rather like a Shetland pony when it fell loose about her small, odd face, was tied back with a ribbon.[2]

"Perhaps some one has left her a fortune," Jessie whispered. "I always thought something would happen to her. She is so queer."

"Perhaps the diamond-mines have suddenly appeared again," said Lavinia, scathingly. "Don't please her by staring at her in that way, you silly thing."

"Sara," broke in Miss Minchin's deep voice, "come and sit here."

And while the whole school-room stared and pushed with elbows, and scarcely made any effort to conceal its excited curiosity, Sara went to her old seat of honor, and bent her head over her books.

That night, when she went to her room, after she and Becky had eaten their supper she sat and looked at the fire seriously for a long time.

"Are you making something up in your head, miss?" Becky inquired with respectful softness. When Sara sat in silence and looked into the coals with dreaming eyes it generally meant that she was making a new story. But this time she was not, and she shook her head.

"No," she answered. "I am wondering what I ought to do."

Becky stared—still respectfully. She was filled with something approaching reverence for everything Sara did and said.

"I can't help thinking about my friend," Sara explained. "If he wants to keep himself a secret, it would be rude to try and find out who he is. But I do so want him to know how thankful I am to him—and how happy he has made me. Any one who is kind wants to know when people have been made happy. They care for that more than for being thanked. I wish—I do wish—"

She stopped short because her eyes at that instant fell upon something standing on a table in a corner. It was something she had found in the room when she came up to it only two days before. It was a little writing-case fitted with paper and envelopes and pens and ink.

"Oh," she exclaimed, "why did I not think of that before?"

She rose and went to the corner and brought the case back to the fire.

"I can write to him," she said joyfully, "and leave it on the table. Then perhaps the person who takes the things away will take it, too. I won't ask him anything. He won't mind my thanking him, I feel sure."

So she wrote a note. This is what she said:

"I hope you will not think it is impolite that I should write this note to you when you wish to keep yourself a secret. Please believe I do not mean to be impolite or try to find out anything at all; only I want to thank you for being so kind to me—so heavenly kind—and making everything like a fairy story. I am so grateful to you, and I am so happy—and so is Becky. Becky feels just as thankful as I do—it is all just as beautiful and wonderful to her as it is to me. We used to be so lonely and cold and hungry, and now—oh, just think what you have done for us! Please let me say just these words. It seems as if I *ought* to say them. *Thank* you—*thank* you—*thank* you!

"THE LITTLE GIRL IN THE ATTIC."

The next morning she left this on the little table, and in the evening it had been taken away with the other things; so she knew the Magician had received it, and she was happier for the thought. She was reading one of her new books to Becky just before they went to their respective beds, when her attention was attracted by a sound at the skylight. When she looked up from her page she saw that Becky had heard the sound also, as she had turned her head to look and was listening rather nervously.

"Something's there, miss," she whispered.

"Yes," said Sara, slowly. "It sounds—rather like a cat—trying to get in."

She left her chair and went to the skylight. It was a queer little sound she heard—like a soft scratching. She suddenly remembered something and laughed. She remembered a quaint little intruder who had made his way into the attic once before. She had seen him that very afternoon, sitting disconsolately on a table before a window in the Indian gentleman's house.

"Suppose," she whispered in pleased excitement—"just suppose it was the monkey who had got away again. Oh, I wish it was!"

She climbed on a chair, very cautiously raised the skylight, and peeped out. It had been snowing all day, and on the snow, quite near her, crouched a tiny, shivering figure, whose small black face wrinkled itself piteously at sight of her.

"It *is* the monkey," she cried out. "He has crept out of the Lascar's attic, and he saw the light."

Becky ran to her side.

"Are you going to let him in, miss?" she said.

"Yes," Sara answered joyfully. "It's too cold for monkeys to be out. They're delicate. I'll coax him in."

She put a hand out delicately, speaking in a coaxing voice—as she spoke to the sparrows and to Melchisedec—as if she were some friendly little animal herself and lovingly understood their timid wildness.

"Come along, monkey darling," she said. "I won't hurt you."

He knew she would not hurt him. He knew it before she laid her soft, caressing little paw on him and drew him toward her. He had felt human love in the slim brown hands of Ram Dass, and he felt it in hers. He let her lift him through the skylight, and when he found himself in her arms he cuddled up to her breast and took friendly hold of a piece of her hair, looking up into her face.

"Nice monkey! Nice monkey!" she crooned, kissing his funny head. "Oh, I do love little animal things."

He was evidently glad to get to the fire, and when she sat down and held him on her knee he looked from her to Becky with mingled interest and appreciation.

"He *is* plain-looking, miss, ain't he?" said Becky.

"He looks like a very ugly baby," laughed Sara.[3] "I beg your pardon, monkey; but I'm glad you are not a baby. Your mother *couldn't* be proud of you, and no one would dare to say you looked like any of your relations. Oh, I do like you!"

She leaned back in her chair and reflected.

"Perhaps he's sorry he's so ugly," she said, "and it's always on his mind. I wonder if he *has* a mind. Monkey, my love, have you a mind?"

But the monkey only put up a tiny paw and scratched his head.

"What shall you do with him?" Becky asked.

"I shall let him sleep with me to-night, and then take him back to the Indian gentleman to-morrow. I am sorry to take you back, monkey; but you must go. You ought to be fondest of your own family; and I'm not a *real* relation."

And when she went to bed she made him a nest at her feet, and he curled up and slept there as if he were a baby and much pleased with his quarters.

CHAPTER XVII

"It Is the Child!"

THE NEXT AFTERNOON three members of the Large Family sat in the Indian gentleman's library, doing their best to cheer him up. They had been allowed to come in to perform this office because he had specially invited them. He had been living in a state of suspense for some time, and to-day he was waiting for a certain event very anxiously. This event was the return of Mr. Carmichael from Moscow. His stay there had been prolonged from week to week. On his first arrival there, he had not been able satisfactorily to trace the family he had gone in search of. When he felt at last sure that he had found them and had gone to their house, he had been told that they were absent on a journey. His efforts to reach them had been unavailing, so he had decided to remain in Moscow until their return. Mr. Carrisford sat in his reclining-chair, and Janet sat on the floor beside him. He was very fond of Janet.[1] Nora had found a footstool, and Donald was astride the tiger's head which ornamented the rug made of the animal's skin. It must be owned that he was riding it rather violently.

"Don't chirrup so loud, Donald," Janet said. "When you come to cheer an ill person up you don't cheer him up at the top of your voice. Perhaps cheering up is too loud, Mr. Carrisford?" turning to the Indian gentleman.

But he only patted her shoulder.

"No, it isn't," he answered. "And it keeps me from thinking too much."

"I'm going to be quiet," Donald shouted. "We'll all be as quiet as mice."

"Mice don't make a noise like that," said Janet.

Donald made a bridle of his handkerchief and bounced up and down on the tiger's head.

"A whole lot of mice might," he said cheerfully. "A thousand mice might."

"I don't believe fifty thousand mice would," said Janet, severely; "and we have to be as quiet as *one* mouse."

Mr. Carrisford laughed and patted her shoulder again.

"Papa won't be very long now," she said. "May we talk about the lost little girl?"

"I don't think I could talk much about anything else just now," the Indian gentleman answered, knitting his forehead with a tired look.

"We like her so much," said Nora. "We call her the little *un*-fairy princess."[2]

"Why?" the Indian gentleman inquired, because the fancies of the Large Family always made him forget things a little.

It was Janet who answered.

"It is because, though she is not exactly a fairy, she will be so rich when she is found that she will be like a princess in a fairy tale. We called her the fairy princess at first, but it didn't quite suit."

"Is it true," said Nora, "that her papa gave all his money to a friend to put in a mine that had diamonds in it, and then the friend thought he had lost it all and ran away because he felt as if he was a robber?"

"But he wasn't really, you know," put in Janet, hastily.

The Indian gentleman took hold of her hand quickly.

"No, he wasn't really," he said.

"I am sorry for the friend," Janet said; "I can't help it. He didn't mean to do it, and it would break his heart. I am sure it would break his heart."

"You are an understanding little woman, Janet," the Indian gentleman said, and he held her hand close.

"Did you tell Mr. Carrisford," Donald shouted again, "about the little-girl-who-isn't-a-beggar? Did you tell him she has new nice clothes? P'r'aps she's been found by somebody when she was lost."

"There's a cab!" exclaimed Janet. "It's stopping before the door. It is papa!"

They all ran to the windows to look out.

"Yes, it's papa," Donald proclaimed. "But there is no little girl."

All three of them incontinently fled from the room and tumbled into the hall. It was in this way they always welcomed their father. They were to be heard jumping up and down, clapping their hands, and being caught up and kissed.

Mr. Carrisford made an effort to rise and sank back again into his chair.

"It is no use," he said. "What a wreck I am!"

Mr. Carmichael's voice approached the door.

"No, children," he was saying; "you may come in after I have talked to Mr. Carrisford. Go and play with Ram Dass."

Then the door opened and he came in. He looked rosier than ever, and brought an atmosphere of freshness and health with him; but his eyes were disappointed and anxious as they met the invalid's look of eager question even as they grasped each other's hands.

"What news?" Mr. Carrisford asked. "The child the Russian people adopted?"

"She is not the child we are looking for," was Mr. Carmichael's answer. "She is much younger than Captain Crewe's little girl. Her name is Emily Carew.[3] I have seen and talked to her. The Russians were able to give me every detail."

How wearied and miserable the Indian gentleman looked! His hand dropped from Mr. Carmichael's.

"Then the search has to be begun over again," he said. "That is all. Please sit down."

Mr. Carmichael took a seat. Somehow, he had gradually grown fond of this unhappy man. He was himself so well and happy, and so surrounded by cheerfulness and love, that desolation and broken health seemed pitifully unbearable things. If there had been the sound of just one gay little high-pitched voice in the house, it would have been so much less forlorn. And that a man should be compelled to carry about in his breast the thought that he had seemed to wrong and desert a child was not a thing one could face.

"Come, come," he said in his cheery voice; "we'll find her yet."

"We must begin at once. No time must be lost," Mr. Carrisford fretted. "Have you any new suggestion to make—any
whatsoever?"

Mr. Carmichael felt rather restless, and he rose and began to
pace the room with a thoughtful, though uncertain face.

"Well, perhaps," he said. "I don't know what it may be
worth. The fact is, an idea occurred to me as I was thinking the
thing over in the train on the journey from Dover."

"What was it? If she is alive, she is somewhere."

"Yes; she is *somewhere*. We have searched the schools in
Paris. Let us give up Paris and begin in London. That was my
idea—to search London."

"There are schools enough in London," said Mr. Carrisford.
Then he slightly started, roused by a recollection. "By the way,
there is one next door."

"Then we will begin there. We cannot begin nearer than next
door."

"No," said Carrisford.[4] "There is a child there who interests
me; but she is not a pupil. And she is a little dark, forlorn creature, as unlike poor Crewe as a child could be."

Perhaps the Magic was at work again at that very moment—
the beautiful Magic. It really seemed as if it might be so. What
was it that brought Ram Dass into the room—even as his master spoke—salaaming respectfully, but with a scarcely concealed touch of excitement in his dark, flashing eyes?[5]

"Sahib," he said, "the child herself has come—the child the
sahib felt pity for. She brings back the monkey who had again
run away to her attic under the roof. I have asked that she remain. It was my thought that it would please the sahib to see
and speak with her."

"Who is she?" inquired Mr. Carmichael.

"God knows," Mr. Carrisford answered. "She is the child I
spoke of. A little drudge at the school." He waved his hand to
Ram Dass, and addressed him. "Yes, I should like to see her. Go
and bring her in." Then he turned to Mr. Carmichael. "While
you have been away," he explained, "I have been desperate. The
days were so dark and long. Ram Dass told me of this child's
miseries, and together we invented a romantic plan to help her.
I suppose it was a childish thing to do; but it gave me some-

thing to plan and think of. Without the help of an agile, soft-footed Oriental like Ram Dass, however, it could not have been done."

Then Sara came into the room. She carried the monkey in her arms, and he evidently did not intend to part from her, if it could be helped. He was clinging to her and chattering, and the interesting excitement of finding herself in the Indian gentleman's room had brought a flush to Sara's cheeks.

"Your monkey ran away again," she said, in her pretty voice. "He came to my garret window last night, and I took him in because it was so cold. I would have brought him back if it had not been so late. I knew you were ill and might not like to be disturbed."

The Indian gentleman's hollow eyes dwelt on her with curious interest.

"That was very thoughtful of you," he said.

Sara looked toward Ram Dass, who stood near the door.

"Shall I give him to the Lascar?" she asked.

"How do you know he is a Lascar?" said the Indian gentleman, smiling a little.

"Oh, I know Lascars," Sara said, handing over the reluctant monkey. "I was born in India."

The Indian gentleman sat upright so suddenly, and with such a change of expression, that she was for a moment quite startled.

"You were born in India," he exclaimed, "were you? Come here." And he held out his hand.

Sara went to him and laid her hand in his, as he seemed to want to take it. She stood still, and her green-gray eyes met his wonderingly. Something seemed to be the matter with him.

"You live next door?" he demanded.

"Yes; I live at Miss Minchin's seminary."

"But you are not one of her pupils?"

A strange little smile hovered about Sara's mouth. She hesitated a moment.

"I don't think I know exactly *what* I am," she replied.

"Why not?"

"At first I was a pupil, and a parlor-boarder; but now—"

"You were a pupil! What are you now?"

The queer little sad smile was on Sara's lips again.

"I sleep in the attic, next to the scullery-maid," she said. "I run errands for the cook—I do anything she tells me; and I teach the little ones their lessons."

"Question her, Carmichael," said Mr. Carrisford, sinking back as if he had lost his strength. "Question her; I cannot."

The big, kind father of the Large Family knew how to question little girls. Sara realized how much practice he had had when he spoke to her in his nice, encouraging voice.

"What do you mean by 'At first,' my child?" he inquired.

"When I was first taken there by my papa."

"Where is your papa?"

"He died," said Sara, very quietly. "He lost all his money and there was none left for me. There was no one to take care of me or to pay Miss Minchin."

"Carmichael!" the Indian gentleman cried out loudly; "Carmichael!"

"We must not frighten her," Mr. Carmichael said aside to him in a quick, low voice; and he added aloud to Sara: "So you were sent up into the attic, and made into a little drudge. That was about it, wasn't it?"

"There was no one to take care of me," said Sara. "There was no money; I belong to nobody."

"How did your father lose his money?" the Indian gentleman broke in breathlessly.

"He did not lose it himself," Sara answered, wondering still more each moment. "He had a friend he was very fond of—he was *very* fond of him. It was his friend who took his money. He trusted his friend too much."

The Indian gentleman's breath came more quickly.

"The friend might have *meant* to do no harm," he said. "It might have happened through a mistake."

Sara did not know how unrelenting her quiet young voice sounded as she answered. If she had known, she would surely have tried to soften it for the Indian gentleman's sake.

"The suffering was just as bad for my papa," she said. "It killed him."

"What was your father's name?" the Indian gentleman said. "Tell me."

"His name was Ralph Crewe," Sara answered, feeling startled. "Captain Crewe. He died in India."

The haggard face contracted, and Ram Dass sprang to his master's side.

"Carmichael," the invalid gasped, "it is the child—the child!"

For a moment Sara thought he was going to die. Ram Dass poured out drops from a bottle, and held them to his lips. Sara stood near, trembling a little. She looked in a bewildered way at Mr. Carmichael.

"What child am I?" she faltered.

"He was your father's friend," Mr. Carmichael answered her. "Don't be frightened. We have been looking for you for two years."

Sara put her hand up to her forehead, and her mouth trembled. She spoke as if she were in a dream.

"And I was at Miss Minchin's all the while," she half whispered. "Just on the other side of the wall."

CHAPTER XVIII

"*I Tried Not to Be*"

IT WAS PRETTY, comfortable Mrs. Carmichael who explained everything.[1] She was sent for at once, and came across the square to take Sara into her warm arms and make clear to her all that had happened. The excitement of the totally unexpected discovery had been temporarily almost overpowering to Mr. Carrisford in his weak condition.

"Upon my word," he said faintly to Mr. Carmichael, when it was suggested that the little girl should go into another room, "I feel as if I do not want to lose sight of her."

"I will take care of her," Janet said, "and mamma will come in a few minutes." And it was Janet who led her away.

"We're so glad you are found," she said. "You don't know how glad we are that you are found."

Donald stood with his hands in his pockets, and gazed at Sara with reflecting and self-reproachful eyes.

"If I'd just asked what your name was when I gave you my sixpence," he said, "you would have told me it was Sara Crewe, and then you would have been found in a minute."

Then Mrs. Carmichael came in. She looked very much moved, and suddenly took Sara in her arms and kissed her.

"You look bewildered, poor child," she said. "And it is not to be wondered at."

Sara could only think of one thing.

"Was he," she said, with a glance toward the closed door of the library—"was *he* the wicked friend? Oh, do tell me!"

Mrs. Carmichael was crying as she kissed her again. She felt as if she ought to be kissed very often because she had not been kissed for so long.

"He was not wicked, my dear," she answered. "He did not really lose your papa's money. He only thought he had lost it; and because he loved him so much his grief made him so ill that

172

for a time he was not in his right mind. He almost died of brain-fever, and long before he began to recover your poor papa was dead."

"And he did not know where to find me," murmured Sara. "And I was so near." Somehow, she could not forget that she had been so near.

"He believed you were in school in France," Mrs. Carmichael explained. "And he was continually misled by false clues. He has looked for you everywhere. When he saw you pass by, looking so sad and neglected, he did not dream that you were his friend's poor child; but because you were a little girl, too, he was sorry for you, and wanted to make you happier. And he told Ram Dass to climb into your attic window and try to make you comfortable."

Sara gave a start of joy; her whole look changed.

"Did Ram Dass bring the things?" she cried out; "did he tell Ram Dass to do it? Did he make the dream that came true!"

"Yes, my dear—yes! He is kind and good, and he was sorry for you, for little lost Sara Crewe's sake."[2]

The library door opened and Mr. Carmichael appeared, calling Sara to him with a gesture.

"Mr. Carrisford is better already," he said. "He wants you to come to him."

Sara did not wait. When the Indian gentleman looked at her as she entered, he saw that her face was all alight.

She went and stood before his chair, with her hands clasped together against her breast.

"You sent the things to me," she said, in a joyful emotional little voice—"the beautiful, beautiful things? *You* sent them!"

"Yes, poor, dear child, I did," he answered her. He was weak and broken with long illness and trouble, but he looked at her with the look she remembered in her father's eyes—that look of loving her and wanting to take her in his arms. It made her kneel down by him, just as she used to kneel by her father when they were the dearest friends and lovers in the world.

"Then it is you who are my friend," she said; "it is you who are my friend!" And she dropped her face on his thin hand and kissed it again and again.

"The man will be himself again in three weeks," Mr.

Carmichael said aside to his wife. "Look at his face already."

In fact, he did look changed. Here was the "little missus," and he had new things to think of and plan for already. In the first place, there was Miss Minchin. She must be interviewed and told of the change which had taken place in the fortunes of her pupil.

Sara was not to return to the seminary at all. The Indian gentleman was very determined upon that point. She must remain where she was, and Mr. Carmichael should go and see Miss Minchin himself.

"I am glad I need not go back," said Sara. "She will be very angry. She does not like me; though perhaps it is my fault, because I do not like her."

But, oddly enough, Miss Minchin made it unnecessary for Mr. Carmichael to go to her, by actually coming in search of her pupil herself. She had wanted Sara for something, and on inquiry had heard an astonishing thing. One of the housemaids had seen her steal out of the area with something hidden under her cloak, and had also seen her go up the steps of the next door and enter the house.

"What does she mean!" cried Miss Minchin to Miss Amelia.

"I don't know, I'm sure, sister," answered Miss Amelia. "Unless she has made friends with him because he has lived in India."

"It would be just like her to thrust herself upon him and try to gain his sympathies in some such impertinent fashion," said Miss Minchin. "She must have been in the house two hours. I will not allow such presumption. I shall go and inquire into the matter, and apologize for her intrusion."

Sara was sitting on a footstool close to Mr. Carrisford's knee, and listening to some of the many things he felt it necessary to try to explain to her, when Ram Dass announced the visitor's arrival.

Sara rose involuntarily, and became rather pale; but Mr. Carrisford saw that she stood quietly, and showed none of the ordinary signs of child terror.

Miss Minchin entered the room with a sternly dignified manner. She was correctly and well dressed, and rigidly polite.

"I am sorry to disturb Mr. Carrisford," she said; "but I have explanations to make. I am Miss Minchin, the proprietress of the Young Ladies' Seminary next door."

The Indian gentleman looked at her for a moment in silent scrutiny. He was a man who had naturally a rather hot temper, and he did not wish it to get too much the better of him.

"So you are Miss Minchin?" he said.

"I am, sir."

"In that case," the Indian gentleman replied, "you have arrived at the right time. My solicitor, Mr. Carmichael, was just on the point of going to see you."[3]

Mr. Carmichael bowed slightly, and Miss Minchin looked from him to Mr. Carrisford in amazement.

"Your solicitor!" she said. "I do not understand. I have come here as a matter of duty. I have just discovered that you have been intruded upon through the forwardness of one of my pupils—a charity pupil. I came to explain that she intruded without my knowledge." She turned upon Sara. "Go home at once," she commanded indignantly. "You shall be severely punished. Go home at once."

The Indian gentleman drew Sara to his side and patted her hand.

"She is not going."

Miss Minchin felt rather as if she must be losing her senses.

"Not going!" she repeated.

"No," said Mr. Carrisford. "She is not going *home*—if you give your house that name. Her home for the future will be with me."

Miss Minchin fell back in amazed indignation.

"With *you!* With *you,* sir! What does this mean?"

"Kindly explain the matter, Carmichael," said the Indian gentleman; "and get it over as quickly as possible." And he made Sara sit down again, and held her hands in his—which was another trick of her papa's.

Then Mr. Carmichael explained—in the quiet, level-toned, steady manner of a man who knew his subject, and all its legal significance, which was a thing Miss Minchin understood as a business woman, and did not enjoy.

"Mr. Carrisford, madam," he said, "was an intimate friend of the late Captain Crewe. He was his partner in certain large investments. The fortune which Captain Crewe supposed he had lost has been recovered, and is now in Mr. Carrisford's hands."

"The fortune!" cried Miss Minchin; and she really lost color as she uttered the exclamation. "Sara's fortune!"

"It *will* be Sara's fortune," replied Mr. Carmichael, rather coldly. "It *is* Sara's fortune now, in fact. Certain events have increased it enormously. The diamond-mines have retrieved themselves."

"The diamond-mines!" Miss Minchin gasped out. If this was true, nothing so horrible, she felt, had ever happened to her since she was born.

"The diamond-mines," Mr. Carmichael repeated, and he could not help adding, with a rather sly, unlawyer-like smile: "There are not many princesses, Miss Minchin, who are richer than your little charity pupil, Sara Crewe, will be. Mr. Carrisford has been searching for her for nearly two years; he has found her at last, and he will keep her."

After which he asked Miss Minchin to sit down while he explained matters to her fully, and went into such detail as was necessary to make it quite clear to her that Sara's future was an assured one, and that what had seemed to be lost was to be restored to her tenfold; also, that she had in Mr. Carrisford a guardian as well as a friend.

Miss Minchin was not a clever woman, and in her excitement she was silly enough to make one desperate effort to regain what she could not help seeing she had lost through her own worldly folly.

"He found her under my care," she protested. "I have done everything for her. But for me she would have starved in the streets."

Here the Indian gentleman lost his temper.

"As to starving in the streets," he said, "she might have starved more comfortably there than in your attic."

"Captain Crewe left her in my charge," Miss Minchin argued. "She must return to it until she is of age. She can be a parlor-boarder again. She must finish her education. The law will interfere in my behalf."

"Come, come, Miss Minchin," Mr. Carmichael interposed, "the law will do nothing of the sort. If Sara herself wishes to return to you, I dare say Mr. Carrisford might not refuse to allow it. But that rests with Sara."

"Then," said Miss Minchin, "I appeal to Sara. I have not spoiled you, perhaps," she said awkwardly to the little girl; "but you know that your papa was pleased with your progress. And—ahem!—I have always been fond of you."

Sara's green-gray eyes fixed themselves on her with the quiet, clear look Miss Minchin particularly disliked.

"Have *you*, Miss Minchin?" she said; "I did not know that."

Miss Minchin reddened and drew herself up.

"You ought to have known it," said she; "but children, unfortunately, never know what is best for them. Amelia and I always said you were the cleverest child in the school. Will you not do your duty to your poor papa and come home with me?"

Sara took a step toward her and stood still. She was thinking of the day when she had been told that she belonged to nobody, and was in danger of being turned into the street; she was thinking of the cold, hungry hours she had spent alone with Emily and Melchisedec in the attic. She looked Miss Minchin steadily in the face.

"You know why I will not go home with you, Miss Minchin," she said; "you know quite well."

A hot flush showed itself on Miss Minchin's hard, angry face.

"You will never see your companions again," she began. "I will see that Ermengarde and Lottie are kept away—"

Mr. Carmichael stopped her with polite firmness.

"Excuse me," he said; "she will see any one she wishes to see. The parents of Miss Crewe's fellow-pupils are not likely to refuse her invitations to visit her at her guardian's house. Mr. Carrisford will attend to that."

It must be confessed that even Miss Minchin flinched. This was worse than the eccentric bachelor uncle who might have a peppery temper and be easily offended at the treatment of his niece. A woman of sordid mind could easily believe that most people would not refuse to allow their children to remain friends with a little heiress of diamond-mines. And if Mr. Carrisford chose to tell certain of her patrons how unhappy Sara Crewe had been made, many unpleasant things might happen.

"You have not undertaken an easy charge," she said to the Indian gentleman, as she turned to leave the room; "you will discover that very soon. The child is neither truthful nor grateful. I suppose"—to Sara—"that you feel now that you are a princess again."

Sara looked down and flushed a little, because she thought her pet fancy might not be easy for strangers—even nice ones—to understand at first.

"I—tried not to be anything else," she answered in a low voice—"even when I was coldest and hungriest—I *tried* not to be."

"Now it will not be necessary to try," said Miss Minchin, acidly, as Ram Dass salaamed her out of the room.

She returned home and, going to her sitting-room, sent at once for Miss Amelia. She sat closeted with her all the rest of the afternoon, and it must be admitted that poor Miss Amelia passed through more than one bad quarter of an hour. She shed a good many tears, and mopped her eyes a good deal. One of her unfortunate remarks almost caused her sister to snap her head entirely off, but it resulted in an unusual manner.

"I'm not as clever as you, sister," she said, "and I am always afraid to say things to you for fear of making you angry. Perhaps if I were not so timid it would be better for the school and for both of us. I must say I've often thought it would have been better if you had been less severe on Sara Crewe, and had seen that she was decently dressed and more comfortable. I *know* she was worked too hard for a child of her age, and I know she was only half fed—"

"How dare you say such a thing!" exclaimed Miss Minchin.

"I don't know how I dare," Miss Amelia answered, with a kind of reckless courage; "but now I've begun I may as well finish, whatever happens to me. The child was a clever child and a good child—and she would have paid you for any kindness you had shown her. But you didn't show her any. The fact was, she was too clever for you, and you always disliked her for that reason. She used to see through us both—"

"Amelia!" gasped her infuriated elder, looking as if she

would box her ears and knock her cap off, as she had often done to Becky.

But Miss Amelia's disappointment had made her hysterical enough not to care what occurred next.

"She did! She did!" she cried. "She saw through us both. She saw that you were a hard-hearted, worldly woman, and that I was a weak fool, and that we were both of us vulgar and mean enough to grovel on our knees before her money, and behave ill to her because it was taken from her—though she behaved herself like a little princess even when she was a beggar. She did—she did—like a little princess!" and her hysterics got the better of the poor woman, and she began to laugh and cry both at once, and rock herself backward and forward in such a way as made Miss Minchin stare aghast.

"And now you've lost her," she cried wildly; "and some other school will get her and her money; and if she were like any other child she'd tell how she's been treated, and all our pupils would be taken away and we should be ruined. And it serves us right; but it serves you right more than it does me, for you are a hard woman, Maria Minchin—you're a hard, selfish, worldly woman!"[4]

And she was in danger of making so much noise with her hysterical chokes and gurgles that her sister was obliged to go to her and apply salts and sal volatile[5] to quiet her, instead of pouring forth her indignation at her audacity.

And from that time forward, it may be mentioned, the elder Miss Minchin actually began to stand a little in awe of a sister who, while she looked so foolish, was evidently not quite so foolish as she looked, and might, consequently, break out and speak truths people did not want to hear.

That evening, when the pupils were gathered together before the fire in the school-room, as was their custom before going to bed, Ermengarde came in with a letter in her hand and a queer expression on her round face. It was queer because, while it was an expression of delighted excitement, it was combined with such amazement as seemed to belong to a kind of shock just received.

"What *is* the matter?" cried two or three voices at once.

"Is it anything to do with the row that has been going on?"

said Lavinia, eagerly. "There has been such a row in Miss Minchin's room, Miss Amelia has had something like hysterics and has had to go to bed."

Ermengarde answered them slowly as if she were half stunned.

"I have just had this letter from Sara," she said, holding it out to let them see what a long letter it was.

"From Sara!" Every voice joined in that exclamation.

"Where is she?" almost shrieked Jessie.

"Next door," said Ermengarde, still slowly; "with the Indian gentleman."

"Where? Where? Has she been sent away? Does Miss Minchin know? Was the row about that? Why did she write? Tell us! Tell us!"

There was a perfect babel, and Lottie began to cry plaintively.

Ermengarde answered them slowly as if she were half plunged out into what, at the moment, seemed the most important and self-explaining thing.

"There *were* diamond-mines," she said stoutly; "there *were!*"

Open mouths and open eyes confronted her.

"They were real," she hurried on. "It was all a mistake about them. Something happened for a time, and Mr. Carrisford thought they were ruined—"

"Who is Mr. Carrisford?" shouted Jessie.

"The Indian gentleman. And Captain Crewe thought so, too—and he died; and Mr. Carrisford had brain-fever and ran away, and *he* almost died. And he did not know where Sara was. And it turned out that there were millions and millions of diamonds in the mines; and half of them belong to Sara; and they belonged to her when she was living in the attic with no one but Melchisedec for a friend, and the cook ordering her about. And Mr. Carrisford found her this afternoon, and he has got her in his home—and she will never come back—and she will be more a princess than she ever was—a hundred and fifty thousand times more. And I am going to see her to-morrow afternoon. There!"

Even Miss Minchin herself could scarcely have controlled

the uproar after this; and though she heard the noise, she did not try. She was not in the mood to face anything more than she was facing in her room, while Miss Amelia was weeping in bed. She knew that the news had penetrated the walls in some mysterious manner, and that every servant and every child would go to bed talking about it.

So until almost midnight the entire seminary, realizing some-how that all rules were laid aside, crowded round Ermengarde in the school-room and heard read and re-read the letter con-taining a story which was quite as wonderful as any Sara herself had ever invented, and which had the amazing charm of having happened to Sara herself and the mystic Indian gentleman in the very next house.

Becky, who had heard it also, managed to creep up-stairs earlier than usual. She wanted to get away from people and go and look at the little magic room once more. She did not know what would happen to it. It was not likely that it would be left to Miss Minchin. It would be taken away, and the attic would be bare and empty again. Glad as she was for Sara's sake, she went up the last flight of stairs with a lump in her throat and tears blurring her sight. There would be no fire to-night, and no rosy lamp; no supper, and no princess sitting in the glow reading or telling stories—no princess!

She choked down a sob as she pushed the attic door open, and then she broke into a low cry.

The lamp was flushing the room, the fire was blazing, the supper was waiting; and Ram Dass was standing smiling into her startled face.

"Missee sahib remembered," he said. "She told the sahib all. She wished you to know the good fortune which has befallen her. Behold a letter on the tray. She has written. She did not wish that you should go to sleep unhappy. The sahib com-mands you to come to him to-morrow. You are to be the atten-dant of missee sahib. To-night I take these things back over the roof."

And having said this with a beaming face, he made a little salaam and slipped through the skylight with an agile silentness of movement which showed Becky how easily he had done it before.

CHAPTER XIX

"Anne"

NEVER HAD SUCH JOY reigned in the nursery of the Large Family. Never had they dreamed of such delights as resulted from an intimate acquaintance with the little-girl-who-was-not-a-beggar. The mere fact of her sufferings and adventures made her a priceless possession. Everybody wanted to be told over and over again the things which had happened to her. When one was sitting by a warm fire in a big, glowing room, it was quite delightful to hear how cold it could be in an attic. It must be admitted that the attic was rather delighted in, and that its coldness and bareness quite sank into insignificance when Melchisedec was remembered, and one heard about the sparrows and things one could see if one climbed on the table and stuck one's head and shoulders out of the skylight.

Of course the thing loved best was the story of the banquet and the dream which was true. Sara told it for the first time the day after she had been found. Several members of the Large Family came to take tea with her, and as they sat or curled up on the hearth-rug she told the story in her own way, and the Indian gentleman listened and watched her. When she had finished she looked up at him and put her hand on his knee.

"That is my part," she said. "Now won't you tell your part of it, Uncle Tom?" He had asked her to call him always "Uncle Tom." "I don't know your part yet, and it must be beautiful."

So he told them how, when he sat alone, ill and dull and irritable, Ram Dass had tried to distract him by describing the passers by, and there was one child who passed oftener than any one else; he had begun to be interested in her—partly perhaps because he was thinking a great deal of a little girl, and partly because Ram Dass had been able to relate the incident of his visit to the attic in chase of the monkey. He had described its cheerless look, and the bearing of the child, who seemed as if she was not of the class of those who were treated as drudges and servants. Bit by bit, Ram Dass had made discoveries concerning the wretchedness of her life. He had found out how easy a matter it was to climb across the few yards of roof to the skylight, and this fact had been the beginning of all that followed.

"Sahib," he had said one day, "I could cross the slates and make the child a fire when she is out on some errand. When she returned, wet and cold, to find it blazing, she would think a magician had done it."

The idea had been so fanciful that Mr. Carrisford's sad face had lighted with a smile, and Ram Dass had been so filled with rapture that he had enlarged upon it and explained to his master how simple it would be to accomplish numbers of other things.[1] He had shown a childlike pleasure and invention, and the preparations for the carrying out of the plan had filled many a day with interest which would otherwise have dragged wearily. On the night of the frustrated banquet Ram Dass had kept watch, all his packages being in readiness in the attic which was his own; and the person who was to help him had waited with him, as interested as himself in the odd adventure. Ram Dass had been lying flat upon the slates, looking in at the skylight, when the banquet had come to its disastrous conclusion; he had been sure of the profoundness of Sara's wearied sleep; and then, with a dark lantern, he had crept into the room, while his companion had remained outside and handed the things to him. When Sara had stirred ever so faintly, Ram Dass had closed the lantern-slide and lain flat upon the floor.[2] These and many other exciting things the children found out by asking a thousand questions.

"I am so glad," Sara said. "I am so *glad* it was you who were my friend!"

There never were such friends as these two became. Somehow, they seemed to suit each other in a wonderful way. The Indian gentleman had never had a companion he liked quite as much as he liked Sara. In a month's time he was, as Mr. Carmichael had prophesied he would be, a new man. He was always amused and interested, and he began to find an actual pleasure in the possession of the wealth he had imagined that he loathed the burden of. There were so many charming things to plan for Sara. There was a little joke between them that he was a magician, and it was one of his pleasures to invent things to surprise her. She found beautiful new flowers growing in her room, whimsical little gifts tucked under pillows, and once, as they sat together in the evening, they heard the scratch of a heavy paw on the door, and when Sara went to find out what it was, there stood a great dog—a splendid Russian boarhound— with a grand silver and gold collar bearing an inscription in raised letters. "I am Boris," it read; "I serve the Princess Sara."

There was nothing the Indian gentleman loved more than the recollection of the little princess in rags and tatters. The afternoons in which the Large Family, or Ermengarde and Lottie, gathered to rejoice together were very delightful. But the hours when Sara and the Indian gentleman sat alone and read or talked had a special charm of their own. During their passing many interesting things occurred.

One evening, Mr. Carrisford, looking up from his book, noticed that his companion had not stirred for some time, but sat gazing into the fire.

"What are you 'supposing,' Sara?" he asked.

Sara looked up, with a bright color on her cheek.

"I *was* supposing," she said; "I was remembering that hungry day, and a child I saw."

"But there were a great many hungry days," said the Indian gentleman, with rather a sad tone in his voice. "Which hungry day was it?"

"I forgot you didn't know," said Sara. "It was the day the dream came true."

Then she told him the story of the bun-shop, and the fourpence she picked up out of the sloppy mud, and the child who was hungrier than herself. She told it quite simply, and in as few words as possible; but somehow the Indian gentleman found it necessary to shade his eyes with his hand and look down at the carpet.

"And I was supposing a kind of plan," she said, when she had finished. "I was thinking I should like to do something."

"What was it?" said Mr. Carrisford, in a low tone. "You may do anything you like to do, princess."

"I was wondering," rather hesitated Sara—"you know, you say I have so much money—I was wondering if I could go to see the bun-woman, and tell her that if, when hungry children—particularly on those dreadful days—come and sit on the steps, or look in at the window, she would just call them in and give them something to eat, she might send the bills to me. Could I do that?"

"You shall do it to-morrow morning," said the Indian gentleman.

"Thank you," said Sara. "You see, I know what it is to be hungry, and it is very hard when one cannot even *pretend* it away."

"Yes, yes, my dear," said the Indian gentleman. "Yes, yes, it must be. Try to forget it. Come and sit on this footstool near my knee, and only remember you are a princess."

"Yes," said Sara, smiling; "and I can give buns and bread to the populace."[3] And she went and sat on the stool, and the Indian gentleman (he used to like her to call him that, too, sometimes) drew her small dark head down upon his knee and stroked her hair.

The next morning, Miss Minchin, in looking out of her window, saw the thing she perhaps least enjoyed seeing. The Indian gentleman's carriage, with its tall horses, drew up before the door of the next house, and its owner and a little figure, warm with soft, rich furs, descended the steps to get into it. The little figure was a familiar one, and reminded Miss Minchin of days in the past. It was followed by another as familiar—the sight of which she found very irritating. It was Becky, who, in the character of delighted attendant, always accompanied her young mistress to her carriage, carrying wraps and belongings. Already Becky had a pink, round face.

A little later the carriage drew up before the door of the baker's shop, and its occupants got out, oddly enough, just as the bun-woman was putting a tray of smoking-hot buns into the window.

When Sara entered the shop the woman turned and looked at her, and, leaving the buns, came and stood behind the counter. For a moment she looked at Sara very hard indeed, and then her good-natured face lighted up.

"I'm sure that I remember you, miss," she said. "And yet—"

"Yes," said Sara; "once you gave me six buns for fource-pence, and—"

"And you gave five of 'em to a beggar child," the woman broke in on her. "I've always remembered it. I couldn't make it out at first." She turned round to the Indian gentleman and spoke her next words to him. "I beg your pardon, sir, but there's not many young people that notices a hungry face in that way; and I've thought of it many a time. Excuse the liberty, miss,"—to Sara,—"but you look rosier and—well, better than you did that—that—"

"I am better, thank you," said Sara. "And—I am much happier—and I have come to ask you to do something for me."

"Me, miss!" exclaimed the bun-woman, smiling cheerfully. "Why, bless you! yes, miss. What can I do?"

And then Sara, leaning on the counter, made her little proposal concerning the dreadful days and the hungry waifs and the hot buns.

The woman watched her, and listened with an astonished face.

"Why, bless me!" she said again when she had heard it all; "it'll be a pleasure to me to do it. I am a working-woman myself and cannot afford to do much on my own account, and there's sights of trouble on every side; but, if you'll excuse me, I'm bound to say I've given away many a bit of bread since that wet afternoon, just along o' thinking of you—an' how wet an' cold you was, an' how hungry you looked; an' yet you gave away your hot buns as if you was a princess."

The Indian gentleman smiled involuntarily at this, and Sara smiled a little, too, remembering what she had said to herself when she put the buns down on the ravenous child's ragged lap.

"She looked so hungry," she said. "She was even hungrier than I was."

"She was starving," said the woman. "Many's the time she's told me of it since—how she sat there in the wet, and felt as if a wolf was a-tearing at her poor young insides."

"Oh, have you seen her since then?" exclaimed Sara. "Do you know where she is?"

"Yes, I do," answered the woman, smiling more good-naturedly than ever. "Why, she's in that there back room, miss, an' has been for a month; an' a decent, well-meanin' girl she's goin' to turn out, an' such a help to me in the shop an' in the kitchen as you'd scarce believe, knowin' how she's lived."

She stepped to the door of the little back parlor and spoke; and the next minute a girl came out and followed her behind the counter. And actually it was the beggar-child, clean and neatly clothed, and looking as if she had not been hungry for a long time. She looked shy, but she had a nice face, now that she was no longer a savage, and the wild look had gone from her eyes. She knew Sara in an instant, and stood and looked at her as if she could never look enough.

"You see," said the woman, "I told her to come when she was hungry, and when she'd come I'd give her odd jobs to do; an' I found she was willing, and somehow I got to like her; and the end of it was, I've given her a place an' a home, and she helps me, an' behaves well, an' is as thankful as a girl can be. Her name's Anne.[4] She has no other."

The children stood and looked at each other for a few minutes; and then Sara took her hand out of her muff and held it out across the counter, and Anne took it, and they looked straight into each other's eyes.

"I am so glad," Sara said. "And I have just thought of something. Perhaps Mrs. Brown will let you be the one to give the buns and bread to the children. Perhaps you would like to do it because you know what it is to be hungry, too."

"Yes, miss," said the girl.

And, somehow, Sara felt as if she understood her, though she said so little, and only stood still and looked and looked after her as she went out of the shop with the Indian gentleman, and they got into the carriage and drove away.

APPENDIX A
FROM *SARA CREWE, OR, WHAT HAPPENED AT MISS MINCHIN'S*

Although Burnett faithfully adhered to her novella's plot in both the 1902 and 1905 expansions and even retained some of her original phrasings, the retellings of Sara's story involved much more than added characters and scenes. For, in the 1888 text, Sara is not yet the extraordinary child she will later become. Whereas the novel immediately adopts the point of view of the pensive girl who scrutinizes Miss Minchin and instructs her father to find Emily for her, the novella subordinates Sara to a narrator who controls the long flashback that follows the opening paragraph. Thus, in the first selection reproduced below, we meet a child who has already been imprinted by her denigration: not only is Sara convinced that she is "the ugliest child in the school" (an assertion the narrator half corroborates rather than disputes), but she also doubts whether she is, or ever was, "Select." Nor is this Sara as inventive and widely read as the child whom Burnett later treats as a junior version of herself. She has no mental store of rich narratives to fall back upon. Quite willing to feed on pulp fiction the later Sara would surely dismiss as "vulgar," she asks "a sentimental housemaid" to lend her "greasy volumes containing stories of marquises and dukes who invariably fell in love with orange-girls and gypsies and servant-maids, and made them the proud brides of coronets."

If the first of the two selections offered below presents us with a heroine who has not yet acquired the powers of resistance of her later, more imaginative incarnation, the second one shows an equally muted handling of the "magic" that so dramatically transforms Sara's attic room. A guarded realism, rather than a willingness to press the resources of romance and myth to their utmost limits, shapes Burnett's first version of this scene.

Whereas the starving Sara of 1905 finds fulfillment for her most desperate "supposings" when she awakens from sleep into a dream that has become true, the Sara of 1888 can exchange her dry crust of bread for "toast" and "muffins" as soon as she enters a fully redecorated room. And she may, subconsciously at least, even fathom the identity of her new friend when, fast asleep in her snug new bed, she soon dreams of speaking Hindustani to this "mysterious benefactor."

I.
[The Novella's Opening]

In the first place, Miss Minchin lived in London. Her home was a large, dull, tall one, in a large, dull square, where all the houses were alike, and all the sparrows were alike, and where all the door-knockers made the same heavy sound, and on still days—and nearly all the days were still—seemed to resound through the entire row in which the knock was knocked. On Miss Minchin's door there was a brass plate. On the brass plate there was inscribed in black letters,

> MISS MINCHIN'S
> SELECT SEMINARY FOR YOUNG LADIES.

Little Sara Crewe never went in or out of the house without reading that door-plate and reflecting upon it. By the time she was twelve, she had decided that all her trouble arose because, in the first place, she was not "Select," and in the second, she was not a "Young Lady." When she was eight years old, she had been brought to Miss Minchin as a pupil, and left with her.[1] Her papa had brought her all the way from India. Her mamma had died when she was a baby, and her papa had kept her with him as long as he could.[2] And then, finding the hot climate was making her very delicate, he had brought her to England and left her with Miss Minchin, to be part of the Select Seminary for

Young Ladies. Sara, who had always been a sharp little child, who remembered things, recollected hearing him say that he had not a relative in the world whom he knew of, and so he was obliged to place her at a boarding-school, and he had heard Miss Minchin's establishment spoken of very highly. The same day, he took Sara out and bought her a great many beautiful clothes,—clothes so grand and rich that only a very young and inexperienced man would have bought them for a mite of a child who was to be brought up in a boarding-school. But the fact was that he was a rash, innocent young man, and very sad at the thought of parting with his little girl, who was all he had left to remind him of her beautiful mother, whom he had dearly loved. And he wished her to have everything the most fortu-nate little girl could have; and so, when the polite saleswomen in the shops said, "Here is our very latest thing in hats, the plumes are exactly the same as those we sold to Lady Diana Sinclair yesterday," he immediately bought what was offered to him, and paid whatever was asked. The consequence was that Sara had a most extraordinary wardrobe. Her dresses were silk and velvet and India cashmere, her hats and bonnets were cov-ered with bows and plumes, her small undergarments were adorned with real lace, and she returned in the cab to Miss Minchin's with a doll almost as large as herself, dressed quite as grandly as herself, too.

Then her papa gave Miss Minchin some money and went away, and for several days Sara would neither touch the doll, nor her breakfast, nor her dinner, nor her tea, and would do nothing but crouch in a small corner by the window and cry. She cried so much, indeed, that she made herself ill. She was a queer little child, with old-fashioned ways and strong feelings, and she had adored her papa, and could not be made to think that India and an interesting bungalow were not better for her than London and Miss Minchin's Select Seminary. The instant she had entered the house, she had begun promptly to hate Miss Minchin, and to think little of Miss Amelia Minchin, who was smooth and dumpy, and lisped, and was evidently afraid of her older sister. Miss Minchin was tall, and had large, cold, fishy eyes, and large, cold hands, which seemed fishy, too, because they were damp and made chills run down Sara's back when they touched her, as Miss Minchin pushed her hair off her forehead and said:

"A most beautiful and promising little girl, Captain Crewe. She will be a favorite pupil; *quite* a favorite pupil, I see."

For the first year she was a favorite pupil; at least she was indulged a great deal more than was good for her. And when the Select Seminary went walking, two by two, she was always decked out in her grandest clothes, and led by the hand, at the head of the genteel procession, by Miss Minchin herself. And when the parents of any of the pupils came, she was always dressed and called into the parlor with her doll; and she used to hear Miss Minchin say that her father was a distinguished Indian officer, and she would be heiress to a great fortune. That her father had inherited a great deal of money, Sara had heard before; and also that some day it would be hers, and that he would not remain long in the army, but would come to live in London. And every time a letter came, she hoped it would say he was coming, and they were to live together again.

But about the middle of the third year a letter came bringing very different news. Because he was not a business man himself, her papa had given his affairs into the hands of a friend he trusted. The friend had deceived and robbed him. All the money was gone, no one knew exactly where, and the shock was so great to the poor, rash young officer, that, being attacked by jungle fever shortly afterward, he had no strength to rally, and so died, leaving Sara with no one to take care of her.

Miss Minchin's cold and fishy eyes had never looked so cold and fishy as they did when Sara went into the parlor, on being sent for, a few days after the letter was received.

No one had said anything to the child about mourning, so, in her old-fashioned way, she had decided to find a black dress for herself, and had picked out a black velvet she had outgrown, and came into the room in it, looking the queerest little figure in the world, and a sad little figure, too. The dress was too short and too tight, her face was white, her eyes had dark rings around them, and her doll, wrapped in a piece of old black crape, was held under her arm. She was not a pretty child.[3] She was thin, and had a weird, interesting little face, short black hair, and very large green-gray eyes fringed all around with heavy black lashes.

"I am the ugliest child in the school," she had said once, after staring at herself in the glass for some minutes.

But there had been a clever, good-natured little French teacher who had said to the music-master:

"Zat leetle Crewe. Vat a child! A so ogly beauty! Ze so large eyes; ze so little spirituelle face. Waid till she grow up. You shall see!"

This morning, however, in the tight, small black frock, she looked thinner and odder than ever, and her eyes were fixed on Miss Minchin with a queer steadiness as she slowly advanced into the parlor, clutching her doll.

"Put your doll down!" said Miss Minchin.

"No," said the child, "I won't put her down; I want her with me. She is all I have. She has stayed with me all the time since my papa died."[4]

She had never been an obedient child. She had had her own way ever since she was born, and there was about her an air of silent determination under which Miss Minchin had always felt secretly uncomfortable. And that lady felt even now that perhaps it would be as well not to insist on her point. So she looked at her as severely as possible.

"You will have no time for dolls in future," she said; "you will have to work and improve yourself, and make yourself useful."

Sara kept the big odd eyes fixed on her teacher and said nothing.

"Everything will be very different now," Miss Minchin went on. "I sent for you to talk to you and make you understand. Your father is dead. You have no friends. You have no money. You have no home and no one to take care of you."

The little pale olive face twitched nervously, but the green-gray eyes did not move from Miss Minchin's, and still Sara said nothing.

"What are you staring at?" demanded Miss Minchin sharply. "Are you so stupid you don't understand what I mean? I tell you that you are quite alone in the world, and have no one to do anything for you, unless I choose to keep you here."

The truth was, Miss Minchin was in her worst mood. To be suddenly deprived of a large sum of money yearly and a show pupil, and to find herself with a little beggar on her hands, was more than she could bear with any degree of calmness.

"Now listen to me," she went on, "and remember what I say. If you work hard and prepare to make yourself useful in a few years, I shall let you stay here. You are only a child, but you are a sharp child, and you pick up things almost without being taught. You speak French very well, and in a year or so you can begin to help with the younger pupils. By the time you are fifteen you ought to be able to do that much at least."

"I can speak French better than you, now," said Sara; "I always spoke it with my papa in India."[5] Which was not at all polite, but was painfully true; because Miss Minchin could not speak French at all, and, indeed, was not in the least a clever person. But she was a hard, grasping business woman, and, after the first shock of disappointment, had seen that at very little expense to herself she might prepare this clever, determined child to be very useful to her and save her the necessity of paying large salaries to teachers of languages.

"Don't be impudent, or you will be punished," she said. "You will have to improve your manners if you expect to earn your bread. You are not a parlor boarder now. Remember, that if you don't please me, and I send you away, you have no home but the street. You can go now."

Sara turned away.

"Stay," commanded Miss Minchin, "don't you intend to thank me?"

Sara turned toward her. The nervous twitch was to be seen again in her face, and she seemed to be trying to control it.

"What for?" she said.

"For my kindness to you," replied Miss Minchin. "For my kindness in giving you a home."

Sara went two or three steps nearer to her. Her thin little chest was heaving up and down, and she spoke in a strange, unchildish voice.

"You are not kind," she said. "You are not kind." And she turned again and went out of the room, leaving Miss Minchin staring after her strange, small figure in stony anger.

The child walked up the staircase, holding tightly to her doll; she meant to go to her bedroom, but at the door she was met by Miss Amelia.

"You are not to go in there," she said. "That is not your room now."

"Where is my room?" asked Sara.

"You are to sleep in the attic next to the cook."

Sara walked on. She mounted two flights more, and reached the door of the attic room, opened it and went in, shutting it behind her. She stood against it and looked about her. The room was slanting-roofed and whitewashed; there was a rusty grate, an iron bedstead, and some odd articles of furniture, sent up from better rooms below, where they had been used until they were considered to be worn out. Under the skylight in the roof, which showed nothing but an oblong piece of dull gray sky, there was a battered old red footstool.

Sara went to it and sat down. She was a queer child, as I have said before, and quite unlike other children. She seldom cried. She did not cry now. She laid her doll, Emily,[6] across her knees, and put her face down upon her, and her arms around her, and sat there, her little black head resting on the black crape, not saying one word, not making one sound.

From that day her life changed entirely. Sometimes she used to feel as if it must be another life altogether, the life of some other child. She was a little drudge and outcast; she was given her lessons at odd times and expected to learn without being taught; she was sent on errands by Miss Minchin, Miss Amelia, and the cook. Nobody took any notice of her except when they ordered her about. She was often kept busy all day and then sent into the deserted school-room with a pile of books to learn her lessons or practice at night. She had never been intimate with the other pupils, and soon she became so shabby that, taking her queer clothes together with her queer little ways, they began to look upon her as a being of another world than their own. The fact was that, as a rule, Miss Minchin's pupils were rather dull, matter-of-fact young people, accustomed to being rich and comfortable; and Sara, with her elfish cleverness, her desolate life, and her odd habit of fixing her eyes upon them and staring them out of countenance, was too much for them.

"She always looks as if she was finding you out," said one girl, who was sly and given to making mischief.[7] "I am," said Sara, promptly, when she heard of it. "That's what I look at them for. I like to know about people. I think them over afterward."

She never made any mischief herself or interfered with any one. She talked very little, did as she was told, and thought a great deal. Nobody knew, and in fact nobody cared, whether she was unhappy or happy, unless, perhaps, it was Emily, who lived in the attic and slept on the iron bedstead at night. Sara thought Emily understood her feelings, though she was only wax and had a habit of staring herself. Sara used to talk to her at night.

"You are the only friend I have in the world," she would say to her. "Why don't you say something? Why don't you speak? Sometimes I'm sure you could, if you would try. It ought to make you try, to know you are the only thing I have. If I were you, I should try. Why don't you try?"

II.
[The Transformation of Sara's Room]

The native servant, whom she called the Lascar, looked mournful too, but he was evidently very faithful to his master.

"Perhaps he saved his master's life in the Sepoy rebellion," she thought. "They look as if they might have had all sorts of adventures. I wish I could speak to the Lascar. I remember a little Hindustani."

And one day she actually did speak to him, and his start at the sound of his own language expressed a great deal of surprise and delight. He was waiting for his master to come out to the carriage, and Sara, who was going on an errand as usual, stopped and spoke a few words.[8] She had a special gift for languages and had remembered enough Hindustani to make herself understood by him. When his master came out, the Lascar spoke to him quickly, and the Indian Gentleman turned and looked at her curiously.[9] And afterward the Lascar always greeted her with salaams of the most profound description. And occasionally they exchanged a few words. She learned that it was true that the Sahib was very rich—that he was ill—and also that he had no wife nor children, and that England did not agree with the monkey.

"He must be as lonely as I am," thought Sara. "Being rich does not seem to make him happy."

That evening, as she passed the windows, the Lascar was closing the shutters, and she caught a glimpse of the room inside. There was a bright fire glowing in the grate, and the Indian Gentleman was sitting before it, in a luxurious chair. The room was richly furnished and looked delightfully comfortable, but the Indian Gentleman sat with his head resting on his hand and looked as lonely and unhappy as ever.

"Poor man!" said Sara; "I wonder what *you* are 'supposing'?"

When she went into the house she met Miss Minchin in the hall.

"Where have you wasted your time?" said Miss Minchin. "You have been out for hours!"

"It was so wet and muddy," Sara answered. "It was hard to walk, because my shoes were so bad and slipped about so."

"Make no excuses," said Miss Minchin, "and tell no falsehoods."

Sara went downstairs to the kitchen.

"Why didn't you stay all night?" said the cook.

"Here are the things," said Sara, and laid her purchases on the table.

The cook looked over them, grumbling. She was in a very bad temper indeed.

"May I have something to eat?" Sara asked, rather faintly.

"Tea's over and done with," was the answer. "Did you expect me to keep it hot for you?"

Sara was silent a second.

"I had no dinner," she said, and her voice was quite low. She made it low, because she was afraid it would tremble.

"There's some bread in the pantry," said the cook. "That's all you'll get at this time of day."

Sara went and found the bread. It was old and hard and dry. The cook was in too bad a humor to give her anything to eat with it. She had just been scolded by Miss Minchin, and it was always safe and easy to vent her own spite on Sara.

Really it was hard for the child to climb the three long flights of stairs leading to her garret. She often found them long and steep when she was tired, but to-night it seemed as if she would never reach the top. Several times a lump rose in her throat, and she was obliged to stop to rest.

"I can't pretend anything more to-night," she said wearily to herself.[10] "I'm sure I can't. I'll eat my bread and drink some water and then go to sleep, and perhaps a dream will come and pretend for me. I wonder what dreams are."

Yes, when she reached the top landing there were tears in her eyes, and she did not feel like a princess—only like a tired, hungry, lonely, lonely child.

"If my papa had lived," she said, "they would not have treated me like this. If my papa had lived, he would have taken care of me."

Then she turned the handle and opened the garret-door.

Can you imagine it—can you believe it? I find it hard to believe it myself.[11] And Sara found it impossible; for the first few moments she thought something strange had happened to her eyes—to her mind—that the dream had come before she had had time to fall asleep.

"Oh!" she exclaimed breathlessly. "Oh! It isn't true! I know, I know it isn't true!" And she slipped into the room and closed the door and locked it, and stood with her back against it, staring straight before her.

Do you wonder? In the grate, which had been empty and rusty and cold when she left it, but which now was blackened and polished up quite respectably, there was a glowing, blazing fire. On the hob was a little brass kettle, hissing and boiling; spread upon the floor was a warm, thick rug; before the fire was a folding-chair, unfolded and with cushions on it; by the chair was a small folding-table, unfolded, covered with a white cloth, and upon it were spread small covered dishes, a cup and saucer, and a tea-pot; on the bed were new, warm coverings, a curious wadded silk robe and some books. The little, cold, miserable room seemed changed into Fairyland. It was actually warm and glowing.

"It is bewitched!" said Sara. "Or *I* am bewitched. I only

think I see it all; but if I can only keep on thinking it, I don't care—I don't care,—if I can only keep it up!"

She was afraid to move, for fear it would melt away. She stood with her back against the door and looked and looked. But soon she began to feel warm, and then she moved forward.

"A fire that I only *thought* I saw surely wouldn't *feel* warm," she said. "It feels real—real."

She went to it and knelt before it. She touched the chair, the table; she lifted the cover of one of the dishes. There was something hot and savory in it—something delicious. The tea-pot had tea in it, ready for the boiling water from the little kettle; one plate had toast on it, another, muffins.

"It is real," said Sara. "The fire is real enough to warm me. I can sit in the chair; the things are real enough to eat."

It was like a fairy story come true—it was heavenly. She went to the bed and touched the blankets and the wrap. They were real too. She opened one book, and on the title-page was written in a strange hand, "The little girl in the attic."

Suddenly—was it a strange thing for her to do?—Sara put her face down on the queer foreign-looking quilted robe and burst into tears.

"I don't know who it is," she said, "but somebody cares about me a little—somebody is my friend."

Somehow that thought warmed her more than the fire. She had never had a friend since those happy, luxurious days when she had had everything; and those days had seemed such a long way off—so far away as to be only like dreams—during these last years at Miss Minchin's.

She really cried more at this strange thought of having a friend—even though an unknown one—than she had cried over many of her worst troubles.

But these tears seemed different from the others, for when she had wiped them away they did not seem to leave her eyes and her heart hot and smarting.

And then imagine, if you can, what the rest of the evening was like. The delicious comfort of taking off the damp clothes and putting on the soft, warm, quilted robe before the glowing fire—of slipping her cold feet into the luscious little wool-lined slippers she found near her chair. And then the hot tea and savory dishes, the cushioned chair and the books!

It was just like Sara, that, once having found the things real, she should give herself up to the enjoyment of them to the very utmost. She had lived such a life of imaginings, and had found her pleasure so long in improbabilities, that she was quite equal to accepting any wonderful thing that happened. After she was quite warm and had eaten her supper and enjoyed herself for an hour or so, it had almost ceased to be surprising to her, that such magical surroundings should be hers. As to finding out who had done all this, she knew that it was out of the question. She did not know a human soul by whom it could seem in the least degree probable that it could have been done.

"There is nobody," she said to herself, "nobody." She discussed the matter with Emily, it is true, but more because it was delightful to talk about it than with a view to making any discoveries.

"But we have a friend, Emily," she said; "we have a friend."[12]

Sara could not even imagine a being charming enough to fill her grand ideal of her mysterious benefactor. If she tried to make in her mind a picture of him or her, it ended by being something glittering and strange—not at all like a real person, but bearing resemblance to a sort of Eastern magician, with long robes and a wand. And when she fell asleep, beneath the soft white blanket, she dreamed all night of this magnificent personage, and talked to him in Hindustani, and made salaams to him.

Upon one thing she was determined. She would not speak to any one of her good fortune—it should be her own secret; in fact, she was rather inclined to think that if Miss Minchin knew, she would take her treasures from her or in some way spoil her pleasure. So when she went down the next morning she shut her door very tight and did her best to look as if nothing unusual had occurred. And yet this was rather hard, because she could not help remembering, every now and then, with a sort of start, and her heart would beat quickly every time she repeated to herself, "I have a friend!"

APPENDIX B
FROM *THE LITTLE PRINCESS: A PLAY FOR CHILDREN AND GROWN-UP CHILDREN*, ACT ONE

The script for the 1902 play production greatly augmented the cast of child characters: Becky and Lottie (as well as a girl called Lilly) were added, and the roles of the lively Carmichael children and a rather pugnacious Ermengarde were greatly expanded. Yet the adult figures, too, were now more fully developed: appearing at Sara's window with a stage crew of "three other lascars" to orchestrate the gradual refurbishing of Sara's room, an exotic Ram Dass became a stellar attraction when he allowed a theater audience to witness this silent pantomime of a step-by-step transformation. And Mrs. Carmichael, who meets a still wealthy Sara at the birthday party at the end of the scene reprinted below, will make an important reappearance when she is called upon to preside over Sara's reunion with Carrisford.

Dialogue, in Burnett's play, must serve to inform the audience about past events that a more leisurely chronological narrative may locate within a series of present moments. Such condensations are often reductive. When Sara simply reminds Lottie of their earlier agreement that she would "be your mamma," we are deprived of the powerful scene in which Miss Minchin and Miss Amelia rely on Sara's talents as a storyteller to tame the screaming child. As a result of such compressions, the play, ironically enough, often turns out be far less dramatic than the later novel. What is more, dialogue and external representation also conspire against a presentation of Sara's inner life. Still, as the ensuing excerpt shows, the lively interactions and the greater intricacies of plot and character make the 1902 drama seem closer to the 1905 novel than to the 1888 prose narrative.

(*Bell rings off* R. *Business of children running into straight lines* R. *and* L. ERMENGARDE *to black-board draws cat on same.* LAVINIA *up stage* R. C.)[1]

CHILDREN: Miss Minchin's coming, Miss Minchin's coming!

LAVINIA: Yes, and leading Sara by the hand as if she were a "Little Princess."

ERMENGARDE: (*pointing to board*) That old cat, Miss Minchin. (*children laugh*)

(*Enter* MISS MINCHIN, *leading* SARA, SARA *first*, MINCHIN *second*, JAMES *third*, WILLIAM *fourth*, EMMA *fifth*, BECKY *sixth*, *servants carry presents.*)

MINCHIN: (*sweeping grandly down* C. R. AMELIA *and* ERMENGARDE *place from* R. *upper to* C. AMELIA *gets* L. *upper behind children*) Silence, young ladies . . . James, place the box (*doll*) on the table and remove the lid. William, place yours there. (*trunk*) Emma, put yours on the table.[2] (*9 books*) Becky, put yours on the floor. (BECKY *looks at the children* L.) Becky, it is not your place to look at the young ladies. You forget yourself. (*Waving servants off* R. *upper*) Now you may leave us.

(*Exit servants* R. *upper.* BECKY *starts to follow them.* SARA *stops her.*)

SARA: Ah, please, Miss Minchin, mayn't Becky stay?

MISS MINCHIN: Becky—my dearest Sara——

SARA: I want her because I'm sure she would so like to see the doll. She's a little girl, too, you know.

MINCHIN: (*amazed*) My dear Sara—Becky is the scullery-maid. Scullery-maids are not little girls—at least they ought not to be.

SARA: But Becky *is*, you know.

MINCHIN: I'm sorry to hear it.

SARA: But I don't believe she can help it. And I know she would enjoy herself so. (*crosses to* MINCHIN) Please let her stay—because it's my birthday. (BECKY *backing into the corner in mingled terror and delight*)

MINCHIN: (*dignified*) Well, as you ask it as a birthday favor—she may stay.

SARA: Thank you.

MINCHIN: Rebecca, thank Miss Sara for her great kindness.

BECKY: (*comes forward making little charity curtseys, words tumbling over each other*)[3] Oh, if you please, Miss—thank you, Miss. I am that grateful, Miss. I did want to see the doll, Miss—that—that bad. I thank you, Miss. (SARA *nods happily to* BECKY, *who bobs to* MISS MINCHIN) An' thank you, Ma'am, for letting me take the liberty.

MINCHIN: Go stand over there. (*pointing grandly to* L. *corner*) Not too near the young ladies. (BECKY *backs into corner, rolls down sleeves, etc.*) Now, young ladies, I have a few words to say to you. (*sweeping grandly up to platform* C.) You are aware, young ladies, that dear Sara is thirteen years old to-day.

CHILDREN: Yes, Miss Minchin.

MINCHIN: There are a few of you here who have also been thirteen years old but Sara's birthdays are different from most little girls' birthdays.

CHILDREN: Yes, Miss Minchin.

MINCHIN: (C.) When she is older she will be heiress to a large fortune which it will be her duty to spend in a meritorious manner.

ERMENGARDE: (L.) No, Miss Minchin—I mean yes, Miss Minchin.

MINCHIN: When her papa, Captain Crewe, brought her from India and gave her into my care, he said to me, in a jesting manner, "I'm afraid she will be very rich, Miss Minchin."

CHILDREN: Oh!—Ah!—Oh!

MINCHIN: My reply was, "Her education at my seminary, Captain Crewe, shall be such as will fit her to adorn the largest fortune." (LOTTIE *sniffs loudly*) Lottie, do not sniff. Use your pocket-handkerchief. (ERMENGARDE *wipes* LOTTIE's *nose.* LOTTIE *sniffs again.* MINCHIN *coughs* LOTTIE *down*) Sara has become my most accomplished pupil. Her French and her dancing are a credit to the seminary. Her manners—which have caused you all to call her Princess Sara—are perfect. Her amiability she exhibits by giving you this party. I hope you appreciate her generosity. I wish you to express your appreciation by saying aloud, all together, "Thank you, Sara."

ALL: Thank you, Sara.

ERMENGARDE: (*alone*) Thank you, Sara.

BECKY: I thank you, Miss.

SARA: (*crossing to* L. C.) I thank *you* for coming to my party. (*crossing to* R. C.) And you. (*retires*)

MINCHIN: Very pretty indeed, Sara. (*down* R.) That is what a real princess does when the populace applauds. I have one thing more to say. The visitors coming are the father and mother of a large family. I wish you to conduct yourselves in such a manner as will cause them to observe that elegance of deportment can be acquired at Miss Minchin's seminary. (ERMENGARDE *bus. of posing in* L. *corner*) I will now go back to the drawing-room until they arrive. (*going up* R.) Sara, you may show your presents.

(*Exits* R. *upper.*)

(ERMENGARDE *imitates her walk from* L. *corner to* C.)

ERMENGARDE: Sara, you may show your presents.

AMELIA: (*coming out from behind*) Ermengarde——

ERMENGARDE: Oh! Miss— (AMELIA *crosses to* R. *door*) Amelia, please forgive me—I did—didn't—

(*Exit* AMELIA R. *upper. Children bus. laugh and flock around the boxes on table* C. *etc.*)

SARA: (*getting chair from piano*) She caught you that time, Ermy. (*getting on chair* C. *behind table*) Which shall we look at first? (*picking up books*) These are books, I know. (*trying to untie them*)

CHILDREN: Oh—books—Oh! (*disgusted*)

ERMENGARDE: (*aghast*) Does your papa send you *books* for a birthday present? He's as bad as mine. Don't open them, Sara.

SARA: (*laughing*) But I like them the best—never mind though. This is the doll. (*uncovering long wooden box*) I'll open that first. (*stands doll upon its feet* R. *Doll is on a metal stand and is made to stand alone*)

CHILDREN: Oh!—Ah!—Oh!

LILLY: Isn't she a beauty? (BECKY *gets stool from above door* L. *and stands on it to see doll*)

JESSIE: She's almost as big as Lottie.

LOTTIE: (*dancing down* L.) Tra-la-la.

LILLY: She's dressed for the theatre. See her magnificent opera cloak.

(LAVINIA *does not get on floor.*)

ERMENGARDE: She has an opera-glass in her hand.

SARA: So she has. (*getting down*) Here's her trunk. Let us open that and look at her things, Ermy, you open the other. (*takes trunk with* JESSIE *to* R. C. *down stage, opens it.* ERMY *takes other one down* L. C. *with help of* JESSIE *and opens it too. Children crowd around trunks, sit on floor looking at the clothes.* BECKY *looks on from behind*) Here is the key.

CHILDREN: Oh!

SARA: This is full of lace collars and silk stockings and handkerchiefs. Here's a jewel case with a necklace and a tiara of diamonds. Put them on her, Lilly. All of her underclothes. Ah, look. (*bus. of showing*)

ERMENGARDE: Here's a velvet coat trimmed with chinchilla, and one lined with ermine, and muffs. Oh, what darling dresses! A pale cloth trimmed with sable and a long coat. (LOTTIE *takes coat and puts it on*) A pink covered with white little buttons and a white tulle dress, and dresses, dresses, dresses!

SARA: And here are hats, and hats, and hats. Becky, can you see? (*rise*)

BECKY: Oh, yes, Miss, and it's like 'eaven. (*falls off stool backwards*)

SARA: (*rises*) She is a lovely doll. (*looking at doll*) Suppose she understands human talk, and feels proud of being admired.

LAVINIA: (*up* R. *of table*) You are always *supposing* things, Sara.

SARA: I know I am—I like it. There's nothing so nice as supposing. It's almost like being a fairy. If you suppose anything hard enough, it seems as if it were real. Have you never done it?

LAVINIA: (*contemptuously*) No—of course not—it's ridiculous.

SARA: Is it? Well, it makes you happy at any rate. (LAVINIA *turns away; changing her tone*) Suppose we finish looking at the doll's things when we have more time. Becky will put them back in the trunk. (LOTTIE *goes up to doll. Bus. with tiara*)

BECKY: (L. *comes forward quickly—shyly*) Me, Miss? Yes, Miss. Thank you, Miss, for letting me touch them. (*down on knees wiping hands*) Oh—my—they are beautiful. (L. *trunk*)

LAVINIA: (*at table, catching* LOTTIE *touching doll*) Get down this minute. That's not for babies to touch. (*takes her* R.)

LOTTIE: (*crying*) I'm not a baby—I'm not—Sar-a, Sar-a—oh!

JESSIE: There now, you've made her cry, the spoiled thing.

SARA: (*runs from* L. *to* LOTTIE; *kneeling*) Now, Lottie, (*puts her on* L. *side*) Lottie, dear, you mustn't cry.

LOTTIE: (*howling*) I don't want to stay in a nasty school with nasty girls.

SARA: (*to* LAVINIA *and* JESSIE) You ought not to have scolded her. She's such a little thing. And you know she's only at boarding-school because she hasn't any mother. (*children sympathetically.* JESSIE *to door.*)

LOTTIE: (*wailing*) I haven't any mamma.

JESSIE: If she doesn't stop, Miss Minchin will hear her. (ER-MENGARDE *gets tiara from doll.*)

LILLY: And she'll be so cross that she may stop the party. Do stop, Lottie darling. I'll give you a penny.

LOTTIE: Don't want your old penny.

ERMENGARDE: Yes, do stop, and I'll give you anything. (*offering box*)

LOTTIE: She called me a baby. (*crying*)

(*Ready lights.*)

SARA: (*petting her*) But you will be a baby if you cry, Lottie, pet. There, there.

LOTTIE: I haven't any mamma.

SARA: (*cheerfully*) Yes, you have, darling. Don't you know we said that Sara'd be your mamma. Don't you want Sara to be your mamma? (LOTTIE *stops crying*) See. (*rising, giving doll to* LOTTIE) I'll lend you my doll to hold while I tell you that story I promised you.

LILLY: Oh, do tell us a story, Sara. (*puts doll* R. *on chair up.*)

JESSIE: Oh, yes, do.

CHILDREN: Oh!

SARA: I may not have time to finish it before the company comes—but I'll tell you the end some other time. (LOTTIE *takes doll to chair* R.)

LAVINIA: (C. L.) That's always the way, Princess Sara. (*passionately*) Nasty (*to* C.) little spoilt beast. I should like to *slap* her.

SARA: (*to* C. R.) (*firing up*) I should like to slap you too. But I don't want to slap you—at least I both *want* to slap you and should *like* to slap you.

CHILDREN: (*in group, interested in fight*) Oh, Oh!

SARA: We are not little gutter children. We are old enough to know better.

LAVINIA: Oh, we are *princesses,* I believe—or at least one of us is—Jessie told me you often pretended to yourself that you were a princess.

SARA: (*getting control of herself*) It's true. Sometimes I do pretend I'm a princess. I pretend I am a princess so that I can try to behave like one.

CHILDREN: Ah!

ERMENGARDE: (*down* R. C.) You *are* queer, Sara, but you're nice. (*hugs her*)

SARA: I know I'm queer, and I try to be nice. Shall I begin the story?

CHILDREN: (*ad lib.*) Story. Oh, oh! Yes, yes, begin, Sara, do.

SARA: I'm going to turn all the lights out. It's always so much nicer to tell a story by firelight. (*turns out brackets with switch above fireplace* R. *gets on sofa* R. *for story. All the children sit, except* LAVINIA, *who stands near the piano. Children on the floor in front of the sofa.* ERMENGARDE *goes up to the window and pulls curtains apart and makes up for ghost with lace curtains.*)

LILLY: It's such fun to sit in the dark.

SARA: Once upon a time—

ERMENGARDE: (*from behind curtain*) Woo-o-oo——

JESSIE: What's that?

SARA: It's nothing but the wind. Once upon a time——

ERMENGARDE: (*coming down in curtains*) Whoo-oo-oo-oopee—(*frightens children.* SARA *turns on lights. Children scream and get up, fall on* ERMENGARDE *and take curtain off her. Laugh*)

CHILDREN: Oh, it's Ermengarde.

LILLY: Begin again, Sara. (SARA *turns out lights*)

ALL: Yes.

SARA: (*all seated as before,* SARA *on sofa*) Once upon a

time—long ago—there lived on the edge of a deep, deep forest a little girl and her grandmother.[4]

LILLY: Was she pretty?

SARA: She was so fair and sweet that people called her Snowflower. She had no relations in the world but her old grandmother, Dame Frostyface.

JESSIE: Was she a nice old woman?

SARA: She was always nice to Snowflower. They lived together in a little cottage thatched with reeds. Tall trees sheltered it, daisies grew thick about the door, and swallows built in the eaves.

CHILDREN: Oh, Lottie!

LILLY: What a nice place!

SARA: One sunny morning Dame Frostyface said, "My child, I am going a long journey, and I cannot take you with me, and I will tell you what to do when you feel lonely. You know that carved oak chair I sit in by the fire. Well, lay your head on the velvet cushions and say, 'Chair of my grandmother, tell me a story,' and it will tell you one."

CHILDREN: Oh!

SARA: And if you want to travel anywhere, just seat yourself in it, and say, "Chair of my grandmother, take me where I want to go."

ERMENGARDE: Oh, I wish I had a chair like that.

LOTTIE: Oh, go on, Sara.

CHILDREN: Do go on.

ERMENGARDE: And so——

LOTTIE: And so——

SARA: And so Dame Frostyface went away. And every day Snowflower baked herself a barleycake, *and every night the chair TOLD her a beautiful new story.*

ERMENGARDE: If it had been my chair, I should have told it to take me to the King's Palace.

SARA: That is what happened—but listen. The time passed on but Dame Frostyface did not come back for such a long time that Snowflower thought she would go and find her.

LOTTIE: Did she find her?

SARA: Wait and listen. One day she jumped into the chair

and said, "Chair of my grandmother, take me the way she went." And the chair gave a creak and began to move out of the cottage and into the forest where all the birds were singing.

ERMENGARDE: How I *wish* I could have gone with her.

SARA: And the chair went on, and on, and on—like a coach and six.

LOTTIE: How far did it go?

SARA: It traveled through the forest and through the ferns, and over the velvet moss—it traveled one day, and two days, and three days—and on the fourth day——

LILLY: What did it do?

SARA: (*slowly*) It came to an open place in the forest where a hundred workmen were felling trees and a hundred wagons were carrying them away to the King's Palace.

ERMENGARDE: Was the king giving a ball?

(*Bell ready and lights.*)

SARA: He was giving seven of them. Seven days feasting to celebrate the birthday of his daughter, the Princess Greedalend.[5]

LOTTIE: Did he invite Snowflower?

SARA: Listen. The chair marched up to the palace and all the people ran after it. And the king heard of it, and the lords and ladies crowded to see it, and when the princess heard it was a chair that could tell stories she cried until the king sent an order to the little girl to come and make it tell her one.

LOTTIE: Did she go in?

LILLY: Oh, how lovely.

SARA: The chair marched in a grave and courtly manner up the grand staircase and into the palace hall. The king sat on an ivory throne in a robe of purple velvet stiff with flowers of gold. The queen sat on his right hand in a mantle clasped with pearls, and the princess wore a robe of gold sewn with diamonds.[6]

LILLY: Oh, what splendid clothes!

SARA: But Snowflower had little bare feet, and nothing but a clean, coarse linen dress. She got off the chair and made a curtsey to the grand company. Then she laid her head on the cushion, and said, "Chair of my grandmother, tell me a story," and a clear, silvery voice came out from the old velvet cushion, and said, "Listen to the story of the Christmas Cuckoo."[7] (*doorbell peals off* R.)

ALL: (*jumping up from floor and sofa, forming two lines, one* L. *and one* R., *in readiness for the visitors*) Miss Minchin is coming—Miss Minchin is coming.

(*Enter* MISS MINCHIN *first from* R. *upper followed by* AMELIA *to* C. BECKY *under table* L.)

MINCHIN: What are you naughty children doing in the dark? Amelia, turn up the lights immediately. (*she does so, switch above fireplace* R.) How dare you? (*lights up brackets and all*)

SARA: I beg pardon, Miss Minchin. It was all my fault. I was telling them a story and I like to tell them in the firelight.

MINCHIN: (*changing*) Oh, it was you, Sara. That is a different matter. I can always trust you.

LAVINIA: (*aside*) Yes, of course, if it's the Princess Sara, it's a different matter.

MISS MINCHIN: (*speaking off* R. *to* MRS. CARMICHAEL) Won't you come in, Mrs. Carmichael?

(*Enter* MRS. CARMICHAEL *followed by first,* DONALD, *then by* MAZIE, NORA *and* JANET *in a line,* DONALD *has mother's skirt in his hand, playing horse, three children are dressed for the street. They follow their mother to sofa* L. *Sit in order,* MRS. CARMICHAEL L. *and so forth. Entering from the* R. *upper door.*)

MINCHIN: She is (*referring to* SARA) such a clever child. Such an imagination. She amuses the children by the hour with her wonderful story-telling.

MRS. CARMICHAEL: She has a clever little face. (*Bus. of* ERMENGARDE *offering to make friends with* DONALD, *who fights her into* R. *corner*)

MINCHIN: Won't you sit here, Mrs. Carmichael? (*indicating sofa* R. C.)

MRS. CARMICHAEL: I hope I won't disturb the dancing if I am obliged to leave you suddenly.

MINCHIN: You will not disturb us, although we shall, of course, be very sorry.

MRS. CARMICHAEL: Mr. Carmichael has just had bad news

from an important client in India. The poor man has suddenly lost all his money and is on his way to England, very ill indeed.

MINCHIN: How distressing!

MRS. CARMICHAEL: Mr. Carmichael may be called away at any moment. He said he would send a servant for me if he received a summons to go. If it comes I shall be obliged to run away at once. The children wanted so much to see the dancing that I did not like to disappoint them.

MINCHIN: Sara, my dear, come here. (*aside to* MRS. CARMICHAEL) Her mother died when she was born. Her father is a most distinguished young officer—very rich, fortunately. (*to* SARA) Shake hands with Mrs. Carmichael. (SARA, *crosses from* L. *and does so. To* MRS. CARMICHAEL) Sara is thirteen years old to-day, Mrs. Carmichael, and is giving a party to her schoolfellows. She is always doing things to give her friends pleasure.

MRS. CARMICHAEL: (*motherly woman, pats* SARA's *hand*) She looks like a kind little girl. (LOTTIE *brings doll over to sofa, shows it to the* CARMICHAEL *children*) I'm sure my children would like to hear her tell stories. They love stories, and some day you must come and tell them one. (*turns and sees doll*) Oh, what a splendid doll! (*bus. to* SARA) Is it yours?

MINCHIN: (*grandly*) Her papa ordered it in Paris. Its wardrobe was made by a fashionable dressmaker. Nothing is too superb for the child.

LOTTIE: (*to* SARA) Sara, may that little boy hold your doll?

SARA: Yes, dear. (LOTTIE *takes doll to* DONALD, *who boxes it away from him, boy fashion*)

LOTTIE: (*taking doll out of harm's way* R.) He's one of the large family across the street—the ones you make up stories about.

MRS. CARMICHAEL: (*good-naturedly*) Do you make up stories about *us*?

SARA: I hope you won't mind. I can see your house out of my window, and there are so many of you, and you all look so happy together that I like to pretend I know you all. I *suppose* things about you.

LILLY: (*all children have been standing in two lines listening to all this*) She has made up names for all of you?

MRS. CARMICHAEL: Has she. What are they?

SARA: They are only pretended names—perhaps you'll think they're silly.

MRS. CARMICHAEL: No, I shall not. What do you call us?

LOTTIE: (R. H. *Solemnly*) You are Mrs. and Mister Mont-mor-ency.

MRS. CARMICHAEL: (*laughing*) What a grand name! And what do you call the children?

SARA: (*shy but smiling*) The little boy in the lace cap is Ethel-bert Beaucham Montmorency—and the *second* baby is Violette Cholomodyely Montmorency, and the little boy with the fat brown legs and socks is Sidney Cecil Vivienne Montmorency.

LOTTIE: (*interrupting and dancing to* C.) Then there's Lillian Evangeline—and Guy Clarence—and Maude—Marion—and Veronia Eustacia—and Claude Audrey Harold Hector. (*laughs and into* R. *corner*)

MRS. CARMICHAEL: You romantic little thing.

SARA: (*apologetically*) I shouldn't have *supposed* so much about you if you hadn't all looked so happy together. *My* papa is a soldier in India, you know, and my mamma died when I was a baby. So I like to look at children who have mammas and papas.

MRS. CARMICHAEL: (*kissing* SARA) You poor little dear, Miss Minchin *must* let you come and have tea with us.

MINCHIN: Certainly, certainly. Sara will be delighted. Now, young ladies, you may begin the entertainment Sara has pre-pared for Mrs. Carmichael.

(*Enter* MAID *from* R. U.)

MAID: A gentleman would like to see you, Ma'am. He says he comes from Messrs. Barrow & Skipworth.

MINCHIN: The lawyers? (*annoyed*) What can he want? I can-not be disturbed at present. Ask him to wait.

MAID: And if you please, Ma'am, a note for Mrs. Car-michael. (*delivers same to* MRS. CARMICHAEL *who rises to receive it and goes down stage. Exit* MAID R. U.)

MRS. CARMICHAEL: A note for me? (*takes it*) Opens note. (DONALD *bus. with* LOTTIE)

MINCHIN: Not bad news, I hope?

MRS. CARMICHAEL: Very bad, I am afraid. My husband's client, poor Mr. Carrisford, has just landed dangerously ill.

Much worse. Mr. Carmichael wants me to go and see him at once. I am so sorry to run away like this. It has all been so charming. Thank you for asking us. Come, children. Say good afternoon. Papa needs us. (*shaking hands with* MINCHIN) Your school is delightful.

(*Exit* MRS. CARMICHAEL *and children in same order as entrance,* DONALD *driving his mother as before.*)

DONALD: Geddap—whoa—go along. (*bus. ad lib.*)

ALL: Good-by. Good afternoon, etc.

MISS AMELIA: What a pity she was obliged to leave so soon. (*bus. down* C.)

MINCHIN: (C. R.) She was evidently very much pleased. (*down* R.)

MAID: (*Entering* R. U.) Will you see the gentleman from Messrs. Barrow & Skipworth, Ma'am?

MISS AMELIA: (*meekly*) The children's refreshments are laid in your parlor, sister. Could you see him in here while the children have their cake and sherry and negus?

MINCHIN: Yes. (*to children*) Now, young ladies, you must go and enjoy the nice things Sara has provided for you. (*children all troop out* 1st *entrance*)

CHILDREN: Cake and sherry and negus.

MINCHIN: (*to servant*) Bring the gentleman in here.[8]

APPENDIX C
"BEHIND THE WHITE BRICK"

Burnett's first story for children was privately written for a little girl in Knoxville, Tennessee, some five years before its publication in St. Nicholas Magazine *and nearly fifteen years before the serialization of the novella* Sara Crewe *in the same magazine. Even though Jemima, the girl who prefers to be called Jem, is an American heroine who must help in chores around the house rather than an upper-class British heiress with her own private nursemaid, her story and that of Sara Crewe are palpably similar. Both of these bookish girls are humiliated and slapped by an abusive mother surrogate who is unsympathetic to their needs; both resort to fantasy as a defense against their humiliation; both learn to curb their justifiable anger. Jem's debasement, to be sure, is of short duration: whereas Sara has to wait for years before she could wake up and find herself restored as her father's "little missus" by his Eton chum, her American counterpart is restored after an escapist dream-turned-nightmare is promptly defused by her returning mother, a girl's best friend.*

The "vulgar" anger Sara manages to subdue in each version of her story is dramatized in "Behind the White Brick" by Jem's alter ego, Baby: this irate dream child is a Lottie who will not be soothed. And there are other originals to be reworked in the later narratives: the animated Doll who squares off with Baby—so unlike the Emily doll that Sara converts into Lottie's placid "sister"—clearly engages in a combative bout of sibling rivalry; and the mild-mannered Mr. "S.C.," a Santa Claus whose existence Jem has started to question, will turn into Ram Dass, a magus whose gifts Sara will most gratefully accept. Despite its interest as an urtext for all three Sara Crewe stories, however, "Behind the White Brick" is an engaging story in its

own right. It is, in fact, a rather stunning first attempt for an au-
thor who had until then only published works intended for an
adult readership.

IT began with Aunt Hetty's being out of temper, which, it must
be confessed, was nothing new. At its best, Aunt Hetty's temper was none of the most charming, and this morning it was at
its worst. She had awakened to the consciousness of having a
hard day's work before her, and she had awakened late, and so
every thing had gone wrong from the first. There was a sharp
ring in her voice when she came to Jem's bedroom-door and
called out, "Jemima! Get up this minute!"

Jem knew what to expect when Aunt Hetty began a day by
calling her "Jemima." It was one of the poor child's grievances that
she had been given such an ugly name. In all the books she had
read, and she had read a great many, Jem never had met a heroine
who was called Jemima. But it had been her mother's favorite
sister's name, and so it had fallen to her lot. Her mother always
called her "Jem," or "Mimi," which was much prettier, and even
Aunt Hetty only reserved Jemima for unpleasant state occasions.

It was a dreadful day to Jem. Her mother was not at home
and would not be until night. She had been called away unexpectedly and had been obliged to leave Jem and the baby to
Aunt Hetty's mercies.

So Jem found herself busy enough. Scarcely had she finished
doing one thing when Aunt Hetty told her to begin another.
She wiped dishes and picked fruit and attended to the baby,[1]
and when baby had gone to sleep, and everything else seemed
disposed of, for a time at least, she was so tired that she was
glad to sit down.

And then she thought of the book she had been reading the
night before—a certain delightful story-book, about a little girl
whose name was Flora, and who was so happy and rich and pretty
and good that Jem had likened her to the little princesses one
reads about, to whose christening feast every fairy brings a gift.

"I shall have time to finish my chapter before dinner-time

comes," said Jem, and she sat down snugly in one corner of the wide old-fashioned fire-place.

But she had not read more than two pages before something dreadful happened. Aunt Hetty came into the room in a great hurry,—in such a hurry, indeed, that she caught her foot in the matting and fell, striking her elbow sharply against a chair, which so upset her temper that the moment she found herself on her feet she flew at Jem.[2]

"What!" she said, snatching the book from her, "Reading again, when I am running all over the house for you?" And she flung the pretty little blue-covered volume into the fire.

Jem sprang to rescue it with a cry, but it was impossible to reach it, it had fallen into a great hollow of red coal and the blaze caught it at once.

"You are a wicked woman!" cried Jem, in a dreadful passion, to Aunt Hetty. "You are a wicked woman."

Then matters reached a climax. Aunt Hetty boxed her ears, pushed her back on her little foot-stool, and walked out of the room.

Jem hid her face on her arms and cried as if her heart would break. She cried until her eyes were heavy, and she thought she should be obliged to go to sleep. But just as she was thinking of going to sleep, something fell down the chimney and made her look up. It was a piece of mortar, and it brought a great deal of soot with it. She bent forward and looked up to see where it had come from. The chimney was so very wide that this was easy enough. She could see where the mortar had fallen from the side and left a white patch.

"How white it looks against the black!" said Jem. "It is like a white brick among the black ones. What a queer place a chimney is! I can see a bit of the blue sky, I think."

And then a funny thought came into her fanciful little head. What a many things were burned in the big fire-place, and vanished in smoke or tinder up the chimney! Where did everything go? There was Flora, for instance,—Flora who was represented on the frontispiece,—with lovely, soft flowing hair, and a little fringe on her pretty round forehead, crowned with a circlet of daisies, and a laugh in her wide-awake round eyes. Where was she by this time? Certainly there was nothing left of her in the fire. Jem almost began to cry again at the thought.

"It was too bad," she said. "She was so pretty and funny, and I did like her so!"

I dare say it scarcely will be credited by unbelieving people when I tell them what happened next, it was such a very singular thing, indeed.

Jem felt herself gradually lifted off her little foot-stool.

"Oh!" she said, timidly. "I feel very light."

She did feel light indeed. She felt so light that she was sure she was rising gently in the air.[3]

"Oh!" she said, again. "How—how very light I feel! Oh, dear! I'm going up the chimney!"

It was rather strange that she never thought of calling for help, but she did not. She was not easily frightened; and now she was only wonderfully astonished, as she remembered afterward. She shut her eyes tight and gave a little gasp.

"I've heard Aunt Hetty talk about the draught drawing things up the chimney, but I never knew it was as strong as this," she said.

She went up, up, up, quietly and steadily, and without any uncomfortable feeling at all; and then all at once she stopped, feeling that her feet rested against something solid. She opened her eyes and looked about her, and there she was, standing right opposite the white brick, her feet on a tiny ledge.

"Well," she said, "this is funny."

But the next thing that happened was funnier still. She found, that without thinking what she was doing, she was knocking on the white brick with her knuckles, as if it was a door, and she expected somebody to open it. The next minute she heard footsteps, and then a sound as if some one was drawing back a little bolt.

"It is a door," said Jem, "and somebody is going to open it."

The white brick moved a little, and some more mortar and soot fell, then the brick moved a little more, and then it slid aside and left an open space.

"It's a room!" cried Jem. "There's a room behind it."

And so there was, and before the open space stood a pretty little girl, with long lovely hair, and a fringe on her forehead!

Jem clasped her hands in amazement. It was Flora, herself, as she looked in the picture, and Flora stood laughing and nodding.

"Come in!" she said. "I thought it was you."

"But how can I come in through such a little place?" asked Jem.[4]

"Oh, that is easy enough," said Flora. "Here, give me your hand."

Jem did as she told her, and found that it was easy enough. In an instant she had passed through the opening, the white brick had gone back to its place, and she was standing by Flora's side in a large room—the nicest room she had ever seen. It was big and lofty and light, and there were all kinds of delightful things in it,—books, and flowers, and playthings, and pictures, and in one corner a great cage full of love-birds.

"Have I ever seen it before?" asked Jem, glancing slowly round.

"Yes," said Flora, "You saw it last night—in your mind. Don't you remember it?"

Jem shook her head.

"I feel as if I did, but——"

"Why," said Flora, laughing, "it's my room, the one you read about last night."

"So it is," said Jem. "But how did you come here?"

"I can't tell you that; I myself don't know, but I am here, and so," rather mysteriously, "are a great many other things."

"Are they?" said Jem, very much interested. "What things? Burned things? I was just wondering——"

"Not only burned things," said Flora, nodding. "Just come with me and I'll show you something."

She led the way out of the room and down a little passage with several doors in each side of it, and she opened one door and showed Jem what was on the other side of it. That was a room, too, and this time it was funny as well as pretty. Both floor and walls were padded with rose color, and the floor was strewn with toys. There were big soft balls, rattles, horses, woolly dogs, and a doll or so; there was one low cushioned chair, and a low table.

"You can come in," said a shrill little voice behind the door. "Only mind you don't tread on things."

"What a funny little voice!" said Jem, but she had no sooner said it than she jumped back.

The owner of the voice who had just come forward was no other than Baby.

"Why," exclaimed Jem, beginning to feel frightened. "I left you fast asleep in your crib."

"Did you?" said Baby, somewhat scornfully.

"That's just the way with you grown-up people. You think you know everything, and yet you haven't discretion enough to know when a pin is sticking into one. You'd know soon enough if you had one sticking into your own back."

"But I'm not grown up," stammered Jem, "and when you are at home you can neither walk nor talk: you're not six months old!"

"Well, Miss," retorted Baby, whose wrongs seemed to have soured her disposition somewhat, "you have no need to throw that in my teeth; you were not six months old, either, when you were my age."

Jem could not help laughing.

"You haven't got any teeth!" she said.

"Haven't I?" said Baby, and she displayed two beautiful rows with some haughtiness of manner. "When I am up here," she said, "I am supplied with the modern conveniences, and that's why I never complain. Do I ever cry when I am asleep? It's not falling asleep I object to, it's falling awake."

"Wait a minute," said Jem. "Are you asleep now?"

"I'm what you call asleep. I can only come here when I'm what you call asleep. Asleep, indeed! It's no wonder we always cry when we have to fall awake."

"But we don't mean to be unkind to you," protested Jem, meekly.

She could not help thinking Baby was very severe.

"Don't mean!" said Baby. "Well, why don't you think more, then? How would you like to have all the nice things snatched away from you, and all the old rubbish packed off on you as if you hadn't any sense? How would you like to have to sit and stare at things you wanted, and not be able to reach them, or if you did reach them, have them fall out of your hand, and roll away in the most unfeeling manner? And then be scolded and called 'cross'! It's no wonder we are bald. You'd be bald yourself. It's trouble and worry that keep us bald until we can begin to take care of ourselves. I had more hair than this at first, but it fell off, as well it might. No philosopher ever thought of that, I suppose!"

"Well," said Jem, in despair, "I hope you enjoy yourself when you are here?"

"Yes, I do," answered Baby. "That's one comfort. There is nothing to knock my head against, and things have patent stoppers on them, so that they can't roll away, and everything is soft and easy to pick up."

There was a slight pause after this, and Baby seemed to cool down.

"I suppose you would like me to show you round," she said.

"Not if you have any objection," replied Jem, who was rather subdued.

"I would as soon do it as not," said Baby. "You are not as bad as some people, though you do get my clothes twisted when you hold me."

Upon the whole, she seemed rather proud of her position. It was evident she quite regarded herself as hostess. She held her small bald head very high indeed, as she trotted on before them. She stopped at the first door she came to, and knocked three times. She was obliged to stand upon tiptoe to reach the knocker.

"He's sure to be at home at this time of year," she remarked. "This is the busy season."

"Who's 'he'?" inquired Jem.

But Flora only laughed at Miss Baby's consequential air.

"S.C., to be sure," was the answer, as the young lady pointed to the door-plate, upon which Jem noticed, for the first time, "S.C." in very large letters.[5]

The door opened, apparently without assistance, and they entered the apartment.

"Good gracious!" exclaimed Jem, the next minute. "Good-*ness* gracious!"

She might well be astonished. It was such a long room that she could not see to the end of it, and it was piled from floor to ceiling with toys of every description, and there was such bustle and buzzing in it that it was quite confusing. The bustle and buzzing arose from a very curious cause, too,—it was the bustle and buzz of hundreds of tiny men and women who were working at little tables no higher than mushrooms,—the pretty tiny women cutting out and sewing, the pretty tiny men sawing and hammering, and all talking at once. The principal person in the place escaped Jem's notice at first; but it was not long before she saw him,—a little old gentleman, with a rosy face and sparkling eyes, sitting at a desk, and writing in a book almost as big as himself. He was so busy that he was quite excited, and had been obliged to throw his white fur coat and cap aside, and he was at work in his red waistcoat.

"Look here, if you please," piped Baby. "I have brought some one to see you."

When he turned round, Jem recognized him at once.

"Eh! Eh!" he said. "What! What! Who's this, Tootsicums?"

Baby's manner became very acid indeed.

"I shouldn't have thought you would have said that, Mr. Claus," she remarked. "I can't help myself down below, but I generally have my rights respected up here. I should like to know what same godfather and godmother would give one the name of 'Tootsicums' in one's baptism. They are bad enough, I must say; but I never heard of any of them calling a person 'Tootsicums.' "

"Come, come!" said S.C., chuckling comfortably, and rubbing his hands. "Don't be too dignified,—it's a bad thing. And don't be too practical and fond of taking unpractical people down,—that's a bad thing, too. And don't be too fond of flourishing your rights in people's faces,—that's the worst of all, Miss Midget. Folks who make such a fuss about their rights turn them into wrongs sometimes."

Then he turned suddenly to Jem.

"You are the little girl from down below," he said.

"Yes, sir," answered Jem. "I'm Jem, and this is my friend Flora,—out of the blue-book."

"I'm happy to make her acquaintance," said S.C., "and I'm happy to make yours. You are a nice child, though a trifle peppery. I'm very glad to see you."

"I'm very glad indeed to see you, sir," said Jem. "I wasn't quite sure——"

But there she stopped, feeling that it would be scarcely polite to tell him that she had begun of late years to lose faith in him.

But S.C. only chuckled more comfortably than ever, and rubbed his hands again.

"Ho, ho!" he said. "You know who I am, then."

Jem hesitated a moment, wondering whether it would not be taking a liberty to mention his name without putting "Mr." before it; then she remembered what Baby had called him.

"Baby called you 'Mr. Claus,' sir," she replied; "and I have seen pictures of you."

"To be sure," said S.C. "S. Claus, Esquire, of Chimneyland. How do you like me?"

"Very much," answered Jem. "Very much, indeed, sir."

"Glad of it! Glad of it! But what was it you were going to say you were not quite sure of?"

Jem blushed a little.

"I was not quite sure that—that you were true, sir. At least I have not been quite sure since I have been older."

S.C. rubbed the bald part of his head and gave a little sigh.

"I hope I have not hurt your feelings, sir," faltered Jem, who was a very kind-hearted little soul.

"Well, no," said S.C. "Not exactly. And it is not your fault either. It is natural, I suppose; at any rate, it is the way of the world. People lose their belief in a great many things as they grow older; but that does not make the things not true, thank goodness; and their faith often comes back after a while. But, bless me!" he added briskly, "I'm moralizing, and who thanks a man for doing that? Suppose——"

"Black eyes or blue, sir?" said a tiny voice close to them.

Jem and Flora turned round, and saw it was one of the small workers who was asking the question.

"Whom for?" inquired S.C.

"Little girl in the red brick house at the corner," said the workwoman; "name of Birdie."[6]

"Excuse me a moment," said S.C. to the children, and he turned to the big book and began to run his fingers down the pages in a business-like manner. "Ah! here she is!" he exclaimed at last. "Blue eyes, if you please, Thistle, and golden hair. And let it be a big one. She takes good care of them."

"Yes, sir," said Thistle; "I am personally acquainted with

several dolls in her family. I go to parties in her dolls' house sometimes when she is fast asleep at night, and they all speak very highly of her. She is most attentive to them when they are ill. In fact, her pet doll is a cripple, with a stiff leg."

She ran back to her work, and S.C. finished his sentence.

"Suppose I show you my establishment," he said. "Come with me."

It really would be quite impossible to describe the wonderful things he showed them. Jem's head was quite in a whirl before she had seen one-half of them, and even Baby condescended to become excited.

"There must be a great many children in the world, Mr. Claus," ventured Jem.

"Yes, yes, millions of 'em; bless 'em," said S.C., growing rosier with delight at the very thought. "We never run out of them, that's one comfort. There's a large and varied assortment always on hand. Fresh ones every year, too, so that when one grows too old there is a new one ready. I have a place like this in every twelfth chimney. Now it's boys, now it's girls, always one or t'other; and there's no end of playthings for them, too, I'm glad to say. For girls, the great thing seems to be dolls. Blitzen! what comfort they *do* take in dolls! but the boys are for horses and racket."

They were standing near a table where a worker was just putting the finishing touch to the dress of a large wax doll, and just at that moment, to Jem's surprise, she set it on the floor, upon its feet, quite coolly.

"Thank you," said the Doll, politely.

Jem quite jumped.

"You can join the rest now and introduce yourself," said the worker.

The Doll looked over her shoulder at her train.

"It hangs very nicely," she said. "I hope it's the latest fashion."

"Mine never talked like that," said Flora. "My best one could only say 'Mamma,' and it said it very badly, too."

"She was foolish for saying it at all," remarked the Doll, haughtily. "We don't talk and walk before ordinary people; we keep our accomplishments for our own amusement, and for the amusement of our friends. If you should chance to get up in the middle of the night, some time, or should run into the room suddenly some day, after you have left it, you might hear—but what is the use of talking to human beings?"[7]

"You know a great deal, considering you are only just finished," snapped Baby, who really was a Tartar.

"I was FINISHED," retorted the Doll. "I did not begin life as a Baby!" very scornfully.

"Pooh!" said Baby. "We improve as we get older."

"I hope so, indeed," answered the Doll. "There is plenty of room for improvement." And she walked away in great state.

S.C. looked at Baby and then shook his head.

"I shall not have to take very much care of you," he said, absent-mindedly. "You are able to take pretty good care of yourself."

"I hope I am," said Baby, tossing her head.

S.C. gave his head another shake.

"Don't take too good care of yourself," he said. "That's a bad thing, too."

He showed them the rest of his wonders, and then went with them to the door to bid them good-bye.

"I am sure we are very much obliged to you, Mr. Claus," said Jem, gratefully. "I shall never again think you are not true, sir."

S.C. patted her shoulder quite affectionately.

"That's right," he said. "Believe in things just as long as you can, my dear. Good-bye until Christmas Eve. I shall see you then, if you don't see me."

He must have taken quite a fancy to Jem, for he stood looking at her, and seemed very reluctant to close the door, and even after he had closed it, and they had turned away, he opened it a little again to call to her.[8]

"Believe in things as long as you can, my dear."

"How kind he is!" exclaimed Jem, full of pleasure.

Baby shrugged her shoulders.

"Well enough in his way," she said, "but rather inclined to prose and be old-fashioned."

Jem looked at her, feeling rather frightened, but she said nothing.

Baby showed very little interest in the next room she took them to.

"I don't care about this place," she said, as she threw open the door. "It has nothing but old things in it. It is the Nobody-knows-where room."

She had scarcely finished speaking before Jem made a little spring and picked something up.

"Here's my old strawberry pincushion!" she cried out. And then, with another jump and another dash at two or three other things, "And here's my old fairy-book! And here's my little locket I lost last summer! How did they come here?"

"They went Nobody-knows-where," said Baby.

"And this is it."

"But cannot I have them again?" asked Jem.

"No," answered Baby. "Things that go to Nobody-knows-where stay there."

"Oh!" sighed Jem, "I am so sorry."

"They are only old things," said Baby.

"But I like my old things," said Jem. "I love them. And there is mother's needle case. I wish I might take that. Her dead little sister gave it to her, and she was so sorry when she lost it."

"People ought to take better care of their things," remarked Baby.

Jem would have liked to stay in this room and wander about among her old favourites for a long time, but Baby was in a hurry.

"You'd better come away," she said. "Suppose I was to have to fall awake and leave you?"

The next place they went into was the most wonderful of all.

"This is the Wish room," said Baby. "Your wishes come here—yours and mother's and Aunt Hetty's and father's and mine. When did you wish that?"

Each article was placed under a glass shade, and labeled with the words and name of the wishes. Some of them were beautiful, indeed; but the tall shade Baby nodded at when she asked her question was truly alarming, and caused Jem a dreadful pang of remorse. Underneath it sat Aunt Hetty, with her mouth stitched up so that she could not speak a word, and beneath the stand was a label bearing these words, in large black letters:

"I wish Aunt Hetty's mouth was sewed up. Jem."

"Oh, dear!" cried Jem, in great distress. "How it must have hurt her! How unkind of me to say it! I wish I hadn't wished it. I wish it would come undone."

She had no sooner said it than her wish was gratified. The old label disappeared and a new one showed itself, and there sat Aunt Hetty, looking herself again, and even smiling.

Jem was grateful beyond measure, but Baby seemed to consider her weak minded.

"It served her right," she said.

But when, after looking at the wishes at that end of the room, they went to the other end, her turn came. In one corner stood a shade with a baby under it, and the baby was Miss Baby herself, but looking as she very rarely looked; in fact, it was the brightest, best tempered baby one could imagine.

"I wish I had a better tempered baby. Mother," was written on the label.

Baby became quite red in the face with anger and confusion.

"That wasn't here the last time I came," she said. "And it is right down mean in mother!"

This was more than Jem could bear.

"It wasn't mean," she said. "She couldn't help it. You know you are a cross baby—everybody says so."

Baby turned two shades redder.

"Mind your own business," she retorted. "It was mean; and as to that silly little thing being better than I am," turning up her small nose, which was quite turned up enough by Nature—"I must say I don't see anything so very grand about her. So, there!"

She scarcely condescended to speak to them while they remained in the Wish room, and when they left it, and went to the last door in the passage, she quite scowled at it.

"I don't know whether I shall open it at all," she said.

"Why not?" asked Flora. "You might as well."

"It is the Lost Pin room," she said. "I hate pins."

She threw the door open with a bang, and then stood and

shook her little fist viciously. The room was full of pins, stacked solidly together. There were hundreds of them—thousands—millions, it seemed.

"I'm glad they *are* lost!" she said. "I wish there were more of them there."

"I didn't know there were so many pins in the world," said Jem.

"Pooh!" said Baby. "Those are only the lost ones that have belonged to our family."

After this they went back to Flora's room and sat down, while Flora told Jem the rest of her story.

"Oh!" sighed Jem, when she came to the end. "How delightful it is to be here! Can I never come again?"

"In one way you can," said Flora. "When you want to come, just sit down, and be as quiet as possible, and shut your eyes and think very hard about it. You can see everything you have seen to-day, if you try."

"Then, I shall be sure to try," Jem answered. She was going to ask some other question but Baby stopped her.

"Oh! I'm falling awake," she whimpered, crossly, rubbing her eyes. "I'm falling awake again."

And then, suddenly, a very strange feeling came over Jem. Flora and the pretty room seemed to fade away, and, without being able to account for it at all, she found herself sitting on her little stool again, with a beautiful scarlet and gold book on her knee, and her mother standing by laughing at her amazed face. As to Miss Baby, she was crying as hard as she could in her crib.

"Mother!" Jem cried out. "Have you really come home so early as this, and—and," rubbing her eyes in great amazement, "how did I come down."

"Don't I look as if I was real," said her mother, laughing and kissing her. "And doesn't your present look real? I don't know how you came down, I'm sure. Where have you been?"

Jem shook her head very mysteriously. She saw that her mother fancied she had been asleep, but she herself knew better.

"I know you wouldn't believe it was true if I told you," she said; "I have been

BEHIND THE WHITE BRICK."

EXPLANATORY NOTES

CHAPTER I

1. *odd-looking little girl . . . the big thoroughfares:* See Appendix A for a totally different opening: the focus here is on the uniqueness of an "odd-looking" Sara, not on her dismal surroundings.

2. *Sara:* The change from "Sarai" (quarrelsome) to "Sarah" (the princess) recorded in the Hebrew Bible carries a special poignancy for the naming of a heroine too dignified to give in to her anger.

3. *Lascars:* The North Indian "lash-kar" was used by the British as a term for Indian sailors as well as soldiers; in *Sara Crewe,* Ram Dass was simply known as "the Lascar."

4. *ayah:* An Indian nursemaid or governess.

5. *Miss Minchin:* The headmistress's name is derived from that of a character in Juliana Horatia Ewing's *From Six to Sixteen* (1875), a novel that also featured an Anglo-Indian girl's English acculturation. Ewing's friendly and generous Mrs. Minchin, however, hardly resembles her mincing and penny-pinching namesake.

6. *"Lady Meredith":* Given the later claim that Sara has no British relatives or acquaintances, it seems curious that both Miss Minchin and Burnett should forget this personal connection.

7. *"Emily":* Sara's choice of name for her doll will become clearer (see note 5 for chapter IV and note 3 for chapter X); notice, however, that Burnett has just alerted us that this child is an avid reader of "grown-up books."

8. *"she wasn't a doll really":* Burnett's own interest in animating dolls is evident in "Behind the White Brick," reprinted in Appendix C, as well as in her 1906–1907 "Racketty-Packetty House," a story about the inhabitants of a dollhouse that was staged by the New York Children's Theater in 1912 with a cast of child actors.

9. *Miss Amelia:* Following the precedent set in Henry Fielding's *Amelia,* Victorian writers such as William Thackeray and George Eliot gave this name to sentimental figures; see the Introduction for a fuller explanation of the Thackerayan resonances involved.

10. *"Valenciennes lace":* The town in northern France is still noted for producing bobbin lace with a distinctive pattern of flowers against a diamond mesh.

CHAPTER II

1. *Lavinia . . . Lottie Legh:* Whereas "Lavinia" is a pseudo-aristocratic, Latinate name favored, according to Yonge, by "those classes in England who have a taste for many syllables ending in *ia*," little Charlotte's surname has more authentic native and rural origins: like "Leigh" or "Lee," it was a term used to designate both places of pasture and spaces of shelter for livestock.
2. *Mariette:* The French diminutive originated when statuettes of the Virgin Mary were called "mariettes" or "marionettes."
3. *"little feet":* The allusion to "Cinderella" becomes even more overt in the next paragraph's discussion of "slippers" and the maternal advice on how to disguise big feet; Lavinia and Jessie will hereafter play the role assigned to Cinderella's older sisters in both Perrault's and the Grimm Brothers' version of the fairy tale.
4. *pretending:* The echoes of Lewis Carroll's *Through the Looking-Glass* are unmistakable here: Alice, whose favorite phrase is "Let's pretend," wishes that the purring Black Kitty might talk back to her; see also notes 8 and 9 for chapter XV.
5. *"Comme elle est drôle!":* "How whimsical she is!"
6. *"Elle . . . petite":* "She has the bearing of a princess, this little one."
7. *a Frenchwoman:* Sara's cosmopolitanism is one of the many links between her and Thackeray's precocious Becky Sharp, who speaks French "with purity and a Parisian accent" derived from her dead mother, "a young woman of the French nation."
8. *did not speak French herself:* See *Vanity Fair,* chapter 1: "Miss Pinkerton did not understand French; she only directed those who did." As explained in the Introduction to this edition, Burnett now cleverly recasts the scene in which Becky Sharp severely embarrasses Miss Pinkerton, the headmistress who already misjudged her rival's maturity when she presented a doll to a girl who has "been a woman since she was eight years old."

CHAPTER III

1. *"always wants to fight":* The pugnacious Frances Hodgson Burnett often described herself in military terms: the aftermath of a fierce weeding, she claimed in her last book, *In the Garden* (1925), made her "go away feeling like an army with banners."

2. *Miss St. John . . . in a window-seat:* Charlotte Brontë's Jane is similarly sequestered at the opening of *Jane Eyre.* Later she is made to feel deficient by her stern cousin St. John Rivers, who not only teaches her German but also wants her to learn Hindustani.

3. *Ermengarde:* The passive child Burnett repeatedly describes as "stupid" is the bearer of a name given to Teutonic women warriors ("universal guard") that ironically clashes with her unguarded behavior; in the stage play, however, Ermengarde was given a much more active role as a prankster and the determined opponent of Lavinia and Jessie.

4. *Mr. St. John:* See note 2, above: Ermengarde's demanding and "clever" father is as unsympathetic a taskmaster as Brontë's St. John.

CHAPTER IV

1. *next two years:* All previous editions retained the misprint "next ten years."

2. *howling, furious child:* Sara's taming of the screaming Lottie bears contrasting to "A Tantrum," chapter 17 of *The Secret Garden,* in which Mary Lennox uses rather different tactics to subdue the hysterical Colin Craven.

3. *"lean . . . look down . . . and smile":* An echo of Dante Gabriel Rossetti's poem "The Blessed Damozel."

4. *"I will be your mamma":* As noted in the Introduction, this is another evocation of Thackeray's *Vanity Fair,* where the little orphan Laura overcomes her separation anxieties by proclaiming that she will call Amelia her "mamma."

5. *"And Emily shall be your sister":* See note 4 for chapter XIX: with Emily as designated sister of a Charlotte, only an Anne is needed to complete the sororal Brontë trio.

CHAPTER V

1. *Of course. . . . was one or not:* See the Introduction's discussion of this chapter.

2. *its . . . its . . . it . . . it:* The depersonalization resembles that of the waif Heathcliff, repeatedly called an "it" when first introduced in *Wuthering Heights.*

3. *sweep up the ashes:* Becky's lowly status anticipates the Cinderella role in store for Sara.

4. *a Prince Merman:* Since Sara, according to her father, reads "poets, and all sorts of things," she probably is familiar with Matthew

Arnold's "The Forsaken Merman," a poem that inverts Hans Christian Andersen's emphasis on a mermaid deserted by a human male lover.

5. *"Revelation. . . . fairy stories?"*: Sara's contention that fairy tales are compatible with spiritual narratives is in keeping with the ideas and practices of George MacDonald, whom Burnett had met and whose work she admired.

6. *ill-used heroine:* See note 3 for chapter VIII.

7. *Sleeping Beauty:* Like "Cinderella," this Perrault fairy tale will become more applicable to Sara's situation than to Becky's.

8. *"arst"*: Ask.

9. *"imperence"*: Impertinence.

10. *"orter"*: Ought to.

CHAPTER VI

1. *the "Arabian Nights"*: Specifically, the story of "Sindbad the Sailor," recalled at a boy's school in Thackeray's *Vanity Fair* and also fondly remembered at the opening of John Ruskin's *Ethics of the Dust* (1866) by schoolgirls who are then asked to regard the hardened gems strewn in the Valley of Diamonds as lesser than the fluid "diamonds covering the grass in showers every morning"; see also note 2 for chapter XIV.

2. *strange, dark men:* The bookish Sara may associate these "enchanting" exotics with goblin miners such as those George MacDonald featured in *The Princess and the Goblin* (1870–71); but the more reality-oriented Burnett hints at the plight of native workers in the diamond mines of either South Africa or, more likely, India.

3. *curled herself up in the window-seat . . . began to read:* See note 2 for chapter III; Jane Eyre's absorption in a book was rudely interrupted by her abusive cousin John Reed.

4. *"It makes me feel as if some one had hit me"*: A recollection of *Jane Eyre* as well as of Burnett's own "Behind the White Brick," where Jem, deeply absorbed in her reading, is first disturbed and then slapped by her Aunt Hetty.

5. *Lavinia commanded:* In the stage version, Lavinia identifies herself even more overtly with Miss Minchin's harsh authoritarianism; Jessie, by way of contrast, imitates the softer Miss Amelia.

6. *"Watts or Coleridge"*: Isaac Watts's *Divine Songs for Children* (1715), parodied by Lewis Carroll, was still reprinted in the nineteenth century; Coleridge's more fantastic "Christabel" and "Rime

of the Ancient Mariner" also found their way into poetry anthologies for children.

7. *forms:* Long benches without a back, used for seats in the classroom.

CHAPTER VII

1. *"James. . . . Emma":* The names of the "man-servant" and "housemaid" mentioned before.
2. *machines:* Carlyle, Marx, Ruskin, and Morris had all attacked the dehumanization of workers.
3. *"a little pauper":* See note 5 below.
4. *"she hasn't a relation in the world":* Yet see note 6 for chapter I.
5. *"pore princess . . . drove into the world":* As princess-turned-pauperess, Sara embodies the identity exchange undergone by royal characters in both George MacDonald's "The Wise Woman" (1874) and Mark Twain's *The Prince and the Pauper* (1882); at one point in her career, Burnett entertained the idea of collaborating with Twain on a book.
6. *"take it away":* Compare with Sara's earlier refusal to part with Emily ("I will not put her down").
7. *"You are like Becky. . . . You are a sharp child":* As the Introduction notes, the sharp Sara is really neither like the scullery maid nor like Thackeray's heartless Becky Sharp.
8. *"just the same . . . just two little girls":* Sara's well-meant analogy is faulty, given the gap in age as well as in education: puberty separates her from the fourteen-year-old Becky.

CHAPTER VIII

1. *wild, unchildlike:* The association of her attic confinement with unrestraint and potential insanity (as well as with the unnerving animal sounds Sara soon hears) links her plight to that of Bertha Mason, the "strange wild animal" caged in the attic at Thornfield (*Jane Eyre,* chapter 26).
2. *"begin to drop my h's . . . six wives":* In her fear of "forgetting" her middle-class education, Sara resembles the Wonderland Alice's attempts to recall the school learning she has received.
3. *"ill-used heroine":* Sara's earlier term for Becky (see note 6 for chapter V).
4. *"Soldiers . . . war":* See note 1 for chapter III.
5. *"Count of Monte Cristo . . . Bastille":* Sara here pairs the dungeon

that holds the falsely accused Edmond Dantès in Alexandre Dumas's 1844 novel with the Parisian prison to which the equally innocent Charles Darnay is sent in Dickens's *Tale of Two Cities* (1859).

CHAPTER IX

1. *almost as if she were a sparrow herself:* Sara's empathy with the sparrow will be carried a step further when Mary Lennox and the robin commune in *The Secret Garden*.
2. *"almost like a nest in a tree":* Another attempt to "naturalize" the urban setting and bring the outdoors inside a room; Burnett rejects the fairy-tale conventions (employed by writers from George MacDonald to Maurice Sendak) that would have transported a confined child traveler into actual or imaginary forests.
3. *a gray-whiskered dwarf:* In Perrault's "Cendrillon," Cinderella chooses a rat that her godmother then converts into a coachman with "the finest whiskers ever seen."
4. *I do not know:* A rare authorial intervention.
5. *"Melchisedec":* In a letter reprinted by Elizabeth Gaskell in *The Life of Charlotte Brontë* (1857), a young Brontë wrote to Wordsworth about the difficulties of relinquishing her childhood fantasizings: "It is very edifying and profitable to create a world out of your own brains, and people it with inhabitants who are so many Melchisedecs, and have no father or mother but your own imagination" (chapter 9). For Burnett, who knew Gaskell's biography, the letter would have held a special meaning in recording a still unpublished writer's despair about her future career. Like the Brontë sisters, Sara draws on her childhood readings and imaginings to find romance and relation in the everyday world. She gives an ordinary rat the name of a biblical figure (*malkhi-tzedek* means "king of righteousness" in Hebrew) valued for befriending Abraham and Sarah yet reputed to have had neither ancestors nor descendants (Genesis 14:18).
6. *"my rat":* Sara's appropriation of Melchisedec places her in the company of Jo March in Louisa May Alcott's *Little Women* (1868); Jo's creativity is abetted by the pet rat who is her garret companion.
7. *"You are a story—I am a story":* Sara's insistence echoes the Cheshire Cat's notion that Alice is as chimerical as he: "We are all mad. I am mad. You are mad."

CHAPTER X

1. *She called them the Montmorencys:* In *Vanity Fair,* Becky Sharp invents an aristocratic Montmorenci lineage for herself. But Sara's droll assignation of names to members of the Large Family is actually Dickensian: in *Our Mutual Friend* (1865), a ballad seller called Silas Wegg affixes imaginary names to the wealthy residents of a nearby house.

2. *One evening a very funny thing happened:* The ensuing account of Sara's relations with the Large Family was added only after the stage version had given the Carmichael children major roles to play. By way of contrast, the novella *Sara Crewe* had swiftly moved from the list of names to the Indian Gentleman, awkwardly introduced in the same light tone: "Next door to the Large Family lived the Maiden Lady, who had a companion, and two parrots, and a King Charles spaniel, but Sara was not so very fond of her, because she did nothing in particular but talk to the parrots and drive out with the spaniel. The most interesting person of all lived next to Miss Minchin herself. Sara called him the Indian Gentleman. He was an elderly gentleman who was said to have lived in the East Indies, and to be immensely rich and to have something the matter with his liver,—in fact it had been rumored that he had no liver at all, and was much inconvenienced by the fact. At any rate, he was rather yellow and he did not look happy."

3. *"more like me than I am":* In chapter 9 of Emily Brontë's *Wuthering Heights* (1847), Catherine Earnshaw describes her relationship to Heathcliff: "He's more myself than I am."

4. *"a nice head":* A fascination with heads severed from the lower body persists in Sara's accounts of the decapitated Marie Antoinette and the Princesse de Lamballe; but it also prepares us to regard Ram Dass, whose head materializes in the next chapter, as a desexualized male friend who plays a role akin to that of Alice's sole Wonderland ally, the Cheshire Cat, whose head could not be cut off, since "there was [no] body to cut it off from" (*Alice in Wonderland,* chapter 8).

5. *"a trac":* Religious tracts were distributed or sold by Victorian proselytizers.

6. *" 'Non, monsieur . . . de mon oncle' ":* "No, sir. I do not have my uncle's penknife."

CHAPTER XI

1. *chrysoprase-green:* A golden-green color (named after a beryl-like precious stone).

2. *floods of molten gold:* Burnett here follows the practice of John Ruskin and George MacDonald, writers noted for using religious imagery to gild a "natural" scene with a supernatural aura: see, for instance, the conclusions to Ruskin's *The King of the Golden River* and to MacDonald's *The Light Princess*.

3. *"a Lascar":* See note 3 for chapter I.

4. *Ram Dass:* Rudyard Kipling had used this name for characters in his 1888 short stories "By Word of Mouth" and "Gemini." As an idealized figure, however, whose first name is derived from "Rama" (an incarnation of the Hindu god Vishnu), Sara's savior comes closer to Kipling's characterization of Sir Purun Dass in the "The Miracle of Purun Bhagat" in the second *Jungle Book* (1895). Burnett and Kipling were both contributors to *St. Nicholas Magazine* and greatly respected each other's work.

5. *ears boxed . . . neatherd:* Burnett here applies to Sara the familiar anecdote about the medieval English king (849–99) who, disguised as a commoner and engrossed in plans to defend his country against Danish invaders, was slapped by a cowherd's wife for having neglected the baking she had asked him to supervise. The story was retold in countless nineteenth-century children's books and magazines.

CHAPTER XII

1. *"Edward the Third . . . lampreys":* The next-to-last Plantagenet king ascended the throne in 1327 and ruled for fifty years; overeating reputedly contributed to the death of monarchs such as Henry VIII, who relished generous helpings of rich, eel-like lampreys.

2. *brain-fever:* In late Victorian fiction, this term was used to denominate what we would now call a "nervous breakdown."

3. *able to speak anything but Hindustani:* A contradiction, since Ram Dass later speaks fluent English when he talks to Carrisford's secretary and to Becky; he has also understood every word he overheard in Sara's soliloquies and in her conversations with Lottie, Ermengarde, and Becky.

4. *"a shrewd, worldly Frenchwoman":* Madame Pascal seems based on Madame Beck, the headmistress of a school for girls in Charlotte Brontë's *Villette* (1853); although devious and almost as self-interested as Miss Minchin, this figure is admired by Lucy Snowe, the novel's narrator, for her managerial skills and independence.

5. *"remember nothing":* The 1939 film version, starring Shirley Temple, gives Carrisford's amnesia to Sara's absent but living father.

CHAPTER XIII

1. *if you will believe me:* See note 4 for chapter IX.
2. *to "move on":* In *Bleak House* (1852–53), Dickens's portrait of Jo, the exhausted street child whom policemen perpetually order to "move on," became a Victorian icon for the pathos of the urban homeless.
3. *brougham:* A closed, four-wheeled carriage, usually drawn by one horse and driven by an outside coachman; *portmanteau:* a suitcase or clothes bag that opens into two compartments.
4. *drosky:* A roofless, four-wheeled Russian carriage.
5. *muzhiks:* Peasants in Czarist Russia.

CHAPTER XIV

1. *"the little friend of all things":* The boy hero of Kipling's *Kim,* an Anglo-Indian child like Sara, is called "Little Friend of All the World" by his Hindu and Moslem admirers.
2. *"being ill and wretched . . . to amuse him":* The analogy to She-herazade, who told her tales to amuse the sick and deranged Sultan Shahryar, not only prompts the secretary's ensuing remark that Ram Dass has added one more story to the *Arabian Nights* but also contributes to the feminization of this nurturing storyteller.
3. *"His God":* As a follower of the doctrines of Sikhism, Ram Dass would reject a caste system as well as adhere to a belief in a single deity.

CHAPTER XV

1. *"Carlyle's* 'French Revolution' *":* Given her thorough grounding in French revolutionary history, it seems curious that Sara should have failed to come across the seminal 1837 book that had established Thomas Carlyle (1795–1881) as a major Victorian literary figure and had also stimulated Dickens to write *A Tale of Two Cities.*
2. *"I might suddenly fly into a rage . . . but I* couldn't *be vulgar":* Another modification of "Behind the White Brick" (reprinted in Appendix C), where Jem is forced to confront the "vulgarity" of her own angry revenge fantasies.
3. *"Robespierre":* The Jacobin leader who ordered mass beheadings was himself sent to the guillotine in 1794.
4. *"I never see her head on her body, but always on a pike":* See note 4 for chapter X; in a gory representation that would now-adays be deemed unsuitable for child readers, *The Prince and the*

Pauper depicted heads impaled on a pike in a drawing Twain caustically called " 'Object Lessons' in English History" (chapter 12).

5. *"chatelaines"*: Ladies in charge of feudal castles.

6. *"ash-barrel"*: A receptacle for household refuse as well as ashes.

7. *"flagon"*: A narrow-necked container used for beverages at medieval banquets.

8. *"There isn't any banquet left, Emily"*: The dissolution of the royal banquet in *Through the Looking Glass* had also ended the "pretends" of a girl who nonetheless still treats a nonhuman creature as a human interlocutor; but "Queen" Alice's return to an everyday reality was hardly as devastating as the hungry Princess Sara's sad admission that her powers of fantasy can no longer keep her body alive.

9. *"I can't pretend . . . while I am awake"*: Walking to her room with a piece of bread in her hands, Sara merely says "I can't pretend anything more tonight" in the corresponding scene in *Sara Crewe*; to appreciate the notable differences in Burnett's handling of "the Magic" that now follows, see the second selection in Appendix A.

10. *hob*: The protruding ledge of a fireplace was used to keep cooking utensils warm.

CHAPTER XVI

1. *"him"*: Why not "her"? The "heavenly kind person" might, after all, be a female benefactress.

2. *like a Shetland pony*: The analogy is probably borrowed from George Eliot's identical description of the disheveled young Maggie Tulliver in *The Mill on the Floss* (1860).

3. *"like a very ugly baby"*: See the description of Baby as a still "unformed" human being in "Behind the White Brick" in Appendix C.

CHAPTER XVII

1. *He was very fond of Janet*: As was Edward Rochester of the young woman he called "Janet"; by curing a self-pitying invalid, however, it is Sara rather than Janet Carmichael who is about to play Jane Eyre to Carrisford's Rochester.

2. *"the little un-fairy princess"*: For a little while this had been the title of the stage version later renamed as "The Little Princess."

3. *"Her name is Emily Carew"*: Hence, a living double for a doll Sara can only deanimate after she has found a more suitable replacement for her father.

4. *"No," said Carrisford:* Unlike the prince who allows a ragged Cinderella to try on the glass slipper, the self-mutilating Carrisford stubbornly resists the notion that a "little dark, forlorn creature" might actually be the object of his desire; despite his ineligibility as a servant and an alien, it is the "dark" Ram Dass, therefore, who far better fits the role of Sara's princely consort.

5. *salaaming:* A salaam is a low bow made with the right hand placed on the forehead.

CHAPTER XVIII

1. *It was . . . everything:* The preeminence Mrs. Carmichael now rather unexpectedly assumes can be traced back to the 1902 play, where she was introduced at the outset in the first act as a maternal foil to Miss Minchin. (See Appendix B.)

2. *"He is kind and good":* Refers to Carrisford, but since the phrasing of Sara's previous question blurs the distinction between master and servant, we are encouraged to consider Ram Dass as the true begetter of Sara's dreams. (See note 1 for chapter XIX.)

3. *solicitor:* In England, any lawyer who is not a member of the bar and hence prevented from appearing in superior courts.

4. *"Maria":* The first name seems to have been delayed as a final piece of irony: Miss Minchin has hardly been an embodiment of the merciful maternal intercessor worshiped in cathedrals all over the world. Moreover, the irony also extends to the novel's Brontëan underpinnings: Maria Brontë, the oldest sister of Charlotte, Emily, and Anne, was not only named after their mother, but also took her place until dying from cholera and malnourishment at a boarding school for girls.

5. *sal volatile:* Smelling salts.

CHAPTER XIX

1. *explained to his master:* See note 2 for chapter XVIII: By stressing his "invention," Burnett now ratifies Ram Dass as a deus ex machina akin to the pagan god who entered a maiden's dark room in the fable of Cupid and Psyche, a source for a variegated host of literary offshoots: folktales and fairy tales such as "Sleeping Beauty" and "Rose-Bud," poems such as Keats's "The Eve of St. Agnes," and even horror stories such as Bram Stoker's *Dracula*. In several Victorian adaptations of this popular myth, the role of a male invader was assumed by a female.

2. *had closed the lantern-slide:* So-called dark lanterns allowed users

to conceal the light by sliding a metal pane over one of the sides.

3. *"I can give buns and bread to the populace":* Informed that there was no bread to feed a hungry populace, Marie Antoinette had presumably remarked "Let them eat cake"; the supposedly democratic Princess Sara can now rectify her favorite queen's insensitivity.

4. *"Anne":* The final naming carries many resonances: the girl can now be identified with two other London street children of the same name: Thomas De Quincey's idealized girl prostitute Anne in *Confessions of an English Opium-Eater* (1821) and the sickly Nanny, a street sweeper in George MacDonald's *At the Back of the North Wind* (1868–69); she also bears the name of Charles Perrault's "Sister Anne," who is rewarded by Bluebeard's heiress after both young women manage to escape a certain death; and, lastly, as noted in the Introduction, she completes a trio of Sara-extensions who carry the names of the three Brontë sisters Emily, Charlotte, and Anne.

APPENDIX A

1. *eight years old:* Sara is only seven at the start of *A Little Princess*.

2. *mamma:* Not a Frenchwoman in this version.

3. *not a pretty child:* The assertion is in marked contrast to the emphasis that will be adopted by the novel's narrator, who claims that Sara is "mistaken" in thinking herself "ugly" and stresses her "intense, attractive eyes" and "big, wonderful eyes."

4. *"since my papa died":* The inference that the still unnamed doll had become a replacement for Sara's father only after his death jars with Burnett's later dramatization of the search for Emily by a girl who has astutely anticipated her need for such a surrogate.

5. *"I can speak French better than you, now . . . in India":* Upon her arrival, the later Sara tries not to embarrass Miss Minchin by boasting about her total command of her mother's native language; this brash child, however, only seems to have perfected her rudimentary knowledge of French under the tutelage of the unnamed teacher who has commented on her "so ugly beauty."

6. *her doll, Emily:* Rather casually (and belatedly) named.

7. *one girl:* Presumably Lavinia's forerunner.

8. *He was . . . a few words:* This casual street encounter will be changed into a momentous rooftop meeting in the novel.

9. *the Indian Gentleman turned and looked at her curiously:* As an observer of this exchange, Carrisford becomes a far more active figure than the invalid who, in the novel, is totally dependent on Ram Dass's investment in Sara.

10. *"I can't pretend anything more to-night":* Changed to "I can't pretend anything else—while I am awake" in the novel, where this concession follows Miss Minchin's cruel destruction of Sara's "banquet."

11. *Can you imagine . . . hard to believe it myself:* This awkward concession is replaced in the novel by a narrator who invites her readers to share Sara's confused blurring of reality and dream, "Do you wonder that she felt sure she had not come back to earth?"

12. *"have a friend":* This sentence marks the end of the January 1888 installment of the story; the next two paragraphs open part III, the concluding February installment; since there is no Becky with whom Sara might share her new bounty, she must keep her secret friend to herself.

APPENDIX B

1. *Business . . . R. and L. . . . R. C.:* "Business," often abbreviated as "bus." in the stage instructions, stands for unscripted activities; "R," "L," and "R. C." mean "right," "left," and "right center."

2. *William:* A servant like James and Emma, whose names the novel retains.

3. *charity curtseys:* Becky presumably learned such marks of respect at the orphanage or "charity home" in which she was raised.

4. *Once upon a time . . . grandmother:* Instead of the story about a merman prince that she tells in the 1905 novel, Sara now embarks on a retelling of Frances Browne's *Granny's Wonderful Chair* (1856), a text from which Burnett had herself drawn in her 1890 story "Prince Fairyfoot."

5. *Greedalend:* The daughter of King Winwealth was called "Greedalind" in Browne's text.

6. *sewn with diamonds:* In Browne's text, Greedalind, also attired in "robe of gold, clasped with diamonds," looks "ugly and spiteful" when she sees that "a barefooted girl and an old chair" have entered the palace; Burnett omits this detail since she wants to suggest Sara's own transformation from diamond heiress into an impoverished Snowflower.

7. *"the story of the Christmas Cuckoo":* The second tale in Browne's collection.

8. *the gentleman:* Mr. Barrow, who, in the conversation that Becky overhears, will now inform Miss Minchin of Captain Crewe's death and Sara's destitution.

APPENDIX C

1. *baby:* The homely chores Jem performs for Aunt Hetty are neither as menial nor as unexpected as those that Sara is asked to perform for Miss Minchin.

2. *flew at Jem:* The phrasing Burnett uses here and in the next few sentences to describe Aunt Hetty's anger is nearly identical to that which she will employ in rendering Miss Minchin's bouts of vindictive fury.

3. *so light . . . rising gently in the air:* An evocation of George MacDonald's levitating heroine in "The Light Princess" (1864).

4. *through such a little place:* Burnett now associates Jem with the Wonderland Alice, who had to shrink before she could squeeze through a tiny door.

5. *"S.C., to be sure":* Young readers looking at the January issue of a magazine named after Saint Nicholas would quickly have identified the figure whose Dutch name (San Nicolaas) had become "Sinter Klaas" before being further deformed into "Santa Claus."

6. *"name of Birdie":* The actual name of the little Knoxville girl for whom Burnett originally had written the story.

7. *"If you should chance . . . you might hear":* In *A Little Princess*, Sara shares this same fantasy with Ermengarde.

8. *stood looking . . . again to call to her:* S.C. reenacts the White Knight's reluctant farewell to Alice in *Through the Looking Glass*.